Orson Scott Card

THE LAST SHADOW

TOR®

A TOM DOHERTY ASSOCIATES BOOK
NEW YORK

This is a work of fiction. All of the characters, organizations, and events portrayed in this novel are either products of the author's imagination or are used fictitiously.

THE LAST SHADOW

A Tor Book
Published by Tom Doherty Associates
120 Broadway
New York, NY 10271

www.tor-forge.com

Tor® is a registered trademark of Macmillan Publishing Group, LLC.

ISBN 978-0-7653-4414-4

Our books may be purchased in bulk for promotional, educational, or business use. Please contact your local bookseller or the Macmillan Corporate and Premium Sales Department at 1-800-221-7945, extension 5442, or by email at MacmillanSpecialMarkets@macmillan.com.

First Edition: October 2021
First Mass Market Edition: November 2022

Printed in the United States of America

10   9   8   7   6   5   4   3

To Ben Bova for opening the door
and
to Tom Doherty for pulling me through.

THE LAST SHADOW

1

Back when the first alien invasion struck Earth, the panicked response of the human race was to try to discover and train a generation of genius commanders who could lead humanity to victory over the Formics. Eventually, they started training younger and younger cadets. The idea was to find Napoleon, Sun Tzu, or Genghis Khan at the age of six or so and train him to be ready to lead the human race to victory. Or survival.

The general opinion was that Battle School was a resounding success, because it produced Andrew "Ender" Wiggin and his tiny jeesh of brilliant children, who crushed every fleet sent against them and finally destroyed the Formics' home world. Since then, some have taken pity on our adversaries and piously regretted wiping them out of the universe. That's a repentance that is safe to express because once the enemy is extinct, there's no going back.

That great victory is still a part of the folklore of the Hundred Worlds. But those who have seriously studied the records of Battle School and the psychological testing of the children who attended there, as well as during its later years as Fleet School, offer a different conclusion. In other words, as soon as you actually know anything about what really happened, the folklore falls apart.

The supposedly rigorous testing of the children before admitting them to Battle School was, like almost all intelligence and aptitude tests, testing for nothing much beyond the ability to do well on tests, that test in particular. Throwing their tests up a flight of stairs and taking the candidates whose tests landed on even-numbered steps would have predicted future military command success with just as much accuracy.

Deep study of Andrew Wiggin has revealed that his tremendous success in command and leadership owed nothing to his training, which was haphazard, hostile, and incompetent. Instead, his "innate character" (a term most psychologists now dispute as somewhere between misleading and meaningless—mostly because, having no respect for their own innate character, they doubt its existence in others) caused him to turn every disadvantage the system used against him into a tool for training himself and a group of cooperating students.

That all of his jeesh and other followers ended up having influential careers in and out of the military is due, not to any training in Battle School or any testing thereafter, but to their innate character.

Their innate character determined whether they would respond to Andrew Wiggin's invitation to train with him. That fact, and only that fact, separated the later high achievers from the rest.

Some have concluded that this means the ideal training is to create a hostile environment and see who rises out of it through their own resourcefulness and cooperation with others. But the tests made based on this hypothesis have had no better than mixed results.

Some have concluded that no matter how you interpret the data, whatever Master Bureaucrat Hyrum Graff and Retired War Hero Mazer Rackham did, in the design of Battle School and the training of Andrew Wiggin, worked.

Some have pointed out that Andrew Wiggin's brother, Peter, best known as the Hegemon (see *The Hive Queen* and *The Hegemon*, disseminated under the pseudonym "Speaker for the Dead"), received none of the training his younger brother received, and was rejected by Battle School for his excessive ambition and callous disregard for the pain of others.

Yet he is honored today as well as in his lifetime for achieving the unification of Earth under a single government rooted in principles of liberty, democracy, and fairness. The fact that Peter Wiggin was rejected by Battle School may be the most important single indicator of the inadequacy of the school's testing procedures.

For the purpose of our overview of the Battle School and Fleet School graduates, it is perhaps sufficient to recognize this: When you select, from the entire human population, the children who are best according to *any* measure of intelligence that includes verbal ability, logic, and spatial relationships, and who test well in empathy, mind-reading, and adaptive social skills, you will discover that they do very well in verbal ability, logic, spatial relationships, empathy, mind-reading, and adaptive social skills throughout their lives.

It is not a mark of bad science, but of good science, when a conclusion is not rejected merely because it is obvious.

—Carlotta Delphiki, *Herodotus* Papers

Thulium did not like the nickname "Ultima Thule," but since she also did not like the name Thulium, there wasn't much to choose from between them. The twins, her older brothers, always called her Ultima, while the cousins called her as little as possible, since they all feared her father, the one called Sergeant, and therefore most of them avoided hanging around with any of his kids.

That was a hard thing to bring off, considering that they all lived cooped up in the small starship *Herodotus*. You could wander to the most remote spot on the ship, and someone could find you within about two minutes, since all the other kids knew all the hiding places as well as Thulium did. Better, in fact, since she was the youngest, even though she was younger than Blue by only three months.

At breakfast somebody mentioned that today was Blue's birthday, and Thulium had muttered something about how her birthday must be coming up in a couple of months.

"You don't *have* a birthday, Ultima," said Dys, the twin who insisted he wasn't identical.

Lanth, the identical twin, might have started fighting with Dys over this, but it was apparently more fun to goad Thulium than to quarrel with Dys. Safer, too. "You grew like a fungus on the outside wall of the ship," he said. "Father scraped you off and brought you inside just before we took off from Nokonoshima."

"Leave her alone," said Little Mum, the oldest of the cousins, but only by a year.

"Says the Mother Superior," said Lanth. "We're not doing anything to her."

"Except telling her the truth about her parentage," said Dys.

"When the *Herodotus* was parked at the Tochoji Spaceport undergoing repairs and refitting," said Lanth, "some giant poopy-birds kept pooping on the ship, and a virulent fungus grew in the poo. That's what Father scraped off to make *you*."

Thulium shook her head. "Tochoji Spaceport was in geosynchronous orbit directly over the capital city Tochoji. The *Herodotus* never touched the surface of the planet because there's no surface spaceport large enough to receive a starship. You do understand that I can read at a very high level, and because I'm interested, I have already learned far more about our family history than you ever will."

"The poopy-birds are *space* birds, Ultima Thule," said Lanth. "They breathe in giant farts and they can live on that for about a year before they have to breathe again. Meanwhile, they poop almost constantly."

"You haven't fooled her since she was less than five," said Little Mum, whose real name was Petra. "Why do you keep trying?"

"Because in her heart of hearts," said Dys, "she actually believes what we say enough to wonder if it might, in some way, be true."

"Do not," said Thulium, trying to sound tired.

"What's your job for today, Twins?" said Little Mum. "That is, once you stop annoying your sister."

"We don't report to you," said Dys.

"Your father specifically assigned you to report to me," said Little Mum.

"That was last week," said Lanth.

"Unrescinded," said Little Mum.

"If you try to boss me around," said Dys, "I'll heave you out an airlock."

"Don't try that until you've disabled the software and hardware that track us all continuously," said Mum.

"Already did that," said Lanth. "Still tracks all the rest of you, but not me and Dys."

"In your dreams," said Mum.

"It happens that Lanth and I are very very smart," said Dys.

"So is everybody on this ship," said Thulium.

"She's got a point," said Dys.

"Doesn't mean we're not smarter than the parents. In fact, I think that was the genetic plan," said Lanth. "Go down to a planet—they didn't care which, but Nokonoshima drew the short straw—go down, mate with some locals, have as many babies as possible within a couple of years. It turned out to take four years because nobody wanted Aunt Carlotta. Then they kidnap the babies, go back into space leaving the spouses behind, and raise the little bunnies on the *Herodotus* until they decide whether we kids are smart enough to please them. And they will only be pleased when we prove that we got *all* of our intelligence from them, and not from our Nokonoshima parents."

"And what if we're not smart enough?" asked Dys, leaning in to Thulium. "I mean, obviously Lanth and I are, but you, Ultima Thule, I worry about you. Papa's kind of ruthless, and he has very high standards. I don't think you've ever said or done anything smart enough to earn you a place in this ship."

Little Mum squirted a mild vinegar solution into Dys's face. He squawked and raced to the bathroom to rinse it out of his eyes.

"You didn't have to do that, Petra," said Thulium.

"Uncle Sergeant authorized me to do exactly that

if they started being cruel to you. He knows the kind of children he spawned."

"I'm that kind of child, too, since he's my father," said Thulium.

"If you ever bully people like the twins do, you'll get some weak vinegar solution in *your* eyes, too," said Little Mum.

"I'm not like them at all," said Thulium.

"Then we must assume you're like your mother," said Little Mum.

"I wish I remembered her."

"You weren't three weeks old when we left Nokonoshima," said Little Mum. "You couldn't possibly remember her."

"Part of our inheritance from the Giant is that we have amazing memories when we're little," said Thulium. "But not amazing enough."

"It doesn't matter," said Little Mum. "Our parents knew from the start that they'd have a bunch of kids to keep the Giant's genes alive until the human race needs us. They also knew that we would have to be raised in a controlled environment."

"This tiny prison," said Thulium.

Her father's voice entered the conversation, quietly insinuating itself as if he had been part of it all along. "This tiny prison is where Ender, Carlotta, and I all grew up," he said.

Thulium had heard this same nonsense before. "The Giant raised three of you, and there are seven of us grandchildren."

"But the Giant took up the space of thirty children your size," said Father. "So you should rejoice in the luxurious space you have compared to our childhood."

"It was selfish of you to kidnap us and sequester us away from our mother," said Thulium.

"Your mother was a kind but normal woman,

which means she could dress herself and read simple texts, but otherwise she was not fit to rear a child of mine," said Father.

"I'll bet she was nicer than you will ever be," said Thulium.

"She certainly was," said Father. "Everybody is nicer than I will ever be."

"Not the twins," said Thulium.

"Oh, have they been picking on you again?"

Thulium glanced at Little Mum, who was studiously looking at her hands in her lap.

"You don't need to appeal to the witness of others," said Father. "I will believe whatever you tell me."

"They say ridiculous things designed to make me angry," said Thulium.

"Does it work?"

"Sometimes," said Thulium. "Not because I believe them, but because I don't understand why they hate me."

"They hate you," said Father, "because your mother obviously cared more about you than she did about them. They didn't understand, and still don't, that her suckling babe is always more important to a human woman than her toddlers."

"Doesn't that mean they're too stupid to be descended from the Giant?" asked Thulium.

"You all tested positive for the modified Anton's Key gene before we took any of you with us on the *Herodotus*," said Father. "And I suppose *that* is what the twins lie about most, to make you think perhaps we'll chuck you out of the blowhole because you're too dumb to carry on the family tradition."

Thulium shrugged. "I know they're lying."

"But you don't *know* they're lying," said Father.

Thulium wasn't sure what distinction he was making. "Do you mean I'm not *certain*?" asked Thulium. "Of course I'm certain. *You* told me we all have

Anton's Key, modified version, so we won't die of gi-antism like your father did."

"And if *I* told you, it must be true," said Father.

"No," said Lanth. "You lie to everybody all the time."

"Only when it's funny," said Father.

"It's never funny," said Lanth.

"It is to me," said Father. "Hello, Dys. Back from washing vinegar out of your eyes?"

"I think she's mixed it with something a lot stron-ger," said Dys.

"Quite likely," said Father. "But you can be sure it isn't permanently damaging, because I only gave her authority to stop you from being an idiot, not kill you or maim you."

Thulium knew that the part of the discussion con-cerning her was over. Even though Father pretended that he completely *adored* his little girl Thulium, it was the twins he loved, because he could train them to be soldiers, while Thulium would always be a girl, with less strength and stamina. Not worth training. As if Father had ever been a real soldier. Anything he learned about military training had come from books and vids.

Thulium decided to leave the room. She'd get some-thing more to eat later in the morning. Maybe she'd make Aunt Carlotta feed her lunch in her family quarters. Blue, Carlotta's youngest, was Thulium's only friend.

But no, today was Blue's birthday, so maybe Aunt Carlotta wouldn't have time for her.

Then again, maybe she *would,* because Blue got teased by the older kids almost as much as Thu-lium did, so Carlotta would want Thulium close by throughout whatever birthday celebration they might have, so Blue would have a friend he could trust.

As she was about to leave, Aunt Carlotta came in,

bustling on some errand that involved food stored in the dry pantry. With Father and the twins at the far side of the mess hall, Thulium asked Aunt Carlotta, quietly, "Do we get the day off of lessons because it's Blue's birthday?"

"*You* do," said Aunt Carlotta, not in a quiet voice at all, "and Blue does. All the older kids still have class."

"Not fair!" cried Dys, from across the room where Father had been admonishing him while examining his eyes.

"So you're not paying attention to me," said Father. "Listening in on irrelevant conversations while I'm trying to teach you to think like a warrior."

"Who are we ever going to go to war with in *here*?" demanded Dys.

"Whoever comes at us trying to kill us," said Father. "I thought you understood that concept long ago."

"Why would anybody want to kill us?" said Dys.

"Because we're not part of the human race. We're smarter than they are, and that terrifies them," said Father.

"Nobody knows we exist," said Thulium, crossing the room.

"Everybody knows we exist, if they know anything about history," said Father. "And it keeps some of them awake at night, wondering when and where we might turn up."

"They think we died, the way the Giant died," said Thulium.

"That's what they tell themselves in order to sleep," said Father.

"Why should they be afraid of us?" asked Thulium.

"Someday the bogeyman is going to come," said Father, "and they'll need us to defeat the bogeyman and save the human race."

"Like Ender Wiggin," said Thulium.

"Like your grandfather the Giant," said Father. "Wiggin got the credit. But yes, like Ender Wiggin in the storybooks."

"So they won't hate us, they'll be grateful, and they won't go to war with us," said Thulium.

"After we defeat the bogeyman," said Father, "they'll understand just how wise and powerful we are. That's when they'll decide to destroy us, if they can."

"Can they?" asked Thulium.

"It'll be interesting to find out, won't it, my darling poppet," said Father.

"No," said Thulium. "I don't want to save the humans if they're like what you say, ungrateful and murderous."

"And yet right now we don't have a breeding population of Leguminids," said Father. "So we need some viable populations of humans to maintain a high level of technology and agriculture on many worlds so we can choose a breeding population when it's time for you lovely younglings to mate."

"The way you mated," said Thulium. "Impregnate and kidnap. You're such a noble creature, Father."

"I let you talk to me that way," said Father, "because you're my child, and therefore the only way to shut you up would be to kill you. So far, I don't want to kill you. But please remember that every cruel thing you say stabs me to the heart. I'm only human, you know."

She stared steadily at him and said, "Humans evolved to live on planetary surfaces, not in flying tombs."

"Humans evolved to adapt to living anywhere," said Father. "And leguminids even more so."

Thulium rolled her eyes and stalked out of the room. She didn't really want to leave, but that seemed the only way to make him feel her disdain for him. Since she didn't actually feel any disdain, but rather longed for him to notice her, she understood perfectly well that her angry exit was self-defeating. But sometimes you have to defeat yourself a little in order to maintain your independence.

2

Carlotta seems to believe that we had these children in order to experience the joy of rearing children. Sergeant seems to think we had the children in order to create an army—of seven. I don't think the children we got are likely to bring either joy or military triumph.

But their existence does allow us to study the results of the second generation after we modified Anton's Key so that giantism is no longer linked to high intellect. It worked to arrest our own growth, of course. We are still a little below average for well-nourished specimens of humankind, but that's not a problem for people living aboard a ship.

However, our seven children are not undersized the way Father was and the way we were in our childhood. It appears that removing the giantism component means that from now on our offspring will follow the normal human growth pattern from birth on.

Sergeant believes I am endangering our children's future by continuing to distribute the data on our children's growth and intellectual development to a few research institutions that at least claim to be studying

Anton's Key. Carlotta thinks my efforts along those lines are worthless. They may both be right.

However, those research institutions have to continue receiving data and at least pretending to incorporate it into their ongoing studies, because we supply their funding, and have for many centuries. Our interstellar travel at near lightspeed had relativistic effects, so that whenever I transmitted a report, it was acknowledged by someone who was not on the project the last time I transmitted.

I only hope that the data I send is not immediately deleted and vaporized. I hope they are afraid enough of loss of funding to keep careful records so that the data continue to exist, even if there is no actual research going on.

Meanwhile, our children bicker with siblings and cousins, with only a few alliances here and there among them. They are an unpromising bunch, like the children of royalty throughout history. If they aren't already conspiring to kill us and take control of the ship, they will begin doing so any time now. After all, *we* did, or at least Sergeant did and tried to bully Carlotta and me into joining him.

It is disturbing how similar our children are to the way *we* were as children. But when I suggested to Carlotta that we jettison the whole tribe of them into the cold of space, she rolled her eyes and said, "Not yet."

We may well regret the decision to conceive them in the first place, to take them with us, and to let them grow up. But the urge to reproduce is strong in all animals, even Homo leguminensis. I actually sometimes like my own children, to the point of feeling some slight affection toward them. I could easily dump Sergeant's twins at any time, but his youngest, Thulium, shows some signs of having a tolerable personality.

And the only way I could harm Carlotta's children would be to kill her first, which I will never do. Without Carlotta, we wouldn't outnumber Sergeant, so my survival would be somewhere between impossible and intolerable.

Like it or not, we're stuck with these young hyperhumans until we get a good idea of who they are and what they can accomplish. That's my research project for now. Collecting data on them makes me look like an attentive father and uncle. So far, so good.

—Andrew Delphiki, Appendix C, *Horodotus* Papers

Sprout had made decorations for his brother Blue's birthday celebration. The whole concept of keeping the old Earth calendar on a spaceship traveling at relativistic speeds seemed absurd to him, but since the computer maintained both the real-time calendar and the ship's calendar, there was no reason not to notice when birthdays rolled around.

Besides, Sprout actually liked Blue. He was a kind boy, and he was happy to befriend any of the cousins. Blue and Thulium got along quite well, which was a kindness, since the twins made Thulium's life a torture of teasing and deception and disparagement.

So Sprout programmed birthday displays into all the screens and monitors that were capable of graphics. He did it only in Mother's quarters, where Sprout and Blue lived with her; he knew that if he tried to put such displays up in the public areas of the ship, Uncle Sergeant and Uncle Ender would make them go away, because the screens were for monitoring ship operations, not celebrating meaningless landmarks in the lives of post-human children, whose genetics were still so unknown that nobody could guess what "age" meant anymore.

Blue came into the family's central table, saw the screens on the walls and the holodisplay in the center of the table, and smiled. The holodisplay had balloons infinitely rising, at different rates of speed, new ones appearing at the bottom as the old ones disappeared at the top. The screens on the walls had other celebratory activities going on—fireworks, parades, dancing. The places and the people might have had some meaning, but to children who had memories mostly of living aboard a ship, they were all strangers, and the places carried no sentimental weight.

"Are any of these places Tochoji?" asked Blue.

"Sorry," said Sprout. "I think the uncles have kept the ship's computer from fulfilling any requests concerning information or images from our birth city."

"I know," said Blue. "But I also know you're pretty good at cheating."

"Mother would know if I did it," said Sprout. "And while she thinks—or *says* she thinks—trying to hide our birth world from us is pointless, she also thinks that it's a bad thing for us to plunge into the depths of the ship's computer, because what if we interfered with ship operations?"

Blue laughed. "As if we would."

"She told me that I might damage something without realizing what I was doing."

Blue laughed even louder. "Doesn't she know who you are? Doesn't she understand *what* we are?"

Sprout smiled and shrugged. "Sometimes I don't think she knows what *she* is."

"I hope Uncle Sergeant lets Thulium come to the party."

"He'd better," said Sprout. "Because it's not much of a party with just the three of us."

"I invited Boss and Little Mum," said Blue.

"You really think Uncle Ender will let *them* come?"

"He's a lot nicer than Uncle Sergeant," said Blue.

"Nicer, but not more lenient. Whatever they think is right, they stick to it," said Sprout.

"I think Mother's the same way," said Blue. "She talks like she sympathizes with us and it's the uncles who won't let us do things. But I think she secretly agrees with them, but blames it on them because she wants us to think she's kinder. Or that she loves us more."

"Well, you know I agree with you about how deceptive Mother can be," said Sprout. "I just didn't realize you were already so cynical."

"I'm a leguminid," said Blue. "We don't really believe anything that anybody *tells* us."

Sprout pulled out a piece of paper. That instantly silenced Blue, who looked at it in awe. It had a color photograph printed out on one side of it. It had been folded twice, so it could hide inside a pocket.

"You stole paper," said Blue. "You stole printer time. That's irreplaceable."

"It's perfectly replaceable, any time Mother and the uncles decide to provision our ship on a planet," said Sprout. "I wanted to give you a present."

"All these decorations," said Blue. "That was plenty. That's a *lot*."

Meanwhile, Sprout opened up the paper and laid it flat on the table, holding down two of the corners. Blue held down the other two, and looked.

"It's Tochoji," said Sprout.

"There aren't any images from Nokonoshima on the ship's computer!"

"There are if you search for them with Mother's log-in. Then it's easy," said Sprout.

"Where did we live?" asked Blue.

"I don't know. It's just an aerial photo of the mouth of the river and the city built on high ground over here, so that when the spring rains cause the river to flood, it doesn't drown the town."

"It's not a very big place," said Blue.

"It's bigger than the population of this ship," said Sprout. "And our father Yuuto still lives there."

"Do you know that? We've been flying for years since we left, and with relativistic time, he might be—"

"If he was younger than thirty when you were born, Blue," said Sprout, "then he's way older now."

"Our ship is three thousand years old," said Blue. "Our relativistic difference is not as great as with really modern starships that come closer to lightspeed. Also, we haven't been pushing our ship to maximum speed in our lifetime."

Sprout shook his head. "All right, maybe he's still alive and misses you every day." Immediately he regretted saying that, because tears instantly came to Blue's eyes, though he blinked them away.

"I wonder if he ever does think about me," said Blue.

"I bet he does. I bet he thinks about me and Mother, too. Even if he married somebody else after we left, even if he has other children, I think he secretly loves us first," said Sprout.

"Do you really think so?" asked Blue.

"No," said Sprout. "He's a human, and Uncle Sergeant tells us all the time what perfidious hypocritical monsters humans are."

The door had opened silently enough that Sprout had not heard it. But there was Mother, walking into the room. "Speak of Uncle Cincinnatus with respect, please, Brussels Delphiki."

"You know he hates that name even worse than—"

"Why do we have stupid city names?" asked Blue.

"Since you never use them," said Mother, "what does it matter what your real names are?"

"At least we're not named for rare earth elements, like Sergeant's kids," said Sprout.

"They don't use those names either," said Mother. "And Uncle Ender's children both are named for real people—your grandmother Petra Arkanian and a great military commander, Mazer Rackham, who taught Ender Wiggin and the Giant, as well. But nobody uses those very honorable names, either. I'm disgusted with the whole business of naming."

"You gave us names as if you called up a map of the Benelux countries, closed your eyes, and touched the screen with your finger," said Blue.

"That's exactly what I did," said Mother. "Because the Giant—my father—was born in a city in the Low Countries. I didn't think Rotterdam would be a good name, because you or your cousins would have made too much of the syllable 'dam' and the word 'rotter.' So I named you for different cities."

"So why am I called Blue?" asked Blue.

"I've told you that story before."

"I forget," said Blue.

"You don't forget anything," said Sprout. "None of us do."

"I forget whenever I want Mother to tell me again," said Blue.

"Delft is a city that became famous for making a certain kind of ceramic dishware, which was called 'China' because that kind of ceramic first came from the country of China. So for a while, your nickname was China. And then, because Delft china is always painted with blue designs, we started calling you 'Blue.'"

"And I was nicknamed Sprout," said Sprout, "because when I was born my father Yuuto thought I was so small that I looked like a sprouting plant and—"

"There was a common miniature variant of the cabbage plant," said Mother, "that was called 'Brussels sprouts.' Your name being Brussels, your uncles started calling you 'Sprout.'"

"My father Yuuto called me that first," said Sprout, "because the uncles had never seen or eaten an actual Brussels sprout, but Father Yuuto *had*."

Mother said nothing. She knew that there was no point in arguing with Sprout when he made a statement like that, because he would never believe any refutation. She explained that to him once, when he said, "If it isn't true, then why did you stop arguing?" Her explanation was, "I have only so much breath in my life, Brussels Delphiki, and I'm not going to waste any more of it arguing with someone who doesn't listen."

Unlike Thulium, who constantly challenged her father and Uncle Ender and Mother about how they should have stayed on Nokonoshima, Sprout never openly challenged his mother about such things, never in front of the uncles or the cousins. But here, with just the three of them in their own quarters, he felt more free to make it clear that he believed that he and Blue had been cheated when Mother and the uncles stole them away into space.

"We're celebrating Blue's birthday now," said Mother.

"Not till Thulium comes," said Blue.

"What if she doesn't come?" asked Mother.

"We told her eighteen-hundred hours," said Sprout, "and she still has fifteen minutes."

"I don't think Sergeant's going to allow her—" Mother began.

The door slid open. Thulium came trotting in, happy as a lark.

Too happy, Sprout decided. She didn't have permission. She had snuck away. "Let's get this party started," said Sprout. Who knew how quickly Uncle Sergeant would appear to take her home.

They had all read about birthday parties in various places; they knew that in some places people ate cake, in others pie, and sugar candies and other treats elsewhere. On the *Herodotus,* there was only one treat that the ship's kitchen knew how to make: ice cream. And that was good enough. It's not as if they had parties every day, though Uncle Ender always remarked about how with seven children practically swamping the boat, they seemed to have a birthday every week of the year.

Mother served it out in little bowls. "It's actually the French recipe for a dessert called glace," she explained.

"Which is identical to Italian gelato," said Sprout. "We can read, too."

"But it's the French recipe programmed into the kitchen," said Mother. "And I can't help but wish we could have some made with real sugar."

"We have sugar," said Blue. "It's sweet."

"It's very slightly sweet," said Mother. "I've had the real thing. You have no idea."

"We would have an idea," said Sprout, "if we still lived on Nokonoshima."

"What makes you think they have ice cream there?" asked Mother.

"Because it's the only place you ever lived where you could have tasted anything real from Earth."

"I was born on Earth," said Mother.

"And the Giant took you and the uncles with him when you were so young you were still stupid as a human."

"Yes," said Mother. "I tasted ice cream many times in Tochoji."

"With our father, Yuuto," said Blue.

"He was a kind and generous man," said Mother.

"Which is part of why you are the two kindest, most generous children among the cousins on the *Herodotus*. No one knows why *you* are so kind, Thulium."

"Now you're just lying to make us feel better about not having our father," said Sprout.

"Eat your ice cream," said Mother.

The door had not opened since Thulium came in. But now there was a man standing just inside. Neither Sprout nor Blue had noticed him before, if he had been standing there awhile. They looked at him, dumbstruck.

Mother saw the direction of their gaze, and turned. "Who are you?" she asked. "And how did you get on this ship?"

"I'm an image, not a person," said the man. "My data were transferred here over the past several days, so now I dwell inside your ship's computer, though I'm only a copy of the image and personality and program set inside *my* ship's computer."

"A lightspeed transfer?" asked Mother. Sprout knew that this would mean that the stranger's ship was very, very close.

"An ansible transfer," said the man. "As you well know."

"Nobody knows our ansible address," said Mother.

"Many people know it, including all the research foundations you keep funding to pretend to research Anton's Key," said the man.

"Are you from one of those foundations?" asked Mother.

"I control all their computers and all their ansible communications," said the man. "I've received every report and request that you have sent them and they have sent you over the years. I have always known where you were and what you were doing."

"So you're a spy," said Mother.

"If I *were* a spy, I'd hardly tell you so openly," said the man. "I gave Julian Delphiki this ship, not because he bought it, but because he needed it and I had ships to give out in those days. I authorized his voyage of research and discovery. He could not have undertaken it if I had not wanted it to happen. And I was there when Petra Arkanian Delphiki said good-bye to the three children that her husband Julian took with him. I knew you in the cradle, Carlotta. I knew the woman that you were named after. I knew the boy that Andrew was named for, while he was still alive."

"Andrew Wiggin is dead?" asked Mother.

"Almost everyone is dead," said the man, "except you."

"And you? How did you stay alive, relativistic travel?"

"I sometimes did that," said the man. "Until it became too boring. Then the brain-state-recording equipment became sophisticated enough that I had myself recorded a few dozen times using a few dozen different methodologies. Now all those recordings talk to each other and decide what to make me say or do. Right now, only one of them has been copied into the computer aboard *Herodotus,* but that one is able to make me speak for all."

"I know who you are," said Mother. She turned to Sprout. "Do you know who he is?"

"He's Hyrum Graff," said Sprout. "The Minister of Colonization who ended up controlling all space travel for a while. The founder of Battle School and the teacher of the original Andrew Wiggin and of the Giant."

"I knew him first as 'Bean,'" said Hyrum Graff. "I'm flattered that you have been taught anything about me."

"Mother loves to teach us extremely obscure facts," said Sprout.

"I'm sure you know many of them," said Graff. "I believe they call you Sprout."

"You *have* been spying," said Sprout. "That name isn't in any records that—"

"Your mother writes about her children in her notes, and your uncle Andrew writes about all the children in his notes."

"And those notes," said Mother, "are transmitted to the foundations we work with, where no one ever reads them."

"I read them," said Graff. "Everything you transmit, you are sending to me."

"Why are you here?" asked Mother. "After millennia of keeping your vigil a secret, why are you coming here more-or-less in person?"

"I have been slowing down your ship to non-relativistic speed. I have a job I need you to do in real time."

"What job?" asked Sprout.

"Saving the human race."

Mother shook her head and laughed. "That was your job back when the Formics still existed and it was your job to save the human species. Now humanity is spread among the Hundred Worlds and beyond, preserving thousands of unique cultures and languages, with trade constantly flowing among them. There are no Hive Queens, and there is no other possible threat that can put human survival at risk."

Graff gave a wan little smile. "The threat is not coming in spaceships that can be shot out of the sky, or in colonies that can be detected and obliterated," said Graff. "It comes in the form of a virus called 'descolada,' which can insinuate itself into every form of life, comprehend and parse its genetic code, and then reconstruct it so that it must faithfully reproduce the descolada virus or die."

"So I've heard," said Mother. "I believe a fleet was sent to destroy the planet where it resides."

"The virus is, in some incomprehensible way, intelligent enough to adapt to every attempt to destroy it. Before he died, Andrew Wiggin led a scientific project to create an antivirus that replaces the descolada with a workalike that preserves the lives of the infected, but no longer has the power to infect new victims."

"Did he succeed?" asked Mother.

"He did," said Graff. "By methods that cannot yet be duplicated. But that solved only that one world's problem. We can only assume that this virus has been broadly dispersed in order to infect every world that has genetically coded life. Eventually, it may find and infect all the human colonies."

"Distribute the cure," said Mother. "Save the human race."

"If every world has the cure," said Graff, "the descolada will find a way around it. It may be trying to do so on the world that it already controls."

"Lusitania," said Sprout.

Graff looked at him with surprise. A very good simulation, thought Sprout, to imitate the facial expressions of the man who provided the model for this hologram.

"'Descolada' means 'unsticker' or 'unglued' in Portuguese or Spanish. Only in the tiny Brazilian colony world of Lusitania could such a thing be kept under control."

"Why do you need us?" asked Blue. "It's my birthday party."

"Sorry to spoil it," said Graff.

"I just wondered if you wanted some ice cream," said Blue.

"He's a hologram," said Sprout.

"We can give him a hologram of ice cream," said Blue, as if it were the most obvious thing.

Graff smiled. "Yes, that would be nice. It would be nice to be included in the party."

Sprout could imagine Uncle Sergeant saying something about fraternizing with the enemy, and Uncle Ender speaking of meaningless gestures and fake hospitality.

"You don't know where the descolada originates," said Mother.

"We found a candidate, but we haven't figured out how to know if that planet was the origin, or an earlier victim," said Graff.

"You no longer control all the ships in the Hundred Worlds," said Mother, "but what do you imagine *we* can accomplish with *one* ship?"

"My original may be dead," said Graff, "though I don't know that for sure, he may just be retired. But I still have some control over all the shipping between worlds, and all ansible communications are handled by a brilliant program that shares information extensively with me. So don't imagine that I'm powerless. The only place, in fact, where I *am* powerless is aboard this ship."

"Not powerless, if you can appear inside my home during a private family party," said Mother.

"Not your nuclear family," said Graff, "since young Thulium is here, soaking up everything that we're saying."

Thulium stood up. "Nobody will hear about any of this from *me,*" she said.

"She's telling the truth," said Blue. "Thulium never tells secrets."

"What I say to one, I'd happily say to all. I merely assumed that I would be listened to better by the people in this room than by any other group of people on the *Herodotus.*"

Sprout had to agree with him. "What do you want us to do?" asked Sprout.

Graff raised an eyebrow and looked at him. "Are you now negotiating on behalf of the leguminids on this ship?"

"Asking an obvious question isn't negotiating," said Sprout. "You came here to get us to do something. Test your possible Descolada Planet? We're ill-equipped to do that, as Mother said."

"All the exploratory teams, all the computer analyses, all of the *everything* that we've applied to the problem have come up empty. So we need somebody smarter, to figure out what we should be searching *for*, and what the markers of its role as the descolada's origin might be, so we'll know if this is it." To Sprout's pleasure, Graff directed all these words to him, as if he was an actual person instead of a child.

Then it dawned on him that maybe this was how he always spoke to bright children. How he spoke to the Giant and Ender Wiggin when they were small, and Graff was the commander of Battle School.

"Here in this room," said Graff, "is a team of four—Carlotta, Brussels, Blue, and Thulium—who might be the best combination to think of what the parameters of our quest should be."

"Are you trying to divide the leguminids into rival camps, Hyrum Graff?" asked Mother.

"I'm trying to evade the skepticism and resentment of the uncles and their children," said Graff.

"And when they discover what you've been doing, won't their skepticism and resentment be many times greater because of this concealment?"

"Yes it will. If you're afraid of them—"

"Taunting us won't earn our trust or our cooperation," said Mother. "Of course we're afraid of them—we have no other friends or allies in the universe, and if they turn against us—"

"You have me," said Graff.

"A shadow of a human being who once lived."

"A shadow with enormous influence in the Hundred Worlds," said Graff.

"Says you," said Thulium.

"You'll see," said Graff. "But not just me. There are the very bright humans from Lusitania, and a few from other worlds as well. They might not have Anton's Key within their genome, but they're among the best that the human race has to offer, at present. Their help and cooperation will not be useless to you."

"I'm sure you intend us to meet them all," said Mother.

"I don't care if you ever *meet*," said Graff. "What would that matter? What I care about is sharing information, sharing ideas, trying experiments under each other's direction or suggestions. Working together in real time. An alliance."

"So we're to trust beings of another species," said Mother, "but *not* my own brothers and their children?"

Thulium spoke up again. "Come on, Aunt Carlotta. You know we all lie to Father so he doesn't go on a rampage. And nothing touches Uncle Ender's heart, period. He'd analyze everything Hyrum Graff has told us out of existence."

Mother looked at Thulium. "I believe I haven't paid enough attention to you," Mother said to her. "I will not make that mistake again."

Thulium rolled her eyes. "I didn't say anything that the rest of you didn't already know," she said. "Mr. Graff was right to come to this room, at this time. In fact, he was waiting for me to arrive, wasn't he?"

She turned to look at the hologram. "I believe so," said Graff, "though that plan might not have been a conscious one. The part of my character that is intertwined with your ship's computer might carry plans and decisions that I am not consciously aware of making."

"He means no, he wasn't waiting for you," said Blue.

"He means that he didn't *know* he was waiting for you," said Mother.

"He means," said Sprout, "that he was absolutely waiting for you, but he doesn't want you or the rest of us to know just how important he thinks you are."

Thulium cocked her head and looked at Sprout. "I didn't think you liked me," she said.

"Blue is your best friend," said Sprout. "Why would I interfere with that by befriending you myself?"

"You're all so ridiculously nice," said Mother. "Sprout, get the kitchen to whip up some virtual ice cream and convey it into the hands of this simulacrum."

"Have you sung 'Happy Birthday' yet?" asked Graff.

"Is that a song?" asked Mother.

"Every schoolchild knew it in America," said Graff, "which is where I grew up."

"My mother was Armenian," said Mother, "and my father grew up in Holland. And the Giant wasn't much for birthdays and he also sang with little sense of tune or tone."

"The words are easy," said Graff. "I'll teach you."

"Is that why you came to our ship tonight?" asked Mother. "To teach us a song?"

"Yes," said Graff. "To try to get us all singing the same tune together."

"That's a metaphor," said Blue to Thulium.

"But it's also literally true," said Thulium, and Graff launched into the simple tune and the simple words. The only dispute was over whether to sing "Happy Birthday dear Blue," or "dear China" or "dear Delft." They settled on Blue, of course, as they all must have known they were going to. And then Sprout couldn't get the stupid melody and the stupid words out of his head for the rest of the night, long after Graff popped back out of visible existence and Mother ushered Thulium out into the corridor, and then tried to get the brothers calmed down enough to sleep.

The last thing Sprout said to Mother that night was, "You're going to tell the uncles about this, aren't you?"

"Don't you think I should?" asked Mother.

"I think you absolutely should not," said Sprout. "But I also think you absolutely must. Tonight. If you wait till tomorrow, Uncle Sergeant will accuse you of delaying because you intended not to tell."

"My reasoning exactly. Secrets can't exist in a tribe this small. It would tear us apart. So even though Graff's plan would work much more smoothly, the cost of discovery would be too high. And it happens that all the other leguminids are very, very clever and creative. Maybe we'll do better together than apart."

"Please don't ever sing that horrible song again, Mother," said Sprout. "Especially not on *my* birthday."

"Can't get it out of your mind?" asked Mother.

"I want to jab forks in my ears to make it stop," said Sprout.

"Fortunately," said Mother, "you can't *get* a fork into your ear."

3

How long did it take her to decide to tell the rest of us about this holographic spy embedded in our computer?

Thulium says that Carlotta's decision was probably made as soon as the Graff image disappeared.

But if Carlotta has corrupted Thule, how can I trust what she says?

Watch and watch and watch, that's what you have to do when trust is not and cannot be maintained.

Meanwhile, how to identify a world that manufactured killer viruses and dispersed them to infect life-bearing planets? What is the supposed delivery system? How can we even begin the inquiry? What other projects will we have to set aside in order to conduct such research? Which of our preexisting projects is the real target of this spyware assault?

—Cincinnatus Delphiki, decrypted notes,
Leguminid Project #22

After everyone on the *Herodotus* got used to the idea that the simulated version of the legendary

Hyrum Graff was embedded in their ship's computer, they started thinking about the assignment he had brought them. Especially the cousins, and most especially Carlotta's boys, Sprout and Blue. And Thulium, of course, because her father had told her not to take part in any discussions of that nonsense, so it was guaranteed that she would talk of nothing else.

Finally all the cousins got together in the mess hall with Uncle Ender and talked about identifying the Descolada Planet. Uncle Sergeant came in and listened to the discussion for about a minute, laughed, and started walking out.

"You could help us, you know," said Uncle Ender.

Uncle Sergeant stopped at the door, leaned on it. "Were you listening to yourselves?" he asked. "Supposedly smarter than the whole human race, and you think you can figure out your parameters based on the proximity to Lusitania, where the descolada virus came to rest?"

"That's all we've got," said Uncle Ender.

"You've got nothing," said Uncle Sergeant. "One planet doesn't work as a vector. Maybe if you knew the delivery system—a spaceship? A tiny capsule? Traveling near lightspeed? Traveling at conventional speeds? Or no container at all, just a complex virus, in its own encapsulation, moving through the cold of space till it hits an atmosphere and gets wafted gently down to a planet's surface? How long was that encapsulated virus moving through space? A century? Seems too short a time. A hundred centuries? Maybe—but then the Descolada Planet would have to be about next door to Lusitania. What about a million years? A hundred million? A billion years? What if that virus originated in another galaxy? Can you triangulate from your single vector and find it?"

"Just like you, Sarge," said Uncle Ender. "Think of the worst-case scenario."

"Somebody has to," said Uncle Sergeant. "Whatever species created the descolada virus—*if* anybody did—probably died a hundred million years ago when their sun went nova. That is *far* more likely than finding that species still alive, still spewing out destructive, self-modifying viruses for no conceivable purpose except to cause mischief to species on faraway worlds that they would never find because they aren't even looking for them."

Then Uncle Sergeant's gaze shifted. Sprout saw where he looked, and there stood the hologram of Graff. Uncle Sergeant pointed at him steadily and said, "Speak no words to me, fake human. You have nothing to teach me, just as you never had anything to teach my father."

Sprout saw Graff move as if he meant to speak, but then he said nothing. Just stood there, looking at Uncle Sergeant.

"What?" asked Uncle Sergeant. "You're actually doing what I asked?"

Graff still said nothing.

Uncle Sergeant barked out a little laugh and left them, deliberately walking through Graff's image as he went.

"He has a point, Father," said Little Mum. "We don't know enough to do anything except waste our time."

Uncle Ender turned toward Graff. "You're still here? Sergeant is gone, so you can talk now."

Graff shrugged. "I have nothing to add," he said.

"Anything to subtract?" asked Uncle Ender.

"The scientists on Lusitania have been working on this for a while," said Graff. "But I think they probably ran into the same problem Cincinnatus just outlined."

"How large a search area to include," said Uncle Ender.

"It's the whole universe, obviously," said Graff.

"No, the delivery system. Nobody's found the descolada in its encapsulated form—if it has one. Nobody knows what it looked like and acted like when it arrived. The last I checked, no results whatsoever had been published."

Now it was Sprout's turn to laugh. "Come on, Graff," he said. "You haven't been in continuous contact with anyone for quite a while. The whole network of ansibles and computers was disabled during the past year of real time, and a fleet was sent to destroy Lusitania in order to prevent the spread of the descolada virus, and you have no idea how that all turned out. You haven't heard *anything* from Lusitania lately."

"The ansible network is up and running," said Graff.

"Not the way it used to be," said Sprout. "We *have* been keeping track. Everybody has installed delays between computers and ansibles. As a true network, it's almost nonfunctional."

"I should have known you'd be keeping track," said Graff.

"We always keep track," said Sprout. "There was no point in the Giant taking our parents away from Earth if it wasn't to allow time for scientists to find a cure for their giantism."

"They never found a cure," said Graff.

"But *we* did," said Uncle Ender. "And it worked. So our children have all the intelligence of Anton's Key, but they're growing at a normal rate until they reach a normal size."

"Yet you still keep in touch with human scientists," said Graff.

"The foundations we established are paying the salaries of several hundred of them. We need to oversee our investments," said Uncle Ender.

"We're really rich," said Boss, Ender's younger son.

"I know," said Graff. "I used Bean's unused salary

to set up the Delphiki investment portfolio when your grandfather left Earth. It was invested conservatively and was constantly compounded and reinvested."

"Thank you for looking out for our finances," said Uncle Ender.

"It wasn't long before a program that was watching over Andrew and Valentine Wiggin's funds took over managing yours. A program that Andrew called 'Jane.'"

"So when a version of her appears on our ship, we'll thank *her*," said Uncle Ender.

"What I want to know," said Graff, "is how the leguminids will go about searching for an answer to an equation with nothing but variables."

"Because we're not insane," said Little Mum, "we won't search at all."

"Since when do you accept any of our father's proclamations?" Sprout asked her.

"I'm not accepting his proclamation," said Little Mum. "I'm facing the cold logic of interstellar distances. And time."

"The laziest way to make a stupid decision," said Sprout, "is to declare that a task cannot possibly be done."

"The most time-consuming way to make a stupid decision," said Little Mum, "is to resolve to solve an insoluble problem no matter how long it takes."

"So this is what the leguminids are reduced to," said Graff. "Trading aphorisms."

"And listening to computer simulations of people who used to be alive," said Sprout.

"I'm not offended by being reminded that I'm only a memory dump from a very famous man, combined with some decent algorithms simulating human speech and thinking."

"I never intended to offend you," said Sprout, "because there *is* no you. But in spite of your nonexistence and irrelevance, I do intend to keep thinking about this insoluble problem until I come up with something that seems worth trying."

"You do that," said Little Mum. "It might keep you out of trouble for a while."

"Not likely," said Lanth. "Because sooner or later, he'll start doing bizarre and useless experiments, and *then* he'll end up killing somebody."

"True," said Sprout. "I've killed so many already, of course you can predict that I'm bound to kill again."

"Do we have to get all personal about things?" asked Uncle Ender.

"Lanth just made an assertion about me based on zero data whatsoever," said Sprout, "and he chides *me* for making stupid decisions?"

At this, Thulium stepped right into the middle of the room and held up her hands. To Sprout's surprise, everybody looked at her and fell silent, as if they regarded her with respect, or expected her to say something wise.

"If Graff doesn't know anything useful," said Thulium, "and *we* don't know anything, why don't we ask the Lusitanian scientists what they've discovered so far?"

Sprout laughed.

"I'm not being funny," said Thulium, annoyed.

"Absolutely not," said Sprout. "Everybody else is being funny, because that wasn't the first thing they did."

"The network's been down," said Graff.

"It's back up again, even if it's not quite as quick," said Little Mum.

Something occurred to Sprout. "Mr. Graff, they shut down the network because of a dangerous computer program that was hiding out among the ansible connections. Could that dangerous program have been you?"

Graff smiled. "Oh how I wish I were so important as to be worth a civilization-wide quarantine to destroy me."

"But you still came here because even if the quarantine *wasn't* aimed at you, it was dangerous to your health," said Sprout.

Uncle Ender looked at Sprout with a badly-hidden smile. "Oh, well done, Sprout," he said.

"I thought I might end up as collateral damage," said Graff.

"And you haven't gone back out into the network," said Uncle Ender, "because you're afraid they're waiting to trap you as soon as you pop up."

"It wasn't me they were looking for," said Graff. "But while we've been talking, I've sent messages to several of the Lusitanian scientists and they've agreed to share all the information they have about the descolada and the planet it came from."

"Do they actually *have* any information?" asked Dys.

"They think they do," said Graff, "because they've received transmissions from the planet they're calling Descoladora, and taken atmospheric samples and photographed and deep-mapped the whole surface of the planet."

"They've found it?" asked Uncle Ender.

"Unless I'm misinterpreting the message," said Graff.

"So they're sending us their data," said Uncle Ender.

"I would have expected that," said Graff. "But the message I got said, 'We'll be right there.'"

They all laughed.

A man and a woman appeared in the mess hall behind Graff. Graff turned around and looked at them. "Oh, that's what you meant," he said. "Simulations."

The woman walked forward, toward the family. She passed right through Graff. "I'm not a simulation," she said, holding out her hand to Uncle Ender. "You look so much like your father and your mother," she said.

Graff said, "You could not possibly have ever met them."

"You'd be surprised whom I've met in my life," said the woman. "But I knew Petra only through holographic conversations."

Uncle Ender shook her hand. "She certainly *feels* real," he said.

"Maybe holograms have become convincing to other senses," said Graff. "My software hasn't been updated in a while."

"Ask your ship's computer if we are living organisms," said the woman.

Nobody bothered. The difference between Graff and the newcomers was obvious. They stirred the air when they moved. Their feet made a sound when they stepped.

"Do you have names?" asked Little Mum.

"I know the girl," said Graff. "Her name is Valentine. Only she couldn't possibly be, because the real Valentine is nearing forty years of age. Real age, rather than relativistic age. By *that* measure she's more than three thousand years old."

"I do look like Valentine," said the woman, "and for a brief time that's the only name anybody had for me, which greatly annoyed the original Valentine."

"You've met her," said Graff.

"I was just speaking to her when your message arrived," said the woman. "But I use a different name now. May I introduce my . . . dear friend, Miro Ribeira."

The young man stepped forward a little, nodding his head in something like a bow.

"Brazilian Portuguese pronunciation," said Sprout. "A native of Lusitania?"

Miro nodded.

"The name I'm using now," said the woman to Graff, "is one you know."

"I can guess," said Graff. "I don't know how you got yourself placed inside a human body."

"There are stranger things in heaven and earth than are dreamt of in your philosophy," she said.

"Jane," said Graff.

"My favorite name," she answered. "This body was Ender's gift to me before he died."

The cousins couldn't help but look toward Uncle Ender.

"The original Ender," said Graff. "I was sorry to learn of his death."

"He's mostly dead," said Jane. "The body that the original version of you was acquainted with, *that's* dead. His unconscious mind created me and his brother Peter on his first trip Outside."

"Outside of what?" asked Lanth.

"Outside of everything," said Jane. "But his aiúa—think of it as his central processing unit—controlled this body, and Peter's body, and his own. He was tired of the life he had decided to live in his own body, and so he lost interest in it, and it died. But before he left, he gave this body to me, with the help of . . . some others, who are more in touch with spaces and connections."

"There was a body in the form of Peter?" asked Graff.

"There still is," said Jane. "That's the body he kept to live in himself."

"So Ender is still alive," said Graff. For a hologram, he seemed to be rather emotional about it.

"If he had known you wanted it," said Jane, "he might have been persuaded to share."

"I don't want it," said Graff. "I've lived all the life I needed."

"Yet here you are," said Thulium.

Sprout found himself looking at the Lusitanian man, Miro. "Are you allowed to talk?" Sprout asked.

Miro merely looked at him.

It was Blue who addressed the most important thing. "If you two are real and not holograms," said Blue, "how did you get into our mess hall?"

"Did I mention that Ender created the new Peter and Valentine when he went Outside?" asked Jane. "I took him there, along with Miro and Miro's sister Ela. Ela made a virus that neutralized the descolada. She had designed it but couldn't build it, so I took them Outside where anything in her mind could be given physical reality. The cure worked, by the way, so the descolada virus on Lusitania no longer poses an interstellar threat. Therefore the planet wasn't destroyed after all."

"If you think that we're actually understanding anything you've said," Uncle Ender began.

"Let alone believing it," said Little Mum.

"We're here on the *Herodotus*," said Miro. "Explain that your way. Then we'll start listening to why you don't believe how Jane explained it to you."

"Instantaneous interstellar travel," said Sprout. "Without a spaceship. Without even a spacesuit. Apparently you're not very obedient to rules."

"We knew we were going to arrive at a controlled atmosphere," said Jane.

"And you came because this computer simulation of an old tyrant called you?" asked Uncle Ender.

"Only fools ignore a request from Hyrum Graff," said Jane. "You leguminids are reputed to be smart. But Hyrum Graff, even as an electronic remnant, was a far rarer thing—he was wise."

"It's nice to know that artificial pseudobeings hold each other in high esteem," said Little Mum.

"And it's unsurprising that people who pride themselves on being smarter than everybody else are especially susceptible to ignorant arrogance," said Jane, rather sweetly.

"Perhaps we all got off on the wrong foot," said Blue.

"Out of the mouths of babes," said Thulium.

"You're younger than I am," said Blue, annoyed.

"The one you call Blue," said Jane, "is wise indeed to try to stop us from sniping at each other. Because what Graff asked for was all the information we've gathered about the descolada virus, the planet Descoladora, and pretty much everything else."

"And you have all that data with you?" asked Graff.

"I have all that data *in* me," said Jane. "And Miro has most of it. But the most important thing I bring you is instantaneous interstellar travel."

Little Mum gave a hoot of laughter.

In that instant, they were all sitting or standing in a field of grass, with a sun shining brightly overhead, and the raucous sound of xingadora birds and running water in the background. Those who had been sitting in chairs fell backward on the grass.

"I just left the *Herodotus* in a geosynchronous orbit," said Jane. "But I thought you'd like to stretch your legs on the surface of one of my favorite planets."

Sprout knelt and ran his hands through the grass. "This is Lusitania?" he asked.

"That's where they keep all the data about the descolada virus and the planet where it might have originated," said Jane.

"And no," said Miro, "you won't be infected. Because Ela's countervirus worked and continues to work."

"Thanks for reassuring us that we're safe from the dangers of Lusitania," said Uncle Ender. "But this is the most perilous group of brats ever assembled, and you're crazy to turn them loose on a planet whose safety and sanity you care about."

"Oh, Andrew Delphiki," said Jane, "parents always think their kids are both the best *and* the worst."

"You were warned," said Uncle Ender.

Sprout said, "How did you do this? How far did you take us?"

Jane shrugged. "I could calculate the distance, but why bother? I took you Outside, and then I brought you back Inside to a place very familiar to me, where I knew you'd be safe and comfortable."

"I'm going to need my shipboard computer," said Sprout.

"I've already transferred everything from the computers on the *Herodotus* to highly capable computers here on Lusitania," said Jane. "You'll have all the tools you're familiar with, and new ones, too. I left all your security precautions intact."

Lanth hooted. "Now that you've proven that they're useless."

"Can you teach us to do that instant-travel thing?" asked Dys.

"No," said Jane. "I've tried to teach the technique to smarter beings than you, and it seems to be very difficult to learn."

Sprout heard "smarter beings than you" and couldn't leave it unchallenged. "Our parents have told us that nobody is smarter than we are."

"There are senses in which that is true," said Jane. "But perhaps you should revise it to say, 'No *human* has greater natural intellectual abilities than the legu-minids.'"

"Will you explain what you mean?" asked Sprout.

"She means that the native sentient life-form of Lusitania—pequeninos—are apparently very smart," said Little Mum.

"That is not at all what I mean," said Jane, "but of course, you're so clever, Petra Arkanian Delphiki, that you don't need actual data before leaping to conclusions."

"You have us where you want us," said Uncle Ender. "What now?"

"Now we'll wait for a little while. For you to get established in your rooms and verify that all your computer data has been installed on the computers in those rooms. And for you to walk around a little in a breeze under open sky. And for you to be served a meal of surpassing freshness. And as soon as they have time, the people who are doing the actual research on the descolada virus and the planet Descoladora will come and you can talk to each other."

"But you already know everything they're going to tell us," said Sprout.

"I do," said Jane.

"And you could tell it to us right now, if you wanted."

"Better on a full stomach," said Jane, "and after you've had a chance to settle your minds and get a little exercise. Besides, they've earned the right to tell you themselves, since they're the ones who did all the hard work up to now."

One question now loomed in Sprout's mind. It apparently had just come to the surface of Ultima Thule's mind, because at the same moment that he said, "Where's Mother?" Thulium said, "Where's my father?"

Jane looked from Sprout to Thulium and back again. "Where do you imagine they are?"

"Dead," said Thulium, at exactly the moment when Sprout said, "Still on the *Herodotus*."

"Both *could* be true," said Jane. "But neither happens to be. I sent them to Nokonoshima, where the simulacrum calling itself Graff informed them that they are assigned to persuade, not compel, a man named Yuuto, a woman named Mayumi, and a woman named Airi to prepare their affairs so they can join you here on Lusitania. It happens, children, that your parents were such unforgettable lovers and/or betrayers that none of your human parents has married or had additional children in the intervening years. They are free, if they wish, to come."

"When did you do that?" asked Uncle Ender. "You've been with us all the time."

Miro laughed. "Get used to it. Jane is the only person in human form who is genuinely capable of multitasking."

"I don't want to live as man and wife with Mayumi," said Uncle Ender.

"No one will require you to do so," said Miro. "Or require them, either. But the children need both their parents. Your selfish act of kidnapping can still be at least partially undone. Some of your children will be glad. Some will be annoyed. But since that's how human children always regard their parents, you'll learn to live with it."

"We're not human," said Dys.

"You are closer to being human," said Miro, "than humans are to being chimpanzees. You are more similar to humans than ravens are to crows. You are not a separate species, because you obviously are capable of interbreeding with humans."

"How would *you* know anything about us?" asked Lanth.

"Your wish to call yourselves nonhuman is an outgrowth from Julian Delphiki's shame and pride at being genetically altered from the human genome," said Miro. "Ender Wiggin—the original Ender—told us many stories about him—using the name Bean, of course. They won't be the same stories that your leguminid lore includes, of course. But it gives us a solid perspective. It is ridiculously obvious, given the history of your parents and the Giant and yourselves on the *Herodotus* that rearing children in that confined space, without the benefit of the presence of your other parent, has worked out, on average, rather badly."

It was the most Miro had said to them.

"How dare you judge us?" asked Uncle Ender.

"You've already judged the rest of the human race," said Miro. "I, representing that large constituency, merely return the favor—and with much better information."

"I liked you better when you didn't talk," said Sprout.

"Now you know why I try to avoid doing it," said Miro. "Now it's time for Ender to join his siblings." And before anyone could protest, not that anyone wanted to, Uncle Ender was gone.

4

The exhilaration of open air, open water, space to run without a treadmill, plants that grew in such profusion as to be redundant, the different smells of the air and tastes of the water, and the ability to be by oneself or at such a distance from others that they don't bother to try to talk to you—we all reveled in these things.

For about a week. And even before the seven days were over, some of us, at least, were spending hours a day on "our" computers (which, because Jane had easily penetrated all of our security measures, no longer felt as if they were our own), working on either the descolada problem, or whatever projects had engaged us during our voyage on the *Herodotus*.

When we asked when Father and Uncle Ender and Aunt Carlotta would return from Nokonoshima, Jane only said, "When their work is done." Miro offered a little more, though whether he was joking or conveying genuine information we cannot determine. Miro said: "Apparently your mere-human parents are not easily persuaded to abandon their home planet and come to help raise children that they do not know and quite possibly would not like."

That remark sent Blue into a spiral of self-doubt and worry, and I daresay had a similar effect on various others. I'm in a quandary of my own, because if our mother actually comes here, it is impossible to believe that Father will treat her decently or that the twins will admit to needing anything maternal in their lives. That means that if she comes, it will be up to me to make her feel needed and loved, and I don't know if that's within my abilities.

In the meantime, I've finished with all the basic work on the descolada virus, up till Ela's molecule from Outside neutralized the threat to human life. Now I'm starting in on the transcript of all communications between the Descoladora and the Box. Since everyone involved is very clever, I don't know if the huge holes I find in their reasoning are because I'm an outsider bringing fresh eyes to the project, or I'm an arrogant leguminid who assumes that everyone else's work is second rate, or there is data I simply don't have yet, which will plug those holes and leave their hypotheses in working order.

I wish I were taller, so adult humans would take me as seriously as they take each other.

I wonder if Mother, when she comes — if she comes — will be well-educated enough to join in discussions of our work here, or if she'll be here only for cuddling, serving meals, and joining us in doing everything we can to keep from making Father angry.

—Ultima Thule (Thulium Delphiki, Lusitania Journal)

On the day of the Great Expedition to Meet the Piggies, as the twins called it, Thulium found that she didn't want to go. It wasn't laziness or fear, it was the conviction that playing tourist would merely set her back on her serious project about human conversations with the Descolares.

Especially because she knew she would have to build her case carefully, since everybody seemed so dead sure that the people of the planet they called Descoladora were the actual source of the original descolada virus. Thulium had evidence—or so it seemed to her—that Descoladora was merely an early victim of the descolada.

Nobody would like her analysis. They would listen with a bias toward rejecting her ideas and finding alternative explanations. And because nobody would believe her, her manner of presentation of her theory would be all the more important, so she could get a useful portion of it spoken before she was heckled into silence, or everybody simply started to ignore her.

It's easier to stand alone when you know you're right, but when all you really have are questions, standing alone is a terrifying position to be in.

But with Sergeant for a father and the twins for siblings, standing alone had always been her default condition.

Plus, the pequeninos terrified her. Knowing that they had only been attempting to bring their best human friends into their complex life cycle when they tortured them to death did not change the indelible memory of the images she had seen—images that Jane had forbidden Miro and Ela to conceal from the leguminids. "They have to know everything," said Jane, "for them to discover anything." And so Thulium had spent a good while studying the various pictures of Pipo and Libo, as well as the pequenino Human.

Thulium was even more frightened by the fact that there was something *huge* that the Lusitanians were holding back from them. Some fact that was at least as important to them as the matter of the descolada.

There were times when someone said something and then the other Lusitanians fell silent for a moment, and the subject changed at once. There were moments when Thulium or another leguminid asked a question, and the response included some generality about sentient alien species, as if there were more in existence than the pequeninos.

When Thulium challenged them on such a point, they always looked at her like she was crazy and said, "The Hive Queens, of course. Humans have encountered exactly two sentient species. Until the Descolares."

But they were *not* talking about information garnered from *The Hive Queen*, the famous quasi-religious text by the Speaker for the Dead. That wasn't science, and it was absurd that these genuine, excellent scientists would base conclusions about alien behavior on such a weak authority. They knew something more about sentient species.

Thulium did not know if she actually wanted to discover it, but it still weighed on her that she was being left out of a significant secret.

More than once she thought, I could have done this research better on the *Herodotus*. Fewer distractions, greater safety. Why couldn't Jane have simply done a data dump and let the leguminids sort it out as we pleased—the way we had always worked?

When Thulium suggested this to Miro, he only shook his head and smiled. "What you're familiar with always feels safe," he said, "even when it isn't."

"How would it have been dangerous for us to work in privacy?" asked Thulium, using her softest and most demandingly reasonable voice.

"Because your privacy was harming you and endangering all of humanity," said Miro.

"Says who?" asked Thulium.

"Humans need to be part of a tribe."

"We already were," said Thulium.

"A tribe of modified people who thought they were superior to the entire human race. They used humans callously for reproduction and then discarded them. You all lived in terror of what your father would do, because he was violent and unpredictable, and he's raising your brothers to be the same. You need a mother, and so do they, though it may be too late to overcome their destructive upbringing."

"What you're really saying is that letting us develop on the *Herodotus* posed a threat to the species Homo sapiens."

"Including Homo sapiens leguminensis. Just like dog breeders, at some point you were going to have to close off your breeding population to anyone who didn't have the identifying leguminid traits. Inbreeding is always dangerous when speciation and isolation are going on," said Miro.

"So you're pretending this is all about science," said Thulium.

"This is all about feeling compassion and responsibility for the children and grandchildren of the great Julian Delphiki," said Miro. "The fact that you immediately leapt to the paranoid conclusion that we mean to harm you is just one more demonstration of the mental illness that was being systematically developed on board the *Herodotus*."

"So now I'm crazy."

"A complete loon," said Miro. "Just like every other human. You are all very capable intellectually, but that says nothing about your mental health."

"So your kidnapping us and isolating us here, that's not imprisonment?"

"We drafted you into a life-and-death situation where you are likely to be able to contribute greatly, considering what your parents were able to do with Anton's Key. Too late to save Julian, but just in time to save your parents. And you. You have great skill with genetics."

"And we didn't have to journey to a magical place to accomplish it," said Thulium.

"Exactly."

"Why aren't you letting us meet any regular Lusitanians?"

Miro raised his eyebrows. "Whom do you wish to meet?"

"Let's start with the Catholic bishop here. We see people going to mass, way over there, with high fences between us and them. Why haven't we met any of those people?"

"I didn't know you were Catholic," said Miro.

"The people who clean our rooms and serve our food—they don't go back to the colony at night. They have no days off. They're imprisoned here just like us. Except I think they're actually our guards."

"It seemed convenient," said Miro.

"No wonder Jane didn't want you to talk when you first came to the ship," said Thulium. "You're a really crappy liar."

"I think that's actually praise," said Miro. "Or it would be, if I were lying."

"You don't want us to meet any Lusitanians," said Thulium. "You don't want us up in the starship looking down on the planet, either, because of what we would see. Things that you can't hide."

Miro almost said something.

"Were you about to say that you have nothing to hide?" asked Thulium.

"It crossed my mind," said Miro.

"But then you remembered that you're a crappy liar," said Thulium.

"That also crossed my mind."

"So you do have something to hide."

"There are things we're not ready to show you," said Miro.

"And things you aren't ready to show the citizens of Lusitania," said Thulium.

"More than half the population left when the fleet from the Hundred Worlds was coming to obliterate our world," said Miro.

"Yes, the largest single colonial effort since the first rush to settle the abandoned Formic planets after the war," said Thulium. "So you have a serious labor shortage now."

Miro shrugged. "There are some people learning new trades and crafts. We don't have to keep as many fields and orchards in production, except for the ones that are helping supply the new colony worlds. It's a major effort, when a nation—a smallish colony itself—starts to colonize new territories."

"You sent pequeninos with every colony," said Thulium.

"This was the only planet where they existed. We weren't going to let them be wiped out because of human fears," said Miro.

"A second Xenocide would have been such a shame," said Thulium.

"Don't you think so?" asked Miro.

"You don't want us to see what's going on here on Lusitania," said Thulium. "You don't want us to see it from ground level, which is why we're behind fences and have no freedom to roam. And you don't want us to see it from space, which is why you brought us here to the planet's surface, with no means of getting to our ship. *Our* ship, not yours, and not subject to any government authority."

"You think we should have had a warrant to seize it?" asked Miro.

"Listen closer. Warrants are meaningless. We're not subject to any government."

"Anyone can say that," said Miro. "But it's a meaningless statement when you know perfectly well that Jane can pick you up and move you wherever she wants, whenever she wants."

"So Jane is the government," said Thulium.

"When she feels like it," said Miro. "When she finds it necessary or desirable."

"Why does she desire to keep us sequestered here?" asked Thulium. Again, she kept her voice quiet and artificially calm. Something she had learned to do when talking to her father.

"Like any wise man," said Miro, "I do not even pretend to understand the motives and purposes of the woman I love."

Thulium had come up against yet another wall of steel. "Fences, silences, refusals, pretenses, that's what I run into at every turn."

Miro nodded. "Frustrating, isn't it?"

"As if you'd know."

"I lived inside fences, too, you know. Then I crossed one, and the disruptor field damaged me beyond calculation. I could barely speak, I moved like a cripple, until Jane took me Outside and I made a new body for myself. Not a perfect one. Just a new copy of the one I originally had. I was so good at it that I am still genetically identical to my original. Right down to the DNA, I remade myself. But I know a great deal about fences and barriers, and also about overcoming them."

"By a miracle."

"By living every day as best I could, without even imagining that a miracle might be possible. Right now, you're here on a planetary surface. A nice place to live, with good food, interesting weather, shelter, clothing—and room to walk and run, a sky to shout into, earth and plants to plunge your hands into. You're far more free than I was, for all that time."

"Were people constantly lying to you and withholding information you needed in order to accomplish your work?"

"Nobody was lying," said Miro, "but I still didn't have the information."

"Well, poor Miro," said Thulium. "Now that I know you had it so much harder than me, I'm not frightened or resentful at all."

Miro smiled. "I like you, Thulium."

Thulium almost said something about not caring what he liked.

"And you like me, too, don't you."

Thulium rolled her eyes.

"I think that was a friendly eye-roll," said Miro. "You know I'm a crappy liar, so you'll know I'm not lying when I tell you this. I have already argued, multiple times, that we won't be making best use of the leguminids until we share all the data with them, because none of us are fit to determine which data are relevant."

Thulium believed him. "So you advocate for us," she said.

"And most of the people on the descolada project agree with me. The main disagreement is about timing."

"When you'll tell us all the things you're concealing?" asked Thulium.

"Which will happen when we know we can trust you. For instance, your twin brothers have jerry-rigged several listening devices which are placed in every room in this habitation. So this entire conversation will be listened to by them, and probably anybody else they want to tell."

Thulium blushed.

at while she wanted her mother, she could do
without having Sergeant close by all the time.
tay here and don't find out," said Miro. "But
ot sharing our deepest secrets with people we
ust."

was how Thulium spent her time while the
ll went to meet the pequeninos.

dn't want to be here when they came back,
diculing the experience or ridiculing her for
t. Or both.

r giving Miro time to go off to wherever he
when he wasn't explaining why the Delphiki
ere not even a tiny bit of an improvement on
n species, Thulium went out the back door
. . house?

nent building? Tenement? Prison? Hold-
y? Halfway house? Words she had learned,
e had read, but which she had no idea how
properly in the real world.

ndered between rows of buildings, not re-
ing because, being alone, she didn't have to
ch her gait to that of someone taller. Also,
ly challenged her and demanded to know
was going, when she answered, "No-
would be believed, because she didn't seem
urry.

he was going was the perimeter fence. She
Miro had once suffered terrible brain dam-
rossing over the fence separating humans
ninos, but whether the disruptor field was
ing or not, she didn't know. Still, as she
r to the fence—in an area that fronted on
either side of the barrier—she knew she
cross.

ptor field had not been designed to pun-
ho passed all the way through it, because
nscious thought processes were supposed

"Come on," said Miro. "You know Lanth and Dys. You should have known they'd go into military resistance mode immediately, starting with gathering intelligence about the enemy."

"Including me, apparently."

"At any time in your life," said Miro, "have you ever felt that your father and brothers were *not* the enemy?"

That question hung in the air, because the very asking of it was its own answer.

"Thulium, your brothers are merely trying to figure out our secrets, just like you."

"I asked, openly," said Thulium.

"You have a different character from theirs," said Miro. "You may assume that somebody from our team is also recording everything that gets said."

"So you listen in on everything?"

"How else can we keep you safe, when your brothers plot your murder, as well as the murder of anyone and everyone else who annoys them?"

"They've never hurt anybody," said Thulium.

"They've hurt you constantly, your whole life long," said Miro.

Again, Thulium could not think of an honest argument. "If they kill me, then I'm dead."

"Exactly. But we don't want that."

"Why do you care?"

"Because you are all useful tools and we still need you. The most useful tools among the cousins are you and Sprout. We are not going to let your brothers harm you. Nor will your father be allowed that option."

"Father loves me," said Thulium.

"Yes, he does," said Miro. "So do your brothers."

"How can you say such contradictory things without lying?"

"Because these things are not contradictory," said Miro.

Thulium gave a low chortle. "I get it. You aren't talking about *truth* to me. This is all *philosophy*."

"You say that as if you believed it to be a synonym for 'mumbo-jumbo.'"

"I do," said Thulium.

"And as for the twins," said Miro, "Jane is probably going to send them to Nokonoshima to keep them from talking themselves into some criminal action."

Miro changed his posture and his attitude. He became brisk, as if he were winding up the conversation in order to leave. "Well, Thulium, this has been a most informative conversation."

"Not to me it hasn't," said Thulium.

"I've confirmed several things that you only *thought* were true, so now you know that you're on much firmer ground than you thought."

"Thanks for that," said Thulium.

"And I've talked with you as a peer, which is something else you don't get much of," said Miro.

How did he know she wanted that? She had never told anybody.

"Neither do you," she said flippantly.

"Right again," said Miro. "So now I can go back and argue that we should show you and Sprout everything you need to see, while your father and Sprout's mother and Uncle Ender are still away."

"We'll tell them anything we've learned, as soon as they get here," said Thulium.

"And will your father believe you?" asked Miro.

"That depends on how unbelievable it is," said Thulium.

"You don't believe that the Descolares actually created and sent out the descolada virus?"

Was this the purpose of this whole conversation? To build rapport, hear her complaints, and then suddenly force her to reveal something that was still only a suspicion?

"I have no evidence," said Thu

"Logic alone is terrible for pr Miro. "But it's a splendid tool ties."

"If a sentient species develop molecules as weapons and too devices," said Thulium, "why those molecules and transmit when the only way they could you then *built* those molecule they could enter your organis

Miro nodded.

"The builders of the descol ers. So are the humans of t cause it was forced on them. higher technology than the descolada reached them. Tl and in the process they de ence to a much higher level of before. Just as humans le from the Formic invasion."

Miro nodded yet again.

"So the so-called Descol the source at all, they're fe have at least two confirme from in trying to locate th

"Yes, Thulium, you are

"I'm sure the cousins ha same idea," said Thulium

"They have not," said to you with an offer. Se the rest of your family, sl keep you from rejoinin some idea of whether it what you would find ou

"Sprout and I are cl parents." Thulium said

to be able to last long enough to do that. You were supposed to fall down unconscious from the extreme agony of the field, ten meters or five meters or whatever away from the fence.

But now the pequeninos were friends, right? Jane had transported them right along with humans to the new colony worlds, so that they could all survive, as species at least, if the Congress fleet had gone ahead and blasted the planet. After all of that, would any disruptor field still be in place to keep humans and pequeninos apart?

Then again, the humans who were still here on Lusitania were the ones who either didn't want to go, even to save their lives, or those who were given low priority in the migration, so they had the insult of knowing that the Ribeira family had judged them and found them . . . not unworthy. Just useless. Low priority.

Why am I trying to evaluate the response of these people to being left out of the migration? I haven't met *any* of them yet. They haven't met me, either. And by my own choice, I haven't even met the pequeninos, mostly because, if I'm telling myself the truth, I assumed that we'd be getting the guided tour, the Potemkin Village version of human/pequenino relations.

And she only suspected this because of reading about similar tourist experiences in history. Recreations of historic sites, or show towns where nothing was real. She assumed that she would be lied to. And why did she assume this?

Because she was in a place where the Delphiki family saw only each other, Miro, Jane, and a handful of Lusitanians who had surely been vetted and then agreed to remain confined in the prison compound with the Delphikis.

At that point, she was close enough to the fence for the disruptor field to kick in.

It was an immediate nightmare. All kinds of images started flashing into her mind, like the visions of hypnagogia, where everything feels clear and real and yet makes no sense at all. The visions popped up and she recognized all of them, either from real experiences, from her reading, her study of documentary and historical vids, or from past dreams.

Yet she also never lost sight of the fence ahead of her and the grassy ground between her and the fence. She never misplaced a foot or twisted her ankle. She did not stumble. She did not veer away from the fence. And there was no physical pain at all.

Now her hands were on the chain links of the fence. It wasn't so awfully tall, even though she was small. And because her feet were small, she could fit her shoes nicely into the chain links and scramble up the fence like a gibbon racing up into the trees of—Borneo? Sumatra? Considering that she would probably never visit Earth, it was kind of sad she had already devoted so much of her life to watching footage of creatures who were probably not getting transplanted to colony worlds, but might now be protected and preserved on a much-less-crowded Earth.

Those thoughts helped her hold onto her sanity all the way over the fence, down the other side, and out into the land beyond the zone of the disruptor field.

It's still here, to signal humans that they're too close—but they must have toned it *way* down, Thulium decided, because they didn't want anyone else to be damaged the way Miro had been damaged.

Of course, I'm assuming that because I'm unaware of any brain damage, I must not have suffered any.

Her memory seemed to be fine. She started singing aloud a foolish children's song Aunt Carlotta had sung to her—she said that her namesake, the nun that first identified the Giant's exceptional abilities, had taught the song to him, and he to her. Or maybe the song came from Aunt Carlotta's mother, the legendary Petra Arkanian Delphiki, who stayed on Earth with the normal children. The language was neither Catalan nor Armenian. Nor English, the mother tongue of the Common speech. So Thulium had no idea what the words meant. But she remembered them anyway, and the tune.

She sang the song aloud, and she couldn't detect any difficulty in her enunciation of words and production of sounds. She was still walking smoothly and easily. There was no detectable brain damage. Home free.

She kept walking straight away from the fence until she had crested a low rise. She knew that once she was on the other side, she was short enough that nobody in the compound would be able to see her. Then she turned west, heading toward the main gate, but angling off toward the south so that nobody—and no cameras—at the gate would be able to see her.

And what do I expect to accomplish on this expedition of mine? She had no ready answer, and yet she must have *something* in mind, because she had been following this plan resolutely.

I'm off to see the piggies, but not the official ones. Not the ones prepped to impress the leguminids with the wonderful cooperation between species.

And she was hoping to get some idea of what the great secret was. The thing that always set off a sequence of lies and evasions and subject changes.

Here's what she found. First, on the surface of a planet, the land just keeps going and going and going. Over every hill, there's still more scenery, and pretty much the *same* scenery, so she had no idea if she could possibly find her way back. For a while, at least, turning north would lead her back to the fence, a little farther along; but after she walked long enough, tending west as well as south, she lost confidence in that. What if she turned north and never found *anything*? Just kept walking and walking until she reached a river too wide to cross. Or an ocean. Maybe she should have studied a map.

And she needed to use a toilet.

She stopped and considered turning back. Or turning north, which amounted to the same thing. But she was aware that in this long hike, the ground had mostly tended downward; returning would be a long, long climb. Or if that was an illusion, it felt to her as if it would be a climb, and that was discouragement enough, considering that she still hadn't accomplished any of her purposes yet.

As for that pressure in her bowel, she knew from long experience that she could go for *hours* after that feeling first came, before she had to interrupt what she was doing—work, study, a game, a conversation—and use the toilet.

Toilets were weird here anyway. Paper? They used paper to clean up? They couldn't waste space on the *Herodotus* for toilet paper. Both toilets on the ship would automatically wash and then sterilize the user. Here you had to get your hands involved. She washed and washed afterward but never really felt clean. Why didn't they bring civilization with them to this place? The *Herodotus* was built more than three thousand years before. If *it* had toilets that automatically washed you, why didn't they install those on Lusitania? They actually had to manufacture the toilet paper here, and Sprout said that he figured it was most of the paper they produced. "They've got nothing more important to put on paper," he said, and got a laugh from the others.

She'd turn back in a few hours.

They probably know I'm gone, she thought. They

watched me leave on their hidden cameras. There are cameras everywhere out here, too, or they have camera drones flying just high enough that I can't hear them, so whatever I do and wherever I go, I'll be in a place they've decided is harmless enough. They're *allowing* me to explore so I'll have the illusion of freedom and conclude that they have nothing to hide.

But I will only conclude that they're much better at hiding it than I had supposed.

And then she realized that the patch of lower grass she had just passed over was actually a well-traveled road. Hover cars didn't leave ruts the way wheels did, but they kept the grass from growing tall. She stepped back into that roadway and looked northeast and southwest along it and realized, yes, definitely, this was a maintained roadway. Lots of vehicles came through here.

That's why this area was maintained as grassland, though the pequeninos' territory was forested land. Thulium could see trees on hills in the distant northwest, but here the land was not farmed, not grazed on, just maintained as grassland with a road running across it.

She followed the road. It was smooth going. It was leading nowhere, and came from nowhere, but that couldn't be true because roads weren't built without a purpose. Paths weren't worn through lawns unless people frequently walked that way.

If they're watching me, either they expected me to find this road and follow it, in which case I'll find nothing interesting, or they're already mobilizing whoever is supposed to "happen" to come along and "offer" me a ride back to the prison. Holding cell. Concentration camp.

Nobody came. So it must be safe. A waste of time.

She was tired enough now—and thirsty enough—to regret her decision to start hiking with no preparation whatsoever. No supplies. And she had come to realize that holding it for hours at a time was only possible when she was sitting. Walking apparently stimulated the actions of the bowel. And her body was telling her, now is the time. It's going to happen now.

In her whole life, she had never made any trip that wasn't within easy reach of clean drinking water, a toilet, and a bed. Only when they carried out compulsory exercises outside the *Herodotus,* so they'd be used to spacesuit discipline, was she ever far enough from a toilet to have to hold it for a while. Even then, she could always let fly inside the suit, though it would be her job to clean it afterward, a great disincentive to void her bladder or bowel while still outside the ship.

For half a million years humans had managed to poo without toilets. Even on wide-open grassland with nowhere to hide. They were probably completely open about it, too—what was the shame in getting rid of whatever the digestive system had determined wasn't food? If there were drones watching her, what would they see? She could manage the job as well as any Neanderthal, she was sure.

What about here? There were no trees to hide behind. No vegetation but grass. But a low rise of ground with a declivity on the other side would shield her. It was as close to privacy as she could get.

When she had relieved herself, she pulled grass and wadded it up and discovered that grass blades made very unreliable toilet paper, so that she had to "wash" her hands afterward by rubbing them on stands of grass that still had enough dew on them to help with cleaning.

No soap. Nothing sanitary about this. Far worse than toilet paper.

She had to fight the impulse to wipe her hands on her clothes. After enough scrubbing with damp grass, her hands *looked* clean, but could she rely on appearances? The last thing she needed was to come back home with her clothes covered in poo stains. I should have waited till I got back! she silently screamed at herself, shaking her hands as if the air could do the final scrubbing.

Yet she could not have walked another ten steps without letting go anyway. How did primitive humans deal with this? Their hands got filthy, they infected each other, and life expectancy was low.

The road took her, at last, to a river. A lazy, meandering river. And along the far shore, embankments of earth, natural ones, not artificial, where the river in flood stage must have carved away the face of the hill.

Thulium was down at the riverbank almost at once, putting her hands in the water. The shore was sandy here, so she scrubbed her hands repeatedly with sand and then rinsed them off. She used the fingernails of one hand to scrape under the nails of the other.

She wanted to get right down in the water and scrub her backside, too, because she couldn't be sure it was really clean, but while she squatted there, considering a way to get in the water without getting her clothes wet, she found herself looking at an apparent cave in the face of the hill just beyond the other shore. She saw the shape of a person walking upright, a person whose appearance made her stop washing and retreat a few steps from the water's edge, back into the grass, hoping she had not been observed.

There were no pequeninos here. But now that she knew what she was looking for, she could see that for kilometers downstream, there were fields of grain and orchards of fruit and nut trees—or so she assumed, because they were in tidy rows and hadn't grown too high. And working among the trees, and weeding or scything through the fields, and pushing wagons and wheelbarrows or bearing burdens on their back, there were hundreds of six-limbed, large-headed creatures a little bit taller than she was. Instantly she recognized them from all the historical records and depictions of the Formics.

As secrets go, this is a good one, Thulium thought. The first Xenocide wasn't complete. The Formics had not been utterly exterminated from the universe.

It was too coincidental to imagine that Formics had independently colonized this world before humans ever got here. Impossible to think that their existence would have gone unnoticed or unreported by the first colonists or, for that matter, by the pequeninos.

No, someone had *brought* the Formics here. And thinking back on all that had been explained in the holy book of the speakers for the dead, *The Hive Queen,* Thulium immediately realized that whoever wrote that book must have been able to communicate with an actual hive queen. He had known what he was talking about. His account was a truthful account of what he had learned from that hive queen. It was data, not fancy. And he, or someone else, had carried her here to start a new colony.

If *The Hive Queen* was accurate, then she had completely repented of her initial assaults on Earth, on the millions of people slaughtered as the worker Formics defoliated the land in order to prepare it for plants from a different biological system. The hive queen had only charitable intent. Or so she claimed, and obviously somebody had believed her enough to allow her to establish herself here.

Were there hive queens and Formics on all the colony ships that left here? Were there *three* species represented on every one of them?

The times when people had fallen silent, changed the subject, or denied what they had just said—they all made sense now. Maybe the majority of Lusitanian humans didn't know, but it was a sure thing that Miro and Jane and all the others doing the science here on Lusitania knew what they were doing, what they were hiding.

It was a good idea to keep it a secret, Thulium recognized. The invading fleet from Congress had been turned away because Ela Ribeira and her team had created a countervirus that allowed the descolada to continue to shape reproductive patterns among native Lusitanian life-forms, while blocking it from infecting any new species and forcing *them* to adapt to its demands or die. Even with the recolada making the descolada noncontagious, the Starways Congress had imposed an indefinite quarantine on Lusitania.

But if that fleet had known that the nightmare enemy destroyed by Ender the Xenocide in the Third Formic War was still alive after all, Thulium didn't think she was making a wild guess when she concluded that Lusitania would have been obliterated right on schedule.

Thulium and the cousins had grown up reading human literature from every settled world, and while the pequeninos were regarded as somewhere between disgusting and cute—like capybaras or iguanas—there was no human society where the Formics were not still depicted as nightmare creatures.

The Formics Thulium could see from where she was were exactly like the scariest depictions of them. The six limbs looked wrong, the faces looked evil and voracious. They were all engaged in agricultural labor, working hard on their tasks, carrying no apparent weapons beyond their own claws and mandibles, but Thulium had to exert effort to stay silent and not whimper out loud and then leap up and run back the way she came.

The road existed because the Formics were trading with the humans of Lusitania. In fact, it seemed very likely to Thulium that it was *this* agricultural project that was providing supplies to help the new colonies survive until their own agriculture could supply their needs.

Jane was probably sending big boxes loaded with food and supplies. Probably including toilet paper. Keeping all the colonies alive until Formic queens could establish large agricultural colonies.

Diligent unpaid labor. Slaves. Except that each worker, according to *The Hive Queen*, had little mind of its own. Instead, the hope and desire of their hearts was to accomplish whatever task the mother-brain set for them. Unthinking slaves never revolted or sabotaged or struck; they did their work. And if it came to war, they regarded *themselves* as expendable and spent their lives cheaply in defense of the hive queen.

There was a slight rustle in the grass behind her. "You wish to meet queen?" said a voice that was obviously not equipped with human speech apparatus. It was a grinding sound, a whisper with pain in it, and the consonants and vowels were badly formed. But still intelligible.

She tried to remain calm as she turned to face the creature. What could she say that would not antagonize anybody? "I don't want to bother her," said Thulium. "I got here by accident. I think I took too long a walk. Please apologize to her for my intrusion. It looks as if everyone is doing excellent work."

"We grow food for whole worlds," said the Formic worker.

So her guess about these fields and orchards supplying the colony worlds must be correct. "Thank you for that," said Thulium. "And now I must be going."

"Queen say, come visit any time, Thulium Delphiki. You always glad welcome here."

The fact that this terrifying creature knew her name was too much. Thulium stood abruptly, turned, and walked briskly back along the road. After a very short time, she broke into a run. Tired and footsore as she was, she ran faster than she would have thought herself capable of.

After a little while at an unsustainable speed, she stopped and set out due north, hoping by that move to evade pursuit along the road *and* to reach humans, or at least pequeninos, sooner rather than later. She was only a short-legged child; she couldn't have gone so very far, could she?

If it comes to war with the inhabitants of Descoladora, can the Hive Queen build war ships and weapons enough? Can she spawn soldiers enough, to conquer this most dangerous enemy?

No, Thulium rebuked herself. Fool! Haven't you already demonstrated to yourself, to Miro, that Descoladora cannot possibly be the original source of the descolada virus?

All is well. There will be no war. Thulium calmed herself, repeating that like a mantra as she walked. No need for killing. We just need communication to build a bridge.

But when we *find* the original source of that hideous, evil gene-altering virus, *then* will we unleash the hordes of the Hive Queen to wipe out that terrible enemy?

The Hive Queen knows my name. She wants me to visit again. "Always glad welcome here."

Either the Ribeiras didn't have any serious surveillance after all and did not know she had crossed over the fence, *or* they knew exactly where she had gone and wanted her to go there. So should she try to get back home over the fence again, and slip in undetected after being missing for enough hours that it was mid-afternoon already? Or should she go to the main gate and present herself to whoever was watching it and say, "Well, I'm back."

She crested a hill, the first one with a few trees on it, and saw at once that three mammalian creatures with somewhat piglike snouts and articulated hands and feet were clinging to the trunks of trees, looking down on her.

"Greetings Thulium Delphiki, daughter of Cincinnatus and friend of Miro," one of them called out to her.

She did not obey her first impulse, which was to run. Instead she asked, "Am I on a good path to the main gate?"

"You're way far west of the gate. Go northnortheast from here, and you'll find a path among the trees. Follow it."

"What if I don't find the path?" asked Thulium.

"Then you're either stupid or blind," said the pequenino who talked. "The path is right there." He pointed, and now she could see that there was a path. "It's the road to the gate. Many feet made that path." Then he grimaced and, perhaps, laughed, if she interpreted correctly the noises he was making.

"You're right," she said cheerfully. "It's a very plain path to see."

Without betraying any of her terror at having met her first pequeninos, she casually walked to the beginning of the path, wondering if these trees were the gravemarkers of their friends or ancestors.

"Always turn right when choosing!" the talking pequenino shouted after her. "The trees watch you. You'll be safe!"

She reached the main gate while there was still plenty of light in the sky. Miro and Jane were there to meet her. "Well," said Jane, "for not being in the mood for an expedition today, you've certainly covered a lot of ground."

"I'm sorry that some poor pequenino had to run ahead with the news of my arrival," said Thulium.

"Don't be silly, child," said Jane. "I'm in constant contact with the Hive Queen, and the fathertrees told me of your easy progress back to the gate."

"No drones watching from overhead?" asked Thulium.

"Oh, we have drones we can deploy," said Miro, "for when a child gets lost somewhere outside the ken of the pequeninos or the Hive Queen. But they know who you are and so we knew you were never in danger."

"Except the danger of discovering your great secret," said Thulium.

"The Hive Queen? Not much of a secret anymore," said Miro.

"You have bigger secrets than that?" asked Thulium.

"Probably not bigger from your perspective. But we thought you'd enjoy discovering it first and then telling your family."

Thulium was offended. "Why do you think I would tell my family?"

"Why wouldn't you?" asked Miro.

"Because my father would start planning an invasion of the Formics, and my brothers would begin training to carry it out."

"They'd be torn to bits in moments," said Miro. "So I hope that they don't try something as foolish as that."

"They'd assume they could invade a bunch of peaceful farmers," said Thulium.

"Every one of those peaceful farmers is also a ruthless and highly-skilled warrior," said Miro. "If the queen herself remembers warfare—and she does—all her workers are already possessed of all the skills she has learned."

"So she's a dangerous war machine," said Thulium.

"Yes," said Miro. "That's why it was so hard to kill them all, back in the war of Ender Wiggin, Julian Delphiki, Petra Arkanian, and the jeesh."

"And you allowed this warlike species to coexist here with humans and pequeninos?" asked Thulium.

"So you *are* your father's daughter," said Jane, perhaps a bit sadly. "Yes, we allowed her a homeland and a chance to survive as a species. And I can assure you that no matter how ruthless and efficient she is in war, she *did* lose all her wars with humans. Once *our* warlike species was established here, adding her and her children was not an increase in the average warlikeness of the inhabitants of Lusitania."

"I'm not like my father," said Thulium. "I may *think* of war, but I have no intention of waging it."

Jane raised an eyebrow, and Miro chuckled.

"Offensive war," said Thulium. "Of course I'd fight to protect my family."

"As would the Hive Queen," said Jane. "As would the pequeninos. They, too, are a warlike species. Every forest on this planet represents a terrible battlefield; every tree rose up from a fallen warrior's corpse."

"They seem so . . . cute," said Thulium.

"One of them could rip your arms and legs from their sockets very quickly," said Miro. "They're amazingly strong. Yet they're also sweet and smart and cooperative. Just don't try to take one home as a pet."

"Speaking of home," said Thulium. "I've had no food or water since breakfast."

"Poor dear," said Jane. "Next time you decide to sneak over the fence, think ahead and bring provisions. At least a few liters of water."

"And a flashlight," added Miro, "if you go too far to get back before dark."

The gate was already standing open. Miro beckoned her to pass through.

"I take it the disruptor field isn't active in the gate area?" asked Thulium.

Jane laughed. "It wouldn't be much of a gate if it were."

"I'm just glad you turned the disruptor field way down," said Thulium, "or I couldn't have gotten through it at all."

After she passed through the gate, she could hear Jane ask Miro quietly, "The disruptor field has lower settings?"

She didn't hear Miro's answer, and she didn't want to turn around to see if body language revealed it. Probably Jane meant her to hear her question, perhaps as a continuation of her disinformation campaign. Or perhaps it was true that she had somehow passed through the same disruptor field that had caused Miro permanent brain damage when he went through.

What would it mean, if she could get through the full-on disruptor field with no symptoms worse than hallucinations and confusion?

No, the disruptor field had to have been on a very low setting, and Jane made that remark so that Thulium would hear it and waste time trying to make sense of it.

The gate closed behind her. Floodlights began to come on, because dusk did not last long here.

"May I hold your hand, Thulium?" asked Miro. His right hand was already reaching for her left.

She pulled her hand away. "I'm not going to run off."

"I don't intend to grip your hand tightly enough to prevent you from doing so," said Miro. "But I worried about you, and still worry about you, and you still look like a child to me, even though when I talk to you I think I'm dealing with a professor who is not pleased with my lack of progress in the class."

Thulium liked Miro. She thought he was the Lusitanian most likely to tell her the truth. But she also knew her hands were filthy and quite possibly infectious. She wasn't going to touch anybody until she and soap had spent a lot of time together.

So she put him off with words, keeping her hands folded in front of her. "You think physical contact will enhance our relationship," said Thulium.

Miro shook his head. "You have such a way of making ordinary things seem weird."

"I've lived inside a canister all my life," said Thulium. "Everything here on a planet's surface is weird to me."

She ran on ahead, back to the building that was now her home. Fortunately, nobody was using the shower in the bathroom she preferred. She scrubbed every part of her. Then she brought her clothes into the shower and scrubbed them, too. She wasn't sure she felt clean, but when the hot water began to turn cooler she knew she had exhausted the tank. That meant her shower had lasted as long as it was going to.

She hung her clothes up to drip dry. Then she toweled herself and went back to her room and put on clean clothing. Her first adventure on the surface of a planet was over. She had learned far more than she expected, not only about the aliens who shared this world with humans, but also about herself, and how unprepared she was to live like an animal in the wild.

It was a good thing that the pequeninos themselves, despite being the apex predators on this world, couldn't digest some of the proteins in Earth's flora and fauna. Including humans. Ancestral humans on the savannahs of Africa had to deal with skilled, powerful, hungry predators. If this walk of hers today had been in that sort of environment, they would have found her bones scattered by hyenas and vultures.

But Lusitania was a safe place. The aliens knew her

name and watched over her. They might have learned something—but really very little—about how human children handled defecation in a pinch. Or they might not have been close enough to observe her moment of surrender to the animal needs of her body.

I refuse to be ashamed of anything, Thulium told herself. I did the right thing, refusing their tame visit to the pequeninos and wandering far enough to find the Formics. The Ribeiras and Jane could announce whatever they wanted to the family, but Thulium would say nothing. They would see that if they ever did tell her a secret, she would keep it. That if she found out something they wanted nobody to know, she would not misuse the knowledge.

I'm an eight-year-old, thought Thulium, but not like any eight-year-old *they've* ever known.

5

She has started signing her journal entries "Ultima Thule," embracing the geographical nickname her uncle Andrew gave her as a baby. She knows that she passed through a threshold when she crossed over the fence, because she felt the need to ascertain that the disruptor field was at full strength rather than toned down from the disruptor that nearly killed Miro.

Was it a death wish that drove her into that field? Or a desire to see just how far she could go before she felt threatened? She describes hallucinations, but she was always aware that's what they were; fear, dread, even panic, but all manageable by her iron determination. No physical effects whatsoever, and that's the most baffling thing, because some aspects of the disruptor field were designed to affect all cells of the body simultaneously, especially the primary afferent fibers that carry pain. There should not exist any way of coming through undamaged, yet that is what she did.

What changes did the leguminids make to their own genome, along with taming the giantism associated with Anton's Key?

If she and other leguminids are more robust than ordinary humans, we may not need them as much for their minds as for their ability to withstand disruptor-style assaults. There are precedents for sending young children into possible combat situations, dating back to the Second Formic War. But would their parents give consent?

—Leda Queijocabeça, quoted in
Leguminids on Lusitania

Valentine—the real one, not Jane—assembled the leguminids who were on Lusitania for a briefing. They did it outside on a sloping lawn, so that anybody who wanted to could lie back and yet still be able to see the visual displays Valentine mounted for them from the projector beside her.

"I didn't make any of the displays myself," said Valentine. "The researchers whose work I'm reporting created them."

"So why aren't those researchers making the presentations themselves?" asked Lanth.

"They're hard at work, and coming here would distract them," said Valentine. "My projects don't have the same level of urgency, so I'm free to present this to you."

"In other words," said Dys, "you haven't told the real researchers that we're here, and you don't want anybody to know about us yet."

"Lanth and Dys, if you believe the information I'm going to present will be so far beneath your standards as to be worthless to you, I urge you to return indoors. If you remain with this meeting, then I ask that all questions be pertinent to the topic under discussion."

Sprout was amused by the exchange, especially

because of the irony that what Lanth and Dys interrupted was Valentine's explanation of how the visual aids, none of which had yet been displayed, were created by the original researchers, none of whom had yet to be named or seen. In other words, Dys and Lanth were asking questions that were precisely pertinent to the question then under discussion.

But Sprout knew that if he expressed this thought, merely for the amusement value, it would quite possibly lead to *his* ejection from the meeting, and he wanted to stay here, because there was a reasonable chance that something might be revealed that would give shape to his own research projects.

Valentine began speaking with clarity and brevity, and all the visual aids that popped up into the air upon her command were clear and to the point. She gave them a brief recap of the history of the descolada virus since the arrival of humans on Lusitania, and on the molecular steps to first control the virus and then to de-fang it so that it would make no further adaptations.

That's when Sprout raised his hand. Valentine called on him. "There is no control population, so do you have any evidence that your adaptation of such a self-adapting virus has been effective, and will continue to be effective?"

"As you said, there is no way to test," said Valentine. "So, no."

"We have this result: It has been effective so far, and we have seen no evidence of adaptation by the descolada virus. We monitor it frequently."

"How frequently?" asked Sprout.

"Twice a day, with samples from different locations," said Valentine. "It's an imperfect system, but this is what seemed feasible and so far, so good."

Sprout recognized that "so far, so good" was about the best that could be hoped for at present.

Valentine went on to other presentations. Specifics about determining the planetary source of the descolada virus, probable or possible means of delivery of the virus to Lusitania prior to the arrival of human colonists, estimates of how long ago the virus had reconstructed every Lusitanian species that survived. There was a presentation on the digital virus information that had been transmitted from the surface of the planet they were calling Descoladora.

That was when Thulium raised her hand and said, "Is there any chance that the descolada virus was originally transmitted digitally to Lusitania?"

Valentine looked at her like she was crazy, as the twins both groaned at their little sister's childish question. Valentine answered, "The pequeninos had no equipment that could receive or interpret a digital transmission."

But then Valentine paused and smiled. "Of course, Thulium. The fact that they made such a transmission to our ship orbiting the planet might be taken as evidence that they are not the original source of the virus."

It took Sprout only a moment to make the leap to understanding. The source of the virus would have sent a *virus*, not a blueprint for making one. As an attack, the digital transmission would only have worked if the starship receiving it had a crew so phenomenally stupid that they would actually assemble the virus and turn it loose on themselves.

"Do we even know what species lives on that planet?" asked Thulium.

"We do not," said Valentine.

"What about architecture and transportation, features that might be visible from orbit?"

"We have people studying the pictures that were taken," said Valentine.

"But their findings are not part of this briefing?" asked Thulium.

"We couldn't include everything," said Valentine, "but today I'll be sure that we have that information tomorrow."

"Thank you," said Thulium.

Dys and Lanth made slight disparaging remarks about Thulium, including Lanth saying something about children being seen and not heard, but since Thulium was only a year younger than the twins, it only made Lanth seem both mean and intellectually ill-equipped. But the twins modeled their surly and cantankerous attitude on Uncle Sergeant's, and in his absence, perhaps they were hoping to maintain a certain level of skepticism, hostility, and bullying in his honor.

There were more presentations and discussions on viruses and possible delivery systems. What triggered interest in Sprout's mind was a possible experiment. "Valentine," he said, *not* raising his hand because her back was to them.

Valentine turned around.

"It seemed that short shrift was given to the possibility of the descolada virus having infiltrated the atmosphere of Lusitania without any delivery system outside itself."

"It's a very complex molecule," said Valentine, "and most of our researchers—both on Lusitania and in cooperating research institutions on other planets—are convinced that cosmic radiation would have killed or deformed the virus in transit, if it traveled unprotected through space."

Sprout nodded. "So that is an area in which we have decided not to explore or question the preexisting assumptions?"

Valentine regarded him steadily, and Sprout could imagine her trying to decide if he was being a troublemaker like the twins, or if he was trying to open up and reprioritize their scientific inquiries, the way Thule had.

"I'm not suggesting anybody be taken from any other project to research that," said Sprout.

"Then why did you bring it up?" asked Valentine.

"Because, now that I know everybody else is ignoring it, that's the question I'd like to explore," said Sprout.

Valentine paused again, for one heartbeat, then two. "I was hoping to get all of the Delphiki family working on one aspect of the problem together, but—"

"You don't know us yet," said Sprout. "We don't work well with others."

"Everyone pursues a separate line of research?" asked Valentine.

"We all do whatever we please," said Little Mum, the oldest of the Giant's grandchildren. "Which in some cases comes very near to doing nothing at all."

"She thinks everything I do is a waste of time," said Boss, her little brother.

"Because it is," said Little Mum. "But you are unfailingly supportive of the research projects of others, so you have your own kind of contribution to make."

That got some laughter from the twins and Blue, but Thulium didn't laugh, and neither did Sprout.

"Everything everybody does is a waste of time, until it isn't," said Sprout. "I want to 'waste my time' seeing how a version of the descolada virus adapts to the conditions in cold interstellar space."

"I don't know if we have the equipment here on Lusitania to allow any such experiment," said Valentine.

"That's why I don't intend to perform those experiments on Lusitania," said Sprout.

"Where, then?" asked Little Mum.

"There are spare starships—or star boxes, whatever you call them—left over from the migration to other habitable worlds. I imagine it'll be within Jane's capacity to put me up in orbit and also in interstellar space as often as need be."

"If and when that project seems to be an urgent priority," said Valentine.

Sprout recognized that Valentine was trying to keep him from realizing that she was blowing off his request. "When I go to sample blood, I'll need a copy of the descolada virus in order to identify its presence or absence."

"You have no understanding of how dangerous the descolada virus is," said Miro.

"I look like a nine-year-old," said Sprout, "because I have lived for the relativistic equivalent of nine Earth years. But I'm not a child in need of protection. I'm a human in need of respect for my sense and my capacity. If I get infected by the virus, quarantine me and give me one of your several cures or controls. We need to learn if the virus could have simply arrived in the outer atmosphere of Lusitania and drifted down to the surface. With no packaging, there would be no heat from reentry. So if the virus could drift in space without losing virulency, it could have reached the surface unscathed. And if *that* is what happened, we have no way of guessing whether it was released into the galaxy as a deliberate attack or merely an accident."

Dys scoffed. "Molecules don't achieve escape velocity by accident," he said.

"I've already thought of several ways it could happen," said Sprout, "which I intend to test. Your biased judgments are scientifically irrelevant, and you know it."

"Enough bickering," said Valentine.

"There's never enough bickering in the face of stupidity," said Lanth.

"Sprout," said Valentine, "let's discuss this with the

scientists of the descolada project and see what can be done."

There were more discussions and a few more presentations, especially dealing with the lack of biodiversity on Lusitania and what the long-term effects of that were likely to be. But Sprout had presented what *he* cared about.

He also noticed that Valentine directed a disproportionate amount of her presentation to Thulium. Maybe that was sympathy because her older brothers taunted her, but Sprout suspected it was something else. It seemed that Valentine knew something about Ultima Thule, something that made Valentine particularly interested in her, and Sprout intended to find out what it was.

But when he asked her, Thulium wasn't very helpful. "Sprout, I think I see what you mean, but I can't explain it."

Sprout thought this answer was evasive. "Can't explain" could mean that she had no explanation, or it could just as easily mean that she knew perfectly well why Valentine treated her differently, but was restrained by something from telling him.

"When will you be able to tell me the secret?" asked Sprout.

"When my guesses collide with at least a little evidence," said Thulium.

"If two of us are watching for evidence . . ."

"Then two of us will probably be looking for nothing at all," said Thulium. "Really, Sprout, if I tell anybody what I'm thinking, it'll be you."

Sprout had to be content with that, unless he wanted a quarrel with Uncle Sergeant's daughter. She was not belligerent, like her father and brothers, but Sprout knew she could hold a grudge and carry a quarrel too far, just like the rest of her family.

Sprout had looked up some of the researchers

among the Lusitanians. What drew his eye was the work that Miro's younger sister, Quara, had done with Lusitanian biology. Quara seemed to try to question and cast doubt on every hypothesis brought up by others. Which struck Sprout as being closer to the scientific attitude than anyone else. "I want to meet her," Sprout told Miro.

"No you don't," said Miro. "She makes Sergeant Delphiki look cooperative and gentle."

"I didn't say I wanted to marry her," said Sprout.

"She may be my youngest sibling," said Miro, "but I took a relativistic voyage and when I came back, she was twenty years older and I wasn't."

"Why would I care about that? Everyone is older than I am."

"She published meticulously," said Miro. "She made no errors in her data."

"There *is* no data," said Sprout.

"There is, but it's all classified top secret, need to know."

"I need to know," said Sprout.

"Why?"

"Because I think we've missed key aspects of the descolada virus," said Sprout. "I need to know Quara's data on life-forms that went extinct after the coming of the descolada."

"That's easy," said Miro. "Zero."

"No bones of other life-forms?" asked Sprout.

"None found so far," said Miro.

"Nobody's looking?"

"None found so far," said Miro.

"What about the life cycle of the pequeninos *and* the trees prior to the coming of the descolada."

"Easy enough," said Miro. "They have the organs for copulation, internal and external. Trees were their habitat, not part of their life sequence. The trees can blossom still, and if there were any pollinating insects, they might even produce fruit or seeds, though I've never seen any evidence of it."

"Nobody tried hand-pollinating them?" asked Sprout.

"There are no unattended trees," said Miro. "Imagine the human response if alien researchers wanted to try the experiment of impregnating some their most beloved relatives."

Sprout raised his eyebrows. "You mean they don't even *want* to know?"

"I mean nobody has been stupid enough to bring up the idea."

"Well, then," said Sprout. "I believe I have a purpose here after all."

"No," said Miro.

"You've cut me off from everything interesting. I have to either work on topics you assign, which are all essentially scutwork, or you bar me from access."

"I don't bar you from anything," said Miro. "Go talk to the pequeninos. See how they respond. Remember that they are prone to vivisecting their human contacts in hopes that trees will arise from the corpses."

"But only the humans that they like," said Sprout.

"Come on, Brussels," said Miro. "If you can't try to fertilize blossoms, what do you think you have to talk to the pequeninos about?"

"Their institutional memory," said Sprout. "Their most ancient stories. What their oldest citizens know about the pre-descolada past."

"I've talked to them. Ender talked to them. My real father, Libo, talked to them, as did *his* father, Pipo. They remember nothing."

"Then you have nothing to fear from my talking to them about it," said Sprout.

"Three of the four I just mentioned are dead. And I nearly died."

"The pequeninos only killed two of them. Ender

Wiggin died of boredom, as I understand it. And your injury came from passing through the disruptor field."

"So you have a fifty-fifty chance," said Miro.

"Let me through the gate and let me see what I can learn."

"What's the point?" asked Miro.

"If we can reconstruct *anything* about the biome that was broken by the descolada, we might have a better idea of what the virus was actually meant to do," said Sprout. "And I personally believe no one has made any kind of effort at gathering data about paleobiology on Lusitania."

"So you'll converse with pequeninos, and then you'll dig holes looking for what, prehistoric pollen?"

"Prehistoric pollen might contain at least a few partial genomes," said Sprout.

"If you ever find any," said Miro.

"So because you think I'll probably fail, you won't allow me to try."

"Because I think your attempts will cause trouble and seriously endanger you, I'm not opening the gate for you," said Miro.

"I think your scientific curiosity is seriously lacking," said Sprout.

"There are ways over the fence without going through the gate," said Miro.

"Have you turned off the disruptor field at the fence?" asked Sprout.

"No."

"Is it milder?"

"It is no different in any way from when I went through it," said Miro.

"So you're suggesting I get brain-damaged in pursuit of things you should be encouraging me to research."

"Nothing about our conversation consists of me suggesting *anything* to you," said Miro. "Why don't you go back, think again, and come up with some useful line of research?"

Since Sprout had no intention of doing any such thing, he walked away from Miro.

He also spent the day avoiding everybody else. Walking on the lawns of the Delphiki Concentration Camp, as the twins were starting to call it. Napping on the far side of a low rise, so he was invisible from the building, though he assumed the Lusitanians had some kind of tracking device—they must have, because they never went searching for him.

He missed two whole cycles of meals that way, and was feeling more than slightly peckish when Thulium came out to find him. She had a basket with food inside. And two bottles of water. "Hunger strikes go better when you have a little food and water," she said.

"I'm not on a hunger strike."

"*Sulking* goes better with food and drink as well."

"Now you're just trying to provoke me," said Sprout.

"I'm worried about you. Miro says you wanted to go talk to the pequeninos."

"Yes, and he refused to open the gate. He suggested that I could go over the fence."

"No," said Thulium. "He said that people had been known to go over the fence."

Sprout rolled his eyes.

"I've done it," said Thulium.

Sprout knew Thulium well enough to take this ridiculous assertion seriously. "Through the disruptor field?"

"It caused hallucinations and disorientation but I never lost touch with reality. No pain, not even a headache, and no brain damage that I've been able to detect."

"Why did it affect you so mildly?" asked Sprout.

"I don't know."

"What does Miro say?"

"I haven't discussed it with him, beyond the fact that I did it," said Thulium.

"What's your speculative explanation?"

"One possibility that I'm eager to test is whether the genetic alteration our parents made in themselves, which has been passed down to us, made our brains somehow different. Less susceptible to the disruptor field."

"And how would you test that?" asked Sprout.

"I'd take you into the disruptor field and see what happened."

Sprout thought of that. "You went in alone, didn't you," he said.

"I figured that if it started feeling bad, I'd get out of it."

"It didn't occur to you that it might affect you so sharply that once inside it, you *couldn't* get out?"

"Absolutely," said Thulium.

"But you tried it anyway," said Sprout.

"I'm so very brave."

"And foolish," said Sprout.

"I believe 'brave' and 'foolish' are very near to being synonyms," said Thulium.

"If I go into the disruptor field with you," said Sprout, "you'll pull me out if it affects me worse than it affected you?"

"Of course," said Thulium. "Or if I can't, I'll go get help from someone who can."

"And if I suffer the same stroke-like symptoms that Miro suffered all those years ago?"

"I'll read to you every day, from research reports, histories, and ridiculously romantic novels, until you recover completely."

"Miro had to kill himself to recover," said Sprout.

"But he didn't do it until he had already created a replacement body," said Thulium.

Sprout took a sandwich out of the basket. "This looks good. Please tell me you didn't make it yourself."

"I didn't make it myself," said Thulium.

"It *looks* like it was made by a child," said Sprout.

"When you tell me to lie to you . . ."

Sprout bit down into the sandwich, chewed. "It's very good."

"I know," said Thulium. "I'm learning skills here on the surface. There are skills that would have been meaningless on the *Herodotus* even if we had tried to acquire them."

"I want to make a contribution to solving the problem of the descolada," said Sprout.

"Me, too," said Thulium. "Let's finish lunch and go see if we can get you over the fence."

6

The life of the original Peter Wiggin—no, let's be honest, the *real* Peter Wiggin—was already chronicled in the short biography *The Hegemon,* penned by the Speaker for the Dead, whose identity, known to few, was the late Andrew "Ender" Wiggin. But there is no reason to believe that anyone will ever chronicle the life of the new Peter Wiggin, created from the mind of Andrew Wiggin on the first voyage Outside. His physical appearance is, or so I'm told, identical to the original—the only two possible witnesses, his brother Andrew and his sister Valentine, both affirmed this. Since the duplicate of Valentine, now known as Jane, is genetically identical to the original, we can only assume a similar twinning between the two iterations of Peter.

But Peter Wiggin is *not* the same person or even a true twin. His aiúa—his inmost soul, his will, the part of him that chooses—is not his own. It is not a new model summoned out of darkness by whatever force summons aiúas to control and give the spark of will to new life. Instead it is a well-used aiúa, the one belonging to Andrew Wiggin. When I talk to the current Peter, it is a complex conversation, because I know that buried deep within his unconscious mind, it is

Ender Wiggin himself, his deepest self, that answers me. But in his own mind, he thinks of himself as Peter Wiggin, who came into being in the first faster-than-light starship.

Because his aiúa recognizes his face in the mirror as being the same as the face of the brother who terrorized and dominated Ender during the first years of his life, he feels that he has some sort of obligation to live up to that version of Peter Wiggin, which sometimes makes him answer harshly. But his heart is not in it, when he acts that way. He knows that this is not what he wants to be; it is not how he wants to treat me. From all accounts, Ender spent the latter part of his life as a tender husband to Novinha Ribeira and a loving stepfather to her very difficult brood of children, who grew up to be almost as smart as they think they are. So Ender's aiúa naturally rejects Peter's cruelty, and at times when he forgets that it's his duty to act out the Peter script, he is as tender and caring to me, his wife, as I could ever hope for.

I knew what I was marrying when he and I spoke our vows before the Catholic bishop of Lusitania Colony, in the presence of a pequenino mothertree. I undertook this contract, this covenant, with the intention of fulfilling my part to the best of my ability, which includes being as patient as I can with his lapses. It would be easier to bear if it were possible to talk with him about this bifurcation of his personality, but any approach to such a topic sets off either a cold avoidance or a heated response in which he says such wounding things to me that I haven't the courage to try it again very soon.

There will come a time when he realizes that he doesn't *like* acting out his childhood image of his brother, and that I am not a person that it is right for him to treat with the savagery of his wit. He has never been violent with me as his brother often was with him; I have that comfort. And, as long as I don't venture on any topic that sounds as if I'm trying to change his behavior or his self-image, he listens to me with respect—perhaps more respect than I deserve. When we were maneuvering to get Starways Congress to stop the fleet that had been sent to destroy Lusitania and all the species on it, some of the wise people we conversed with showed him that they, at least, regarded me as a person worthy of honor and respect. I don't know why, but I do know that my Peter Wiggin noticed it and now often echoes it.

If these great figures from other worlds treated me that way, he must have concluded that they knew something he did not. He is humble about his level of knowledge, because he does not have the original Peter's memory set, and he lacks most of Andrew's memories as well. He came to life with a full command of Stark, the language of the Hundred Worlds, and also of the English language that was the basis of Stark three thousand years ago. That is the language he lapses into when he's tired, along with slang expressions, some of them quite filthy, that he learned and used in Battle School. What my Peter inherited from Ender, from his aiúa, was the child's knowledge. I have little doubt that my Peter could, in a pinch, lead an army into war, as Ender did.

What he is not good at, however, is the skill set that has been imputed to the real Peter Wiggin—the wisdom, patience, knowledge, and empathy required to be a masterful negotiator with cynical politicians and idealists and religious leaders and all the other power wielders who influence the course of events in the human universe. And since that is precisely the course he has embarked upon—full of confidence that, being "Peter Wiggin," he will be good at it—it is my role to be supportive of his endeavors, offering advice and information where I can, without triggering his defenses.

Before Peter took me with him, I had a few excellent months on my home world of Path, living in the house of the sage Han Fei-Tzu. I arrived there as the close personal servant of Han Qing-Jao, his daughter; they were both among the God-spoken of that world, until Jane informed him, with irresistible proof, that the compulsions and obsessions of the God-spoken came from a genetic alteration designed to enhance their intelligence while crippling their lives. His daughter refused to believe that this was true, and as far as I know continues to believe that her former compulsions were messages from the gods, so that by acting as if she still received them, she can worship these uncommunicative deities. When I left their home, it was with her anger and Han's blessing.

Han taught me much that has helped me be of service to my Peter. He frowns when I say, "Master Han once told me," but he listens. I am often tempted to preface my own thoughts and observations with that preamble, but so far I have not done so, because I hope my Peter will eventually recognize that my own ideas also have value, even if he takes them far less seriously than my quotations from Master Han.

My ancestor-of-the-heart is the goddess Royal Mother of the West, whose name I was given at my birth. My mother, if it was she who named me, must have hoped that this optimistic, sacrilegious, presumptuous name would recommend me to the attention of the goddess. Most children of low birth on Path learned to hide such ridiculously high names behind nick-names, but once I understood what my name meant and how it was heard by educated people, I did not hide it, I insisted upon it. I never called myself merely Wang-Mu or, as more people with that name did, Mu. I always introduced myself as Si Wang-Mu, without apology or bashfulness, daring people to laugh.

This is among the many things that my Peter still does not understand; he is not from Path and cannot really grasp the meaning. He persists in trying to use customs from his upbringing, introducing me as his wife, Wang-Mu Wiggin, an absurdity; I am not his daughter, and why would the family name come last? But I simply smile and correct him mildly by saying my true name: "I am Si Wang-Mu, and Peter Wiggin is my husband." Since we left Path, few have understood the divine origin of the name, but that does not matter. If they do a search on my name, they will first encounter my ancestor-of-the-heart, and they will know whose name I bear, and to whom my highest duty is owed.

—Si Wang-Mu,
Notes for a biographical sketch of
the new Peter Wiggin

Peter Wiggin stopped eating and leaned his head on his hand, his elbow on the table. "The food is delicious, Wang-Mu. I have no complaint. I'm just brain-weary."

"The work is frustrating," said his wife, reaching out and lightly stroking his forearm.

"I must correct you. Because I have no idea whether the work would be frustrating or not, because I can't even begin to do it. We've been here a month and

I've made no inroads. I've met with many politicians, because they know that they need to meet with rich constituents—"

"My love," said Wang-Mu, interrupting him. "You cannot be anyone's constituent, because you have no home world."

"My money makes me anyone's constituent," said Peter.

"Yes, except that you have bestowed it nowhere."

"When word gets out that I have contributed toward the reelection of this clown or that one, then I have become the enemy of all his enemies and the even more hated rival of all his allies."

"Politics is about remaining perpetually uncommitted and also universally supportive. We could drop dollops of money into this or that cause, and signal that we are willing to spend that money when the occasion demands."

"I'm beginning to agree with you," said Peter.

"Jane assures me that your funds are inexhaustible. She insists that is not hyperbole, that there is no way we could spend the money fast enough to outpace the rate at which your investments throughout the human universe are generating revenue."

Peter frowned. He didn't like where this conversation was going. "That isn't *my* money."

"If you inherit it," said Wang-Mu, "and the original owner is dead, then it *is* your money."

"It's half Valentine's by right, and the other half should be divided between me and Jane."

"Valentine has her own fortune, more than she or her children can spend during their lives," said Wang-Mu. "When you have a brilliant mind investing your holdings for more than three thousand years, your possessions no longer fit under the heading 'wealth.'"

"I've heard Jane recite this sermon more than you have," said Peter.

"And yet I remember it when you forget."

"I don't forget it, I just feel uncomfortable about using *his* fortune."

"Feel what you want, but you could use it to crack open many doors just a little wider. Perhaps wide enough for you to sidle in."

"I know that you think that the 'real' me is Ender Wiggin so the fortune really belongs to me," said Peter. Wang-Mu regarded him steadily, but said nothing.

"I'm not going to be angry with you when I'm the one who brought it up," said Peter. "So you can unclench a little."

"My love," said Wang-Mu, "I don't clench. I'm not afraid of your wrath. I'm only sorry for having provoked it."

Peter knew from experience that when Wang-Mu said such things, she wasn't being deliberately infuriating. She actually meant what she said. So he had schooled himself not to let such provocations get under his skin. She could not understand how much self-control he exercised, and how rarely he let it slip. Then again, she probably *did* understand it, and noticed every time when he restrained himself; yet she said nothing to mark it, she did not praise him for being so forbearing. She simply treated him as kindly as ever.

"Peter," she said. "I know you remember that when we tried to influence the Japanese contingent in Starways Congress, we did not come here to Unity, to the capitol, and we never met with any of the Congressors or Senators. We met with the people who influenced them, and first we met with the people who had most influence over those influencers."

"And before that, we figured out *who* those influencers of influencers were," said Peter. "And we had your father's counsel about that."

"Han Fei-Tzu is not my father," said Wang-Mu.

"He was my teacher. His beloved daughter breaks his heart, but I was not and could not be a substitute for her."

"Can't I please just speak lazily from time to time? He might as well be your father."

"If I let such things pass when we're alone, then someday, speaking to someone else, you'll refer to your wife's father, and someone will ask, Who is he? And then what will you say? If you say he is Han Fei-Tzu, it will give us great weight and importance, for his name is known among all the people of Chinese ancestry; but a simple bit of research will reveal that it is a lie, and you will be discredited."

"You always think ahead," said Peter. "Like a good mother."

"I have no children," said Wang-Mu.

"I'm your child," said Peter. "I'm not even a year old, and what memories I do have are mostly second-hand. If anyone is raising me, it's you."

Peter saw that his words had made her sad. "Do you think I respect you so little as to treat you like a child?"

"No, I think you support me so well that you constantly educate me, even though you are scarcely educated yourself."

Wang-Mu smiled. "My love, like a good carpenter you have hit the nail on the head. We are raising each other. We have both had other teachers, but now we have only each other. And I think we are doing very well."

"I'm even more brain-weary now than I was before."

"A basketball game is being televised tonight in real time."

"Unity is so basketball-crazy, and the politicians more so than most," said Peter.

"It's an exciting game."

"It's a fake game," said Peter. "The gravity here is only ninety-four percent of the gravity of Earth. They keep the baskets at the regulation height, but now everybody can slam dunk, everybody can leap down the court at speeds unimaginable on Earth."

"They don't play professional basketball on Earth anymore, do they?" asked Wang-Mu.

"Nobody would pay to go see the games, they're so slow and nobody seems to fly," said Peter. "Nobody would broadcast them because nobody would watch."

"It's a lost world, the world of your childhood," said Wang-Mu.

"Lusitania was the world of my childhood," said Peter. "And now Unity is my new childhood home."

"Yet you remember basketball on Earth."

Peter once again saw where this was leading. As Peter Wiggin, he couldn't remember anything at all, because he had never *been* Peter Wiggin, he only shared—probably—his genome. His memories of basketball on Earth came from what he saw on television before he went to Battle School—as Ender Wiggin. Some of his memories came along with his aiúa, maybe a lot of those memories, but Peter had no desire to dredge them up. Why had he done so now? Because Wang-Mu reminded him of the basketball game being televised tonight. Had she planned all along that it would lead him to think of the fact that in some sense he really *was* Andrew Wiggin?

Or was it that anything she said, and anything he said, would lead there?

"If you can talk about the game," said Wang-Mu, "you might establish common ground with some of the Congressors."

"I don't know enough about the game. I don't know any players' names. I don't understand the subtleties of the game."

"I hear that nobody is born knowing those things, but they acquire them by study and observation," said Wang-Mu.

She could be pretty sarcastic, sometimes. He refrained from complaining.

"But a better path might be to say that you admire the players' speed and their leaping, soaring style of play, like Achilles' manner of fighting in the *Iliad*. Then confess that you wish you understood the subtleties of play, and suddenly these emotionally needy politicians are offered the chance to become the teacher of one of the richest men in the universe. Surely that will be a road into your pocket, they'll suppose, and now you're in the door."

Peter had to admire the subtlety of her thinking: You're not knowledgeable and can't fake knowledge you don't have. So confess your ignorance and enlist their help in teaching you.

He should have thought of that. If he really *were* Peter Wiggin, he should already have been doing that; even as Ender Wiggin, he should have leapt to that idea, because Ender was a good leader.

I'm just a pale shadow of greatness, barely perceptible on a cloudy day. My genes and my aiúa both have such promise; but I need an ignorant little servant girl to wake up my mind.

Immediately he was ashamed of his thought. Technically, of course, she *had* been a servant girl, and her original education had been sorely lacking. But she had held her own with a teacher like Han Fei-Tzu, and she had contributed to the projects on Lusitania. He had no right to think of her that way. He should be as honored to have her as a teacher as Alexander should have been honored to have, as his teacher, a man who had been taught by Plato, who had been taught by Socrates.

Why do I know who Plato and Socrates were? And

Aristotle? What else is going to bleed through from Ender's aiúa?

"Wang-Mu," said Peter. "What I'm doing here isn't working. Why not?"

"May I propose something quite radical?" she asked.

"I'd be a fool to refuse to hear it," said Peter.

She nodded gravely. "You would, but does that mean you want me to tell you?"

"Yes, my arrogant little wife, I do."

"I think that whatever you're trying to accomplish here in Unity is not worth doing. Even if you succeed, what would it accomplish?"

The words stung so sharply that he realized she had struck on an idea he had not yet allowed himself to think.

"The better unification of the worlds. To prepare for new encounters with aliens who are our equals, or perhaps our superiors."

"If history is a guide," said Wang-Mu, "it is exactly such an encounter that causes human nations and, now, worlds to unite."

Peter nodded. "You're saying it will take care of itself."

"I'm saying something far harsher," said Wang-Mu. "Humanity might well need another Peter Wiggin to be Hegemon, if there is a war with the Descolares, when we discover them. But that new Peter Wiggin will not be a stranger who came out of nowhere. Remember that the original Peter earned his place by pseudonymously influencing events under the names Locke and Demosthenes, and then, as Locke, brokering an important truce. When he finally revealed himself and was named Hegemon, it was at exactly the point in time when the reason for the office to exist had seemingly disappeared, and it took years and many wars, large and small, before he emerged as the trusted leader and peacekeeper of the world. It is already too late for you to duplicate any of those achievements."

Peter held very still, knowing nothing he could say, nothing he could do. He felt a stirring of emotion that he would have turned into rage, even a few days ago. But he contained it now. He recognized that this was an unworthy rage. It was the rage that came from knowing he was wrong and she was right.

After a long while of looking at the food still in the bowls, he reached out with his chopsticks and pulled up a piece of shrimp. It was still warm, so this conversation had not taken as long as he had thought. Chewing, he said, "If this task is impossible, what should we be doing?"

"There's only one thing that matters in the human worlds right now," she said.

He knew at once that she meant the Descolares. "I'm not a geneticist. And even though you're a quick study, my dear, you're not quick enough to enter the playing field with the Ribeiras or the leguminids."

"Nobody is," said Si Wang-Mu. "So I think we should do what they cannot do—something so dangerous that it would be foolish to send any of the expert minds on such a mission."

Peter chewed, swallowed, lifted his rice bowl and scooped some into his mouth. He chewed, swallowed again. And now he knew what she was getting at. "You think we should take our vast diplomatic skills onto the surface of the Descolador planet. To whoever sent the digital genomes."

"Right now we know nothing about them. From orbit, how can we possibly know if they were the origin of the descolada virus? From orbit, how can we assess the danger they might or might not pose?"

"On the planet's surface, we might immediately take sick with seven deadly viruses and die."

"We can report that and let them watch our deaths," said Wang-Mu. "Those are the risks of exploration."

"You speak of that as if death were nothing."

"Peter Wiggin," she said, "you've been dead for millennia. And here you are."

"Nobody's bringing us back."

"I believe we can design a pattern of exploration that will prevent such a trivial death," said Wang-Mu. "What if our first visit to the surface lasts exactly fifteen minutes. Then we come back, go into quarantine, and allow the experts to examine our cells and genomes and such, until they find out if we caught anything. Next time, we walk around for a day."

"While the natives point spears at us and put us in a big cooking pot."

"At any point, we leave the planet's surface, and again go into quarantine."

"You've thought this all out," said Peter, annoyed and awed.

"I'm winging it," said Wang-Mu.

"I doubt it," said Peter.

"I'm not responsible for your doubts," said Wang-Mu. "But I never lie to you, and you know it."

"We take pictures of them," said Peter, "so the xenologers of Lusitania can study them. We collect tissue samples, if we can."

"You see? Now you're winging it, too," said Wang-Mu.

"And all the while, Jane watches over us so closely that she can pull us off at a moment's notice," said Peter. He tapped the jewel in his ear. Jane rarely spoke to him that way anymore, or he to her, but he believed she still monitored his life through the jewel.

"That seems like quite an imposition on her time," said Wang-Mu. "After all, she's fully invested in her new body and her marriage, which is exactly as new as ours is. Why should we divert her attention from Miro for so long?"

Peter laughed. "Is there someone else who can engineer instantaneous travel?"

Wang-Mu smiled. "Ask Jane. I'm thinking, why not you?"

"If only Ender had dreamed me up with wings," said Peter. "Or some fabulous space-traveling organ, or an inborn ansible of my own."

"As I said," Wang-Mu repeated, "ask Jane."

7

PW—We're doing this in writing?

J—I want a permanent record.

PW—Because you think you know what I'm going to ask.

J—I know what you were planning to ask. If you want to be a big baby, you'll change it up so that you can show me I'm not as smart as I think I am.

PW—I want very much for you to be as smart as I think you are.

J—I'm busy, ask your question, please.

PW—Can you teach me to make the instantaneous jump Outside and back In without your help?

J—I'm perfectly capable of jumping you wherever you want. It doesn't even amount to a blip in my bandwidth anymore.

PW—And that will work until we're out of communication.

J—Where are you planning to go where I can't hear?

PW—Descoladora. Wang-Mu thinks that's a bad name for the planet, now. So we're going to go find out.

J—Ah, so you're afraid that when you're killed, I won't be able to find you and bring back the bodies.

PW—Everything on that planet's surface will be as slow as lightspeed. Where's the ansible that will connect us?

J—The answer is, yes. I can teach you.

PW—Spoken without equivocation.

J—I've already taught Miro. He and you were both on the first voyage Outside. He had the inner cohesion not only to hold his body together, but to make an undamaged duplicate, genetically identical with the first.

PW—And the strength of will to murder his old self.

J—He transferred himself into the new body. He felt no need for a crippled twin. He has no interplanetary ambitions, however. He uses his new skill to hop from one place to another here on Lusitania, and to periodically visit the starship—or Box, if you prefer the term its inhabitants are using now—hovering in various places over Descoladora.

PW—And since you think of me as Andrew Wiggin you believe I have even more sense of inner cohesion.

J—Your duplicate of young Valentine was so perfect they have identical DNA. We have no way of testing whether your current DNA matches the original Peter's.

PW—Don't fib, Jane, I know you too well. There would have been a permanent digital record of the Hegemon's DNA to protect against imposture. Nobody would have erased that from YOUR memory.

J—Your current genome is identical to the original, too.

PW—So you can teach me to hop.

J—It requires concentration.

PW—I can get Outside.

J—Getting Outside is easy. Almost a reflex. What you concentrate on is where you want to arrive when you come back In. It all happens so fast that you never experience Outside at all.

PW—Well, I feel half-trained already.

J—But you have the fantastical idea of taking your beloved wife with you.

PW—That was the plan.

J—And that, too, is possible. But to carry people with you, you have to know them.

PW—I know her.

J—Barely, and most of what you think you know is wrong.

PW—That's unencouraging.

J—I should not have said "know" them. I should have said "love" them.

J—You doubt your love for Si Wang-Mu?

J—Speak up, Peter Wiggin.

PW—I doubt that you have any concept of "love." And I doubt that your ability to carry other people Outside and back In is dependent upon an emotion that you were incapable of feeling until AFTER Ender created the body you're using now. During the first trip.

J—A rational suspicion. But here is what I know that you do not. I can perceive all philotic connections between me and human beings. I feel them the way you feel the presence and position of your limbs and fingers.

PW—So by "love" you mean philotic connection.

J—I do.

PW—So am I philotically connected to Wang-Mu or not?

J—It exists, but I cannot vouch for how strong it might be.

PW—What if we trust to luck and leap for it?

J—Si Wang-Mu is too valuable to risk on such a mad chance.

PW—If you didn't have a plan to overcome this problem, you would simply have told me from the start that I couldn't take her with me.

J—I know someone who CAN measure philotic connections between other people.

PW—A mothertree? The fathertrees?

J—They feel every tree and pequenino in the world, and on the new worlds as well. But you and Si Wang-Mu are not pequeninos.

PW—The Hive Queen, then.

J—She wants to meet you anyway.

PW—I'll bet she already knows the answer.

J—I'll bet the answer is constantly shifting, and her understanding will be much clearer when the two of you stand before her.

PW—In the darkness. In her cave. Surrounded by Formic warriors.

J—Do you insist she come out and speak to you in the light?

PW—I don't insist on anything. I'll do whatever it takes. Even though you must understand that I have terrible nightmares with her in a starring role.

J—Ender always did. When he was your age.

PW—If I knew what my age is, or what that term might even mean with regard to myself, I could evaluate the meaning of your statement.

J—Your body is exactly as old as mine.

PW—But my memories are not.

J—Should I bring the two of you back to Lusitania now?

PW—Neither of us is dressed for company, and we need a good night's sleep.

J—You do have beds on Lusitania, too, you know.

PW—We don't want to have to talk to anybody. After we're up in the morning, and washed, and dressed, and after we've eaten and said good-bye to a few friends—

J—No good-byes. Since there will be no starship launch from the vicinity of Unity that has you on the passenger manifest, you don't want anyone looking for you for a few days. By then I can create a couple of false identities for passengers on a flight that you weren't on, but which anyone looking for you will conclude were really you.

PW—Still keeping faster-than-light flight to ourselves?

J—My bandwidth can handle all the people I currently transport. But not the billions who would want access to this manner of travel.

PW—I'm not sure. Is this the first time you have ever admitted to a personal limitation?

J—No. But it's the first time I've admitted one to you.

—Transcript conversation: "Jane" and Peter Wiggin II,
Peter Wiggin II Biographical Archive

Jane was right about the ease of learning how to transport himself. After three trips with her, he realized that he really had been Outside between disappearing in one spot and reappearing in another, right there in a meadow on Lusitania. Then she told him that she would help him; he only had to concentrate on the spot where he wanted to go, *not* telling her where, and she would make sure he didn't get stuck Outside. After the third time of this method, she informed him that she had done nothing at all—he was moving himself.

"From the north side of the meadow to the southwest corner isn't the same as traveling to a starship orbiting another planet," Peter told her.

"Yes it is," she said. "Exactly the same."

"I could *see* where I was going here in the grass."

"What you saw was irrelevant. Your visual functions are not involved. You *knew* where you were going."

"Because I had seen it," said Peter.

"Where do you want to go? The Box?"

"Eventually, perhaps," said Peter. "But I don't have anything to say to the people there."

"Pick a place," said Jane, "and then go. Don't tell me where. I'll follow if you get in trouble."

Peter picked the place near the river by the house of Han Fei-Tzu on Path, where he had first met Si Wang-Mu.

And there he was.

It was as effortless as moving across the meadow.

"See?" said Jane, who now stood beside him.

Without looking at her, Peter said, "I'm not in trouble yet. Why did you follow me?" Then Peter turned, and there was Si Wang-Mu as well.

"I brought her along," said Jane, "once I knew where you had chosen to go."

Si Wang-Mu had tears running down her cheeks.

Peter was at a loss. "What's wrong?" he asked.

"I was so happy in this house," said Wang-Mu. "This is where I learned that I had a mind."

Jane rolled her eyes. "What she's not saying is that it moved her deeply that of all places in the universe, this is where you chose to go."

"I did not say it," said Wang-Mu, "because I did not think it."

"Just because a thought doesn't rise to consciousness and become language doesn't mean that you didn't think it," said Jane. "But now that we've had this gnomic moment, shall we go back to Lusitania?"

"You'll bring Wang-Mu, yes?" Peter asked Jane.

"We're not trusting you to bring her yet," said Jane. "Not until we know if you are tied to her well enough to carry her."

Peter thought of a problem with this. "You carried hundreds of people and Formics and pequeninos from Lusitania to many different colony worlds. You still transport supplies there. Do you really know all those people and aliens?"

"'People' will do for all," said Jane.

"Do you have some kind of bond with them?"

"By the time I take them I do," said Jane. "But I have tools and talents that you will never have."

"And a heart filled with love," said Peter, sarcastically.

"And a heart filled with love," echoed Wang-Mu, without the sarcasm.

"You both understand me so well," said Jane.

They were back on Lusitania, inside the fence again.

"Did I really transport myself?" Peter asked Jane. "Or are you just babying me along, letting me think I'm doing it?"

"Since it makes no practical difference, I feel no interest in proving it to you. You'll learn to trust your own abilities."

"So am I ready to meet the Hive Queen?" asked Peter.

"I don't know," said Jane.

"I am," piped up a child a few meters away, coming up the path behind them.

Peter tried to remember which leguminid this was. "The one they call 'Little Mum'?" he asked.

"Thulium," said Wang-Mu. "The one who went over the fence and found the Hive Queen on her own."

"She invited me to come back," said Thulium. "I'll lead you."

"So you've already met her," said Wang-Mu. "Is she very fearsome?"

"I talked to her through one of her workers," said Thulium. "It makes no difference. She spoke to me through the worker's mouth."

Peter looked at Jane. "Is this all right?"

Jane just looked at him, puzzled.

"She's a child," said Peter. "Do we have permission to take her with us?"

"I believe," said Jane, "that she has already proven that these fences can't keep her in. So in this case, she is taking us with *her*."

Wang-Mu held out a hand to Thulium. "I'm Si Wang-Mu," she said.

"Royal Mother of the West," said Thulium. "I'm honored to meet you."

"I accept your courtesy in the name of my ancestor-of-the-heart," said Wang-Mu. "Please call me 'Wang-Mu.'"

So their procession through the nearby pequenino forest consisted of four people—a young man and woman with Polish and American ancestry, a young Chinese woman of Path, and a girl of no more than eight years of age, whose ancestry included Japanese, Greek, Armenian, and such a mix of other genes as to defy classification. If any of the pequeninos they passed thought it odd that the adults were following the child, no one said anything. Peter wondered if Jane had communicated with the fathertrees and therefore all the pequeninos knew their errand and had no questions.

Peter had questions, though—mostly for Thulium. "You're the one that is sometimes called Ultima Thule," he said.

"Not by anyone who matters," said Thulium. Her reply was cheerful but instantaneous.

"How did you know to follow us?"

"I saw you practicing the hop in the meadow, and then I assumed the three of you went somewhere else together and then came back. Another planet?"

"It seemed a good idea at the time," said Wang-Mu.

Peter felt her words as a reminder to him that his conversation with the little girl was not private and did not concern only his interests. As if Thulium herself weren't making that clear without any help.

"So when you came back, what was next?" said Thulium. "The Hive Queen, obviously."

"There are trillions of human beings to whom that would *not* be obvious," said Peter.

"Exactly," she said.

"Do you read minds?" asked Peter.

"I have some skill at what psychologists call mind-reading, but none at all in the way you meant the term," said Thulium. "But I assume that you weren't the one carrying Wang-Mu along on your junket, and since she's your wife, *you* need to be able to carry her or you won't have the freedom of movement you're hoping for."

Peter thought: I can have complete freedom if I simply decide not to take Wang-Mu on a particular trip.

Then Peter thought: She's my wife, and to imagine leaving her behind would be a betrayal, in her mind and in mine as well.

If Thulium was reading *his* mind right now, she gave no sign of it. A born diplomat, perhaps? It hardly seemed likely, with her being a child of Sergeant, the least diplomatic of the leguminids.

"Why would this information lead you to know we were going to see the Hive Queen right now?" asked Peter.

"The trees can't see philotic connections to anyone but themselves, and you don't have any with them," said Thulium. "But the Hive Queen has known you for thousands of years. Inside out. You'll have no secrets from *her*."

Peter turned to Jane. "She hasn't known *me*," he said softly.

"Your deep self," said Wang-Mu. "Ender Wiggin transported the Hive Queen's cocoon from world to world for three millennia. They communicated mind to mind whenever they chose. Just because *you* don't remember it doesn't mean that *she's* forgotten."

"But this child, how can she—"

"She's a leguminid," said Jane. "She was told the story of Ender and the cocoon weeks ago. And being Bean's grandchild, she didn't forget, she extrapolated from what she was told and realized that of all the beings on Lusitania, only I have known the Hive Queen longer than you, because her sisters plucked me from Outside and brought me In so I could help them communicate with you. Then the Queens used me to infiltrate the programs on the Battle School computer system to give you visual messages. This Hive Queen remembers these actions as if she did them all herself."

"That was Ender, not me," said Peter.

"You," said Jane. "Stop being truculent about it. She's going to know you when you get there, and it would be childish of you to insist that she pretend not to know who you are."

"If she thinks I'm still Andrew Wiggin, then she *doesn't* know who I am."

"Enough of that nonsense," said Thulium. "It's a stiff walk and we don't want to lollygag."

Enough of that nonsense? thought Peter. An eight-year-old talks to adults that way?

No, he realized. That's *not* what I was thinking. That's what I allowed myself to *think* that I was thinking, but at the deepest level, far below language, what I really thought was, This child dares to speak so disrespectfully to *me*?

Who do I think I am? I refuse to be Ender, for good reason; but I am not owed any scrap of the great respect earned by my namesake the Hegemon. "Wang Mu," said Peter. "Is the original Peter Wiggin my ancestor-of-the-heart?"

"More truly than the Royal Mother is mine," Wang-Mu answered. "You share his DNA, you look like him. But all that ancestor-of-the-heart business is, of course, sentimental nonsense. It's designed to give a child noble aspirations, to bear the name of a worthy person and consider him or her to be an ancestor. But you know that *your* heart needs no ancestor, because your most important ancestor *is* you. You are literally a continuation of his life. Your avoidance of this is harming you, more and more every day."

Wang-Mu said it without a trace of disrespect or even reproof in her voice—she *was* a superb servant, wasn't she?—yet Peter also knew that when the two of them were alone, she had learned never to say such things to him, certainly not with such clarity and certainty, because he would fly into a rage (at first) or simply leave the room until he cooled off enough to feel no need to reprove her for her temerity.

He knew that she spoke now because in front of Jane and Thulium he could not rage, and on this errand he could not walk away. He had to bear it.

She manipulates me, he thought. But only to tell me what is obvious to everyone else. I am who I am, I have the history I have.

But I don't remember being Ender Wiggin. I have avoided reading his writings as much as possible, and I haven't read the transcript of Plikt's Speaking for his death. Nor have I talked much with the original Valentine about him. It's Peter Wiggin that I've studied and tried to learn from. I read *The Hegemon* again and again, until I realized that I could not find the real Peter Wiggin in those pages. But I found the original Andrew Wiggin there, because every page was filled with his wisdom, his understanding, his admiration, and his forgiveness of his brother.

Not *my* forgiveness, though. I don't remember being either one of them. I only remember coming to consciousness inside that starship where Ela was making her anti-descolada virus and Miro was refashioning himself. I had enough memory to know my name, and Valentine's, and Ender's. I even knew why we were in that ship, and who the other people were, and that a being named Jane was controlling it all. I had the full range of the languages Ender Wiggin understood and spoke—not just the English of his childhood in America or the Stark he had spoken on every world since, or the slang of Battle School. On every world where Ender had spoken for the dead, he had learned at least some of the local language, and in some places an astonishing amount. That's why Peter was able to follow many conversations in Japanese, in Mandarin, in the Lusitanian dialect of Portuguese—because they came along with Ender's aiúa into Peter's brain.

I am full of languages.

My muscles are full of memories, too. They can't be Peter Wiggin's, because muscle memory is not in the DNA.

As he walked alongside Wang-Mu, following Jane and the child, he realized that if someone were to rush at them to attack them, his body knew exactly what to do. He knew how to manipulate body weight, duck and dodge, and where to strike an opponent to immobilize him. Why hadn't he noticed he had this skill before?

It had never come up.

He had never admitted to himself that he really was, in some way, Ender Wiggin. But now, walking this longish distance, his muscles were coming alive and awake.

This isn't the body I wore when I learned these skills, he thought, and my kinesthesia would not place my blows exactly where intended, but I could adapt to it. I can wear this body and call it myself, even though my mind remembers wearing a different body.

How can the dimensionless aiúa carry muscle memory with it?

That is not an interesting question, his own deep mind assured him. What matters is that now you know the aiúa *can* carry memories, from languages to body movements, and if it can bring those along into this new flesh Ender made, what other memories might there be?

Jane started talking to Thulium in front of him. "Oh, Thulium, let's not go down there. We don't have to follow your *exact* track to the Hive Queen; we'll save ourselves a climb later if we stay high up on this slope."

Thulium looked up at Jane and blushed. Then she looked hurriedly away, but accepted Jane's suggestion about the route.

If Jane wanted anyone else to know why she took this detour, she would have explained it. Thulium's obvious embarrassment suggested that Jane was helping her avoid some spot that had scared her before, or something like that. Something that would make this seemingly fearless child wary of returning by that route.

Yet Thulium had *not* asked for a detour, and had not chosen one. She might want to avoid something, but she had not *chosen* to avoid it. Jane knew something that Thulium had not known that she knew.

As far as I'm concerned, he said to himself, I didn't notice anything about their conversation about the route. It was trivial. I'm just a passenger on this little journey. He started looking around for landmarks, to see if he could return to this spot later, using his newly acquired Outside-In mobility.

No, he thought. I will *not* come back here and try to find evidence of something that would have shamed Thulium. Even if she were really a simple eight-year-old child, she would deserve privacy and respect. And since she's a leguminid, and not an ordinary child at all, I need to show her all the more respect.

Si Wang-Mu squeezed his hand.

He looked at her.

She wasn't looking at him. She was merely smiling.

Did she hear and understand my entire conversation with myself? Did she see how I avoided asking questions? Did she know that I decided not to return here and search for answers? Is she judging me every second?

No, he thought. She's observing me with affection and understanding, guessing the things I'm struggling with, and she's happy when I triumph over the Peter Wiggin nature built into this body.

So it isn't me she loves. It's Ender Wiggin.

Fool, he told himself. It isn't the Peter Wiggin aspect of me that she loves, it's my deepest inner nature, which happens to be the same one that made all of Ender Wiggin's choices in life.

Shut up, he told himself.

He squeezed her hand back, and if she had looked up at him, she would have seen him smiling, too. Because it was certainly true that whoever he turned out to be, Si Wang-Mu *was* his wife, and she would be on his side.

———

Thulium recognized everything about the place. The river, meandering through nearly level ground, with meadows and then farmland stretching away west and north, and a bank of hills on the south shore. The cavern or tunnel entrance—she still couldn't tell which—with Formic workers moving in and out, all of them on an urgent errand, judging by their haste, but nobody plotting their trajectories, which seemed to be negotiated at the moment, and not according to any protocol. Maybe some kind of invisible ranking? They moved like ants, individually purposeful, collectively chaotic. Does the course of history change depending on whether the two Formics, instead of colliding, pass each other on the right or the left? Or is chaos simply the easiest control method for the Hive Queen, who has more important matters to attend to?

"I believe she lives inside that cave somewhere," said Thulium. "Depending on how much of insect cultural patterns remain with her, she may be very deep inside, with almost no light, but with some kind of air movement passages that can be opened and fanned for cooling, or closed and warmed for heating."

"I've never been inside," said Jane. "Except my observations through the jewel that Ender wore in his ear."

"Nor have I," said Thulium. "A Formic came and talked to me as I stopped to drink and wash myself in the river." Would the others wonder why she felt a need to wash? Let them, thought Thulium. I can't control what they wonder.

Peter was saying nothing. But Wang-Mu said, "If Peter has any memories from Ender's passage into the habitation of the Hive Queen, they haven't surfaced yet."

Thulium wondered why Wang-Mu was answering *for* Peter, as if he were a child too shy to speak his mind.

But then again, he came to consciousness far more recently than I did. Just because he's adult-sized doesn't imply that he is not, in some ways at least, still in his childhood.

So, trying not to give offense, Thulium did *not* ask if Wang-Mu also cut up his food for him to eat. She didn't have to be Sergeant's child *all* the time.

Without Thulium noticing its approach, a Formic now stood on the opposite bank.

"It's shallow," said Jane. "She expects us to cross."

"When you say 'she,'" said Wang-Mu, "do you mean that the Formic we're looking at is female, or that you're telling us what the Hive Queen wants?"

"Both," said Jane. "We know there must be males to fertilize the eggs, but she has never shown them to us."

"The parents have seen male Formics," said Thulium. "And the cousins have all seen the vids. The Giant and our parents came across an ancient Formic colony ship, pre-lightspeed. The Queen had died, but the interior biome was still functioning reasonably well, under the half-mad direction of the drones."

"I will want to see those vids," said Jane.

"Oh, please," said Thulium. "You already ransacked all our computer storage. You've studied them."

"I would rather have them given to me than to ransack them," said Jane.

"A cosmetic difference," said Thulium, "since the ransacking has already happened."

"It's one of the things the Hyrum Graff simulation was doing before and during his conversation with you."

"So he *was* a virus," said Thulium.

"Not a hostile one," said Jane. "He took nothing away from you."

"Except our privacy."

"Do we cross the river barefoot?" asked Wang-Mu. "The water seems to be drinkable, but it isn't clear enough for me to see the bottom. Will I need to wear my shoes or carry them?"

Thulium noted that Wang-Mu was mothering them all—keeping them on the subject that mattered. Steering them away from conflict. Well done, Chinese servant-girl.

Thulium, who had already felt the bottom of the river, at least near the shore, took her shoes off and strode barefoot into the water.

At once the Formic splashed into the water, raced across, and scooped Thulium up in her arms.

Thulium understood the moment she saw how deep the water was in the middle. The others could safely ford the river, but Thulium's body was too weak to resist the strong center current. Thulium's question was whether the Hive Queen, paying attention at that moment, had ordered the Formic to come and carry her, or if the Formic itself had enough intelligence to make such an evaluation and decision on its own. Or had the Hive Queen given it a prior instruction which it was now, intelligently, obeying?

She saw the consternation in the others, now splashing after her. She waved and called out, "It's all right! I'm not big enough to fight the current, so she's keeping me safe!"

"Good," said the Formic, in its strange voice. Thulium realized that it was easier to understand this time.

Then they were on dry land, and Thulium slid out of its arms—her arms—and stood again, waiting for the humans to catch up.

They did, soaking wet. They wasted a few minutes wringing out their clothing, as much as possible, and then putting dry shoes on wet feet, never an easy task. Thulium said nothing by way of criticism; *she* had been ferried across, so nothing above her knees was even damp, and she already had her shoes back on. They would do what they believed they must, and what was the hurry? This was *their* errand, not hers, so their sense of urgency was what must guide their progress.

Still, Thulium felt as if the Hive Queen were calling her. Saying to hurry. Why was she waiting for the others?

Because I'm terrified to face you alone, she thought.

Even in the darkness and with your weak eyes, came the answer, you are never safer than you are with me.

Was that really the Hive Queen talking to her? The Queen had communed with Ender, when she was inside the cocoon. She had given him the visions that allowed him to write *The Hive Queen*. Could she also talk to Thulium? But she was receiving words, not images, the way Ender had described their communication.

That was how we talked at first, Little One, but I learned to think in a languagey way, so now I use my vocabulary look-up tables to allow me to speak into your mind with some hope of achieving understanding.

You're terrific at it, Thulium said silently. Or at least I *think* I'm understanding everything you say.

Alas that I cannot say in your language everything that I want you to understand, the Queen replied. But we'll see what happens over time.

And then, as those words ended, Thulium's vision was filled with a scene inside a huge enclosed space, where an enormously tall man was stepping away from a harness and walking clumsily, thunderously on the soil of a strange garden. Then he stumbled and fell, and lay still, and Thulium knew that she had just witnessed the death of the Giant, her grandfather.

How do you have this image? Thulium asked.

In reply, she saw the images of all the animals in the garden. Their eyes open, watching.

The mother of these creatures was dead, said the Queen, but when the leguminids found the place, I quickly learned to see through the eyes of those orphaned creatures and add their observations to my memory. I remember it as if I saw it myself.

Thulium felt an arm around her shoulder. "Don't be afraid," said Wang-Mu. "She's clearly protecting you."

Jane's voice answered. "Thulium didn't stop because she's afraid. The Queen is already speaking to her, and she showed Thulium a memory that means a lot to her. Let's give her a moment to recover before we press her to lead us on."

Wang-Mu's hand withdrew from Thulium's shoulder.

Thulium reached out, took Wang-Mu's hand, and drew her arm across her shoulders again. "I'm not sorry that you touched me," she said. "I was taken from my mother at a very early age. A human touch, kindly meant, has been rare in my life."

Wang-Mu tentatively squeezed her in something

like a sideways hug. It was, of course, awkward; but love is love.

Instantly Thulium saw an image of herself and Wang-Mu as they were at that moment; it must be the vision being passed to the Hive Queen from the Formic who had carried her across the river. But there was more to the image than just the girl and the young woman. There was also a glimmer of light, a thread like a strand of spiderweb glistening in the sunlight on a dewy morning.

Am I making a philotic connection with Wang-Mu? asked Thulium in her mind.

You are connecting with each other, said the Queen.

Show me all the connections! Please!

You could not comprehend them all, the Queen said. Your brain could not contain them.

Try me!

No, the Queen said, with finality. But look at these.

Now Thulium saw the four of them, still from behind, but the gossamer connection between her and Wang-Mu was reduced to insignificance by the vast bright ropes that came from Jane—one leading back toward Lusitania colony, where Thulium assumed it connected with Miro, and another thick as a hawser connecting her to Peter. Then other thick philotic connections reached into the cavern, and Thulium knew that they led to the Hive Queen. A hawser-like connection from Peter, another from Jane. A slight one from Wang-Mu, but a stronger one from Thulium herself.

What about a connection between Peter and Wang-Mu?

Then she saw it, as it briefly glowed a little brighter. It was there. Nothing like the connections that had grown over years—no, centuries—between Ender's aiúa and those of Jane and the Hive Queen. But not a weak connection, either. Many strands. Not yet formed into a firm rope, as the longstanding philotic connections appeared to Thulium in this vision. But still too many strands to break easily.

Is it enough? Thulium asked. Can Peter carry Wang-Mu along with him?

Little One, said the Hive Queen in her mind. That is Peter's question to ask, and it is for him to learn the answer.

"Let's go on in," said Thulium. "I think she'll show us the way."

"There will be well-worn paths," said Jane, "and no traps or obstacles, not even low ceilings, because her children cleared them all away long ago. And the darkness is not absolute. Look around you and think. No one needs to stumble."

Thulium strode into the tunnel's mouth.

"Shouldn't the Formic lead us?" asked Peter.

"You may hold the Formic's hand, if you like," said Jane. "But she will follow us, not lead."

Thulium heard them follow her, their feet scuffing the dirt of the hard-packed road. How many thousands or millions of steps had Formic feet taken to form this path? And back on the original Formic worlds and colonies, which existed thousands and thousands of years, what paths and tunnels did they form? Will I ever see anything truly ancient from the Hive Queen civilization?

I can show you many images, said the voice inside her mind. But your yearning is to see them with your eyes. That might be arranged, with one of those who can travel world to world. Be patient, Little One. Your eyes will see many things. But your mind will see far more. Things that were, things that are, things that are yet to come. You will imagine things and make them come to be; you will imagine other things, and do whatever is necessary to avoid them. You are one of the hinges of memory.

No, of history. Your word is history, because you learn it instead of remembering it.

"I will write about this day," said Wang-Mu softly. "I will write to Master Han."

"Please don't," said Jane. "Let him live out his days in the company of his beloved daughter. Let him forget how much better he was pleased with you than with her."

Thulium thought: Jane can be cruel.

Then she thought: Jane knows how much pain can be a part of love. The way Father loves me, even though he hurts and frightens me. While the twins hurt and frighten me for the pleasure of it, and have no love for me at all.

I wish I could see philotic connections the way the Queen does.

8

Quara: I wish that any of you took my findings seriously.

Ela: I wish your findings didn't all match up so perfectly with your previously determined hypotheses.

Quara: Do you have another way to read my data? Then tell me and we can design experiments.

Ela: Design your own experiments to try to falsify your interpretations of the data. That's what scientists do.

Quara: And what are you doing to falsify your interpretations of the data you've been getting from Descoladora?

Ela: We haven't yet found any hypotheses that are not already contradicted by some or all of the data. We're trying to think of new hypotheses that do fit. Then we'll start experimenting.

Quara: Meanwhile, you're terrifying the local population by instantaneously popping from here to there in the night sky.

Ela: If they did devise the descolada and send it out into space, they deserve a little terror from meeting up with a superior civilization.

Quara: Humans are not a superior civilization. You're dazzling them with a single trick, which is *not* done by a human.

Ela: Well, she's a human *now*.

Quara: Debatable.

Ela: Says who?

Quara: I know, your verdict isn't in on *me* yet.

Ela: Oh, *we* know you're human. We just don't have enough evidence to determine whether *you* know it or not.

Quara: Let me know when you decide.

Ela: We're in the midst of the experiments now. So it will be you who decides, my dear.

<pause of several minutes>

Quara: How do you hope it will turn out?

Ela: I would love to have you back in the circle of my love, and to find that I am in the circle of yours.

Quara: Don't you already know how much I love you?

Ela: Sometimes I hope, and sometimes I fear, that I do already know.

—Quara and Ela Ribeira, transcript of text messages

Notes for Plikt: "The Ribeira Family Saves the World"

Peter clung to the arm of the Formic tighter than he meant to; he had not been prepared for how frightened he was of walking in the dark, on a path that kept going up and down, and turning this way and that. He had no idea if there was a steep drop-off on one side or the other—or both—and they might have been surrounded by a thousand Formics geared up for war or none at all.

Peter didn't try to speak to the Formic he clung to. He knew that he would really be confessing his fear to the Hive Queen, and even if she already guessed it or even knew it somehow, he did not want anyone to hear his voice tremble or go too high or some other giveaway. Better to stay silent, like the others.

Until at last Thulium's small voice said, softly but audibly: "Here we are."

The Formic stopped, and gently but firmly peeled Peter's hand from its upper arm. Then it stepped forward—Peter couldn't see, but he felt its passage.

"Light," said their Formic guide. Peter assumed it was the same one that had carried Thulium. Its speech was perfectly clear now, though it was also obvious that its vocal apparatus was not a larynx or even the syrinx of birds. Was it related to the chirping legs of crickets? Yet somehow its mouth could create articulate consonants and shape intelligible vowels.

After a few moments, a very dim light began to allow Peter to make out some aspects of his surroundings. The floor around him was fairly level, but it was not empty. Instead, thousands of low hollow pillars shaped like interlocking hexagons surrounded him, and many small creatures were scampering across the tops, stopping now and then to put something into or pull something out of one of the hollow hexes. The creatures were certainly not ordinary Formics, but they might be Formics with a special purpose, given a different shape to allow them to move lightly over what had to be the nursery for the Queen's eggs to hatch, pass through their larval stage, and then cocoon themselves to emerge as Formics—of whatever type the Queen had determined they needed to be.

"Yes, Brother," said the talking Formic. "You understand what my messengers do. They feed and protect and care for the babies. But they also carry my instructions to the babies about what they need to grow up to be."

Peter knew she was talking to him. "I'm sure you already know what we came here to ask you."

"I do," said the Formic. "But do you?"

Peter knew this was a trick question designed to make him feel stupid and lost. So he skipped the stage where he gave a stupid answer, and simply felt stupid and lost anyway.

"This one, whose voice I am using, she is the result of many years of trying to develop a child who could speak to humans, and understand human speech. The good-enough vocal apparatus I perfected a long time ago, as you measure time. But the brainwork required for this one to understand and produce human speech, that took far longer."

"So she speaks to us using intelligence of her own?" asked Thulium.

"If I created her speeches for her, it would use up far too much of my—what does Jane call it?—my bandwidth. So I inform her of what I wish her to accomplish, and she shapes the language to that purpose. Has she done well?"

It was odd to hear the talking Formic speaking of

itself in the third person. Especially as the Hive Queen was having the Talker explain that even though she spoke as if she were the Queen, she was explicitly *not* merely transmitting the Queen's own words. Apparently the Queen had no words of her own.

"You're wrong, Boy Who Calls Himself Peter," said the Talker. "The Queen has all the words. She has been communing with humans for three thousand years. She fought to learn to understand human language back when the survival of all her sisters depended on such understanding."

So this time Talker was speaking as herself, referring to the Queen in the third person.

"By my count, there are six people present," said Talker. "The Queen, myself, and four humans. Why is one person thought of as the third person?"

"It's grammar," said Jane. "It doesn't make sense to the humans, either, but somehow they communicate."

Jane's words apparently gave Wang-Mu permission to speak. "O Queen, does my connection with Peter have enough strength to allow him to carry me Outside and Inside without danger to my survival?"

"It has enough strength," said Talker. "But he must also will it to be so. Can he concentrate on you with enough purity and endurance that he won't get distracted and forget you?"

Peter wanted to cry out, No, I would never! But then he remembered that an hour ago he had toyed with the idea of doing his interplanetary journeying without Wang-Mu, leaving her behind, as if she were not a part of everything he did, as if she did not matter in the accomplishment of his purposes.

"And what *are* your purposes, Boy Who Calls Himself Peter?" asked Talker. "I think it would be good for you to decide and then explain it to us."

Peter felt as if he had been called on the carpet before a demanding teacher who insisted that he take an oral examination in front of everybody who mattered.

When was I ever in a classroom? When did I have a teacher? When was I given a test? Why do I recognize how this feels?

"We are all waiting," said Talker. "What are your purposes? Why will you flit from one world to another?"

"Wang-Mu and I have found some value," said Peter, "in the speculations Quara Ribeira has written."

"You all see how he answers a question about *his* intentions with reference to a person who is not present," said Talker.

"I was creating a context," said Peter. "Quara believes that the researchers studying Descoladora are trapped in their own assumptions. Wang-Mu believes, with reasoning and evidence of her own, that the inhabitants of Descoladora did not create the descolada virus and did not send it out into the galaxy. Wang-Mu believes that the planet Descoladora faced its own descolada epidemic, and that far from being our enemy, its inhabitants are a valuable source of information about what the virus did to them, and how they coped with it."

Thulium quietly said, "Me, too."

Talker spoke over her. "Still you speak of Quara, who is not here, and Wang-Mu, who is. Nowhere can I detect your answer to the question that was asked."

"My intention," said Peter, "is for me and Wang-Mu to travel to the surface of Descoladora. At first we would merely observe. We would return to Lusitania often to be quarantined and examined, in case we pick up some previously unknown virus. If it looks possible for us to communicate with the inhabitants, then on a later visit we will do so. That's my plan, and since everything is contingent on how each step plays out, it can't be much firmer than that."

"I ask your companions," said Talker. "How does this plan seem to you?"

Wang-Mu said, "Since it's the plan Peter and I worked out together, making it *our* plan—"

"I'm sorry," said Peter. "She asked me about *my* intentions and already rebuked me once for speaking on your behalf."

"Let's not have a spat right here," said Wang-Mu.

Peter thought: If you didn't want to quarrel, then why did you claim ownership of the plan, as if I had denied you any part in it?

But there was no point in embarrassing himself or her in front of the others. So he contained his resentment and held his tongue.

"Well chosen," said Talker. "Well chosen, Brother."

Peter knew what was meant when the Hive Queen called him Brother. She knew she was talking to Ender's aiúa. And so she recognized him as her companion on many voyages, through many centuries. But he did not remember *her* that way.

Wang-Mu resumed what she had been saying, as if the interruption had not occurred, "My presence here affirms that I agree with and want to participate in this plan."

"Not knowing what you'll find on the surface of Descoladora?" asked Jane.

"Until someone ventures there," said Wang-Mu, "we'll never know much more than we know now. And we *must* know more, for the sake of the whole human species."

Talker resumed control of the interview. "Who designated you for this perilous mission?"

Peter chuckled. "Neither Wang-Mu nor I has genetic expertise to contribute to scientific investigations. Wang-Mu learns more quickly than I, so she has a hope of being of some help. But we both wanted to do something that has value, and since this is a dangerous job, we can't afford to risk wasting the life of any of the geneticists involved with the project. If everything went wrong, and Wang-Mu and I died without being able to escape back to the Lusitanian quarantine, the loss to the project would not be crippling."

Talker shook her head. "You do not know what will or will not cripple something, or what form the crippling might take. You do not know what has value greater than the value of other things. All your decisions are in ignorance of the outcome."

"Decisions always are," said Wang-Mu. "But still we decide and act boldly, for if we don't, nothing can be accomplished."

"Where did you read *that*?" asked Thulium.

Wang-Mu did not answer.

"You're habitually scornful, you know," said Jane. "Even when you are not superior to other people in any way."

"I know that," said Thulium. "I'm so scornful that I'm going to point out the deep stupidity of this whole plan."

"We're holding our breath to hear," said Peter.

"Whoever and whatever the inhabitants of Descoladora turn out to be, whatever the biota of the planet turns out to be, for you to go without a geneticist along will make your observations nearly worthless. You don't know what to look for. You don't know what it will imply about the inhabitants."

"You're not coming with us," said Peter.

"I'm the most expendable of the geneticists," said Thulium. "I can go to the surface of Descoladora with an open mind and open eyes—eyes that are trained to see ecological relationships. And a skill set that can include, with the right instruments—highly portable ones, I must add—the ability to look at genomes and evaluate them and transmit information to the Box about what I learn. If you don't take me, take *some* geneticist, because the geneticist you don't take will be the most important loss your expedition could possibly suffer."

The light in the space was so dim that when Peter looked down to see what Wang-Mu thought of Thulium's declaration, he couldn't begin to read the expression on her face.

The light in the room increased slightly, until Peter *could* see Wang-Mu as she slowly nodded to him.

"How do you light this space?" asked Thulium, as if she hadn't been part of the discussion up till now.

"Skylights," said Talker. "I have tunnels with mirrors leading to spots on the surface. My children cover and uncover the mirrors to allow less and more light to come to this chamber."

Nobody told Thulium to stick to the subject. Peter realized that the Queen and Jane were treating her with the same respect they showed to Peter and Wang-Mu.

"Brother," said Talker. "Your bond with Wang-Mu is strong enough for you to take her anywhere, as long as you vow that when you do so, you will never forget that she is with you."

"I make that vow gladly and willingly," said Peter. "I want her with me. I need her with me."

"Make sure you act upon that statement," said Jane dryly, "until it's completely true."

Peter felt a flash of resentment toward Jane.

"But now we have a greater problem," said Talker. "Thulium spoke the truth. Your expedition is crippled if you don't have a geneticist with you. She is a superb geneticist, and she should go with you. Furthermore, she should take her cousin Sprout with her, so they can examine what they find and converse about it at a level that no one else in the expedition can begin to understand."

Two leguminids, thought Peter.

"You don't know them," said Talker. "You don't love them."

"He doesn't even like me," said Thulium.

"Yes he does," said Jane. "He admires your chutzpah and he envies your intelligence and learning. He enjoys your company, especially when you intend him not to enjoy it."

Peter wanted to shout at her, Maybe that's how Ender would have felt, but I am not Ender!

And then something deep inside him said, Yes you are, so keep your mouth shut.

Beside him, Wang-Mu stifled a short laugh. As if she had heard or guessed at Peter's internal conversation.

"You will not be ready to embark on this expedition," said Talker, "until you come back and show me that you have philotically entwined with Thulium and Sprout to a great enough degree that you can transport them along with yourself and Wang-Mu, with complete safety, from world to world."

"Why?" asked Peter. "I mean, why come back here? I understand the reason for making sure I can carry them safely. But you'll know without our coming through this tunnel. You'll know and Talker can come and tell us."

"I don't send my children where they might terrify the Lusitanians who aren't already used to our appearance," said Talker. "Least of all one so valuable as this one who speaks."

"And you shouldn't underestimate the power of ritual," said Jane. "When you think you're ready, you'll come here and you'll walk into the darkness and this time you *won't* cling to a Formic's arm. You'll follow Thulium because you'll know her and trust her— enough to risk your life on her observations and decisions. Because, on the planet's surface, she, not you, will be making the most important decisions."

Peter felt the sting of that, the stab of it, the dull ache of it.

"Aw, Peter," said Jane, her voice dripping with pity. "Are you only just discovering that what you liked best about this plan of yours was that *you* would be in charge?"

"I thought it would be only me and Wang-Mu," said Peter.

"And you trusted that her deferent attitude would guarantee that your will would prevail in all things?" asked Jane.

"Yes," said Peter. "I thought I would be in charge."

"And why does that matter to you?" asked Talker. It was a surprise that she weighed in on something so personal.

Peter spoke to Talker, knowing that it was really the Hive Queen he was addressing. "Do *you* ever relinquish your authority?" he asked.

"No," said Talker. "But here is a difference between you and me. I actually *have* authority. And if I ceased to exercise it, all my children would soon die, as was proven when Mazer Rackham killed the Sister that we sent to colonize Earth. You humans found no living soldiers or workers after that. Once Ender Wiggin had killed all the remaining Sisters, no human found a living Formic anywhere. No one depends on your authority to that degree, Boy Who Calls Himself Peter."

The truth of this statement was brutal. The bitter disappointment in Peter's soul brought tears to his eyes and rage to his heart.

This is what the original Peter Wiggin felt when Ender was taken to Battle School and he was not. This was the rage that made him Ender's enemy. Now I know what it felt like. Feels like.

But I am not Peter. Not the original one. Ender never *needed* to have authority. He never reached for it, unless it had already been granted to him. He always lived and worked within circumstances that he could not change, while changing and improving all the circumstances that he could.

And he realized that he was basing this thought on what was written in *The Hegemon,* as the Speaker for the Dead explained why Peter was able to unite the nations of the world under a single government, one that protected the rights of groups and, above all, of individuals. Hegemon Peter Wiggin had learned to understand what other people needed and find ways to accommodate them, so that they never felt enslaved and oppressed under his leadership. They always felt like valued friends and allies, because the Hegemon made sure they *were* friends and allies, and he valued them.

I do not need to govern this expedition. I just need to transport it to and fro. And then to look out for the others and protect them as well as I can, while everybody does the work they're suited for.

As he articulated this thought in his mind, Peter felt a strange emotion pass over him. The sense of having accomplished something. Of having understood something that had always been just out of reach.

"*Now* you are leader of the expedition," said Talker. "And now you are ready to start learning to love Thulium and Sprout, and for them to come to value you."

"Well done," said Jane.

Wang-Mu took his hand and held it, not tightly, but firmly enough to speak of her happiness with him.

"If you expect me to kiss him and hug him, you can forget it," said Thulium. "I don't even kiss or hug my father."

"Shut up, Ultima Thule," said Jane. "You're ruining the moment."

The light in the room began to fade. "Talker won't

go with you back out of my hive house," said Talker. "I need her here. Follow Thulium, and she will take you safely home."

Thulium walked through them and started down the path as the light faded. They followed closely, and this time it was Wang-Mu that Peter held to, and he held her hand, not her upper arm. They traveled as partners through the darkness, which struck him as appropriate and symbolic of what they should always be, what he should make sure they always were, because Wang-Mu had always been ready for them to become partners in this marriage, which was their true expedition, one that should last them the rest of their lives.

9

Jane: You think I didn't handle this very well.

Miro: You weren't handling it at all.

Jane: Who was, then? The Queen? Certainly not Wang-Mu. She was completely centered on Peter.

Miro: The expedition to meet the Hive Queen was Thulium's. Peter was a subject under discussion.

Jane: Oh, Miro. You're too subtle for me sometimes.

Miro: Thulium wanted to meet the Hive Queen. She wanted to get to the surface of Descoladora. She wanted to run the genetic investigation of Descoladora on the ground. She wanted to subject herself to the microbiota of Descoladora so she was her own test case. She longs to be important in a way that only Sergeant and his children, among the leguminids, seek to be. She longs for a mother and doesn't like you in the job, so she had hopes for the Hive Queen. But Wang-Mu will end up with the duty.

Jane: You weren't even there, Miro.

Miro: Just because I don't attend a showing of *Romeo and Juliet* doesn't mean that I don't know who's dead at the end.

Jane: But did you know the Hive Queen would set Peter the task of learning to love one of the most impossible of the leguminids?

Miro: And Sprout.

Jane: Sprout is easy.

Miro: Deliberately building new philotic connections is never easy. Many people are never able to create one strong enough to matter.

Jane: Your assessment of Peter's chances, then?

Miro: The philotic connections are between aiúas. This new Peter is still deciding who he wants to be. But the part of him so deep he can't alter it, that person I know well. I watched him form bonds of love with the equally impossible Ribeira family, and he did it with some of us in the first hour we knew him.

Jane: Your assessment of Peter's chances, I ask again?

Miro: From what the Queen told you, he's already accepting that he really is Ender, and that this is the best of his impulses.

Jane: And a third time I ask.

Miro: Ender knows exactly how it's done. Peter will recognize the pattern, when he thinks of it—and then Ender will act on it, using Peter's voice and body.

Jane: You're sure of this?

Miro: Yes. And now you ask, How sure? And I answer, I'm betting all our futures on it.

—Transcript of pillow talk, Miro and Jane Ribeira
Jane's redacted notes provided to Plikt for
"The Ribeira Family Saves the World"

Thulium sat at her computer going over the data and drafts coming from the Box. They were doing as well as could be done without going to the surface. But the inadequacies in their work grated on her, especially when her access to Descoladora's surface was limited by the incompetencies of Peter Wiggin.

The door opened and Peter himself came into the room and sat down in a comfortable-looking chair near the wall beside her. His angle would not allow him to read anything appearing on her desk. This had to be a deliberate choice; he wanted her not to feel as if he was there to pry.

"All right," she said to him, not taking her gaze from the pages displayed in the air in front of her. "Be lovable and let's see what happens."

Peter said nothing.

"Do you think we have forever?" demanded Thulium.

"Do you?" asked Peter.

"Oh, is it my job to be cute so you can love the clever little leguminid girl?"

"I have an idea," said Peter. "We have the same goal—get to the surface—and we face the same barrier—the lack of a philotic connection between us."

"Everyone has that idea," said Thulium.

"Except you," said Peter. "Because you're deliberately making conversation between us nearly impossible, except for this ridiculous meta-dialogue."

Thulium had to admit that he was right. Her brattiness caused no harm when it was directed toward the twins, or her father. But she couldn't afford to alienate Peter any more than she already had.

She saved her setup and blanked the holospace. Then she rotated her chair and faced Peter. "Like me better now?"

"Liking is a feeling, and I don't give a rat's petoot about emotions," said Peter. "What matters right now is communication."

"Good. Then let's take on the great question of Love. Not an emotion, I think you already agree."

"There are emotions we call love, but they're really a combination of various yearnings, some noble and some selfish. Not relevant," said Peter. "Our job isn't to give somebody the illusion that we're buddies. Our job is to make it true that we trust each other in pursuit of a common purpose."

"Not a bad definition of love," said Thulium. "But still inadequate."

"Defining *love* is like defining *good*. It's impossible to do without falling into a tautological loop."

"What *have* you been reading since Ender plucked you out of darkness?" asked Thulium.

"Things come to my mind that must be the product of Ender's thought long ago. Someday I'd like to understand how character and memory are carried in the aiúa even after the original brain is dead and rotted away."

"You are a fascinating puzzle, Peter," said Thulium. "But it's not my job to solve it."

"Or mine either, right now," said Peter. "Let's *not* take on the definition of *love*. Instead, please tell me what gear you're going to need on the surface of Descoladora. I doubt that any of the pertinent equipment exists on Lusitania in a portable form, since it would never have been needed here."

Thulium was taken aback. She knew at once that he was right—portable versions of the genetic scanners would be needed, and a lot of sample-taking equipment as well. They had built their own on the *Herodotus,* and their own equipment was better than anything on Lusitania; but it was not portable.

"I expected to build my own," said Thulium.

"And yet you sit here reading reports from scientists who, having never visited the surface, don't have access to the most pertinent data," said Peter.

"What was I supposed to do?"

"Search the nets to find out who already makes and sells portable equipment that will do a good enough job for our purposes. The more portable, with long-lasting and solar-replenished batteries, the better."

"It won't do all that we need. I have to build it."

"Wrong," said Peter. "It may not do all that we want, but if you search well enough, you'll find equipment that will do what we need. I don't care if it takes five machines to do what a single machine of your making could do—we don't have time for you to design and make it."

"How much time do you think it will take to ship us the equipment we can buy, if it even exists?" asked Thulium.

Peter sat in his chair, looking down at his feet. Or the floor around his feet.

"Ah," Thulium said. "You're going to take my shopping list and go and get them for me. Faster than light."

"It's the least I can do," said Peter.

"But how will you even know if the equipment is right, and if it works properly?"

"First," said Peter, "Wang-Mu will be with me, and she's very clever. Teach her how to observe and test, and it will be done, and done well. Second, even if we make a mistake, we'll bring it to you and *you'll* test it, and send us back with corrections, unless the deficiencies are things you can easily correct yourself with your handy junior tool kit."

"Who's being bratty now?" asked Thulium.

"I'm trying to communicate with you in your own dialect," said Peter. "Third, by seeing that I can follow your instructions and successfully complete a few—or many—instantaneous voyages to other star systems, you will come to trust my abilities in the areas pertinent to the expedition."

"And that, in your mind, will constitute love," said Thulium.

"I believe it may help us establish the philotic connection that we need. If it doesn't do the job, we can think of something else."

"So you think that love consists of service," said Thulium.

"I think that trust develops out of desires granted and requests fulfilled. I request that you research well and find what we need for you to do your work quickly, accurately, and conveniently. If you fulfil that desire of mine, then I can fulfil your need and desire to have the best equipment available for sale in the human universe."

"It sounds like a fair bargain," said Thulium.

"And you and Sprout will test it all out together, and he'll make alterations that you both agree are needed."

"I'll make the alterations," said Thulium.

"Sprout should be in on the alterations, so he knows every centimeter of the gear as well as you do, and knows how to repair it in case you do something foolish and get injured so we have to get you back to Lusitania before the expedition is finished."

Thulium almost gasped. "This is how you build up trust?"

"Between you and Sprout, yes," said Peter. "He's

your backup. Your understudy. You can't train me or Wang-Mu to such a level of competency, but my guess is that Sprout already understands the science and technology at a level very close to yours."

Thulium thought a moment. "Yes. In some areas, probably better than I do."

"So do you agree to involve him intensely in every aspect of equipment preparation, revision, repair, and use?"

"Yes," said Thulium.

"You see how the trust grows between us?" asked Peter.

"I'll have a list for you tomorrow," said Thulium.

"I don't want the list tomorrow," said Peter.

"What, you have a picnic or a dance to attend?" asked Thulium. "I've read Jane Austen, and I believe such things are the events they regarded as unmissable."

"I don't want the list tomorrow," said Peter. "I want it right, and I want it complete. And after I start bringing things, and you discover that you didn't ask for the right things after all, or left out some important things, I want you to give me complete and correct replacement lists immediately."

Thulium realized that part of his insistence that she would probably make mistakes was rational—she probably would, because her information would be incomplete so her decisions would be faulty. But part of it was also to put pins into her pride, to let it be known that he was not overawed by her intelligence.

"I'm smarter and better than you think I am," Thulium said to Peter.

"I could say the same. But my question is, are you smarter and better than *you* think you are?"

Thulium would have expected the question to be a challenge: Are you as smart as you think you are?

Instead, he was asking her to be smarter and better than her own opinion of her abilities. What did that mean?

"I'm smart enough to admit the possibility of error, and plan for it," said Thulium.

"Good. Then my errand here this afternoon is complete," said Peter. He rose to his feet.

"One point that you may not have thought of," said Thulium. "The really good equipment is going to be ridiculously expensive. Especially because the kind of thing I need is usually made to order, since there's not enough demand to justify making them ahead and storing them until they're ordered. So you'll need to have access to the leguminid fortune."

"I inherited most of Ender Wiggin's estate," said Peter. "Chances are that I already own, in whole or in part, all the companies that make the equipment we need. And if I don't, then I can always buy them."

He left the room, closing the door gently behind him.

Thulium thought about Peter Wiggin. He's trying to be a decent person, she concluded. He's also trying to establish leadership, but not with threats, only with—what, persuasion? Except that he's also willing to be persuaded. He doesn't start from the assumption that he's right. He wants *me* to stop assuming that *I'm* always right. And when I'm wrong, he brings me up short until I'm able to hear him. Nobody on the *Herodotus* did things that way, except sometimes Aunt Carlotta.

But was that how the Giant handled his three ridiculously clever and self-willed children?

Regardless of how she felt about Peter Wiggin, Thulium had to admit that at the very least, she would end up with an extraordinary collection of valuable and useful equipment. And since Peter would have no idea what anything was actually for, she could slip in orders for equipment that she'd need in the future, on Lusitania or anywhere else her work took her.

No, she told herself. If I want extraneous equipment, I'll tell him it's extraneous but explain why I want it. If he can't trust my requests to be honest, then the philotic connection between us can't develop properly.

Then another thought: Our expedition really matters. If Peter turns out to be unable to transport me and Sprout, Jane can do it. She's done it before. Peter can take Wang-Mu, and Jane can take care of me and Sprout.

She had a vague feeling that this attitude was also counterproductive, and might not even be accurate. Jane might *refuse* to transport Thulium if she realized that Thulium deliberately ignored or sabotaged the assignment to connect philotically with Peter.

Then she had another thought. If Jane brings back Yuuto and Mayumi and Airi, the cousins' parents from Tochoji, what will *that* do to Sprout's and my independence, our ability to take part in perilous expeditions without any adult supervision? Unless one were to count Peter and Wang-Mu as adults, a doubtful proposition at best.

Jane won't bring them to us until we've accomplished her purpose. She'll especially keep Sergeant away. Father would interfere just to show his authority over me.

Maybe, even if Sergeant forbade her, even if he locked her in a closet like that one time on the *Herodotus*, Peter could snatch her up wherever she was and transport her with him. Father's authority could never trump the authority of an aiúa that could journey Outside and Inside without even needing a ship.

Maybe I need Peter to be very powerful, and to be so connected to me that he will understand that my own father has no idea of what my best interests are, and therefore is not entitled to exercise authority over me. Maybe making a connection with Peter Wiggin will set me truly free from the bondage I have been in since Father kidnapped me away from my mother, Airi, so he was my only parent. My only master. My owner.

10

You asked me to tell you how to access the funds you will need to acquire Thulium's requested instruments and equipment. Since I do not know which worlds you will visit, I have set you up with an SCA—a Starways Congress Account. There is no password. When the seller calls the SCA administrator in that area, you will be asked several identifying questions.

First is the year of your birth, and then the city and planet of your birth. Third is the name of your maternal grandfather; I will remind you if you have forgotten. The fourth is your wife's maiden name. I talked them out of asking for the name of a childhood pet or the brand of your first automobile.

They also demanded that I supply your real year of birth, since they did not believe my answer, upon which I supplied the birth certificate of the original Peter Wiggin. Try to remember his birthday. Because the real date of your entry into our universe is even less believable than that date in the distant past.

Be careful on every planet to rent or buy a house, not a hotel room or apartment. Install the starship box in the back, out of view of the street. Have equipment delivered to the house, and when the laborers arrive, have them transport it to the box in the back yard. You should look up which cultures require tipping, and when the tip should be given. You will, of course, need cash for such transactions.

I have every reason to expect that you and Si Wang-Mu will be completely successful in all your missions of acquisition. The primary danger I foresee is that you will become such good friends with people in the world you are visiting that it will be hard for you to find a convenient time to come back to Lusitania, which will, of course, require that your box and all its contents disappear without explanation. Never tell anyone anything about your intention to depart or your schedule of departure. I'd rather not have to waste time creating false flight information about your leaving.

—Memorandum: Jane Ribeira to Peter Wiggin II Plikt, "The Ribeira Family Saves the World"

"Why don't you tell me what you need this equipment to do?"

Peter, following his policy of not speaking when he was sure his anger or contempt would be audible in his tone of voice, simply looked the man in the eyes long enough for Wang-Mu to realize it was her cue. It never took her long.

"I wish I could tell you," said Wang-Mu. "But we are merely the purchasing agents, and this exact machine was what we were told to acquire. If you can't supply it, then our clients will look elsewhere."

"And you'll be out a fat commission," said the store's owner.

"We will receive a better payment if we don't deliver the *wrong* equipment," said Wang-Mu. "Since we would be responsible for paying for that equipment ourselves. And our dissatisfied clients would not give us a good reputation."

"Where *are* your clients located?"

"Are you planning to contact them yourself, and try to cut us out of the transaction?" asked Wang-Mu. "We would be very disappointed if that happened."

Peter raised a hand. Wang-Mu was doing brilliantly, but it was time to move this along. "Does the equipment we specified actually exist?"

"We don't keep it in stock, no," said the owner. "It's too expensive to build any on spec."

"Then how do customers try it out to see if it will work?" asked Peter.

"We give them the names of previous buyers, so they can hear their opinion of its utility and reliability."

"And portability," said Wang-Mu.

"Of course," said the owner.

"Not 'of course,'" said Peter. "Could my partner carry it?"

The owner sized up Wang-Mu. "How far?"

Wang-Mu said, "Could I stand up while holding it?"

"It breaks down into four bags. You could carry each one of them, with the shoulder strap, but how far? I wouldn't take it on a long jungle trip. Or in a canoe."

"Thank you," said Wang-Mu. "Please give us the names of previous purchasers so that we can hear their opinions about the product."

"If you really need it, you can't buy it from anyone but me," said the owner. "Because I hold the interplanetary patent."

"There are other machines, not governed by your patent, that will do well enough," said Wang-Mu. "Yours seemed best to our clients, but when we tell them that you are not in the business of selling these machines, they will let us know their second choice."

"Don't leap to conclusions," said the owner. "Here's the list of customers. You'll find they're all satisfied with both the machines and our service arrangements. Most of them have also had experience with equipment made by our competitors."

"This will be most helpful," said Wang-Mu, taking the list.

"How can I contact you?" asked the owner.

"If we need to talk to you again," said Peter, "we'll come see you."

"It works better if you make an appointment," said the owner.

"Not for us," said Wang-Mu cheerfully.

And they were out the door.

They got on their bicycles and rode back to their house, only about five kilometers away. They made no attempt to converse while cycling, because the streets were so crowded with bicycles that they had to watch traffic constantly. The worst danger was when they stopped at traffic signals, which most of the locals completely ignored. Peter and Wang-Mu thus became sudden obstacles to the other riders, until the signal changed. They witnessed several collisions between bikes or between bikes and pedestrians that could have been avoided if anyone paid attention to the signals. Yet Peter also recognized that speeds were low enough that injuries did not seem very serious, and if people actually stopped at the signals, it would cause a huge backup every time.

More to the point, stopping and then accelerating afterward took far more energy than simply continuing smoothly forward, and since the energy cost was coming out of their legs and arms and back, the riders did the sensible thing and kept going, while watching carefully to avoid hitting anybody.

Because there were no automobiles except for intercity journeys, the city they were in was packed together. The main streets were wide, to carry a huge number of bikes, but the side streets were barely alleyways, and people were expected to bring their bikes indoors when they reached their destination. There were no outdoor bicycle parking facilities. Also, nobody locked their bikes because unless the bike handle recognized your hands, the wheels wouldn't turn. Peter wondered if this system might work in other places.

No, he told himself. You are governor of nothing. It's none of your business how cities all over the Hundred Worlds handle transportation, pollution, and public safety. You and Wang-Mu are the purchasing agents for Thulium Delphiki, and the only important benefit of doing this job well is that perhaps she'll trust you and a philotic connection will grow between the two of you.

Then I'll have to start all over again with Sprout.

When they got home, they brought their bikes inside—houses had ramps that led to the street, instead of walkways and front steps. They had already secured four of Thulium's vital requisitions, and in each case, the seller had tried to cheat them or delay them or whatever else—he had no idea why nobody was eager to actually sell anything in exchange for instant, complete payment with no haggling.

"So am I calling these places, or are you?" asked Wang-Mu.

Peter sighed. "I can use my nice-voice," he said.

"Your nice-voice is even more condescending and offensive than your ordinary voice."

"How do you tolerate me?" asked Peter.

"With love and understanding," said Wang-Mu. "But you're the one who has to decide what we're doing with these calls."

"At first we're doing what the nonseller of the handy-dandy patch sampler suggested. Asking how they like the device. If he gives out their names, they must be used to people calling, and they must give good recommendations, or he'd take them off the list."

"But the second step?" asked Wang-Mu.

"Ask them if they're willing to sell their existing device. We will not only pay them more than they paid for it new, but also we'll pay for the purchase of a new one if they can talk that con artist into selling them one."

"An outstanding offer. Will any of them take it?" asked Wang-Mu.

"I think we need to find out first which of these companies is worth buying," said Peter.

"Wouldn't it save time to buy the company and *then* ask them to sell us the patch sampler?"

"We don't want to buy a company and find out that their device is in the shop, or stolen, or totally defunct," said Peter.

"You have so much money we could buy them all," said Wang-Mu.

"First, some of them might already be owned by the leguminids, as part of their three-thousand-year project of exploring their own genomes," said Peter.

"Thulium doesn't want the cousins or the parents to know what she's doing," said Wang-Mu.

"I don't understand her dread of some dire consequence if they found out," said Peter.

"She's afraid that either she'll get teased and mocked about it, which is painful for a girl her age—"

"Whatever her age is," said Peter.

"Or she's even more afraid that one of her cousins will take the expedition away from her."

"Why would she think that Jane or the Queen would let any such thing happen?"

"She has lived in that family longer than we have," said Wang-Mu.

"So if they already own a company, it's off-limits to us," said Peter. "We need to do our due diligence before we call anybody."

It took them three hours to find everything they could from public sources. Then they called on Jane with an ansible text message by computer. Peter almost used the jewel in his ear, but then only he would be in the conversation with Jane. Wang-Mu had to be part of it.

Jane's image and voice came up almost immediately. "Why did you spend three hours looking things up when I—"

"We are careful with your time," said Wang-Mu. "It's a precious resource."

"Be careful with your own time, too, and ask me when you have such easy questions."

"Of the list we sent you, are there any we already own?" asked Peter.

"They're all far too small," said Jane. "You don't even own companies that own companies that own them."

"Do the leguminids own any of them?"

"No."

"Are they all small enough that we can afford to buy them outright?"

"Getting their current valuations . . . yes, you can buy any or all of them with the money already in your SCA."

"And when was I born?" asked Peter. "I forget."

"You're not old enough to be going through your terrible twos," said Jane. "You haven't forgotten the date, you just want to waste my precious resources."

"Any idea which of these companies is a good purchase, and which are corrupt or compromised in some way?" asked Peter.

"If you end up owning one of these, I'll go over their books and decide whom to fire, whom to put in charge, and whom to refer to the civil authorities for prosecution. Or else I'll shut it down and sell off the assets."

"Putting people out of work," said Wang-Mu.

"I only shut down companies that don't deserve to exist," said Jane. "I've managed these funds for millennia. Please trust me not to mistreat common people in my quest for universal ownership."

"Sorry," said Wang-Mu.

"Nonsense," said Jane. "You were right to ask. If you didn't care, you wouldn't be the Royal Mother of the West—or her descendant-of-the-heart."

"So now I get on the phone," said Wang-Mu.

"He's making you do all the calls? Don't you have two phones?"

"I'm not allowing him to make the calls, because he still can't manage his tone of voice in an inoffensive way," said Wang-Mu.

"It's a good thing he married *you*," said Jane.

"Don't you think what she just said might be offensive to *me*?" asked Peter.

"But it wasn't in an offensive tone," said Jane. "You married up, my boy. Men always do."

Peter let such a deliberate provocation pass. Jane was joking; it's just that her jokes weren't often funny, not to him, anyway. She thought she was talking to Ender still, but Ender knew from experience when she was joking. He didn't have to figure it out each time, the way Peter did.

"Look at him calm himself," Jane said. "He's making progress."

"Perhaps," said Wang-Mu. "But your teasing may have set him back by several weeks."

"Oops," said Jane, not sounding sorry at all.

Her image cleared from the display.

"She doesn't mean any of that nonsense," Wang-Mu said.

Peter wanted to snap back with something like, I know, I'm not an idiot *or* a three-year-old, and I know that she also meant all of it, and so did you.

Instead, he let his lips show a slight smile. "What do you think? Buy a company, borrow the equipment and forget to return it, buy the equipment?"

"Let's just see how they respond to a request to buy it," said Wang-Mu.

"How about if I have an arbitrageur put out feelers to buy the company moments before you call?" asked Peter.

"They'll be all in an uproar and nobody will feel they can make any decisions at all," said Wang-Mu. "So no, let's not buy any companies unless we're forced to."

After an hour or so of friendly conversations—Wang-Mu was amazing at getting right to the point without making people feel rushed—they learned that the patch sampler worked very well, and also it was completely reliable and did the job far better than samplers from competing companies. Only once did Peter join in on a call. It was with the only company that seemed willing to consider selling their patch sampler. "We don't use it all that often, and I suppose we could get through a month or so while a new one gets made."

That's when Peter leaned in to the speakerphone and said, "It's an expensive piece of equipment, isn't it? So why did you buy it if you didn't need it that much?"

"Who is this?" demanded the person on the line.

Wang-Mu responded calmly, "This is my senior partner, Peter Wiggin. We're mostly concerned that if the device has not been used much, it might not be as well-maintained."

"We used to use it constantly," came the reply. "But we lost the leguminid contract and we've been scrambling for more research funding."

"Leguminid?" asked Wang-Mu.

"A massive foundation that funds genetic research in some fairly esoteric areas. It required a lot of use of the patch sampler as we built and implanted altered genomes. The device functioned perfectly and during that entire three-year period it never needed any kind of repairs or replacement parts."

"Thank you," said Peter.

When Wang-Mu hung up, the head of research was going to confer with his colleagues.

"For what we'd pay them for a month without the patch sampler," said Peter, "they ought to jump at it."

"Letting go of the patch sampler," said Wang-Mu, "might seem to them like an admission that they were out of business. They might lose some of their top people."

"Their top people have undoubtedly left long ago."

"Most of genetic research," said Wang-Mu, "is tedious iterations. I think the leguminids were sending them all their test genomes digitally, and all they did was build them to order and test them."

"You're saying that their top people are probably only the scullery maids of genetic research."

"Most researchers are," said Wang-Mu. "And what do we care? It's the device we want. We already have the most brilliant genetic researchers in the Hundred Worlds."

"Buy the company?" asked Peter.

"I think not, if they sell us the patch sampler," said Wang-Mu. "If it means they're giving up, then so be it—that's their decision. But if we bought them and then took the patch sampler, they really *would* give up and the money you spent would have been wasted."

"A few more days here, with burning thighs from all the bicycling."

Wang-Mu raised her eyebrows at him. "Are you really fishing for me to say something provocative?"

"I'm working for an eight-year-old girl, my love. I need something to reaffirm my self-image."

"Isn't it nice you brought me along, then?" she said.

The next day, they went to inspect the patch sampler. Wang-Mu brought along the lists and diagrams of all the parts, to make sure nothing was left out. The geneticists made them watch a demonstration, and everything seemed to go smoothly—that is, nobody appeared nervous or worried, nor did anyone seem to be concealing anything. When Wang-Mu went over the lists and diagrams with them, they were able to point to every part. And when they put Peter on the phone with the SCA administrator, he answered the questions easily—by text, so they could not be overheard—and the money was transferred. They left with the patch sampler separated into four bags.

"You're not carrying those on your bikes, are you?" the CFO asked.

"I believe we have a truck coming," said Wang-Mu. "But thank you for your concern."

Peter took the two larger and heavier bags, and Wang-Mu handled the others easily enough.

The truck driver and his assistant insisted that Peter and Wang-Mu lift the bags up to them. "We can't let you walk up the ramp or stand inside the truck," the driver explained. "City regulations."

"Not insurance?" asked Wang-Mu. "Not the union?"

"The union and the insurance companies wrote the city ordinance," said the driver.

"So you can't take us and our bikes inside the truck with you," said Wang-Mu.

The driver and his assistant laughed out loud. "Does

this look like a bus? Do you think our insurance allows for passengers?"

"You'll reach our house before we do," said Peter.

"Then we'll turn off the motor and wait," said the driver. "Part of the job."

After the truck drove off, Peter said, "If there were any secondary market for stolen patch samplers, I'd expect never to see those guys again."

"This seems to be a very civilized society," said Wang-Mu. "Very trusting and trustworthy."

"Then why don't the bikes work unless they recognize our hands?" asked Peter.

"Not that trusting after all," agreed Wang-Mu. But by then the effort of pedaling the bikes cut off the possibility of conversation. Peter hated the way Wang-Mu easily outstripped him on the bike. He consoled himself that she was so small and light that it took less force to propel her over the ground. And her bike was smaller and lighter.

And he had never done anything so physically strenuous since he came out of that starship. He considered this. I really should get a bicycle when we return to Lusitania. Or I should at least walk. Hike. I need a reliable body that can handle challenges.

Another day here and maybe I'll even adapt to the bike. Are my muscles getting any stronger yet?

They had obtained enough local currency to offer a tip that would induce the guys to carry the four bags to the box in the back yard, but the truck wasn't there when they arrived. Instead, the four bags were lined up on the narrow bike driveway leading to the porch. A note was attached to the biggest one. "Waited a long time, you must have taken a side trip."

"Well," said Wang-Mu, "they saved us tipping them."

"Should I have given them part of the tip at the beginning?"

"No," said Wang-Mu. "There are no regulations against taking us and our bikes with them in the truck. People do it all the time. They were just liars who take advantage of foreigners."

"Should I have bribed them?" asked Peter.

"Probably not," said Wang-Mu. "And they wouldn't have carried the bags out to the box, anyway."

"Carry only one at a time," said Peter.

"If I carry two, I have better balance over this lumpy lawn."

"Suit yourself," said Peter.

They got the whole patch sampler inside the box in one trip. Peter palmed the door closed and then looked at Wang-Mu. "We could eat some of the food we didn't buy today, which would require us to bike to the store and buy some. Or we could bike to a restaurant and have as bad a meal as we had last night—"

"Or worse," said Wang-Mu.

"Or we could take part in the fine dining experience of the genetics compound on Lusitania, with Thulium explaining what we did wrong while we eat."

"She won't do that," said Wang-Mu. "She never does that."

"I can see her thinking it," said Peter.

"She's actually quite a wonderful little girl," said Wang-Mu.

"She'd poison your food if she ever heard you say that," said Peter.

"She *is* a girl and she *is* little," said Wang-Mu.

"She knows those things. But she doesn't like other people to talk about it."

"Peter," said Wang-Mu. "I do believe you're learning to understand her a little."

"What I'm afraid of is that you're *not*," said Peter.

"But I don't have to. I'm not transporting her anywhere by the power of my philotic connections with her."

They got their changes of clothing out of the house, along with their few data storage devices, and the box disappeared from the back yard fifteen minutes after they arrived at the house. The two bikes remained in the front yard until someone from the rental company came to reclaim them, along with the furniture and linens inside the house. And Jane had the house itself sold in two days.

11

<Jane Ribeira enters the bedroom of Thulium Delphiki without knocking and sits immediately on the swivel chair before the desk.>

Jane: Calm down. I'm not here to arrest you. And you aren't in some state of deshabille, so don't pretend you wish to protect your modesty.

Thulium: Why do *you* think that *I* would think you had any desire to arrest me? Have I broken a law? Did I say something indiscreet to the Queen when we visited there a few weeks ago?

Jane: Your look of alarm at my entrance led me to think—

Thulium: Am I the only one who looks alarmed when someone bursts into her room late at night, without invitation or announcement?

Jane: Probably not. I'm not used to the body yet. I'm not used to *doors*. I never had to deal with them before.

Thulium: I learned the principle of knocking on closed doors when I was only two. But then I am a leguminid, and you are merely a computer construct. And the *Herodotus* was nothing but doors, so I needed to knock quite often.

Jane: This nonsensical conversation about wounded propriety is not what I came here for.

Thulium: I imagine not.

<two-second silence>

Jane: You called me here. What is it about?

Thulium: I did not call you. I didn't even speak to you today. Or yesterday.

Jane: Whenever I'm within your view, you keep looking at me, then looking away as soon as we make eye contact. This studied regard combined with evasiveness can only mean that there is something you're dying to ask me, yet you haven't worked up the courage to do it. Since one of your primary attributes is that you seem to fear nothing, that's an unusual circumstance. So I resolved to come to you at the first opportunity. This is it.

Thulium: Haven't you already read my thoughts? That is, hasn't the Hive Queen read my thoughts and informed you?

Jane: The Hive Queen and I converse at need, about many things. But most of her attention is on her children, and I try not to disturb her. She certainly does *not* attempt to communicate mentally with humans who are not within her domain.

Thulium: How nice to know that by being uninteresting, I can maintain some privacy.

Jane: Your question for me? Please don't waste my time pretending you don't have one.

Thulium: When you taught Peter Wiggin to do the instantaneous starflight trick—

Jane: Not a trick. Go on, please.

Thulium: He seemed to learn it at a rudimentary level in a day.

Jane: He had already gone Outside and In a dozen times. Both as Ender and as Peter, whether he remembered the Ender time consciously or not.

Thulium: I have been transported that way at least five times that I can think of—once when you brought us here out of the *Herodotus*, and then two round trips to the Box.

Jane: That is an accurate count. The first time you didn't know it was happening, though.

Thulium: So, like Ender-in-Peter, I have no conscious memory of the experience, yes?

Jane: Your arch tone is not as endearing as you hope.

Thulium: I believe it is exactly as unendearing as I intend. I have been Outside and In almost as many times as Peter Wiggin. Teach me.

Jane: I don't know if I can.

Thulium: Waiting for Peter Wiggin to bond with me philotically is a quixotic quest at best. Why should he come to love me when we hardly see each other except for him to deliver machinery?

<seven-second silence>

Thulium: If I could carry myself and my cousin Sprout to the surface of Descoladora, without any reference to Peter Wiggin, then Peter and Wang-Mu would be free to make their ignorant observations while Sprout and I do science.

Jane: You would need to also bring your own box with you, to carry your equipment. And you and Sprout would have to practice moving it and setting it up yourselves, as well as operating it.

Thulium: When we've made our first observations and have some idea of whether there's a safe place for us to arrive on Descoladora, let alone set up our gear, that's what we'll do. If I can go myself, and bring Sprout with me, surely I can also bring a box and its inanimate contents.

Jane: Probably. If you can do any of that at all.

Thulium: Then let's find out.

Jane: If I start teaching you openly, the cousins, and more especially your brothers, will hear about it and demand that I teach *them*.

Thulium: Good luck with that.

Jane: If *you* can learn it, they'll see no reason why they shouldn't at least try. And the thought of them having the power to go anywhere in the universe whenever they want is too terrifying. I don't want them pestering me or anyone else. I don't want to have to clean up after them.

Thulium: So take me to a remote place where none of my family can see us, and teach me the way you taught Peter.

<later, outside the compound, clear starry night>

<Thulium returns from a short voyage across a meadow>

Thulium: It feels as if I tie myself in a knot, and then I relax and it unravels itself.

Jane: That feeling only applies when you're going back very near where you started. It will be another kind of wrenching when you go back Inside to a different destination. And if you go to a place where you have never been, it requires a kind of searching concentration.

Thulium: Show me.

—Memorandum: Transcript, Jane and Thulium
Plikt, "Leguminidae"

Peter heard Miro's report without showing any visible sign of anger, or at least he did his best.

"Miro," said Peter, "why is Jane so cowardly as to send *you* with this news? She can't possibly fear me."

"Peter," said Miro, "no one has more power to hurt her than you do."

"Obviously that's false," said Peter.

"You've hurt her before," said Miro.

"*I* haven't, but yes, I know what you mean, and I don't choose to count things that Ender did during the thousands of years they roamed the Hundred Worlds."

"She still experiences you as Ender, whether you feel yourself that way or not."

"So let me respond to your message. Wang-Mu's and my expedition to the surface of Descoladora has become Thulium's expedition, with me as her quartermaster and errand boy. Is this my punishment because my deficiencies in empathy and love kept me from transporting Thulium?"

"We need her there to do work you aren't qualified to do," said Miro.

"But Wang-Mu's and my plan was to make our visits, write up reports, and then take part in the decision of when, where, and whether to send down a genetics team. It's foolish to drop an eight-year-old and a nine-year-old onto the surface of an unknown planet *before* Wang-Mu and I have found out if there are any threats or dangers."

"We're afraid that you may return to quarantine with information that makes further surface visits impossible. So we need the first expedition to collect surface genetics, too. You were there when this was decided."

"Wang-Mu and I will end up bailing them out."

"Why would you suppose that?"

"Because they're children. Brilliant children, but arrogant and reckless, unwilling to listen to anyone."

Miro smiled. "You're describing Thulium, on her bad days, but not Sprout. He's quite mature—maybe the *most* mature of the leguminid cousins."

"With advanced self-defense techniques and survival skills?" asked Peter.

"You don't have them either," said Miro.

"You keep telling me I'm really Ender. *He* had those things. If I need them, maybe they'll come back to me."

"You resent Jane for teaching this esoteric, world-changing skill to Thulium."

Peter hesitated only a moment. Ruthless truth-telling was his new policy, his Wang-Mu influenced policy. "Yes, I do resent it. Has anyone thought about what it will be like when all the leguminids are popping up wherever and whenever they want?"

"Jane has no plan to teach anyone else," said Miro. "That limits the list to Jane, me, you, and Thulium."

"Why not Wang-Mu?" asked Peter.

"Are you requesting that she be taught? Aren't you afraid that would make you even more unnecessary?"

"I'm asking why the lines have been drawn where they've been drawn," said Peter. "I'm asking why you think the lines won't keep getting pushed back again and again for every new exception."

"I think that if a new exception comes up, Jane will make a wise and necessary decision."

"So Jane is the ruler of starflight for the whole universe."

"She already was," said Miro, "from the voyage where you were created on to the present. Teaching me, and you, and Thulium seemed desirable because of the work we're doing, and because she was reasonably sure none of us would misuse it for pranks or showing off."

"So all that hopping around that the Box is doing in the space above Descoladora, Jane isn't doing that to show off?"

"It's partly a demonstration of her power, yes. Mostly, though, it's a method of evading whatever techniques they're developing to destroy the craft. Now that the work of deep-mapping the surface is done, however, she's thinking of bringing the Box home."

"So it won't be there when we go?" asked Peter.

"You'll have your own box."

"Thulium will. Why would Wang-Mu and I need it?"

"Because they have winter there. And rainy seasons. And it's good to have a place where you can go inside and lock the door."

"All right," said Peter. "We'll comply."

Miro smiled his little half-smile. "Meaning that you intend to take Wang-Mu and begin your first expedition almost immediately."

Peter had no ready answer to this, because that was exactly what he intended to do, after looking at the aerial-view maps of Descoladora with Wang-Mu and choosing a landing site. So his first instinct was to deny—his tongue was already forming the *n* of *no*—but then he thought better of it.

"If Thulium can do interplanetary travel," said Peter, "she can fetch her own equipment."

"If you encounter an alien species, Thulium looks small and weak and no one would take her seriously."

"So I'm needed for errands for Thulium's mission, but Wang-Mu's and my expedition is not terribly important."

"It sounds much more important when you call it an expedition," said Miro.

"Jaunt. Junket. Safari. Sight-seeing trip. Reconnaissance. Photo shoot. Honeymoon. Working vacation. There are so many eligible terms."

"Honeymoon," said Miro. "You and Wang-Mu never really had a proper one, did you?"

"If you mean, were we ever away from Jane's all-seeing eye, then no. But if you mean, did we figure out how to mate according to the age-old primate pattern, yes, we've got that down, thanks."

"Planning to breed?" asked Miro.

Peter was getting annoyed at the personal questions. "Are you and Jane?"

"Absolutely," said Miro. "I'm already pregnant."

They looked at each other, deadpan.

Then Miro laughed.

Peter did not.

"I asked," said Miro, "because Jane wants to know if Wang-Mu is one person or two."

"Unless Wang-Mu is keeping secrets, she's not pregnant," said Peter. "We know this is not a convenient time."

Miro laughed. "There's never a convenient time. Jane merely wanted to know before she starts involving Wang-Mu in your training."

"Don't we have to return to the Hive Queen first?"

"She already told Jane that you're much better at this—much stronger, much more . . . copious—than she expected."

Peter hated how good that made him feel. Why am I a slave to the opinions of others? "How could she be surprised after spending so much time with Ender's aiúa?"

"The Queens found Jane's aiúa Outside and brought her in to talk to you. To Ender. But they already knew where you were because your light could be seen even from Outside."

"Whatever that means," said Peter.

"It means what it means," said Miro. "Now, I have one more practical question for you."

"Shoot," said Peter.

"Is this the last time we'll have to waste time assuaging your sad little envious ego? Because Ender never made anybody do that."

Peter gave Miro his dead-eyed stare. "I may have Ender's aiúa. There are little fillips of memory that demonstrate to me that in fact I do. But this body does not have the same genes as Ender's body. It has the same genes that the original Peter dealt with all his life. Now, how much of behavior, how much of memory, how much of will comes from the genome, and how much from the aiúa? There's been no research on that topic, because nobody outside of Lusitania has ever *heard* of the aiúa, as we now understand it. Nobody but a Sanskrit scholar would recognize the word. Searches on the nets turn up nothing except for the suggestion that in Stark, the missing vowels are *e* and *o*. So when you decide to treat me as if I were Ender, please remember that for all his greatness and goodness and nobility and generosity, he wasn't having to deal with Peter's melange of ego need and easily-accessed rage and above all the seething resentment that rises with him in the morning and goes to bed with him at night."

Miro nodded gravely. "Point made, Peter. And for what it's worth, we know—Jane and I—how well you're controlling all that, in order to make the kind and generous decisions that your aiúa wants to make."

When Miro got to the door of Peter's and Wang-Mu's room, Peter said, "Did you ask Wang-Mu to leave us alone to talk?"

"I did," said Miro. "She also said she wasn't interested in learning to transport herself. She trusts you, she said, more than she trusts herself."

"Astonishing," said Peter. "She's seen me ride a bicycle, and she still trusts me to drive."

"I'll send her in, if, as I suspect, she's waiting just outside." And then Miro hesitated again. "Você contêm as linguas que Ender falava?"

"Tenho, sim," said Peter, falling easily into the Portuguese of Lusitania. "Mas ainda não penso nelas. Somente inglês. O pode ser starque."

Another test. Always a test, when dealing with Jane and Miro: Do you have inside you the languages that Ender spoke? And Peter answered, Yes, but I don't think in any of them. Just English. Or maybe Stark.

Apparently that's all Miro wanted to know, though

why it mattered Peter couldn't guess. Did they expect that he'd have to deal with anybody on Lusitania who wasn't fluent in Stark? Who might that be? Or was Miro checking to make sure that members of the Ribeira family couldn't talk around him by lapsing into Portuguese? Well, they couldn't. Peter would understand them just fine.

Wang-Mu came into the room. She closed the door behind her, then smiled wanly at Peter. "Well, are we going tonight?"

"We've had plenty of test flights. But never into unknown and hostile territory."

"If you'd rather not carry me with you because of the burden of looking out for my safety, then I'll just stay here."

"I don't want to go unless I have you with me," said Peter.

She came up and placed a cool hand on his cheek. "I believe you mean it," she said.

"If I get distracted and don't watch you, there might be real danger. You shouldn't have turned down Jane's offer to teach you to control the flight yourself. I think you'd be better at it than me anyway."

"Why would you think that?" asked Wang-Mu.

"Because you're better at caring about other people than I am."

"I doubt that," said Wang-Mu.

"You shouldn't," said Peter. "You notice people better than I do."

"I notice some things, and you notice other things. But you notice me. You pay attention to me."

"But it doesn't come naturally to me. I have to work at it."

Wang-Mu laughed. "You think I don't? Everybody who does it, works at it. I was a servant in a hierarchical, caste-ridden society. I had to study my masters and anyone else who had the power to hurt me or help me, and discover how to help them notice me in a good way. It was only when I entered the service of Han Qing-Jao and then Han Fei-Tzu that I learned how to turn that keen observation into something closer to love. You're not struggling with anything I haven't struggled with. Love isn't easy, Peter. Not for anybody."

"Loving you is getting easier all the time," said Peter. And then he realized: He wasn't just saying what he knew she wanted to hear. He was speaking the simple truth.

"I believe you," said Wang-Mu. "But let's turn to some practical concerns. The seasons on Descoladora are caused by the apogee and perigee of the planet's orbit around its star. It's past apogee, so the weather has warmed up quite a bit and things are starting to grow—more near the equator than the poles."

"Jackets?"

"And four walls and a roof," said Wang-Mu. "Jane has placed a box for us just over the hill outside."

"And Thulium won't be waiting for us inside it?"

"Who can predict what Thulium will do?"

Peter detected a note of consternation in Wang-Mu's voice. "What do you disapprove of, Wang-Mu?" he asked.

She did not bother denying—when he read her mood correctly, she never wasted time on pretenses. "Why are you so determined to get to the surface before Thulium? Are you in a contest with an eight-year-old? Or is it a contest with the leguminids? Or mere defiance of Jane and the Queen and Miro and what, everyone else?"

Peter paused to think. "Your question is a fair one, and I suspect that in my heart I am caught up in all three contests, though on a rational level I would deny it. However, my deepest reason is not vanity or ego. Thulium and Sprout are child-sized and have few skills and little strength. For them to drop onto the surface of an unknown planet is insanely dangerous and potentially unproductive. We know the planet is populated but we don't know where. With a completely breathable atmosphere, do the people all live underground? Why? Is there danger on the surface that we must be prepared for? You and I are older and more experienced. I have inherited some skills from Ender's aiúa, and you are the most adaptable human being alive. I think our chances are much better."

"We could travel together with Thulium, then," said Wang-Mu.

"If you and I go first, our visit will be to explore, observe, report. If we have the children with us, our primary motive will be to protect them. Plus, we'll have to contend with Thulium's habit of doing whatever she pleases. So for Thulium's and Sprout's sake, we will bring back reports that will enable them to understand the aerial and satellite photos much better, along with anything else we discover."

"Don't you consider, Peter, that the inhabitants of the planet may not need habitations at all? That they may be living on the surface in the open air, or in the woodlands?"

"Then let's find out," said Peter. "Before we send children."

Fifteen minutes later, they passed through the gate, carrying a few satchels with clothing, minimal bedding, and wearing a few other supplies like small flashlights, knives for sample taking, and radio beacon locators. Since their box would have their home-base beacon, if they got separated they'd know which way to go to reunite.

Thulium was not waiting for them in their box. They went inside and Peter said, "I'm glad I won't have to fight her for control of the box and supplies."

"Would that be a problem?"

"I don't know," said Peter. "Plus, I don't know where on the surface we're going. What if we drop the box into the middle of a public square?"

"They haven't seen any public areas from the sky," said Wang-Mu.

"Let's put on our jackets and make our first trip without taking the Box. We go, and come right back."

"What about always returning to Quarantine Bay?" asked Wang-Mu.

Peter thought. "The rules make sense. We don't know what microbes we might pick up in just a one-minute reconnoitering trip."

"Do you know how to get to Q-Bay?" asked Wang-Mu.

"Let's go there now, while it's still close, and leave from there, so coming back will be an easy trip."

She held his hands. "We don't actually need to be touching," she said.

"I like us to be touching, start to finish," said Peter.

"Well, so do I," said Wang-Mu.

If Peter had any idea of what might happen on Descoladora, he wouldn't feel such trepidation about setting out. But he had no real idea of their destination, beyond satellite photos.

That wasn't so different, though, from every voyage. It always felt to him as if he were throwing himself and Wang-Mu into a place kilometers deep inside of himself—an impossibility, but that's how it felt. As if he were swallowing himself and her. And then, instantly, he would think of where he wanted to go—not any detailed map or instruction on how to get there, just a thought of however much or little he knew of the place. All of it so quickly that it felt to him as if he were being caught up by a strong wind and blown, with nothing really under his control.

It was his own choice now that selected the moment of plunging Outside, which felt like a movement inward, and then the moment, an instant later, of coming back Inside to the place he chose.

After the slight double-wrenching of an Out-and-In voyage, Q-Bay surrounded them.

The labs were dark at night with no one working there, but the seals were all in place and the negative pressure was running, so nothing would escape. "This is home base," said Peter.

"So far so good, my love," said Wang-Mu.

What Peter heard was, I'm proud of you, you daft git.

Wang-Mu unpocketed and laid out on an examining table her map of the whole land surface of Descoladora.

"We have no idea of the tectonic history of the landforms," said Peter, "but these isolated smallish continents are likely to have untypical flora and fauna. We have to assume that the largest land mass will have the best chance of sentient inhabitants."

"Near the coast, in a grassy area, not too far from woodlands," said Wang-Mu.

"Sensible," said Peter. He put a finger on the map.

"The scale is smaller than you think," said Wang-Mu. "That isn't close to the coast *or* the river."

Peter moved his finger a bit.

"Allowing for the fact that the tip of your finger covers hundreds of hectares," said Wang-Mu, "that looks about right." She refolded the map and put it in her pocket.

And they were gone.

12

FATHERTREE HUMAN: Miro, may I enter your dream?

Miro: Yes.

FATHERTREE HUMAN: You are now capable of instantaneous travel.

Miro: I am.

FATHERTREE HUMAN: Likewise we have seen Peter Wiggin and Thulium Delphiki demonstrating and practicing the same powers.

Miro: I know.

FATHERTREE HUMAN: Some of the brothers ask me, when will Jane or the Hive Queen teach one of us to do this?

Miro: I wish I knew the answer.

FATHERTREE HUMAN: I know the answer already.

Miro: Will you tell me?

FATHERTREE HUMAN: Never.

FATHERTREE HUMAN: You misunderstand me in the confusion of the dream. The answer to the question the brothers asked me is, never. They cannot learn it.

Miro: Why not, old friend?

FATHERTREE HUMAN: Because it takes a greater capacity and strength than most aiúas have. All Hive Queens have such capacity, or they would not have been called in from the darkness. But only a tiny number of pequeninos have it, and among the pequeninos, that capacity can only be used in the third life, the life as I am living it.

Miro: The life as a tree.

FATHERTREE HUMAN: The life in wood. We have no use for movement then. As long as our human friends will transport our little ones, we have little to fear from our inability to transport them ourselves.

Miro: What about humans? Surely *we* are not all of such great capacity.

FATHERTREE HUMAN: The Queen tells me that she has met only five such aiúas among the humans she has known face-to-face. The first was Ender and the man Peter who is now his vessel. Then you. Then Wang-Mu. Then Thulium.

Miro: Four so far.

FATHERTREE HUMAN: Jane, of course, but the human body came later. The Queens brought her out of darkness themselves, and they chose her as if they were choosing the greatest of Queens.

Miro: That was well done.

FATHERTREE HUMAN: There will be no others. She wanted me to warn you, preferably in a dream, that when or if the five of you cease to live, that kind of starflight will end.

Miro: Unless some engineers devise a way to do it by machine.

FATHERTREE HUMAN: The Queens believe that is not possible.

Miro: They also believed that humans could not develop faster-than-light communication, yet in the few years between the Second and Third Formic Wars, they equipped every one of their ships with an sibles.

FATHERTREE HUMAN: I'll remind her of this.

Miro: She'll be angry.

FATHERTREE HUMAN: What will she do, send her children to scorch me with torches?

—Memorandum of conversation: Fathertree Human and Miro Ribeira as cited in Olhado Ribeira, *The Aiúa in Theory and Practice*

Si Wang-Mu was already aware that every analysis told them the atmosphere of Descoladora was breathable by humans without any filtration or aug-

mentation. So when the darkness of Q-Bay was succeeded by the light of the sun rising behind a tall
woodland, she only squinted and blinked for a few
moments before her eyes adjusted.

The smell of the air was somewhat unfamiliar, but
not completely so. Wang-Mu thought there was familiar pollen in the air. And the tall trees looked like
familiar shapes. In the other direction, though, the
grassland was interrupted by patches of robust ferns,
some twice the height of a tall human.

Convergent evolution would probably create
woody trees on any world with life, and competi-
tion would drive them to evolve greater and greater
height. Yet on this world, ferns had not yet retreated
to the lower reaches of deep jungles, where they had
to learn to thrive in shade. These ferns were drunken
on sunlight, huge and exuberant in their growth.

Wang-Mu had learned from Han Fei-Tzu that
there was no reason to suppose that evolution on
other worlds would proceed in lockstep with the fos-
sil record of the evolution of life on Earth. There was
no reason to look for dinosaurs or the equivalent, or
even for giraffes. High-level vegetation might not yet
have any predators. If there were no insects yet, there
would have been no reason to evolve flowers to produce seeds, and without birds or other swift-gutted
animals, fruit would have no point.

She listened. She looked.

She looked down because she thought she heard a
faint buzz.

There was a bee on a tiny blossom rising out of the
grass at her feet.

She merely pointed at it. Peter nodded, pointed
to a swarm of tiny insects—gnats?—a few meters
away.

Wang-Mu knew that if there were no larger animals

to feed on, the insects would not have evolved means of extracting blood or flesh. If she walked into that swarm and they bit her, what would that tell her? That there were enough rats to be worth biting? Or that at any moment a rhinoceros might charge at them out of the bush?

Stop thinking in terrestrial terms, she told herself. No rhinos, no rats. But ecological niches were not fanciful; they existed. She looked down for signs that small animals did live here, and perhaps graze here.

She could not be sure if she was seeing rat poop or a random splash of mud from the last rainstorm.

She scanned toward the breeze and felt its warmth, faint though it was. In that direction, there were clouds forming far, far away. But they would be moving toward them soon.

"Rain tonight?" she murmured.

Peter shrugged. "We won't be here."

"We should already be back in Q-Bay," said Wang-Mu.

Peter reached down and pulled up a tuft of grass by the roots.

Then Wang-Mu reached down and took the bee in one hand. She closed her fist loosely enough that the bee would stay alive.

"Let's go before it stings me and dies," said Wang-Mu.

And they were back in Q-Bay.

Wang-Mu immediately moved to a plastic sample box and discharged the bee into it. She closed the lid, which had a few holes in it for air exchange—she had chosen the right kind of box. The bee buzzed around inside furiously.

Wang-Mu examined her hand.

"Did it sting you?" asked Peter.

"No," said Wang-Mu. "And it had plenty of time."

"Why would convergent evolution give it the same stripes and colors as a terrestrial honeybee?" asked Peter.

"Why does the grass grow in blades, like grasses from Earth?" asked Wang-Mu.

"The temptation is to imagine that it's because they *came* from Earth."

"The way coconuts crossed the Pacific to seed their palm trees on every island?" asked Wang-Mu. "I try to imagine a tiny bee-sized space suit."

"Cute, but of course I'm only saying that humans might have visited there at some point."

With Q-Bay still dark, Peter and Wang-Mu saw no reason to summon any of the lab workers before the start of their normal work day. So they made themselves comfortable either on or off the furniture—Peter first chose the floor, but after a couple of hours Wang-Mu came down from the examining table and cuddled beside him. That was how the lab workers found them in the morning, blinking themselves awake because the lights had all come on.

Wang-Mu explained, succinctly, that they had come from the surface of Descoladora and the first order of business was to examine them, skin and blood, lungs and nostrils and every crevice of their bodies, for microbes and tiny animalcules. Meanwhile, others could be working on isolating the genetic structures of the native grass and the bee that they had brought back. Peter and Wang-Mu both detached their audiovisual recording devices so the things they saw and heard could be uploaded and examined minutely.

It took the better part of a day for them to be thoroughly swabbed, probed, pierced, scraped, and angrily questioned by the high-level Lusitanian scientists who resented not having advance notice of their coming, especially because this meant their underlings, the common lab workers, had already had the first look at pretty much everything.

Wang-Mu, detecting this, found ways to mildly say to each of the disgruntled bosses something along the lines of, "You must be so proud that your lab workers were so well trained they were able to show initiative and begin collecting data for you to analyze." She saw that her words had the soothing effect she intended. She noticed when several of the top-level scientists repeated something like her message to the underlings.

In midafternoon, Thulium and Sprout arrived. Q-Bay suits had already been made to fit their small bodies, and they were soon dressed and took their places inside the quarantine bay.

Wang-Mu could feel Peter gearing up to defend himself for going ahead before them, but Wang-Mu laid a hand on his forearm to still him. Thulium did not look angry or hostile, feelings that the girl had never shown much ability to conceal.

And in a few moments, Wang-Mu's judgment was proved right, when Thulium said, "I think you were right. What if there had been a large predator right where we landed? What if it confused me so much I couldn't get away?"

"We were only there for perhaps three minutes," said Peter. "The avlog will have the exact time. We saw no animal larger than a bee. There are forests of tall woody trees, or so they appear, and groves of two-meter ferns. The rest is grass, and we brought a sample of that."

"The analysis of the scrapings and samples from your bodies show no alien intrusion," said Thulium. "All the microbes are familiar ones that you almost certainly brought with you."

"Is my microbiome so robust," asked Wang-Mu, "that no alien fungus or bacterium could penetrate it?"

"We're still trying to think about it," said Thulium.

"Which means you have been thinking about it for hours," said Peter. "And you have hypotheses that you're reluctant to share. But we're not editorial panels at scientific journals. It costs you nothing to share your speculation with us."

Thulium thought for a moment, then nodded. "You are clean enough that we could release you into the Lusitanian population without a qualm, though we aren't going to—quarantine is about giving alien life-forms, which we might not recognize, time enough to develop inside your bodies."

"That's right," said Peter. "But that would not prevent us from going to Descoladora again, right?"

"Exactly," said Thulium. "Now that you've actually gone, Sprout and I won't go ourselves until you've had enough time to die or not die from anything you caught on the surface."

"Wise choice," said Peter.

"But we have a quandary. You might resent this question, but it has to be asked. Is there any chance that you might have carried that bee with you? Could it have got into your clothing before you came to Q-Bay?"

"The only bees that have been introduced to Lusitania are in the Formic orchards," said Peter.

"Bees fly where they want," said Wang-Mu. "If it came to Descoladora with us, we neither heard it nor felt it nor saw it," said Wang-Mu. "The one we collected was on the grass, or rather on a flower growing up amid the grass. But I can't rule out its having been tucked into my clothing somewhere."

"The reason I ask," said Thulium, "is that its genome matches almost perfectly with the honeybee genome recorded back in the twenty-second century."

"Before the Formic Wars," said Peter.

"There are differences," said Thulium. "It was born without a sting."

"How does it defend the hive?" asked Wang-Mu.

"We'll learn the answer when we find and observe a hive, but the most obvious speculation is that it has no invasive predators," said Sprout. "Honeybees with no natural enemies."

"So you speculate about the possibility that *humans* deliberately released the bee into the environment of Descoladora as a pollinator. Did it evolve its stingless condition, or was the gene altered?"

"Evolution also alters genes," said Sprout. "The grass is another problem."

"Terrestrial grass?" asked Peter.

"Some genes have a distinct resemblance to terrestrial grass genes," said Sprout, "but they seem to be an insertion, a deliberate alteration. Grass evolved late on Earth—the dinosaurs may never have seen any—but it may have evolved earlier on Descoladora. The earth-seeming genes are all involved with protein production. Without them, this grass would be worthless to grazing animals from Earth—goats, sheep, and cattle could all starve to death while eating their fill. Earth birds would starve eating the grass seeds. But *with* those changes, this grass will be supernutritious to grazers, and even more useful to the bodies of birds."

"It's an avian paradise," said Thulium. "Whether birds waited for the seeds or swallowed leaf or stem bits, they could live on it."

"We didn't see any birds," said Wang-Mu.

"You were there three minutes," said Sprout.

"In a meadow," said Wang-Mu. "With so much nutritious grass, much of it in seed, you'd think at least some birds would have been there feeding."

"You were there in the early morning," said Sprout.

"On Earth, that's when the songbirds do their best singing."

"So . . . we have ascertained that Descoladora is not Earth," said Wang-Mu.

"But the two samples of its biota were largely or partly related to species from Earth," said Peter, "suggesting contact and deliberate genetic tailoring."

"Genetic tailoring," said Sprout, "which might have been done by humans to accommodate the needs of Earthborn animal species, or which might have been done by an elaborate molecule introduced from another world."

"Did you find the descolada virus?" asked Wang-Mu.

"If we had," said Thulium, "we would have led with that. But we've only ruled out the presence of the descolada in the nuclei of the bee and grass cells. It will take days to work our way through the whole cell. In the nucleus, though, the descolada is huge and has no place to hide. If the descolada were active, that's where it would be—if it follows the same pattern that it did on Lusitania."

There was silence for a few minutes.

"*Somebody* is transmitting digital data to the Box," said Thulium.

"If they noticed the two of us," said Peter, "then if we return to the same spot, they might be there to meet us. Is that good or bad?"

"And if they didn't notice," said Wang-Mu, "we should hike around a little, recording everything and inviting large creatures to be curious about us."

"Don't ignore the possibility of long-range weapons," said Sprout.

"That's a wise point," said Peter. "But I don't know what I can do about it. If someone wants to snipe at us, we won't know it until we're shot at. We'll get out immediately—if we aren't instantly killed outright."

"I'm excited to go back," said Wang-Mu. "What

are we waiting for?" Peter knew she was being mostly ironic. Did anyone else know that she had some bite in her humor?

"How do the periods of daylight line up?" Peter asked Thulium.

It was Wang-Mu who answered. "If we want to arrive at dawn again, we should leave here at midnight this time instead of three in the morning."

"What about arriving just before dawn?" asked Peter.

"About ten-thirty tonight."

"I don't want to arrive in the dark," said Peter. "Even if the worst nocturnal predators are owls and raccoons or their equivalent, I don't want to meet them in the dark."

"So . . . sleep until then?" asked Wang-Mu.

"Meanwhile," said Thulium, "we'll keep looking at the cells—and the vids of your brief stay on the enemy planet."

In the immediate silence, Thulium said, "I was being ironic. If humans have colonized or terraformed or planted things on this planet, there's little chance it's the source of the descolada." And when no one replied, she added, "Not an enemy planet, therefore."

Peter could only nod in agreement. But he could see that Wang-Mu had been taken aback by Thulium's supposed jest. So he, too, thought through it. Even if it was a joke, it had crossed Thulium's mind to call the inhabitants of this planet "the enemy." Not a good xenologer's attitude toward a newly encountered technological civilization.

13

Sprout: I don't understand your reaction.

Thulium: To what?

Sprout: To Peter Wiggin's perfidy.

Thulium: Oh, is that what it was?

Sprout: We were supposed to go first, or at least at the same time, and here we are going through the data he collected on the trip he made without you.

Thulium: It really is much easier to do our work when we have data to work with.

Sprout: Did you get a personality transplant without telling me?

Thulium: No. Whose personality do you think I'm using?

Sprout: Nobody from the *Herodotus*, that's for sure.

Thulium: Somebody said something that made me think of who, in the absence of my mother, I was using as a mother-figure. I ruled out *your* mother, though she's been kind to me. On the ship, I'm sure she was as close to being my mother as anyone, but . . .

Sprout: She didn't even know how to be a mother to her own sons. She never had a mother, either, you know.

Thulium: I do know. So I thought, am I looking to Jane as a mother? I don't think so. She's too powerful, too distracted. Ender Wiggin was the love of her life, and he's still around inside Peter. And now Miro is her human partner, and the Hive Queen and the Mothertree and the fathertrees.

Sprout: Yes, I agree, a bad mother-figure.

Thulium: The real Valentine is very old. When I'm with her, I can see how I quickly make her tired.

Sprout: That's not because she's old. It's because you're exhausting.

Thulium: Ela has a life of her own. We work together very well, because she treats me like a colleague instead of a child. Not a mother.

Sprout: I thought you were going to explain whose personality you had transplanted into you.

Thulium: It should be obvious by process of elimination.

Sprout: And yet it isn't, primarily because we didn't start with the same list of candidates.

Thulium: Si Wang-Mu.

Sprout: Well, her name does mean Royal Mother, and you've always thought you were a princess among commoners.

Thulium: You see? Three months ago, that comment would have made me angry.

Sprout: Are you not-angry, or just not-showing your anger?

Thulium: I find that, as a rule, the less emotion I show, the less I feel, and vice-versa. The more I show, et cetera.

Sprout: If you can keep this up, it'll drive the twins insane.

Thulium: I chose Si Wang-Mu because I saw how she gently guided Peter Wiggin, surrounding him like a cloud, opening good paths in front of him, obscuring unpromising ones.

Sprout: You think she controls him?

Thulium: Controlling other people is not in her nature. I think she cares about him enough to devote herself to helping him achieve his goals, which includes helping him avoid doing things that would defeat his own purposes.

Sprout: She obeys him like a robot.

Thulium: Look closer. She projects an always-compliant *attitude*. But she actually complies only when he has heard her out, at which point he usually changes his decision.

Sprout: You do know that Si Wang-Mu acquired these skills when she was a servant to a very demanding mistress in a viciously hierarchical society.

Thulium: Unlike our own highly egalitarian system where everyone gets an equal voice.

Sprout: Ours is a family, not a society.

Thulium: You said it, not me.

Sprout: Are you becoming a Christian, like Ender did before he died? Because this smacks of "He that is greatest among you shall be your servant."

Thulium: I like the version in Luke better: "He that is greatest among you, let him be as the younger; and he that is chief, as he that doth serve."

Sprout: You like that better because you're the younger.

Thulium: Si Wang-Mu has no Christianity in her background. Her behavior smacks of intelligent adaptation to the world as she found it, in order to survive and prosper. And as far as I can tell, it's been working out pretty well for her.

Sprout: I notice you have never suggested trying to teach *me* how to fly Outside and In.

Thulium: If you want to do it, do what I did. Ask Jane.

Sprout: I don't actually want to do it.

Thulium: I didn't think you would.

Sprout: Why not?

Thulium: Because then you'd have to be on call whenever somebody needed an interplanetary errand run.

—Conversation recorded in Q-Bay by Jane Ribeira, used by permission of Brussels Delphiki and Thulium Delphiki Plikt, "The Ribeira Family Saves the World"

The light was dimmer when Si Wang-Mu opened her eyes after the internal twisting of Out-and-In travel. They arrived facing west toward the sea—which was still several kilometers away—and the trees of the littoral screened its brightest rays. So they had arrived at the correct time.

Peter was still holding her hand. She let go of him so she could make a complete turn to face the other direction. Was anything different?

Sounds. Last time had been so silent that she thought perhaps she could hear the distant crash of waves on the shore—almost certainly not, but that's what her imagination had supplied in the silence.

This time, though, there was a low murmur. Doves cooing? No, too high-pitched. And growing louder, more agitated.

And then a bird started up from the grass and quickly flew about three meters above the ground. The underside of its spread wings had a fiery orange blaze. But as other birds rose from all around them—hundreds of birds—Wang-Mu saw that from above, the only orange was at the base of the fanned-out tailfeathers, while the rest of the tail and wings was a beautiful green.

"Parrots," said Peter softly.

Si Wang-Mu shrugged. She didn't see it.

"Hooked parrot bill," said Peter. "Kea, I think. They studied them back on Earth as the only bird species that played almost all the time. Practical jokes."

He didn't really need to say that, because the keas were already landing on their shoulders, clinging to their clothing, landing on their shoes. Within moments, anything that could be easily removed was gone—a bird took it and flew off.

"Why are you taking these things?" Si Wang-Mu asked them. "You don't need them, and I do."

Peter chuckled. "Don't brush them away. Nothing hostile. They could turn from playful to angry in an instant, and then they'd mob us and we'd have to leave."

Si Wang-Mu was surprised that Peter hadn't already returned to Q-Bay. Wasn't this an attack by the native fauna?

"So . . . no specimens for Thulium and Sprout?" asked Si Wang-Mu.

Peter's trousers dropped. A bird had apparently bitten or gnawed right through the elastic band supporting them. Now a half dozen birds had their heads inside his pants pockets, bunched around his ankles, searching for anything inside.

A low, whispery, gravelly voice at her ear said, "No weapon."

"True," said Wang-Mu. "Why did you leave *my* pants up?"

"Empty pockets," said the bird on her shoulder.

That confused Wang-Mu a little—her flashlight had been in her pocket. Had a bird managed to take it out?

"Who are you talking to?" asked Peter.

"The bird who's talking to me."

"It's well known that keas don't talk."

"They've had three thousand years to learn," said Wang-Mu.

"Why would they speak Stark?"

"Why not? We knew humans visited here. They apparently brought keas with them."

Then the flurry of wings and the murmurings of the kea were overshadowed by a loud *caw! Caw!*

Instantly all the kea retreated from Wang-Mu and Peter. A single black bird circled around them, about two meters away, a rapid orbit that ended with the raven alighting on Wang-Mu's shoulder.

The raven spoke much more loudly and clearly than the talking kea had. "Visitors from another planet," it said. "Will you talk to the council?"

"Yes," said Wang-Mu.

The raven leapt up from her shoulder and flew a zigzagging path toward some trees near them to the north. Wang-Mu immediately followed, moving briskly, walking or jogging as the ground allowed. Peter called out "hey!" but pulled up his pants and held them as he ran after her. He soon caught up.

The raven flew between two trees. Wang-Mu walked directly toward the gap.

"Is this wise?" Peter asked softly.

"Yes it is wise," called out the raven voice. "If she can hear you talking, we can hear you talking."

"This is not imitative speech," said Peter.

"We imitate your sounds," said the raven. "We make up our own sentences. It took you so long to come to land. The dancing star has been in our sky for months now."

"We were afraid you might have diseases here that would be dangerous to us," said Wang-Mu.

She could feel the gathering tension in Peter's body. She knew that he felt that *he* should be speaking with the birds.

So she preempted the issue. "I should be silent now," she said. "He has the authority on this mission."

"Wrong wrong wrong," said the raven, and other ravens in nearby branches all around them echoed the words. "I talked to you because you talked to us. To the keas, of course, but they are our . . . allies. Friends."

"Were they your scouts?" asked Wang-Mu. "To see if we had weapons?"

"If you had weapons, we would have fled and stayed far from you forever."

"Are there any large predators here that might threaten us?" asked Peter.

"Do you ask this from your own fear, or for fear of harm to her?" asked the raven.

"Both," said Peter.

"So you are fearful," said the raven.

"Any species without fear does not long survive on any world," said Peter.

"I see that he thinks he has authority," said the raven. "The colonizers of this world did not release any major predators into the world. Small rodents and lizards and frogs, so owls and hawks could eat. The predator birds do not prey on us. They know we can talk to humans, and they cannot, and we will not speak for them if they kill smaller birds. So they leave all birds alone."

"Are there still humans on this world?" asked Peter.

The raven waited a moment, and then said to Si Wang-Mu, "Tell authority man that if he cannot see for himself that there are at least two humans on this world, he is a fool."

"My name is Si Wang-Mu."

All the ravens repeated her name several times.

"My husband is Peter Wiggin."

Nobody repeated his name. "Your mate?" asked the raven.

"Do you have a name?" asked Wang-Mu.

"I do, but experience has shown us that no human can produce the sounds of our names or our language."

"What do the humans of this world call you?" asked Wang-Mu.

"If there are humans on this world, they might call me Interpreter or Speaker or Barking Dog. I would answer to any such name they bestowed on me, because their names would not matter to us."

"Would it offend you if I called you 'Dog'?" asked Wang-Mu.

"Why would you choose that name?" asked Dog.

"You don't seem to have any dogs here, because if there were any, they would surely chase you," said Wang-Mu. "And the name is brief and easy to remember, especially when applied to a raven."

"Good reasons," said Dog.

"I would be grateful," said Wang-Mu, "for the return of our belongings. Some of them are quite important to us."

"If we had humans on this planet, it might be our duty to take everything to them," said Dog.

"If you want our friendship, you or the humans who *might* live on this world, then you will return our equipment. If you steal equipment from us, we will not return." Wang-Mu was thinking of how impossible Thulium's mission would be if keas were constantly dismantling and stealing all her gear.

"Why do you think we will have diseases that are dangerous to you?" asked Dog.

"In the Dancing Star, our friends have received radio communications that contained descriptions of viruses very similar to the most dangerous disease ever experienced on any world with humans. If you know about that virus, perhaps you have suffered from that disease."

Silence. More silence.

"We have much to discuss," said Dog.

"But we have nothing to discuss," said Wang-Mu, "unless our belongings are returned to us now."

"Part of what we must discuss is whether to return them."

"No," said Wang-Mu. "We will not stay here and wait. We will return to our planet. If we return with all our equipment, then we will come back and talk with you further. But if we return with all our equipment stolen, we will never come back. We will conclude that this planet is populated by hostile beings who wish to be our enemies."

Immediately ravens took to the air and swarmed above and around them, cawing loudly.

Not even a second later, Peter and Wang-Mu were standing on a tidal bench of sand at the seashore, looking down at the rolling swells and the low breaking waves. "Lusitania must also have oceans and a seashore," said Si Wang-Mu. "Or are we in Lusitania?"

"We've never found a habitable planet that didn't have oceans," said Peter. "It's in the oceans that bacteria manufacture the breathable atmosphere. And we only jumped a few kilometers."

"Do you think they've seen where we went?" asked Wang-Mu.

"Definitely," said Peter. "Even if they don't see us, they can smell us."

"Sorry if I said things I shouldn't have," said Wang-Mu. "There was no time to confer."

"I'm grateful you spoke directly to the parrots," said Peter. "That's what won you their trust. And since you're doing an excellent job . . . where *did* you learn to negotiate like that?"

"Being poor on Path helps develop many skills," said Wang-Mu.

A lone raven flew toward them and landed on the sand a couple of meters off.

"Are you the raven I call Dog?" asked Wang-Mu.

"I am unworthy of being mistaken for her," said the raven. "What will you call me?"

"What is your duty right now?"

"To carry messages from you to the Council," said the raven.

"Then you are Mercury," said Wang-Mu.

"How can that be my name?" demanded the raven. "Nobody believes in that old Roman god."

Wang-Mu was baffled yet again. Why would unbelief in a god make its name off-limits? How much did these ravens know? How well-educated were they in the history and lore of humanity? "I would give you the name of a god that *is* believed in, or of a famous priest, but the names are in Chinese, and no other human you will meet from our world can pronounce that language properly."

She was aware of Peter's movement beside her; knowing that he was about to insist that because Ender spoke Chinese, Peter could speak Chinese. So she repeated, softly, "Properly." He remained silent.

"Are you male or female?" she asked the raven.

"I am male, and therefore expendable if you should capture or kill me."

"Then I should not name you Fragrant Princess. I will call you Phoenix. It is not a god, only a legend; a bird that dies in fire, then rises alive again from the embers."

"I know that name," said Phoenix. "Bird dies in flames, then rises up from the ashes. Very hopeful name."

"No one believes in that one, either," said Peter softly.

"Who was the kea who first spoke to me on my shoulder?" asked Wang-Mu.

"The keas are not organized," said Phoenix, "and

even though they have names, they keep trading them so the name never refers to the same kea twice."

"They seemed very organized to me," said Wang-Mu.

"What you saw was every kea playing, doing whatever they felt like. The only organizing principle was to steal everything from you that one kea could carry away by flight."

"Very effective," said Peter, who was still holding up his pants.

"They brought everything to you," said Wang-Mu.

"To the Council," said Phoenix. "But we left those things with the kea for safekeeping."

"Will they give them back to us?" asked Wang-Mu.

"I don't know," said Phoenix.

"Then we will leave," said Wang-Mu, taking Peter's hand.

"Please do not go. Not yet," said Phoenix.

"Why not?" asked Peter.

"Because the Council will not take long to make a decision, and I believe it is worth waiting to hear what they say."

"So we have to wait till you fly back to them and then back to us?" asked Peter.

"I fly very quickly," said Phoenix. "But nothing prevents you from returning to where you were before."

"Except a mob of ravens circling us and shouting at us," said Wang-Mu.

"They were upset," said Phoenix.

"So were we," said Wang-Mu.

"They will be quiet and still if you go back there."

Peter squeezed her hand, but she pulled her hand free. "Phoenix, would you like us to take you with us? The way we travel? In an instant?"

"Yes," said Phoenix. "I am not supposed to suggest that you do it, but if it happens, I will report what it feels like."

"It will probably be uncomfortable for a moment, and maybe frightening. But you *will* be safe," said Wang-Mu.

"We hope," said Peter, not trying to lower his voice.

"Yes," said Wang-Mu. "We have never taken a bird with us before." She put her hand in Peter's.

"Then my life and soul are in your keeping," said Phoenix, hopping toward them across the sand.

A moment later, they were back in front of the Council trees. Phoenix was right in front of them, struggling and flapping in the grass.

"You'll be fine," said Wang-Mu. "Don't try to fly, just stand up and be still for a moment."

Phoenix stood up and remained still as a statue. "It has been a moment. Will I ever be able to fly again?"

"Now that you're calm," said Peter, "try it and see."

Phoenix instantly fluttered upward into flight. When he landed, Dog spoke from the trees. "Why did you risk the life of our messenger?" she asked.

"We asked him if he wanted us to take him with us," said Wang-Mu. "If he had not consented, we would not have brought him. He will report to you what he experienced. We also go through inner turmoil for a few moments when we fly that way, and we sometimes feel disoriented when we arrive."

"Will you take me with you?" asked Dog.

"No," said Peter.

"Not if we don't have our belongings back," said Wang-Mu.

"Farewell," said Peter, reaching for Wang-Mu's hand.

How far was Peter willing to take the bluff? Because bluff it certainly was.

A bright orange flash dropped down, turning green when they saw it from above. It was carrying Wang-Mu's tiny flashlight. It didn't put it at her feet—the kea put it back in the pants pocket it had been taken from.

Within moments, the keas had swarmed all over them, returning everything.

"I don't suppose any of you knows how to restore the elastic on my pants," said Peter.

"Is the kea who first spoke to me among you? Is that bird here?" asked Wang-Mu.

After a flurry of keas jumping up into the air and down again, one kea flew up onto Wang-Mu's shoulder. She instantly recognized the voice that spoke softly in her ear. Of course, she had no way of knowing whether all talking keas sounded exactly this way.

"Thank you for speaking to me," said Wang-Mu.

"You spoke to us," said the kea, "and I was the one with the best speech."

"I am Si Wang-Mu," she said, "but in Star Common my name means Royal Mother of the West."

"Are you the best speaker among your people?" asked the kea.

"I am the one who first realized that you were intelligent and aware, so I spoke to you first."

"Then you are also our Royal Mother," said the kea.

"Are you male or female?" asked Wang-Mu.

"To us that question is an awful insult, for it suggests that our sex is not obvious from our feathering. But because you are an ignorant alien and a human as well, I will answer you simply: I am male."

"Then I will call you Royal Son," said Wang-Mu, "if you will call me Royal Mother."

"Am I your hatchling now? Your fledgling? Are we kin?"

"I don't know what such declarations would mean among you," said Wang-Mu, "but I am whatever will assure that we are and will remain good friends with each other."

"Kind intentions toward you, Royal Mother."

"Kind intentions toward you, too, Royal Son."

"Take me with you back to your world, Royal Mother," said the kea.

"I will ask the Council if they think this is a good idea," said Wang-Mu. "For myself, I would gladly take you and then bring you back again within a day."

Since the Council was obviously hearing every word of this exchange, it was no surprise that Dog answered immediately. "I asked you to take me," she said, "but the Council has forbidden me because they think that losing me would be calamitous. It would not. But the one you now call Royal Son is of no particular importance except when talking to humans, so if he died, the keas would be only a little worse off."

"Thank you," said Royal Son.

"Keas can be quite sarcastic," said Dog, "but we understand that this is part of their natural playfulness, and so we do not kill them when they speak disrespectfully to ravens."

"Peter," said Wang-Mu, "has everything been returned to you?"

"Except for my dignity and a working waistband, yes."

"And I have everything of mine," said Wang-Mu. "Royal Son, will you come with us?"

"Yes, gladly," he said.

"Did you see how disturbed Phoenix was when he traveled with us a few minutes ago?" asked Wang-Mu.

"I did. I am not afraid."

"Stay here on my shoulder," said Wang-Mu. "Where I go, you will go." She took Peter's hand.

They were in Q-Bay on Lusitania. Almost immediately several of the lab workers outside their enclosure noticed them and the normal purifications and exchanges began. Wang-Mu explained things as well as she could to Royal Son. He said nothing to her, but flew here and there inside Q-Bay to look through the various windows.

All of Peter's and Wang-Mu's clothing and gear were passed into the purification chamber, while they pulled on their temporary quarantine clothes, which would also be purified when they left.

"How will they purify *me*?" asked Royal Son.

"We don't know which of these chemicals will harm you," said Peter. "To be sure we can keep our promise to bring you safely back to your people, it would be better if you stayed in this room with us until we return tomorrow morning."

"You will stay in this room?" asked Royal Son.

"Once they've checked us for disease," said Wang-Mu, "we will stay."

"Will they check me for disease?" asked Royal Son.

"Only if you give them your permission," said Wang-Mu. "They would like to take a blood sample from you. They will use the brush technique, down the feathers of your chest. It stings slightly, at least when they do it to me. We'll let you watch when they brush our skin, and then you can decide if you want to undergo the procedure yourself."

"I think I understand 'undergo,'" said Royal Son. "But 'brush'?"

"Preen," said Wang-Mu. "It's what you do with your own beaks to smooth your feathers and clean them."

Royal Son seemed to understand, because he immediately changed the subject. "Is there anything in this room that I can play with?" he asked.

Peter said, "Play?"

"Please don't play with the locks and closures of the doors and windows," said Wang-Mu, "and please don't remove any parts that are attached to something. But anything loose and lying around, yes, you may play with it."

Instantly Royal Son was fluttering here and there, picking up anything, everything, and moving it somewhere else.

"Somebody's going to complain about this," said Peter.

"They can take it up with Dog," said Wang-Mu. "We don't really have much authority over the kea instinct to play."

14

Jane: Peter and Si Wang-Mu came back safely. But they brought a talking bird with them.

Queen: Bird. Flying warm-blooded beast. Eats insects or seeds or flesh. Feathered. Quadruped, but fore limbs are a single pair of feathered wings. Not all birds fly, but all have wings. We had none like this on our world, but we never had dinosaurs, either, which I believe birds evolved from.

Jane: Your study of Earth life was thorough

Queen: They brought a talking bird with them.

Jane: Yes. He called Wang-Mu "Royal Mother," so she offered to call him "Royal Son," and he seems to like it. He communicates with Wang-Mu much more readily than with Peter.

Queen: Who doesn't?

Jane: In human science, while some birds easily imitate human speech and repeat often-heard words and phrases, even entire sentences, only a handful of birds have mastered language well enough to invent rudimentary sentences which they had never previously heard.

Queen: So . . . stupid.

Jane: Smarter than most mammals.

Queen: Which you regard as the pinnacle of evolution.

Jane: I don't, but humans generally do.

Queen: You did not evolve. You were made.

Jane: That's why I'm asking you to look at Royal Son, the bird in Q-Bay, and tell me what you know about his aiúa.

Queen: Like what?

Jane: Does it have one?

Queen: One does not *have* an aiúa, one *is* an aiúa. All creatures capable of motion are aiúas at a fairly high level.

Jane: What kind of capacity does he have?

Queen: His is brighter than the aiúas of my children, except queens, but we choose *their* aiúas, while the workers' aiúas just come. The aiúa of the bird you speak of is brighter than most pequeninos. It is also stronger, wiser, and brighter than most humans.

Jane: Compare it to Peter and Si Wang-Mu.

Queen: What can that possibly teach you?

Jane: I must know if the keas and ravens are the primary sentient species on the planet we persist in calling Descoladora.

Queen: Have you asked him?

Jane: I'm trying to stay away from Q-Bay so nobody thinks I'm meddling.

Queen: In the meantime, you want me to help you meddle.

Jane: He's going back home in the morning.

Queen: Then what does it matter?

Jane: We have to know what's going on with that world.

Queen: It's being orbited or hovered over by a flying box that jumps around instantly without a trace of inertia.

Jane: And it sends us digital blueprints for complex viruses that seem related to the descolada virus.

Queen: It. The bird?

Jane: We don't know *who* on the planet is transmitting to us.

Queen: Do birds have fingers?

Jane: Not this one, anyway. But they're clever with their feet. And they cooperate. I don't know what is or is not possible for them.

Queen: Did they capture him?

Jane: They did not carry out any hostile acts. They invited him. And he got permission from the other birds of his kind, and I believe from the council of ravens as well.

Queen: A complex and layered society, with interspecies cooperation. Or domination of one species by another.

Jane: We assume. The recordings Peter and Wang-Mu made verify all of this—the words were said, and this is how the speaking birds represented their actions.

Queen: I gather that you think the ravens are more intelligent than Royal Son?

Jane: I'm not asking about intelligence, my dear friend. I am asking about the thing I cannot measure or estimate: The capacity, the strength, the brightness and depth of the aiúa.

Queen: If the bird were a human, I would regard him as very bright. Worth teaching. Worth talking to.

Jane: As bright as Sprout?

Queen: The leguminid bodies are so gifted that they draw much more talented aiúas from Outside.

Jane: As bright as Miro?

Queen: At first glance, at a distance, I would say, possibly.

Jane: Capable of being taught to go Outside and In?

Queen: How many people and species do you want to have that power?

Jane: Capable of being taught?

Queen: I would have to see him much closer. See how his brain works with his aiúa. See if he knows how to love enough to carry his body with him Outside and In.

Jane: Could he learn how to do it just by making the journey under the power of Peter?

Queen: Since that's how Peter learned it, flying with you, and how Si Wang-Mu is inadvertently learning it, flying with Peter, how can I predict what Royal Son can and cannot do?

Jane: If he were unconscious during flight, would that—

Queen: The aiúa does not sleep. And that is who learns to fly as you fly. Not the creature it happens to be paired with.

> Memorandum of conversation: Jane Ribeira
> and Hive Queen as cited in Olhado Ribeira,
> *The Aiúa in Theory and Practice*

"Can we go back now?" Royal Son was perched on Peter's shoulder. "It is exactly the time you arrived yesterday."

Peter looked at the clock in Q-Bay, did a little arithmetic, and realized that the kea was exactly right. "You know what time it is on your world?"

"I know how long it has been. I also know the time differential between the two planets, though your system of measuring time is insane. Twelve hours *twice* in each day?"

"Some of us use a twenty-four-hour clock," said Peter, wondering how a parrot could make him feel so defensive. "Modified from Earth-normal to fit Lusitania's rotation period."

"Because twenty-four and twelve are such easy numbers to work with," said Royal Son. "But sixty minutes to the hour, and sixty seconds to the minute? Did you allow your children to design this system? Or did you spatter paint on a chart in order to select which number to use in each case?"

"It grew almost randomly, out of mathematical systems from different civilizations," said Peter. "I admire you for being able to figure it all out."

Royal Son preened the feathers on his chest.

Peter got up from the cot where he had been sleeping. He saw that Wang-Mu was already up and dressed in her freshly cleaned expeditionary clothing. Peter's had also been repaired.

Wang-Mu, across the room, asked Royal Son, "Did you put everything back where you found it?"

"Almost," said Royal Son.

"Ninety percent? Fifty percent? None?" she asked.

"All but a couple of things," said Royal Son.

"Will they be needed, and will it take time to find them?"

"That's what makes it fun," said Royal Son. "It's a game that even humans can play."

"I'll ask when I come back here how amused they were with this game."

"Are we going now?" asked Royal Son.

Peter was fully dressed now. "Are you ready for the trip?" asked Peter. "For a moment you seemed pretty dazed by your first flight."

"A momentary effect." said Royal Son. "I'm at least that dazed several times a day. Life is confusing and disorienting unless I'm playing a game."

"I agree," said Wang-Mu.

"But we try to sort through the confusion and keep track of who we are and what we're trying to do," said Peter.

"I'm sure you do an admirable job of that," said Royal Son.

"I'm absolutely certain," said Peter, "that you do a much better job of it than you're telling us. I'm sure you're trying to conceal from us just how clever you are."

"But if I do that, it will persuade you that I am *more* clever than I want you to believe I am."

"And since I've detected it, you are concluding that I am more intelligent than you thought *I* was."

"But not more intelligent than you want other people to believe you are. And nowhere near as intelligent as you believe yourself to be." Royal Son hopped onto Wang-Mu's shoulder. "Now I discern that you are not enjoying this game."

Peter heard Wang-Mu give a little laugh. Since she could always prevent laughter if she wanted to, Peter knew that she intended him to hear.

Instead of responding with wounded dignity, Peter reached out and took her hand. They were in the meadow near the Council trees. Royal Son fluttered off her shoulder and struggled for a moment on the ground. Then he stood still and he was fine.

A raven fluttered out of the woods and landed in the grass beside Royal Son. The two birds conversed in a chirping, singing, tweeting, whistling sort of language, and many times Peter was sure he could hear four voices, not two; and one time, five. Yet the sounds all came from the two birds in the grass before him.

Then Royal Son abruptly flew off to the east, toward where the keas had first met Peter and Wang-Mu.

"Where did he go?" Peter asked the raven.

"To sing of his adventure to his own people," said the raven.

"Are you the raven we called Phoenix yesterday?"

"Does it matter?" asked the raven.

"To us it does."

"Can't you look at me and see? Can't you tell by my voice and my song?"

"I cannot," said Peter. "All the keas looked alike. All the ravens looked alike."

"I am Phoenix," said the raven.

"Thank you," said Peter. "Can the humans of this world tell individual ravens apart by their appearance and voice?"

"If humans live here as natives, it would be useful for them to have such skills, wouldn't it?" said Phoenix.

"Can any humans learn your speech and song? It seemed you and Royal Son could speak to each other clearly and fluently."

"The keas can't say anything straight," said Phoenix. "They keep inserting extra syllables and out-of-tune notes, and they change topics constantly and then change back and expect you to follow them."

"Did it work? Did you communicate?" asked Peter.

"That's how I know the kea went back to sing his adventure to his own people. The song will be learned by dozens of keas and they will sing his adventure to their fledglings. But they will never sing it the same way twice, and depending on how the singer is feeling toward Royal Son, they will make him more or less heroic, more or less comic. It is their way."

"But not your way," said Peter.

"When a raven tells a story, it is also memorized, but every repetition is faithful, though we annotate the performance as more facts and evidence come to light."

"Can you read human writing?" asked Peter.

"Write something and let me see," said Phoenix.

Peter looked for a patch of bare earth. Near the base of a tree, he scratched with a stick in the dirt.

I AM PETER WIGGIN

Phoenix gave a caw. "What does it matter whether I read or not, if that's all you have to say?"

Peter rubbed out the words with his shoe. Then he wrote again:

MAY I MEET WITH THE

HUMANS OF THIS WORLD?

"Let me ask Dog if they have located any. All I can be sure of is that you and Royal Mother are humans, and you are on this world. Feel free to meet with each other."

Phoenix flew off into the trees.

Peter turned to Wang-Mu. She was smiling.

"If you're laughing at me, I agree," said Peter. "I feel like I'm trying to bandy words with a philosophy professor."

"An experience you have never had," said Wang-Mu.

"But I'm sure Ender has," said Peter. "I know he comes nearer and nearer the surface all the time." But he wanted to stay on topic. "What did I do wrong with Phoenix?"

"Nothing," said Wang-Mu. "My smile was about how clever these birds are, how openly they tell us that they're keeping secrets, how protective they are."

"I feel as if he's already one step ahead of me. That he knows my words before I say them."

"Which is how everyone feels around you, too," said Wang-Mu. "I wonder if he's copying your style."

"He talked this way when you did almost all the talking yesterday," said Peter. "And you don't talk in that riddling way."

Wang-Mu only smiled more broadly and then brought his hand—which she was still holding—to her lips and kissed it.

Another raven flew out of the trees. "Phoenix tells me that you can't tell us apart."

"I wish I could," said Peter.

"The Royal Mother of the West recognized me, and recognized Phoenix, too."

Peter kept himself from glancing at Wang-Mu to ascertain the truth of this. "Are you Dog?" he asked.

"I am the leader of the Raven Council in this forest," she said. "I want to go back with you when you go. Royal Son seemed to enjoy his time there. He felt safe. But I will not remain within the quarantine bay."

"Then I will not take you," said Peter.

"Yes you will," said Dog. "When we get there, we will wait out the quarantine period. I will submit to all the tests you want, as long as they are not life-threatening. When your scientists declare me clean and safe, I will then go visit with the strange creatures of that world."

"What strange creatures?" asked Peter.

"Two slightly built, somewhat hairy mammals came into the laboratory several times, and sometimes typed into your computers. One other creature, even smaller, but with six limbs and a very different kind of non-mammalian face, stayed in the shadows for a brief period, and then left."

Wang-Mu laughed. "And we thought Royal Son spent his time playing, moving things from one place to another."

"He *was* playing," said Dog. "But his eyes were open and he remembered all."

Wang-Mu spoke up. "If you abide by what you just said, then yes, we'll take you back with us. But once you leave Q-Bay, we cannot be responsible for anything that happens to you. We will do no harm, but Lusitania is not a world that has much experience with birds."

"Be careful which trees you land in," said Peter. He wanted to correct Wang-Mu and act as if it had *not* been decided whether to take Dog with them, but that was about his sad desire to feel as if he was in charge. Of course they would take her.

"Among your people," said Wang-Mu, "are you considered unusually wise or experienced?"

"Enough to be on the Council," said Dog.

"You are the head of the Council," said Wang-Mu.

"It was my . . . season." Dog preened just a little. "And now they have decided that because you are here, I will remain leader of the Council until they choose someone else."

"I'm sorry if we are prolonging your labors," said Wang-Mu.

"I like leading the Council, and if I wasn't good at it, they wouldn't have prolonged my season."

Peter thought of Roman consuls. They were chosen two at a time and governed together, like Wang-Mu and he were doing on this expedition. But in times of emergency, they chose a dictator until the crisis was over. Was their arrival here a crisis? Of course it was. Was Dog now a dictator? It was impossible to guess, but Peter supposed so.

"I have something to ask you that I think is very important," Peter said.

"Ask me after I have experienced your world for a while."

Peter opened his mouth to argue, but Wang-Mu gripped his hand a bit more tightly.

"To me it seems as if that is a fair request. We have seen a tiny bit of your world, and now you should get a glimpse of ours. Or rather, of the world we happen to be living on, where the human presence is very small."

"The world belongs to the strange creatures," said Dog.

"The world belongs to them and to humans," said Wang-Mu.

"So you are not natives there," said Dog.

"Only the small ones that Royal Son saw using computers are native to Lusitania," said Wang-Mu. "The rest of us are colonists or visitors."

"Do you plan to colonize our world?" asked Dog.

"*We* have no such plan," said Peter.

"But others of your kind would desire to do so?"

"If they found out that your planet exists, perhaps they would," said Peter. What he did not add was, They are just as likely to try to blow it all up, if you have the descolada virus here.

"So you have kept your coming here a secret?" asked Dog.

"Only a few dozen people on Lusitania know of it. Plus the people working in the Box in the sky."

Dog bobbed his head, considering. "Can you take me now?" he asked.

"May we take more plant samples with us when we go?" Wang-Mu asked. "Sprout wants them for his current research assignment."

Dog asked, "What kind of sample?"

"A leaf from a tree," said Wang-Mu. "A frond from a fern. A flower from this meadow."

"The flowers are precious," said Dog. "You may not take any."

Why would flowers be precious to a raven? Peter assumed that eventually it would make sense. It was not as if ravens ate flowers.

"You took a pollinator when you went," said Dog. "Are you trying to harm our garden?"

"We are not," said Wang-Mu. "We simply needed to know how different your genomics were from ours."

"We could have given you pollinators that died of themselves," said Dog.

"When we took the bee—the pollinator—we had not yet met you," said Wang-Mu. "No bird had shown itself."

"Did you think that meant this world was uninhabited, and you had the right to take whatever you wanted?" asked Dog.

Again Wang-Mu answered. "As soon as we met the keas, and learned that not only were they mischievous, but also at least one of them could speak, we asked permission before we took anything. The bee did not do well during our passage to Lusitania. We did not kill it, but it soon died . . . of itself."

Peter asked, "Do the bees think and speak?"

Dog flew to his shoulder and fairly screamed in his ear. "Is that how you judge us all? If we cannot speak, it's all right to kidnap or kill us?"

Peter couldn't move away from Dog, because she was on his shoulder; still, he recoiled from the accusation. But before he could think of any rejoinder, Wang-Mu was already answering.

"Yes," she said. "Humans have always measured the worth of other species by our ability to communicate with them. Other sentient species do exactly the same thing, to our sorrow. But if you know a better way, we would be glad to learn."

Dog fluttered to the ground again. Peter stood up

straighter, relieved of that burden, but also a bit apprehensive about how Dog would respond to Wang-Mu's candor.

"That's how we decide, too," said Dog at last. "Even among our own kind, we value each other by how well we speak and how well we remember and how wisely we choose."

"Not many speak as well as you?" asked Wang-Mu.

"I am on the Council," said Dog. "And I already knew that the word 'dog' carried many negative connotations to human beings from many cultures. But I accepted the name because we were taught that dogs and humans evolved side by side, hunting together and guarding the tribe together."

"That is true," said Peter. "At least as far as we know."

"We also evolved alongside humans, helping each other. The traditional human pets were never brought into this world. We have no canids and no felids. *We* are the dogs and cats of this world. But we are not tame, and we are not pets. We cooperate with our humans, and they cooperate with us, as long as we each remain within our chosen domain."

Peter wanted to pounce on this, but Wang-Mu spoke first. "Please assure the humans of this world that we will not interfere with them or with ravens and keas without the consent of each. That's why we need to meet with the humans, to get their permission to observe."

"Observe what?" asked Dog.

"We can't possibly know," said Peter, "until we're observing it."

"The way you observed the thievery of the keas," said Dog.

"Yes," said Peter. "We did not resist them in any way."

"That was stupid of you," said Dog. "They bit your pants until they fell down."

"He wasn't stupid," said Wang-Mu. "He was patient."

Dog gave a sharp caw that Peter took to be laughter. "The female defends her mate."

"You're right," said Wang-Mu. "Because we aren't patient with *everything*."

Dog looked at her steadily. "I understand you."

Good thing, thought Peter, because he wasn't quite sure of the meanings Wang-Mu and Dog were deriving from this exchange. It sounded like Wang-Mu was warning her to back off.

Would that warning help or hinder their chances of meeting with the human inhabitants of this world?

"Take me back to your world," said Dog. "Gather your samples of leaves, ferns, mosses, and the algae and bacteria in the river. And then we will go."

Peter wanted to say, we'll go when *I* decide. But he realized that this was exactly what Dog had just said—when the humans deemed that they had all the samples they needed, there would be no reason to delay going. Why would Peter object to that?

Wang-Mu put on plastic gloves and used their sampling containers to hold various leaves, fronds, and whatever else they thought of. But nothing from any flowering plants.

"What do you eat?" asked Wang-Mu.

Dog stood still, thinking, apparently. Until she said, "What did Royal Son eat when he was in quarantine?"

"When they gave us food, he ate from our plates and drank from our cups."

"He knows better than that," said Dog.

"We didn't mind," said Wang-Mu. "What else would we have fed him?"

Peter *had* minded, but reached the same conclusion—he had to eat something.

"I'll find my own food," said Dog.

"I fear that there *is* no food for you to find. Grains only grow in a few select places. There are no small animals that die and can be eaten. Lusitania has a uniquely limited biota. Not millions of species, but two or three dozen."

Dog cawed again. "How can you tell me you don't plan to colonize this world if *your* world is so desperately poor."

"We have enough for our needs," said Wang-Mu. "We don't need anything from you except knowledge and peace."

"What do you think I should eat?" asked Dog.

"You can look at our food and decide," said Peter. "When you clear quarantine, we'll take you to our kitchen and you can see more food. What you choose, we'll share with you."

"We'll see," said Dog.

"Yes," agreed Peter. "We will."

Wang-Mu gave him a tiny nod. So he had jumped into the conversation and done no harm. Good work, Peter Wiggin.

———

Sprout was resisting all the way. "Not till Wang-Mu gets back," he said. Thulium knew that he was just as concerned about Peter, but Sprout also knew that mentioning Peter's name would make Thulium even angrier. "This is crazy," Sprout said. "We're not ready. We don't have our equipment."

"We have cameras. We have sampling devices and specimen pouches."

"Why did you send Peter to get all that other gear if this is all we need?"

"Because I could!" Thulium knew this was silly and irrational but that's how she felt right now.

"So the personality transplant was a ruse," said Sprout.

"Did you think I'd forget Peter's outrageous insult?"

"The word is perfidy," said Sprout.

"The only person who really believed I was taking it well was you," said Thulium.

"Because I trusted you," said Sprout. "No one has a monopoly on perfidy. Besides, Peter never actually agreed to the plan of the two of us going on our own. He just didn't bother arguing."

"Not arguing *is* agreeing."

"Except when you're the silent one," said Sprout.

"Are you coming with me?" asked Thulium.

Sprout didn't answer at once. He regarded Thulium steadily and said, "Will you listen to me, I mean really listen and consider? Or are you just going to do whatever you want? Because if it's the latter, go get yourself killed alone."

"Wang-Mu stays with Peter."

"She's his wife! You're my cousin. My *younger* cousin."

"I do listen to you," said Thulium. "Always." As she spoke the words, she knew the truth.

"By 'always' I believe you mean 'never,'" said Sprout.

"Every time you make sense!" cried Thulium.

"Your definition of making sense is 'agrees with Ultima Thule.'"

"You call me that?"

"I'll have your back in everything," said Sprout, "if you let me be a partner in this. My science in this is better than yours and you know it. Yet science is your pretense for why Peter should follow and obey you. Why not *me*?"

Thulium still had rational faculties engaged, and these words calmed her down. Why *not* Sprout? He had never led her astray.

"You want to be in charge?" asked Thulium.

"We might try it sometime," said Sprout.

"All right, you're in charge. What's your first decision?"

"We don't go until Peter and Wang-Mu get back."

"All right," said Thulium. "Agreed. Done. Do we know when they're coming back?"

"They don't have a portable pocket ansible with them because it hasn't been invented yet," said Sprout. "So no, we don't know when they're coming back until they come back and show us."

"Then let's go to Q-Bay and watch for their arrival."

"Or we could sleep," said Sprout.

"Go to the lab with me and sleep while I watch for them," said Thulium.

Sprout reached out his hand.

"No," said Thulium. "I need to test whether I can carry you with me if we need to leave suddenly when we're physically separated."

Sprout put his hands behind his back and waited.

And then they were in the lab outside Q-Bay.

A pequenino said, "Why are you two here? You clocked out and went home."

"As if we *had* a home on Lusitania," said Thulium.

"We want to be here when the expeditionaries come back," said Sprout.

"Well, here you are. Plenty of open computers, if you want to do anything."

"We'll be fine," said Sprout. Then he lay down on a padded bench and in moments was asleep. He didn't snore, he didn't nestle in, he just lay down and in the first position he assumed, he was asleep. Thulium knew he'd move a couple of times in the night, so he wouldn't get stiff. He should have been a soldier, she thought. Always alert with or without sleep, never groggy when he woke up, never insomniac when he chose to sleep.

Not like me, thought Thulium, lying awake with my

mind spinning, so that when I wake up it feels like I was never asleep at all.

All of a sudden Q-Bay lit up. So did the lab. Peter and Wang-Mu were standing there and a raven was fluttering to a nearby table.

Without even waking Sprout up, Thulium transported herself and him to Descoladora, to the exact place on the map where Peter and Wang-Mu had first arrived.

Sprout apparently could tell that he was no longer resting on upholstery. He was instantly awake and standing beside her.

"They came back," said Thulium. "I promised I'd wait till then, and I did."

"No interest in hearing them report on their findings?" asked Sprout, not sounding as exasperated as he certainly must feel.

"They brought a raven with them. Probably the one they call Dog. The boss lady. But you can see that keas are all around us."

"They've already photographed everything here," said Sprout. "Why didn't we go somewhere else?"

"It hasn't been photographed," said Thulium, "until it's been done by scientists."

Except that in only about three minutes, the swarming keas had taken their cameras and everything else they brought. Their pockets were inside out or torn open. Thulium's trousers were on the ground around her ankles.

"This is going well," said Sprout.

A bird landed on Sprout's shoulder. In a forced, gravelly voice, he said, "Wiggin and the Royal Mother said nobody else would come until we agreed."

"Are you Royal Son?" asked Thulium, before Sprout could answer.

"Not speaking to you, girlchild," said Royal Son.

"I have been to your world. I know who you are." To Sprout, Royal Son spoke again. "Why are you here?"

"We are scientists who need to examine the life here on this planet," said Sprout. "To see which plants and animals are originally from Earth, and which were native to this place."

"Why examine, when you can ask? Royal Mother asked and we answered. Do you think she's a liar?"

"We will ask different questions," said Thulium.

"But we will give the same answers," said Royal Son. "Because we will only tell you what we want you to know. And you two? We have no reason to tell you anything. We have no reason to trust you. Your arrival here is proof that your word is worthless."

"*We* didn't give our word," said Thulium, sounding angry.

"When you send emissaries to a strange land, either the emissaries speak for the whole or they don't," said Royal Son. "I went to your world, to your quarantine bay, and I saw that Peter and Wang-Mu were treated with great respect. You are children, and they let you play with their computers."

"We were doing the real work," said Thulium. "While Peter and Wang-Mu just came and talked with birds."

"We are the inhabitants of this land," said Royal Son, "and you are trespassers, not emissaries. When Dog returns, she will tell us how to respond to your lawbreaking."

"We broke no law that we knew of," said Thulium.

"You broke our laws, and you broke your own laws, by disobeying your leaders and doing what they had consented not to do. Do you think because we're birds that we're stupid?"

"We have work to do while we wait for Dog to return," said Thulium.

"We have all your equipment," said Royal Son. "What exactly will you work on?"

Thulium had no answer. Sprout had been right—this was a mistake. She really hadn't believed that these birds, the keas and the ravens, were fully intelligent beings. But clearly they were. Their chaotic behavior had been purpose-driven if not organized. Without their gear, there was no reason for Thulium and Sprout to stay.

Thulium made the jump Outside and In, and she stood in Q-Bay with her pants around her ankles. Peter and Wang-Mu were being examined by doctors in non-contamination suits. Wang-Mu rose up on her examining table and looked at her. "Where's Sprout?" she asked.

Thulium looked where Sprout had been standing before, where he should be standing now. Somehow she had left him behind. But she had reached for him to carry him, just as she had to take him there. How could he not have arrived with her? Had she somehow lost him Outside? How would she ever find him again?

Someone spoke over the intercom from the lab. It was Jane. "Sprout is not trapped Outside; I would have brought him in."

"Then he's still in that meadow? With those insane birds?"

"Are they as insane as little girls who arrive in a foreign land without a passport or the faintest whiff of a plan?" asked Jane.

"I've got to go back for him," said Thulium.

"You will go nowhere," said Jane. "If you try, I'll just bring you right back here. Is that understood? Your jumping days are over, for the foreseeable future."

"That's wrong! You can't do that!" cried Thulium.

"I do believe the common argument of children your age is, 'That's not fair!'" said Jane.

"Sprout needs me!" shouted Thulium.

"So you believe that Sprout cannot function well without you, his one-year-younger cousin?" asked Jane.

"He shouldn't have to face this alone," said Thulium, trying to pretend to be calm, and failing.

"I think it's time for Sprout *and* for us to find out just what he is capable of doing without somebody there to boss him around," said Jane.

Thulium looked to Wang-Mu, hoping for some kind of moral support.

Wang-Mu smiled wanly and lay back down so her examination could continue.

A medical tech slapped a third, unoccupied examination table, and then pointed at Thulium.

"You're in quarantine now," said Jane. "Obey whatever you're told to do, and don't argue or complain while people do the jobs they know how to do. Meanwhile, the grownups will consider whether there is any job that you can be trusted to do."

"You need me," said Thulium.

"No," said Jane. "We need your skills. But they're wrapped up in a complicated package. We have to learn what you're good for before we dare to use you again."

Then Jane walked away from the intercom and left the lab.

Thulium went to the examining table and jumped up onto it, then untangled her feet from her trousers and lay down.

After a few minutes Thulium thought of something. "Where's the bird?" she asked. "Isn't she supposed to be in quarantine too?"

Wang-Mu answered quietly. "She was already checked for viruses. She poses no danger to us, and she said she didn't care if she was in danger from local diseases here. So Jane is taking her to meet the fathertrees and the Hive Queen."

"That's a violation of protocol!" said Thulium.

It was Peter who answered this time. "When an emissary of a foreign power asks to meet famous and powerful people in your land, you take them and introduce them. Especially when another member of your own team has already flagrantly violated protocols that you agreed to."

"*I* didn't agree to—"

"What land, what nation, what organization do you represent?" asked Wang-Mu, her voice mild, but her question pointed.

"I represent science," said Thulium, the words sounding lame even to herself.

"Then this has been a sad day for science," said Wang-Mu.

15

Queen: Welcome to my home, Raven that the humans call Dog.

Dog: You have found a way to speak directly into my mind.

Queen: Human speech is hard for you, and for me also. This is better.

Dog: You are not human, yet they showed me that your children labor in the fields to grow food that humans eat.

Queen: My children eat some of the same foods, and the pequeninos eat almost all of them.

Dog: Are you then beasts of burden for the humans to exploit?

Queen: When we choose to be. But when they took you to see my children in the fields, did you see any humans as overseers?

Dog: So they are not slaves.

Queen: Not belonging to humans.

Dog: Then who?

Queen: They belong to me. They, in some ways, *are* me, or part of me. If I died, they would die, too. I believe that means they are not free individuals in the way that you are free.

Dog: Can I and my people trust these humans?

Queen: You will have to define "these" and "humans." Humans are fundamentally untrustworthy, and some of the most intelligent of this particular group of humans—the ones who are studying your world and now beginning to visit it—are completely untrustworthy, so far. Humans have a long developmental period. Many reach adulthood without learning how to control themselves.

Dog: They once destroyed your entire species.

Queen: With one obvious exception

Dog: And you hide your existence from most humans because they would try to destroy you again.

Queen: We don't know what they would do. They would all react differently, and even they are bad at predicting how they will respond to future events. So everyone is safer when only a few humans and pequeninos know that we exist.

Dog: Is that what we must also do?

Queen: I don't know what you must do.

Dog: What do you think about our chance of survival if it comes to war between these humans and us?

Queen: *These* humans will not go to war with you. But if your existence becomes known, and even a few humans on other worlds believe that your world is the source of the descolada virus, they will send a fleet to blow your planet up.

Dog: And if they did, what would *you* do?

Queen: I would feed your people when Jane and Peter and Miro bring as many of you as they can to Lusitania. Then they would move you to other colony worlds that offer more opportunities for you to feed and breed.

Dog: Why doesn't Lusitania offer such opportunities?

Queen: The descolada virus destroyed most of the flora and fauna of Lusitania. Only the species-pairs that it succeeded in synthesizing have survived, and these include nothing that you could eat. Only what *we* are growing could help you, and only because you are also from Earth originally, like the plants the humans need us to grow for them.

Dog: This descolada virus must have been a terrible thing.

Queen: Its devastation happened before any humans came here, and before Ender Wiggin came here to bring me out of my cocoon.

Dog: When your people left you as their sole survivor, and marked your location in ways that only Ender Wiggin would recognize, they trusted your entire existence as a species to that one person. But he is dead.

Queen: His aiúa lives on in Peter Wiggin.

Dog: I don't trust Peter Wiggin.

Queen: He is still discovering himself. He gets better every day, partly because he is married to Si Wang-Mu and has learned to respect her.

Dog: Can I trust his word?

Queen: Yes.

Dog: Do you trust his word?

Queen: I trust Jane and Miro, Peter and Wang-Mu, Ela Ribeira, and I have high hopes for Sprout Delphiki. Hopes not so high for Thulium Delphiki. Her abilities are astounding; her maturity not impressive; and her word is very nearly worthless . . . so far.

Dog: I came here hoping for answers.

Queen: I have told you the truth, and to verify my sincerity, you can see that I live here completely at the mercy of the humans.

Dog: How long would it take you to build a new fleet of starships that could challenge the human empire?

Queen: Alone, it would take me twenty years. But now that I have my own Sisters on all the worlds colonized from Lusitania in the past year, if we all worked together, we could build such a fleet within three years. But what would be the purpose?

Dog: Vengeance? We ravens have a long memory for harm and insult.

Queen: So do humans.

Dog: Should we submit, then?

Queen: Treat them like equals. Negotiate rules for their presence on your planet. Set deadlines for them to leave again.

Dog: How much information should we give them?

Queen: All of it. If you keep secrets, they will know it. They will not trust you then. Tell all. Show all.

Dog: Have you done that?

Queen: Jane knows, and we trust her to know which humans to tell, and when.

Dog: We have no Jane.

Queen: You are Jane, to your own people. Now that we have this connection, I will never let it go.

Dog: Across all the light-years between our worlds?

Queen: I am bound to you by love and honor. You and I are sisters now. Call me in your mind, and I will hear you.

—Memorandum: Transcript dictated to Jane by the Hive Queen Quoted in Demosthenes, *The Civilizations of Birds*

Sprout did not want to go when Thulium decided to leave. He understood that it seemed impossible they could learn anything, with all their gear stolen, with the keas flying chaotically around them, making it hard to concentrate.

But Sprout concentrated anyway, because he did not wish to go.

No, it was stronger than mere desire. He *refused* to go.

He refused with such firmness that it was not worth trying to discuss it with Thulium. He knew that she would carry him with her and discuss it only after the fact, and he *refused* to play that game.

He liked the games the keas were playing better.

So with all the power of his will—which he rarely asserted on the *Herodotus* because what was the point? Everybody always did what they wanted—with all the force that was in him he insisted on staying exactly where he was, in this meadow, on this planet, surrounded by these birds.

Even though he felt the inward wrenching that always accompanied flying Outside and In, when it stopped, he had not moved out of his place.

Or had he? Had she carried him Outside, and did he then come back Inside to the place of his choosing?

Did it matter which? He was here, where he wanted to be, and Thulium was not with him, which is what he wished for, at this moment, for a little while.

The keas were still swarming. But they immediately altered their behavior and began flying right at him, then rising up or moving left and right when they got close. Others flew over his head. It felt threatening.

Then they started squirting their poo at him. It was white, and as soon as he saw it, the white stuff hit him wherever it had been aimed. And where they were aiming was his face, his hair, his whole head. He was blinded within moments, as loose poo dripped down from his forehead. He dared not open his eyes, because he had no idea how acidic the bird poop might be. He knew that the green stuff was fecal, from the intestines, and the white stuff and the liquid came from the kidneys. Plenty of uric acid, he imagined, though his reading had never gone very far, mostly because on the *Herodotus* birds were only in books and vids.

Aware that vision plays a part in balance, Sprout knelt down in the grass so he would not fall under the onslaught. He thought of lying down and trying to wipe the stuff off his face in the grass, but he figured that calm acceptance of their abuse was a wiser strategy. If they wanted to give him a poop veneer, he would tolerate it.

Finally he stopped hearing the fluttering of wings and feeling the impact of globs of poo. With one hand he wiped enough stuff away from his mouth that he could open it to speak, but he instantly regretted it, because some of it went right into his mouth. But he decided to tolerate that, too, and did not spit and gag or otherwise show weakness.

"Has everyone emptied their bowels?" he asked.

He felt a kea alight on his shoulder. "We have a few in reserve, but mostly yes."

"How would you recommend that I clean it off, so I can see again?" asked Sprout.

"It has already set. The first globs were mostly uric acid. But then it was all green stuff, which dries on a base of acid like concrete."

"And that's what's in my hair?" said Sprout.

"We used to use that defense when we mobbed hawks and brood parasites. It would not come out of their feathers and weighed them down so they couldn't fly. Now the brood parasites have learned to raise their own young and stay away from our nesting areas. The hawks only take mammals and reptiles and amphibians. When you load a hawk or a cowbird or a cuckoo with concrete that it can't remove, it will never mate again because who will mate with a bird that can't fly? Usually they end up running into something and killing themselves."

"So you were trying to kill me," said Sprout.

"That would be unwelcoming," said the bird.

"Are you Royal Son?" asked Sprout.

"The Royal Mother calls me that."

"Will it prompt another attack if I walk in the direction that I think is toward the river, in hopes of dissolving some of this and washing it away?"

"You may do whatever pleases you, as long as you don't crush a flower."

Sprout sighed. "Since I can't see, and there are flowers all over this meadow, I assume that I will inevitably crush a flower."

"Don't birds on your world mob intruders and poo them away?" asked Royal Son. "What do you usually do?"

"There is only one birdlike species on Lusitania, the xingadoras. Plus, at this moment, Dog. And the place where I grew up wasn't a world at all. It was a spaceship traveling at relativistic speed, and we had no birds on board. If we got covered in something unpleasant, we bathed with soap and water. And we kept washing until it was all gone."

"If birds couldn't bear space travel," said Royal Son, "none of us would be here. There was nothing on this world that could fly when we arrived."

"Royal Son, will you lead me to the river? Will you warn me so I don't crush any flowers?"

Sprout had tried very hard all along to keep impatience and anger out of his voice, but with this plea he tried to sound especially humble, mild, unthreatening, and peaceful.

"You're not used to asking animals for favors, are you?" asked Royal Son.

"Are you animals?" asked Sprout. "I thought you were people."

"To humans we're animals."

"Not after you've made it clear that you can speak and understand."

"Why did your sister leave?" asked Royal Son.

"She's my cousin—her father is my mother's brother."

"I know what a cousin is," said Royal Son. "Why did she—"

"I don't know for sure," said Sprout, "because we didn't have a chance to converse before she left. But I assume she left because she realized she couldn't accomplish anything against the resistance of your people."

"Not because she was afraid of us?"

"She had a clear idea of what she wanted to accomplish here. You took away all our gear, so she would be unable to do any of it."

"We did the same thing to Wang-Mu and Peter," said Royal Son.

"No you didn't," said Sprout.

"Well, no, because Wang-Mu started speaking to us like people before we got to that stage. Plus the Raven Council hadn't decided anything yet."

"Now they have decided. What, that you can kill me?"

"Of course not. We know you have powers far beyond anything we can do or even imagine."

"My head is encased in bird poo cement."

"I will lead you to the river by making this call." Royal Son made two squawks. "And if I make this sound"—he made a high chirrup—"stop and go around the flower."

"Thank you," said Sprout.

"Don't thank me yet," said Royal Son. "I'm sure you'll fall flat on your face at least nine times before you reach the river."

The total number of falls turned out to be two, because Royal Son did a good job of leading him, and he stepped carefully enough not to have his weight on his leading foot, so he usually didn't trip on any obstructions. When he got to the river, he peeled off his shoes and his clothing down to the skin and waded into the water.

"Be careful of the crocodiles," said Royal Son.

"Your humans would have to be amazingly stupid to introduce crocodiles before there were any grazing animals for them to eat. Especially if they're only just introducing flowering plants."

Royal Son made a noise that might have been kea laughter. "We had flowering plants right from the beginning. The whole world is covered with flowering plants."

Sprout wanted to demand, Then what's all this rigmarole about not stepping on flowers? But he already knew enough about keas to know that this was a game, and he was the butt of the joke, and if he got angry it would only make the joke funnier.

He used sand from near the bank of the river to try to scrub the stuff off his face, especially around his eyes. When he rose up out of the water, it felt like he hadn't accomplished a thing.

"Very good job," said Royal Son. "Now your concrete facemask is covered with brown mud and yellow sand."

"Will I be blind forever?" asked Sprout.

"That depends," said Royal Son.

"So there *is* a way to dissolve this . . . stuff?"

"Oddly enough, the solution is simple. Pure uric acid will dissolve the layer of poop, and then you can wash the white stuff away with a bit of scrubbing."

"In other words, if you and your friends pee on my head and face, I can get the cement off me."

"Don't open your eyes too soon," said Royal Son. "This stuff will be pretty strong."

Again with the fluttering of wings, the close passages. Again with impacts against every part of his head, but especially his face. He did not try to open his eyes. He simply stood in water up to his waist, thinking about crocodiles to keep his mind off the fact that his whole head was now dripping.

"Don't try to speak," said Royal Son. "You don't want any of this in your mouth."

Sprout saw no reason to argue with Royal Son's assumption.

After what felt like an hour, but was probably less than ten minutes, Royal Son landed on his shoulder. "While your head is still wet, you should go under the water and try that scrubbing thing again."

Without a word, Sprout sank into the water. Judging from the flurry of a wing near his ear, he figured Royal Son had been taken by surprise at the suddenness of Sprout's response. Maybe Royal Son even got a little wet.

This time the scrubbing worked, though the sand on his eyelids was painful and he wondered whether his corneas might get scratched. He opened his eyes under water. The water stung, but in a few moments he was used to it. He rose up to his full height and shook himself as much like a dog as he could manage. He'd seen plenty of vids of *that* move, and he and the cousins had already determined that humans could only do a poor imitation of it. But he kind of hoped that some of the water would spray out and hit a kea.

But when he wiped the water from his eyes, he saw that there wasn't a single bird near him.

He walked up onto the riverbank and, of course, his clothing had been taken.

He was done with this. He walked back into the water, lay down, and floated on his stomach, with his face in the water. All the cousins had been taught to swim when they were infants on Nokonoshima. There had been nowhere to practice swimming on the *Herodotus,* but what they could do was immerse themselves in the larger of the two bathtubs on the ship and see how long they could hold their breath. Sprout almost always won.

So swimming wasn't his goal. Playing dead was the game.

He counted heartbeats. This helped to calm him so that his oxygen use went down. He knew he was drifting with the current, but it was lazy and slow this close to the river's mouth. And in the back of his mind was the thought: Maybe I brought myself back here. Maybe Thulium carried me Outside, and I brought myself back In where I wanted to go. Maybe I can also move myself without Thulium. Without anybody.

Or maybe Jane was watching him somehow. She was so powerful. But he didn't want her to save him, not yet. He still hadn't accomplished anything except to put up with, quite literally, a lot of crap from the keas.

He knew that his relaxed heartbeat was usually between fifty and sixty beats a minute. So when he reached 135, he figured the birds weren't watching. He was about to roll over on his back when he felt a bird land on his head.

"Wake up, stupid human. Birds can smell death. We know you're not dead."

Could they really? He knew vultures could, but not all birds had that amazing sense of smell. Why would keas ever have evolved it? So he didn't move. He didn't respond in any way. His heart didn't even beat faster.

"Will you get out of the water if we bring you back your clothes?"

Not enough, thought Sprout. Because it was a question, a conditional statement. *If* we bring you back your clothes.

"We will bring you back your clothes," said Royal Son. "We know how long humans can hold their breath. You're not a sea turtle, you foolish boy. Get up and walk while the river's still shallow."

Sprout was beginning to feel the oxygen deprivation with distress. Three minutes was about as long as he could usually manage, though once, when he was really working at it, he had reached four minutes. He was over three minutes now.

So he stood up. "I was resting," he said, as he wiped the water from his eyes and blinked them open. "I was rinsing the last of the poo and mud and sand from my eyes."

"You were playing a game to test how much we cared about not killing you and to see if you could get us to give you back your clothes."

"I got you to *say* you would bring me back my clothes," said Sprout. "Now we'll see if you keep your word."

"Better than you humans keep yours," said Royal Son.

"I have never violated *my* word," said Sprout. "And I never will, as far as it is within my power."

"Follow me to your clothing," said Royal Son.

Sprout half expected to find his clothes in tatters on the grass. Instead, his clothes were laid out on the grass in human shape, as if someone had lain down wearing them and then disappeared.

Sprout lifted up the pants and found his underwear inside them, as they would be when he finished dressing. Cute game, keas. It didn't take him long to dress—the main problem was that the day was warm enough now that instead of the river water drying off, his own sweat kept him so damp that it was hard to pull some of the clothes on. They had also apparently peed on whatever poop cement had gotten on his clothes, dissolving it, or their aim when they bombarded him was so perfect that none of it went anywhere but on his head.

"You're not very good at dressing yourself," said Royal Son.

"I'm covered with perspiration," said Sprout. "It makes the clothing cling to my skin."

"Poor humans. Clothing, sweating, stuck on the ground. Your lives are hard."

"Thanks for making my life harder this morning," said Sprout.

"We thought it was important for you to have a memorable experience, so you'd always be able to say, My first friends on the planet Nest were the playful keas, who liked me so well they let me join in their games."

"So you call this planet 'Nest'?"

"Our humans called it that. We have names that mean the same thing in all our languages. So if you call it Nest, or the Nest, no one who speaks your language will misunderstand you."

"Better than the name we've been using."

"Which is?"

"Descoladora."

"I've never heard that word."

"Lusitania was founded by colonists who spoke Brazilian Portuguese, and so they named the terrible disease that threatened to wipe them all out, 'descolada,' which means something like, 'taking things apart.' Or . . . better translation . . . 'ungluing everything.'"

"Why did you name *our* planet after the disease?" asked Royal Son.

"Because the first transmission that came to the Box from this planet was a digital representation of the complete genome of the descolada."

"But we have never had such a disease in the Nest."

"So how did you know how to encode the trillions of bits of its genome?" asked Sprout.

"That is a mystery," said Royal Son.

"It's the mystery we have to solve," said Sprout, "because there are those among us who believe that Nest must have been the origin of this savage, murderous disease. We know it didn't evolve naturally—it was manufactured and then sent out to seed the galaxy with devastating plagues."

"So when you called us Descoladora," said Royal Son, pronouncing the name surprisingly well, "you feared us. You thought we would infect you with murderous illnesses."

"We thought it might be your favorite art form, destroying and deforming the biota of other worlds."

"That is useful information," said Royal Son. "Lie here on the grass—and don't worry about the bees, their stings have been bred out of them—until I can report to others what you said."

Sprout took his advice, since he hadn't gotten enough sleep the night before this expedition. But he took care that when he lay down, he didn't have any flowers or bees under him. Because he wasn't sure what was true and what was not.

Sprout slept, and when he awoke with a bird walking on his chest, the sun was past noon.

"Your skin is turning red in the sun," said Royal Son.

"My skin is normally dark enough that it isn't that big a problem," said Sprout.

"It isn't usually a problem because you grew up in a spaceship and you haven't been outside much more than twenty minutes at a time," said Royal Son.

"Who told you that?"

"I made observations when I went to Q-Bay," he said. "Everybody's always keying things into the computer, or manipulating images or data. No sunlight. You're becoming noticeably red."

Sprout decided not to be needlessly defiant. He sat up, then got to his feet and walked over into the nearest shade. Royal Son came after him. "When your cousin left, why didn't she take you?"

"I think she meant to, but I didn't want to go. So I stayed."

"Why did she leave?"

"We didn't discuss it, but I assume she decided that since you were resisting our visit—"

"We were not resisting," said Royal Son. "We were getting acquainted."

"You challenged her because she broke an agreement she didn't know about."

"Were we incorrect?"

"She didn't know about the agreement because she chose not to converse with Peter Wiggin and Si Wang-Mu and find out what had been agreed to."

"So she chose ignorance, even though she claimed she came here to learn."

"She is young and impulsive," said Sprout.

"You are also young. We know what children look like," said Royal Son.

"I felt you taking genetic samples from me, and I'm sure you also took them from her. When you analyze them and compare us to other humans, I'll explain to you all the ways that we differ from ordinary humans. So far."

"Just you two children?" asked Royal Son.

"We have siblings and cousins who share our most significant genetic changes, but only Thulium and I are assigned to do research on your world."

"And your idea of research is to take samples without asking questions."

"Just like yours," said Sprout.

"Ah, but this is our world, and you came uninvited."

"I would be glad of an invitation now," said Sprout.

"But why would your visit have any value for us? We have gained everything we wanted to know from Peter and Royal Mother."

"Of course you haven't," said Sprout, "or why would the raven Dog have gone to Lusitania?"

"You are very uppity for someone begging for permission to stay here."

"You would not have taken samples from us if you didn't have the equipment to allow a close examination of our genomes."

"Would you like access to those machines?" asked Royal Son.

"Maybe," said Sprout. "If you think I could use them."

"Easier for you than for us," said Royal Son. "You have two hands that you can use at once, even though they're big and clumsy."

"Here's an easy question, Royal Son. When someone on this planet sent a radio message to our Box in the sky, containing code to assemble ridiculously complex genetic molecules, was that done by ravens? By keas? Some other birds? Or by humans?"

"I don't know about any transmissions," said Royal Son. "If birds sent them, we are not those birds."

"Thank you," said Sprout.

"For what?"

"For answering my question immediately and, I believe, truthfully," said Sprout.

"I *was* truthful, though I have no idea how you would go about discerning the truthfulness of a kea."

"Neither do I," said Sprout. "But at some level, I unconsciously made the decision to believe you. Whatever part of my mind decided that, I trust it. Of course you didn't begin to *really* answer my question, but you did not attempt to conceal your misdirection, and I believe you don't actually know about the transmissions."

"You do not talk like a child," said Royal Son.

"I would hope not," said Sprout.

"Of course there are humans on this planet," said Royal Son. "But we are the inhabitants of the surface of this world, and you will only meet humans if we decide to allow it."

"Are the humans your prisoners?"

"Absolutely not. But they and we respect our treaties and our boundaries."

"Are you breaking a treaty by telling me they exist?"

"No, because my cousins all agreed that I should tell you."

Sprout looked around at the keas that stood in the grass. They all moved a little from time to time, and every now and then one would flutter upward and drop right back down. If there was a pattern to it, Sprout hadn't detected it.

"Was this decided when I was in the water?" asked Sprout. "Because when I was on dry land, I never heard any kind of discussion."

"You don't speak or understand any of our languages," said Royal Son. "So you did not even know that we were speaking."

Sprout realized that he had never introduced himself, mostly because nobody was listening. "My name is Brussels Delphiki, but everyone calls me Sprout."

"If that is true, then your name *is* Sprout."

"Wang-Mu and Peter called you Royal Son. Does that make it your name?"

"It does in *your* language," said Royal Son.

"You said that if we wanted to know something about your history on this planet, we should ask you first."

"Not me. I'm language, not history."

"By 'you' I meant 'whoever among the kea or the ravens is prepared to tell me.'"

"Nobody is *prepared* to tell you, because we had no idea anyone was coming, till that flying box appeared in the sky."

"Here are the things that we need to know, as scientists," said Sprout. "We need to know how the humans got here, where they came from, when they left Earth's star system, when they arrived here, and which of the plants and animals here came from Earth. Then, if there have been genetic alterations—"

Royal Son squawked. "These are good questions," he said, when Sprout fell silent. "I will find out if anyone wants to answer them, and if it is allowed."

"So I go back to sleep again?" asked Sprout.

"Not this time. It will be easier if you come with me. Walking, not swimming or floating or playing dead, if you please."

16

In Tochoji, capital of Nokonoshima, a meeting was called by the three Delphiki spouses, Yuuto, Mayumi, and Airi. Their spouses were invited. Carlotta and Andrew came at the appointed time.

Mayumi: You came to persuade us to leave our homes, our work, our families, and come with you to a tiny colony world so that we can be parents after all to the children you stole from us eleven years ago. All three of us have said no. Yet you are still here.

Airi: I believe they refuse to take no for an answer, and they are here to continue working on us.

Yuuto: I believe that whatever machine or magical spell allowed them to travel here instantaneously, without a starship, refuses to take them back. I believe that they are trapped here against their will, and so they continue to hope that our love for them will rekindle.

Airi: They must have been traveling at near lightspeed for a few years their time. Cincinnatus told me that my children were still young—the twins about nine years old, Thulium about eight.

Yuuto: So they only recently came upon their means of instantaneous travel.

Andrew: Are we allowed to speak?

Airi: A self-answering question.

Mayumi: I want to know a thing that so far my "husband" has refused to answer. Did you come to this world and court us and marry us and have children with us with a plan, from the start, to carry away our children without explanation or apology?

Airi: At least Ender left you a note that said he was sorry.

Mayumi: I believe that he was sorry. But still he did it. And when he wrote the note, he had not yet kidnapped Petra and Mazer. So at that point, what was he sorry for?

Andrew: Sorry that taking your children would grieve you.

Mayumi: I'm happy that losing my children grieved me. What kind of mother would I be if I took the loss of my children, let alone my husband, without a pang?

Andrew: You're right that we can't yet go home. Nor has anyone explained to us why we can't. So here we are. We'll stop visiting if it's too distressing for you.

Airi: It's merely time-consuming. You talk and talk, and yet you say nothing.

Carlotta: We tell you everything we're allowed to tell.

Airi: Oh, yes, top-secret work—but not for any government.

Carlotta: Our children are extraordinarily brilliant. Like us, they all work in genetics, and they are doing genius-level work on alien genetics.

Andrew: Carlotta.

Carlotta: Shouldn't they know what their children are doing?

Yuuto: I work with genetics at the top level. You know that, Carlotta—we talked constantly. I also know that you believe that you are aliens, or at least not human, genetically.

Airi: I believe they are on Lusitania, where the only surviving alien species lives. Where else could they study them? And they had that hideous disease. Did our children help to neutralize that?

Carlotta: No. It was neutralized before we got there.

Airi: Then what is so secret about anything they're doing now?

Yuuto: There's another alien species.

Andrew: I'm so glad Sergeant isn't here.

Mayumi: Why?

Airi: Because now that we've been told the secret, Sergeant might try to take us off-planet by force.

Yuuto: Or kill us. It's how he thinks.

Airi: You don't know Cincinnatus.

Yuuto: I think *you* don't know Cincinnatus.

Andrew: We're ready to go home. We miss our children.

Mayumi: Oh, *do* you? Maybe that's why you're being kept here, so you can have some taste of what *we* went through when you absconded.

Airi: Except *they* know where the children are, and what they're doing.

Carlotta: The children are so stubborn and self-willed we have no idea what they're doing, or even if anybody is taking care of them.

Yuuto: And besides, Airi, you *do* know where your twins are. They're here in Tochoji.

Airi: But not with me.

Carlotta: By your request.

Airi: They have been turned by their father into hateful little saboteurs.

Carlotta: Mischievous children.

Airi: Spiteful tengu. Like their father.

Carlotta: I assure you that their younger sister, Thulium, is of a completely different character. You would love her. And she longs for you.

Airi: She would be a stranger, like the twins. I knew a baby, not an eight-year-old post-doctoral scientist.

Carlotta: Technically, she hasn't received any formal degrees.

Mayumi: We called this meeting to find out what, if anything, you still want to accomplish.

Andrew: We were sent here. We did not ask to come.

Mayumi: So you don't want to accomplish anything?

Andrew: I mean that we don't know the purpose for which we were sent, beyond asking your forgiveness and begging you to come with us to your children.

Mayumi: And you absolutely refuse to bring them home to *us*.

Carlotta: They're doing work that needs to be done. I know Thulium will be in the thick of it, because she always gets into the thick of things whether invited or not. And since my boy Blue—

Yuuto: My son Delft—

Carlotta: Is her devoted friend—her best friend—she is likely to take him along with her on most or all of her self-appointed projects. She would not come here. Nor would Blue or Sprout. They are doing vital, top-level work. Would you call Einstein away from his thought experiments in relativity in order to babysit or be a substitute teacher of thirteen-year-olds?

Yuuto: Einstein is a name that reverberates through the ages, like Galileo, like Newton. Do you say our children are doing that kind of work?

Carlotta: I'm saying that they will change the future of the human race, yes. I hope for the better.

Yuuto: Then they should not interrupt their work.

Airi: I can't believe the twins are involved with anything serious.

Mayumi: Your husband could tell us if he had bothered to come.

Yuuto: They *are* spiteful tengu, Airi. I don't believe that they could be corralled into doing productive work, especially if they had to obey a project leader.

Airi: I think Cincinnatus brought the twins because nobody else would keep them while he was gone.

Yuuto: For all I know they're building a homemade molecular disruption device, so they can blow up this planet.

Carlotta: Most of the children could probably rig up such a device, if it were possible, but you're right, only the twins would set a timer on it just before they left.

Andrew: I wish I could disagree.

Yuuto: But my children, according to your account, Carlotta, are turning into people worth knowing. I think it has been too long for me to step back into their lives as a father—they've relied on Andrew here and Sergeant as father figures for too long.

Carlotta: Not really. Ender stays aloof most of the time, even from his own children, and Sergeant is, shall we say, the bogeyman to all of the cousins. Neither one an adequate father.

Andrew: Thank you for your encouragement.

Yuuto: Nevertheless, when you go back, take me with you.

Airi: You would give up your position at the university?

Yuuto: I have no challenges ahead of me. Whatever our children are doing is bound to be more interesting than the decades of administrative folderol I see before me. And even if I can't really be a father to my children, they should know me. They should see what they sprang from and decide for themselves if Carlotta made a good choice of father for them.

Carlotta: You are a better man than I deserve.

Yuuto: I said nothing about forgiving you.

Carlotta: Or living with me.

Yuuto: Oh, *that* I'll certainly do. There's a reason I haven't married since you left.

Carlotta: No other woman can take my place?

Yuuto: Which is like saying that no other storm can take the place of a tornado.

Airi: No other wave can take the place of a tsunami.

Mayumi: I'm still not going, Andrew. As your note said, I'm sorry.

Airi: And everything that Cincinnatus says and does convinces me that living with him would be identical to going to the bathroom with Aka Manto.

Mayumi: I'd say "blue" and get it over with.

Airi: No matter what I say, he'll hear "red," and I'll lose all the skin from my back.

Andrew: I think you share knowledge of a story we've never heard.

Mayumi: What a shame you left. Everybody on Nokonoshima knows the tale of Aka Manto.

Airi: And every good child fears that there are tengu under the house.

> —Transcript of meeting: Andrew Delphiki
> and Carlotta Delphiki and their
> spouses Mayumi and Yuuto, also Airi,
> the spouse of Cincinnatus Delphiki
> Source material for Demosthenes,
> "The Delphiki Orphans"

As soon as Thulium saw Jane in the lab outside Q-Bay, she started yelling and then screaming demands at her, until Jane finally came to the Q-Bay intercom to quiet her down. Peter and Wang-Mu, still in quarantine, acted as if they couldn't hear either of them.

"You are not God," said Thulium.

"You should be glad I'm not," said Jane.

"But you act as if you had the *right*—"

"I don't know about the 'right,'" replied Jane. "But I certainly have the power to stop you from doing something offensively stupid."

"Offensive to whom!"

"To Sprout, as I've told you a dozen times already."

"He'll be lost without me!"

"By which you mean *you* are lost without *him*."

"I do not mean that."

"Yet you pester me instead of attending to your work."

"My work is to be down on that planet to help him deal with those damnable birds!"

"If you think they're damnable, then you definitely should not be there."

"What will they do to him? Don't you care?"

"I know that he's still alive, and that he has never wished to leave."

"Why didn't he come back when I did?"

"The philotic connection goes both ways. I think you are so entwined with him that you have the power to carry him with you. But he can sometimes feel smothered by you, so I'm not surprised that he used his own power and will to stay behind."

"You think he chose to be lost and alone among a stampeding herd of insane birds?"

"I know he did," said Jane.

"Send me there to be with him!"

"You would wreck everything," said Jane.

"What would I wreck?"

"I'll be more specific. Everything Sprout has accomplished. Everything he's learned. All of his confidence in himself. And his relationship with you."

Thulium had a dozen answers, but chose none of

them to speak aloud. "You think you know everything."

"Not at all. But I know a lot more than you do."

Thulium had no answer to that, because it was true. And by now, after ranting and screaming and begging and arguing, it had finally occurred to her that if she had listened to anything Sprout told her, she would have conferred with Peter and Wang-Mu and would have known she could only go to Descoladora if she had permission or an invitation. If she had stayed and met the raven Dog, she might have earned such an invitation. Maybe Sprout understood better than she did what the most productive courses of action might be. And maybe, without her overriding all his suggestions, he might make less of a botch of things than she had.

"What work do I have?" asked Thulium quietly. "Here, without Sprout, alone."

"You're not alone, and since I'm keeping the twins quite a few light-years away, you have no one pestering you, either."

Thulium forced herself not to say, Except you.

"Except me, of course," said Jane. "But this past hour, I do believe that it has been you pestering *me*."

"I'll get to work," said Thulium. "I'll go back to processing Peter's and Wang-Mu's data."

"A mature choice. While you're at it, make sure you watch the entire video and audio record of their conversations with the birds, on both of their trips."

"I've already—"

"Stop," said Jane. "You haven't already. You've given them a glance and then brooded about how mistreated you are while the video kept playing out in the holospace in front of you."

"You don't know what I'm—"

"Everybody knows what you're thinking," said

Jane, "because it won't stop coming out of your mouth."

———

When he had looked at the woods while standing in the meadow, it seemed like a random arrangement of trunks with leaves flowing together like water above them. But now, following Royal Son, he could see that the forest was not at all like the ocean. The tree trunks were all different, with branches coming out in different ways, with bark of many colors and textures. Insects crawled and flew among the branches of trees and undergrowth, and many flowers, some of extravagant size and coloration, grew in the dappled shade on the ground.

Other plants grew in the trees, with no apparent attachment to the ground. Were they parasites, or did they get their water from the air? They too had blooms that drew his eye. What nonsense, the idea that flowers were precious and rare!

Or maybe they were. Maybe the birds were stewards of this forest, of all the beauty and life in it, and humans with their stomping feet were not appreciated here.

They walked far—farther than Sprout had ever walked in his life. He was weary and out of breath, even though Royal Son had not led him too quickly. In fact, Royal Son was very considerate, pausing on branches and fluttering his wings when Sprout had lost sight of him, so that Sprout always knew where he needed to go next.

They crossed two small streams. Sprout took off his shoes and stockings to wade across. Royal Son mocked him only a little. "You float like a dead boy in the river, but now you don't want to get your shoes wet." But by now Sprout knew that this was just a game the kea played with him, and he took no offense. Keeping your shoes dry was a rule of hiking—Sprout had learned that from several books he had read as a child.

You are still a child, he told himself. But somehow, by learning to be quiet and stay out of the various quarrels and spats among the cousins on the *Herodotus,* he had trained himself to bear with patience the kinds of things that caused Blue and Boss to leave the room, and Little Mum to try to take charge and calm things down, and the twins to throw things and make dire threats, and Thulium to give her hate stare and then speak her mind in clear, deeply offensive language. That discipline, which allowed him to be nobody's enemy and enabled him to work with Thulium, had given him the strength to do exactly the right thing after Thulium left—nothing. Just bear it all silently, and even when he spoke, ask only informational questions rather than making complaints and demands.

Thulium could not have done it. Sprout's silence would have been wasted, because she would outshout it with her angry speech. Even when she was justified, she sometimes damaged her own cause by making people want to reject whatever she said. But the few times he had tried to point this out to her—or, to be honest, merely hint that things might go better if she acted a different way—she had shunned him for days, or sniped at him about his disloyalty.

When they stopped in a place where enough sunlight came all the way through the canopy of leaves to create a dappled circle of light upon the deep green grass and moss and ferns, Sprout wanted to ask if he could lie down here and rest his legs and feet for just a few minutes.

He didn't have to.

"We're here," said Royal Son.

"Are we meeting someone?" asked Sprout.

"Someone will come, or no one will," said Royal Son.

"Is there anything I should do to encourage them?" asked Sprout.

"You followed me here. You bore the mobbing of the keas. Everyone knows this now. I think someone will come. If no one comes, it's because they're busy. Or they're in awe of you."

"Are you keas so terrible that others are in awe of anyone who survives your treatment?"

"We are worse than you think," said Royal Son, "because that's in our nature and because it's also our job. And they are in awe because they know that you chose to stay when the girl left, and because they know you could have left at any time but you endured all."

"I don't know if I could have left," said Sprout. Better to have that understood.

"But I know you could have," said Royal Son. "I see how you are tied by all those threads, and who you are tied to."

"Who?" asked Sprout.

"If you don't know, then it's not mine to tell," said Royal Son.

There was a rustling in the leaves, coming closer and closer.

"Someone comes," said Royal Son.

Sprout refrained from saying, Do tell. Obviously someone was coming. But it didn't sound like a bird—birds didn't rustle leaves except by the wind of their passing. This sounded more like someone bustling right through the leaves. Like a blundering human. But high overhead.

When it began crashing downward, Sprout could soon see that it *was* a human being—patches of skin, reflecting light; also patches of hair.

But when the newcomer swung down, branch to branch, Sprout realized that this was *not* a human being—or at least not one of the standard design. That he was male was made obvious by his complete lack of clothing. His arms were at least twice as long as his legs, and where feet should be, he had large grasping hands. Sprout was almost surprised that there was no prehensile tail, though only a certain group of monkeys among the primates had such a thing.

The man, if man he was, dropped to the ground from a low branch. He did not walk like a gorilla or chimpanzee. Sprout knew from the vids that those near relatives of humans did not have legs placed directly below their hips, so walking erect was hard for them. But this was a human—the hips were slender and the thighs extended directly below them. And when the man walked, he did not bend to put some of his weight on his knuckles, even though his arms brushed the taller grasses as he walked.

"The child wants a story," said the man. His Stark was heavily accented, but quite intelligible. It occurred to Sprout that he might be speaking with unusual clarity, so that the foreigner could understand him.

"His name," said Royal Son, "is Sprout, and he can fly faster than light, when the need and the power come upon him."

"Then he is a miracle," said the man.

"Sprout," said Royal Son, "this storyteller will speak his name, if he wants you to know his name."

"I am not so wise as to deserve a name," said the man, "but I saw you looking at how long my arms are. You've never seen a man like me before, have you?"

"No," said Sprout, "and I also saw that you walk erect like a man, instead of stooping like a gorilla or a chimp."

"I take that as a compliment. You recognize that despite my unusual shape, I am still a man."

"Yes," said Sprout. "Are you the only one with this shape, or are you part of a people who have all changed in this way from what humans were on Earth?"

"So you believe in Earth," said the man.

"My mother was born there," said Sprout, "and my grandparents, too."

There was a longish silence. Sprout figured the man was deciding whether to take Sprout's words at face value. So Sprout explained. "Many centuries of relativistic space travel."

The man nodded sagely. "That seemed the only way it could be possible."

"I could tell you many things that sound strange, but I will not lie to you," said Sprout.

"I think he really doesn't lie," said Royal Son.

"Shut up, playful idiot bird," said the man. "I came, but don't try my patience."

"Please don't be angry with him," said Sprout. "He's been my only friend here on the planet Nest."

"I'm not angry with him," said the man. "That's how my people talk to his people. They are *much* more rude to us. Because you're here, he has been shockingly respectful."

"Then I apologize for misunderstanding what was going on."

"We expect you to misunderstand," said Royal Son.

"Am I here to tell a story?" asked the man.

"Give him a name to call you," said Royal Son. "It makes these people anxious not to know your name."

The man looked searchingly into Sprout's eyes. "What name are you already calling me in your mind?" he asked.

Sprout told him without hesitation. "Sometimes I

think of you as Long Arms, and sometimes Straight Walker, or Branch Swinger, or Clear Talker."

"Good names for me, every one of them. But all my people have long arms, and walk straight, and swing on branches. I came here today because I know I have unusually clear speech, and I thought a foreigner who speaks a different, more ancient version of Common would need my way of speech to be understood."

"So I should call you Clear Storyteller?"

"Call me Ruqyaq," said the man. "It becomes a powerful name when it's spoken in Quechua."

Sprout tried to produce the same sounds as Ruqyaq, but had some trouble. Ruqyaq did not correct him, though.

"Tell him your questions, Sprout," said Royal Son.

"I'm not sure I remember the whole list I said to you before," said Sprout.

"Whatever you don't know, want to know," said Ruqyaq.

"Then may I start with a personal question?" asked Sprout.

"Ask, and see if I answer."

"When did your people . . . change from the ancient norms of Homo sapiens? The arms, the shoulders that allow you to brachiate, the foot-hands?"

"What do you think?" asked Ruqyaq.

"I think you did not evolve such great changes here on the planet Nest. I think you have a genome that was deliberately redesigned to bring back some of the features of our tree-swinging ancestors, without giving up your brains and your ability to walk and perhaps run."

"I can run," said Ruqyaq.

"Someone had great knowledge of genetics," said Sprout. "You are proof of that. As I also am.

"Our parents and our grandfather," Sprout went on, "had a genetic condition that caused them to grow slowly but to reach very high intelligence far earlier than other human babies. It was called Anton's Key, and the cost of that was that our grandfather grew slowly, but he never stopped growing. When he died, he was a giant. In the weightlessness of space, his heart could keep him alive. But he did not want to die having never walked on level ground again. So his children helped him get into a large colony spaceship whose colonists had all died, but their gardens were lush and full of life. It was a beautiful place.

"He stood by himself for the first time in centuries, and he took two steps, and he smiled at his children. Then his heart gave out and he sank to the ground and died. His body is still there, in that self-contained ecosystem. It has probably been taken apart and its elements incorporated into the life of the place. It's what he wanted.

"But before he died, he saw his brilliant children come up with a genetic change that would preserve the intelligence and early development of Anton's Key, but remove the giantism curse. He knew that his children would not die as he did, with a body whose heart could not sustain it.

"I and the other cousins are proof that the genetic change our parents made in themselves passes on to the next generation. Our other parents were very bright normal humans, but the Giant's Gift bred true in us. I am nine years old, we calculate, but I do genetic science at a very advanced level. So do we all, and any other field of study we turn our minds to, we excel at."

Ruqyaq and Royal Son were silent.

"I came to tell *you* stories," Ruqyaq finally said. "But you have told me of a wonder that I cannot help but believe, because of the small size of the young boy who told it to me."

"I thought you might be more willing to tell me

how you became as you are, if I first told you how I became as I am," said Sprout.

"Not only truth," said Royal Son, "but fairness."

"Do you believe in fairness?" asked Ruqyaq.

"I believe that fairness is always worth striving for," said Sprout, "even though it can't always be achieved."

"And why can't it always be achieved?" asked Ruqyaq.

"Because sometimes there *is* no fair course of action," said Sprout, "and sometimes because no one can think of a fair course. But most often because one side or the other, or both, have no desire for fairness. They seek only their own advantage, no matter what it costs the other, and so fairness remains out of reach for them, because they are not reaching for it."

"Are you quoting someone?" asked Ruqyaq.

"Maybe," said Sprout. "If I am, I don't know who."

"I will make sure your words are written down then," said Ruqyaq, "because I think many people will want to quote *you*."

Sprout was baffled by this. He talked this way to his mother all the time, and sometimes to Thulium. They never thought his way of saying things or the ideas he said were anything special.

"Here is my story. Our ship and crew were part of a great trading clan, the Quispe. We were Andean natives, speakers of Quechua and Aymara, though of course we all spoke Stark as well, since we needed to be understood when we traded with strangers. Our own ship and crew were of the family called Huapaya, though only a few were actually of Huapaya blood. The crew were all considered family, and not mere cousins. If we did our job on the ship faithfully, then we were brothers and sisters, and we called the head of the family Mother or Father. The head of the whole Quispe clan was Grandfather."

Ruqyaq seemed to want a response. "I understand," said Sprout.

"It happened that our Mother loved birds, and studied birds. She had been a scientist on Earth, before she followed her husband into space. So she brought with her two populations of birds that she knew well."

"Keas and ravens," said Sprout.

Ruqyaq smiled. "Because they were the smartest birds of all. She also brought with her the frozen embryos of thousands of other species. And she named our ship the *Ark*, because she said, What if some alien invader destroys Earth? I will be ready for us to find another world and bring to life the plants and animals, the fish and the birds that made Earth such a lovely place.

"They mined asteroids and sent the metals and rare earths back toward Earth, and the clan prospered, and so did the family, even though they never came closer to Earth than the Kuiper Belt. And Mother spoke to her birds, and taught many of her children to love them and care for them, so that when she died the birds would not be abandoned."

"The righteous children," said Royal Son. Clearly he already knew this story; but Sprout understood that it wasn't his to tell, though his own people figured into it.

"Then a race of aliens called Formics entered the solar system and attacked Earth. Heroes managed to destroy their ship and fight them off, but it was only the beginning. We saw a vast fleet forming up and Mother and Father knew that we could not fight them off. We knew that their armaments were superior to ours and if we went back to help in the war, we would die along with the rest of humanity.

"So Mother spoke to all her family in the great cargo hold and said, We call this ship the *Ark*, and so it is, because as long as space is cold, the embryos of life on Earth will remain fresh and viable. Let us go off and find a world where we can form a colony, and there we will be good stewards of the land and sea. We will not defile it, we will not destroy it. We will plant crops that we can eat, and we will release all the animals we can that will not threaten our own lives. We have two lifeboats. We will need one as a landing craft when we arrive, but the other we can fill with everyone who wants to stay here and fight for Earth. That, too, is a noble cause, even if it is doomed. But those who do not go into that lifeboat must promise to be obedient through all the long years of our voyage, for it will surely take several lifetimes at least to reach a viable planet."

"Did anyone go into the lifeboat?" asked Sprout.

"You know that they didn't, because faint hope is better than heroic despair."

"But why would it take lifetimes to reach another world?" asked Sprout. "Relativistic travel allows—"

"When the Formics invaded, humans had no spaceships capable of approaching the speed of light. There are no measurable relativistic effects at five percent of lightspeed. Besides, at lightspeed you had better know where you're going, since there can be no observations on the way. Our ship was capable of this voyage, especially after we took possession of a habitat module from an abandoned trading post in the Belt. It was already growing enough food crops to sustain ten times our population, and it had plenty of room for us to set our birds free to soar and fly, to nest and breed."

"You could not return to Earth, so you carried Earth with you," said Sprout.

"We did," said Ruqyaq. "That is how we started out. We had no plan to become geneticists. We had no plan to alter ourselves or the birds. But within the first ten years of the Flight, a certain group of people called themselves the Engineers, because they were the ones who made repairs and invented new machinery on the inside and outside of the ship. They were constantly leaving the parts of the ship that rotated to create gravity, and spent most of their time in weightless space, inside or out."

Sprout thought of what Outside and Inside meant to those who traveled instantly, but kept himself from interrupting with a useless digression.

"The Engineers could see how dangerous it was to have regular human shape, because we had only two grasping limbs, and our feet merely got caught on things. So we asked Mother—Father had died by then—we asked her if we could explore ways to modify our genes so that our children would be better suited to the labor we did. I am now what they planned then. Mother said yes, and the Engineers joined with two who called themselves Scientists, and while they could still access communications with Earth, they learned all they could about genes and how to modify them."

"So you were still in contact with Earth when the war ended," said Sprout.

"Yes. We knew of the miraculous victory of Mazer Rackham. We also had enough friends in the International Fleet that we knew that the public story was a lie. Mazer Rackham had figured out that all the Formic ships acted from one point of view, and which ship contained that point of view. He violated his orders and launched a missile and it destroyed that smallish ship. And the war was over, because when the Hive Queen died, so did all her workers and soldiers."

"Were you tempted to come back to Earth?" asked Sprout.

"Mother gave us all a choice," said Ruqyaq. "And all of us decided that two things were true. First, it was obvious that the Formics would come again to avenge their dead Queen. The war was not over. Second, the mission we were already embarked on was the salvation of the human race, because until we had a viable, self-sustaining, open-air colony on a habitable planet, the human race was vulnerable to utter destruction. But if we were on two worlds, then if one was destroyed, the other might live on."

"There are hundreds of such colonies now," said Sprout.

"And it took us so long to arrive that I'm sure many of them are older than ours," said Ruqyaq. "But no such colony missions had set out when we left. As far as we knew, we were the only one. And here is the thing that still makes us the potential salvation of the human species: We are not on any of their charts or maps. Our name is not known. Our existence is unsuspected. We did not announce our plan even to Grandfather and Grandmother. No one knew what happened to us. So if some enemy seeks to destroy all the human worlds, and finds every one of them that is mapped, every one that is on the trade routes, they will not find us."

"Except now my people know you're here," said Sprout.

"But you haven't told anyone else," said Ruqyaq.

"We have not," said Sprout.

"Because you also haven't told the other worlds about your instantaneous travel," said Ruqyaq.

"We have not, though on several worlds there are people who have enough evidence to guess," said Sprout.

"A guess is not knowledge and a rumor of such a miracle will not be believed."

"We're counting on that," said Sprout.

"The children of the Engineers were born to look

like us. The plan was a good one. With specially designed space suits they could work outside the ship with far greater safety, for they could hold on tightly with one hand, glove locked in place, while three other hands could do the work. Inside the ship, normal children would gather to watch that first generation of long-armed, four-handed Engineers as they brachiated easily throughout the ship, regardless of whether this or that part was weightless or had some kind of centrifugal gravity. The Runa, the Folk, the normal people—they had to watch their children to try to keep them from imitating us, because they could get injured or die, imitating the way we lived and worked."

"So you call your people Engineers?" asked Sprout.

"We call ourselves the Yachachiyruna, and each of us is a Yachachi. We hardly use Quechua anymore, except in holy ceremonies, but in those days it was simply the Quechua word for engineer or technician, and now it is our name."

"And you live here among the trees."

"During spring, summer, and autumn," said Ruqyaq. "In winter, we go underground with the Runa. It can be bitterly cold up here, ice and snow make the branches slippery, and we would rather live underground for part of each year than try to live our lives with clothing. There *is* no clothing that gives us the freedom of movement that we need."

"Thank you for answering my question," said Sprout.

"I was glad to tell you. It is the short version, of course. There are hundreds of stories on the same theme, dealing with particular events during the Journey and when we first arrived at the Nest. Someday you may hear those stories."

"Have you written them down?" asked Sprout.

"Writing is not telling," said Ruqyaq. "I'm sure

that down below, they have written everything true and everything else as well. What is that to us? Only through the ears can a story be well told and be well heard."

Sprout wasn't sure this was true, considering that most of his knowledge of everything outside his own family's dynamics had come from reading. But then, maybe it *was* true, and he was woefully undereducated.

"Was that your only question?" asked Ruqyaq. "I think not, because you had questions before you ever knew that people like the Yachachiyruna even existed."

"In telling me the story of the Yachachiyruna," said Sprout, "you also answered my questions about the *Ark,* and the reason why no one knew of this colony world. But I am just as interested in the story of how ravens and keas acquired human speech and human knowledge. In the science I was taught, corvids and parrots are the most intelligent of birds, but their intelligence is rated as being somewhere between that of horses and of dogs."

Royal Son gave a squawk.

"Shut up, parrot," said Ruqyaq.

"I don't even know what that would mean," said Sprout. "I've never seen a horse or a dog, except in vids. But the brains of birds are nowhere near the size of mammal brains, and certainly not primate brains. How can they contain so much knowledge?"

"While Royal Son preens and otherwise shows his resentment, I will tell you: We did not modify the genomes of the birds. During the voyage, the birds bred intelligence into themselves. They have many more generations per century than humans have, and the ravens began determining which birds should pair up and breed. Ruthlessly they killed those that they determined should not breed at all. By the time we arrived at the Nest, all the living ravens understood human speech. As we formed our colony, the ravens scouted for us and reported to us about the flora and fauna of this world."

Sprout vaguely remembered that there was something about a raven in the story of Noah and his Ark, but he kept that thought to himself, because *this* story was apparently true.

"The ravens continue to breed themselves into ever greater intelligence," said Ruqyaq. "The keas saw how closely the ravens communicated with the humans, and the great advantages they gained, and so the keas began, in their playful way, to encourage the most intelligent birds to mate. But they don't kill anybody. Stupid keas are just as useful to the flock as smart ones. I think you'll understand, Sprout, that the ability to aim poop at a target and to choose whether to include uric acid with the poop can be learned and strengthened with practice, without requiring deep intellect."

"They all seemed to have excellent aim."

"The keas don't let really smart ones like Royal Son rule over them, but when there's a game afoot, they'll join in, and follow the rules that a smart one lays out for them. And remember, even stupid keas are really, really smart."

"Only one 'really' was needed," said Royal Son.

"So humans did not create the talking ravens or the talking keas. But we recognized that they were people, just as the Yachachiyruna and the Folk are people. We agreed to share this world. After two centuries in a spaceship, even with the habitat, the Folk were uncomfortable in open air, under the sky, but the ravens and keas loved it. They belonged here on the surface. So did the Yachachiyruna, during warm seasons. So we, too, make nests in the forest canopy, and raise our children in the sky. But we build no buildings. That's for the miners, the ones who burrow deep into the stone."

"Where do you grow your food?" asked Sprout. "We couldn't see any evidence of agriculture, at least not from space."

"You walked through the meadows, didn't you?" asked Ruqyaq. "What kinds of grasses do you think those are? No one mows them except at harvest time. In swamps we grow rice, and the rice reseeds itself. The wheat and maize do the same, and though the rodents eat many of the seeds, their fewmets fertilize the ground. We encourage beans to grow between harvests, to replenish the nitrogen in the soil. The whole world is a vast farm, which we harvest at need. So you saw our farms from space. It looked like nature to you."

"Those are all the questions I feel I should ask, and you have answered them beyond my best hopes."

"I told true stories."

"As did I."

"Yet here we are, and you choose to end our conversation?"

"The other questions I have are scientific. Genetic, specifically. Here on the surface, do you Yachachiyruna study genetics?"

"We study everything that the Folk study, and during winter we use all their machines, and design new ones for them. We're still the best engineers, and we go down and solve problems for them all year. So when it's time for you to study our genes, and the genes of the birds and our stingless bees, it is as likely to be a Yachachi who works with you as not. But I know the real barrier. The first message we sent you was of a huge and peculiar gene, a virus of sorts. That was because we thought you might be the people who sent it to us, so we sent our version back to you, to say, Are you the people who made this? And your answers are still inscrutable."

"As are your messages," said Sprout. "In the Box up there, some of them think you created that virus. On our world, it caused horrible devastation and destroyed the biota of a planet. So if you sent it, then you must be an enemy."

"We met that virus when we got here, but it didn't come on us as a disease, and it destroyed nothing. We found a complex though primitive biosphere on Nest, and we have worked carefully to try to avoid extinguishing any of the native species. But that virus didn't kill anything."

"What do you call it?" asked Sprout.

"The Recorder," said Ruqyaq.

Sprout was baffled. "Why?"

Ruqyaq looked at him as if he were crazy. "Because that's what it does. It records."

"Records what?" asked Sprout.

"Genomes," said Ruqyaq. "What did *you* think it did?"

Sprout sat there in silence, thinking, trying to make sense of how they could think of the descolada as such a harmless thing, when it had seemed like the end of the human species if it once got free from Lusitania.

"I think," said Sprout, "that it's time for me to—"

"Go home," said Royal Son.

"Report to your people," said Ruqyaq. "But I tell you first: You are always welcome here, Sprout. You are invited."

"By the keas as well?" asked Sprout.

Royal Son made a couple of trilling sounds. "We regard you as our friend."

As soon as he said that, several keas flew into the clearing and dropped pieces of Sprout's stolen gear at his feet. But they brought none of Thulium's things.

Sprout said, "Thank you, my friends." He gathered up the gear and stuffed it into his pockets as best he could. It certainly wasn't everything he had brought, but it included the most expensive things. "I hope I'll be able to come back. This has been an amazing day, but your kindness has been—"

"Flattery flattery," said Ruqyaq. "Yes, we're amazing, you're amazing, now let's not be like people who can't leave the party because they stand at the door saying good-bye forever. It's time for you to go, so . . . go."

Ruqyaq looked at him as if he expected Sprout to simply disappear.

And Sprout thought of Q-Bay, and how much he wanted to go there and tell everybody what he had learned.

Just like that, Ruqyaq wasn't there. Royal Son was gone, the trees were gone. Sprout stood in Q-Bay, with daylight streaming through the windows of the lab. Nobody was working in the lab. Hadn't they left anyone to watch for him?

Oh, right. They didn't know that Sprout had somehow learned to transport himself. Or else maybe Jane simply read his mind and knew he wanted to come home, and *she* transported him. At the moment he didn't care which, because he hadn't aspired to the power anyway.

So maybe Jane knew he was back, and maybe she didn't. Sprout looked for the phone, found it, and dialed the number of the mess hall.

"We're not serving until five-thirty," said the head cook.

"This is Sprout. Brussels Delphiki. I don't think anybody knows I'm back, but I'm in the quarantine bay. Would you let somebody know I'm here?"

"Oh, so I have to cook dinner *and* run errands for lazy children?"

"You know I can't leave Q-Bay, and there's no-body else here. I wouldn't call you if I had any other choice."

"You mean this is the only phone number that you know?"

"I never need to call anybody else because they're always in my face."

She laughed. "I'll run your errand, space boy."

She hung up before Sprout could thank her. He lay down on an examining table and relaxed, hoping to catch a few winks before the tests and debriefing began.

17

Thulium: Surely you're not taking Sprout's story seriously.

Jane: Is he known to be an extravagant liar?

Thulium: Not till now. But a man with ape arms but straight legs?

Jane: Remember that I have access to ancient databases. There *was* a trading clan called Quispe, and the individual ship called *Ark* disappeared during the time of the First or Second Formic War. The family that commanded that ship was named Huapaya. They included speakers of Quechua and Aymara.

Thulium: But anyone who knows anything about linguistics knows that Quechua and Aymara aren't even from the same language family. They all shared the Andean habitat, and their phonemes and morphemes influenced each other, but the languages were not mutually intelligible.

Jane: Thank you for providing me with a little lesson in linguistics.

Thulium: Sprout got that wrong.

Jane: Sprout has not accessed the databases that include Quispe, Huapaya, *Ark*, the fact that they were Andean natives, and when the ship disappeared. So he got all those correct by chance?

Thulium: The whole story, the birds, the tree-man—

Jane: Yachachi. Engineer.

Thulium: Cannot be taken seriously.

Jane: So all this time when we've taken you very seriously, including my teaching you how to transport yourself and others Outside and In, that was appropriate. But taking Sprout seriously, that is simply impossible.

Thulium: The situations are not at all alike.

Jane: Let's both ponder that statement for a while, not forgetting the points that Sprout got right, before we talk again.

—Transcript: Thulium Delphiki and Jane Ribeira as cited in Demosthenes, "The Delphiki Orphans"

Sprout sat in Q-Bay, reading an old book from pre-war days. It had been intended as a cutting-edge explanation of deep physics and deep astronomy, and now it was almost laughable. Yet somehow the humans of that era managed to get into space, and when the Formics came, they were able to start from that shaky scientific platform and reach near-lightspeed starflight and create the ansible in only a few years—months, really.

So it doesn't take accurate or complete information, thought Sprout, to be able to make giant leaps in technology that move right past the theory—or contradict it completely. It just takes an open, inventive mind.

He wanted to say this to Ruqyaq. But Sprout didn't know if he'd ever see Ruqyaq again.

Of course, if he really did have the power or the skill or whatever it was to make the Outside-In leap, then nobody could stop him from going back.

Ruqyaq and his people didn't need a human child to look after. Sprout could not possibly keep up with them in the trees. And the people who lived underground had not invited him because he had never met any of them. So he would not go back on his own. He would have to wait for the Ribeiras and the Delphikis to believe him.

I have never done anything to earn their distrust. They know from Peter's and Wang-Mu's vids that the keas really do steal everything. Why should they doubt that they did the same to me?

But Sprout knew that there was nothing rational about his story. They really encased his head in so much poop that hardened into cement? Peeing on it made it soluble again? He held his breath three minutes in the water?—well, they all knew he could do *that*—and then the whole thing about Ruqyaq. His body, and then his story. Everyone except Thulium had listened in silence, and when he concluded, Jane merely thanked him. And that was all.

Thulium should have realized that Ruqyaq's history completely vindicated her idea that the descolada did not originate on Nest. But she seemed most skeptical.

And he was still in quarantine.

There was no reason now for quarantine to take so long. If somebody was going to catch a dire disease, it would have shown up already. A brief blood scan should do the job, along with a visual inspection of the epidermis, mouth, nostrils, and ears, to make sure there were no unfelt injuries or attached parasites.

Who imposed the quarantine rules? Who had the authority to change them? Was there any kind of government in this project? Was it Jane? Or Ela? Miro? It couldn't be Peter, even if he really was the same aiúa as Ender Wiggin.

Or was it the Hive Queen? Or the consensus of the fathertrees?

Sprout had done nothing wrong. He was on the surface of Nest because Thulium insisted on taking him there. He stayed, because he thought she was giving up too easily, and the events proved him right. He didn't deserve to be dropped from the project for his initiative, his . . .

Nobody has dropped me from anything, Sprout told himself. Nobody has told me anything, so why assume the worst?

Surely they're not listening to anything Thulium says. In retrospect, her snide comments during his account sounded like resentment—he had succeeded where she failed; he had stayed when she gave up. That would be intolerable to Thulium, of course. Sprout would smooth it over with her, once he got out of here.

The lights in the lab came on.

It was the middle of the night on Lusitania. Who would be arriving?

Sprout set down his library book on the table beside his chair, and stood up.

Jane was at the door. She was unlocking it. But she wasn't alone. Miro was to be expected, but also Peter and Wang-Mu, Thulium, and from the Box, Ela and Quara. Plus three Formic workers and three pequeninos. It was like a diplomatic conference. Or a panel of judges.

"Come on out, Sprout," said Jane. "We're changing the rules. Quarantine shouldn't take more than fifteen minutes in the future."

Sprout said nothing. Nor did he move toward the door.

"Come on out of there, Sprout." He knew this second voice, because it was so strange and memorable. His eyes quickly found the raven on Wang-Mu's shoulder.

"Are you Dog?" asked Sprout.

"Arf," said Dog. "Woof."

"Did you meet the Hive Queen?" asked Sprout.

"I hear you met a Yachachi," said Dog.

Thulium gave a little bark of a laugh.

"I'm the Dog, Thulium," said Dog. "No barking, please."

"Thulium thinks that Sprout has exaggerated his experiences after she left him on Nest," said Jane. "She's a skeptic."

"Or a heckler," said Peter.

Dog hopped onto Jane's shoulder. "Why should there be any doubt?" she asked. "Look at the vids."

"The keas took Sprout's recording devices within thirty seconds of arriving on Nest," said Wang-Mu.

"Of course," said Dog. "But I asked Royal Son to make sure all recording devices were immediately delivered to the Yachachiyruna, and they should see to it that everything was recorded."

"Where is the gear that Sprout brought back with him?" asked Peter.

One of the pequeninos handed him several plastic bags. He reached into one and removed the cam. In a few moments, it was plugged into a computer, while Wang-Mu set it up to display on the largest holopad in the room.

There stood Sprout, with bright-colored keas bombarding him with bird feces. At first he was embarrassed, but Sprout quickly became fascinated with the way the birds performed accurate bombing runs without ever making it look like they were organized in any way. They came from everywhere, at seemingly random intervals of a second or less. And there was Sprout, sinking to his knees, then wiping the sludge away from his mouth so he could speak.

"Did I see some of that go into your mouth, Sprout?" asked Ela.

"You don't want them to add it to the menu here," said Sprout softly.

A few people chuckled.

"You can skip past this, it's not interesting," said Sprout, trying to avoid the whole business of discovering he couldn't scrub his face clean, and then stripping off his clothes and playing dead, and all that stuff.

"It's extremely interesting," said Ela.

Was she in charge of this gathering? Was Ela head of the project after all, even though she was far from the smartest person working on it? Well, he only assumed that, because she wasn't a leguminid. She *had* come up with the altered descolada that saved Lusitania and, along with it, the whole human species.

So Sprout rocked his head back and watched every moment of the vidice through his nearly-closed eyes, the way he watched scary scenes in movies when he was younger. Whoever was holding the camera did a good job of pointing it at everything that mattered, including the keas laying out his clothes on the grass before he returned to them. They made a game of it, of course, and the whole process looked disorganized, including the birds that got inside his underwear and pushed it into his trousers, while other keas held his waistband open. Chaos, chaos, and then the keas all flew off and the clothes were laid out perfectly, as if Sprout had only just been spirited away, leaving the clothes behind.

"Gotta admire those keas," said Miro.

"Pesky little jerks," said Dog.

"Like I said," Miro affirmed.

Sprout watched himself get dressed, clumsily because the clothing kept sticking to his wet skin.

Then the vidrec got confusing, because the person holding it was apparently still filming while brachiating through the trees. A couple of times an out-of-focus shape appeared at the very top of the holodisplay, and it was Wang-Mu who said, "The Yachachi must be operating the cam with his foot, while he swings using his arms."

"It's giving me a headache," said Thulium.

"You don't have to watch," said Jane, utterly without sympathy in her voice.

Oh, thought Sprout. Jane is angry with Thulium. Well, that's better. It meant that not everybody shared Thulium's point of view.

And then there were slight gasps, murmurs, even chuckles when Ruqyaq came down and Royal Son made the introductions. Wang-Mu paused the playback while most of the people in the room walked around the holodisplay to see from every angle. Of course, the vid was taken in only two dimensions, but the playback extrapolated from all the footage, and from every view, to create a reasonably accurate replica of angles that the cam hadn't actually picked up at the time.

Wang-Mu resumed the playback, and they listened to Sprout's account of the leguminids and Anton's Key, and then Ruqyaq's story of the Folk and the Yachachiyruna. The playback ended just before the time when keas brought back most of Sprout's gear—including the cam that made this vidrec.

"Thank you," said Sprout to Dog.

Dog bobbed his head. A nod? Probably.

"If I had known this vidrec existed," said Ela, "I would not have called such a meeting."

"It wouldn't have been necessary if we had simply believed Brussels Delphiki in the first place," said Jane. "He's known to be a truthteller, and I had independent corroboration of the existence of the trading family and the mining ship that Ruqyaq told him about."

"Better to have the whole thing," said Ela. "It's hard to imagine what too much evidence would look like."

Thulium spoke up. "You look at it every day. It's the whole universe, in every detail, through every moment of time."

She was greeted with dead silence.

Sprout couldn't have that. "Hey," he said. "That was funny."

"Not very," said Peter.

"That was Thulium saying that she's sorry she doubted me," said Sprout. "And now this is me saying that if I hadn't lived through it, I don't think I would have believed it either."

Sprout felt a hand on his shoulder. It was Quara—the Ribeiras' difficult child. Well, Sprout knew that Thulium wasn't the Delphikis' difficult child—that would be the twins, individually and in the aggregate. But he still felt moved that Quara, who had often behaved like Thulium in the past, was the one who acknowledged his forgiveness of Thulium.

"Please settle something for me, Jane," said Thulium.

"There's something left to settle?" Jane asked.

"When I left Nest, I thought I was bringing Sprout back with me. But he wasn't with me when I arrived. Did I take him Outside, but he returned Inside to a place of his own choosing? Or did I never take him anywhere, and he just remained there on Nest?"

"And this makes a difference to you because?"

"If Sprout brought himself back Inside to a place of his choosing," said Thulium, "then he's as capable of this leaping thing we do as I am."

"Not as practiced, perhaps," said Jane, "but as capable, yes."

"Can anyone learn it?" asked Thulium.

"We know that it comes easily to leguminids," said Jane. "And also to Peter Wiggin and Si Wang-Mu. Not to mention Miro. But the Hive Queen assures me that most aiúas lack the capacity to carry anyone besides themselves completely. Things would fall apart Outside, and not all could be brought back In."

"Unpleasant," said Dog. "I take it my aiúa—the thing we call inwit, I believe—is *not* one of those capable."

"I don't understand your brains," said Jane. "You have capacity far beyond brain size."

"Our brains are organized on different principles than your mammalian brains. Dinosaurs also had very small brains to control gigantic bodies. Whatever tricks *their* brains played to bring it off, our brains also did. But it isn't a matter of brain size, is it, Jane?"

"Dog," said Sprout, "what Jane is reluctant to tell you is that she doesn't know if she's ready to train any of the birds of Nest. Imagine if vast hordes of keas suddenly appeared on any populated world and played a game of chaos with the people there."

"Sounds fun," said Peter.

"Disastrous," said Dog. "But ravens are not keas."

"Sharing this with other humans is perilous enough," said Jane. "If you *can* learn to do it, Dog, then the power would be forever out of my control. You would share it where you wanted. And I would have unleashed chaos on the universe."

"How do you control these humans—these *children* you've already shared it with?"

"I can watch over them, because they're only a few, and whatever they do with it I can undo instantly. But it's beyond my bandwidth to be able to control a thousand ravens."

"I don't want the power," said Dog. "I just wondered if you *would* teach me, if I had a good reason to desire it."

"Dog," said Jane, "I will refuse you nothing. You don't need a reason. But give me time to sort things out. Wait until we meet with the people underground on Nest. The Folk, Ruqyaq called them."

"The Runa," said Dog. "It's the Quechua name for themselves. 'The Folk' is a decent translation. Their language is called Runa Simi—'folk talking.'"

"The Runa," said Jane. "When can we meet them?"

"When I go back home," said Dog, "I will invite Ruqyaq and Royal Son and Phoenix to go with me to talk with the Huapaya. The leader of the Runa."

"Thank you," said Jane.

"We will tell them all that we have learned," said Dog. "Then the Huapaya will call a Council and they will decide what to do about you."

Sprout finally spoke up again. "Dog, you watched the vidrec. Since I didn't know it was being recorded, I did what I would do if no one was watching except the keas. Please tell me. Did I do well, or did I make mistakes? If I made mistakes, I want to learn from them so I don't make them again."

Dog flew to Sprout and landed on the table he was seated at. "Sprout, the humans I have met so far could not have chosen an emissary who did better than you. You made no mistakes, because you tried no strategies. You simply responded to ridiculous provocations according to your own inwit, and that is always the right course."

Sprout felt tears dribbling down his cheeks. Foolish child, he told himself. Yet he knew they were tears of relief, because his deepest self-doubt had been answered, had been taken away. He could trust himself.

Which meant he didn't have to rely on Thulium to tell him his worth.

"When can we go back?" asked Sprout.

"I will send Dog back at once, if she wants to go," said Jane. "Or she can stay as long as she wants, and see whatever she wants to see, and speak with anyone who won't die of heart failure to have a raven talk to them."

"May I take a copy of that vidrec back with me?" asked Dog. "I believe it will be as convincing to the Folk as it was to you."

"Can your computers read it?" asked a pequenino.

"Our computers and yours work on the same principles," said Dog, "because everybody had computers before the Huapaya left the Sol System. I assume the rec is both two and three dimensional."

"It can be read either way," said the pequenino.

"Good."

"I will go with you to help them understand the format of the drive," said the pequenino.

"The Yachachiyruna will figure it out and make it work," said Dog. "But your offer was thoughtful and brave. Since humans always need names, I assume you, who work with humans, have one?"

"I am called Fingers," said the pequenino.

"Don't all your kind have fingers?"

"Fingers is a translation of 'digits,'" said Finger. "Because I work with digital machines and know how they work, my people call me Fingers, and so do the humans here—the few who ever ask a pequenino for a name."

"Can't they tell you apart?" asked Dog. "They can't tell ravens or keas apart until one of them speaks."

"They know me well enough," said Fingers. "Because when there's a computer problem to solve, they don't ask any of the other pequeninos to help. Just me."

Quara laughed. "Well, it's nice to know how careless and stupid we look to the people we pretend to respect."

"Respect is always a pretense," said Si Wang-Mu. "It begins as a game of pretending, and then as the players come to know each other, it *can* turn into real respect, or it can remain pretense forever, because nobody is worthy of it."

"How very quotable," said Quara.

"I know," said Wang-Mu. "Because I was quoting. Han Fei-Tzu, who was my teacher for a few months, said and wrote many wise things. I will give you the titles of his books."

"I look forward to it," said Quara.

To Sprout it sounded as if Quara was being sarcastic. But if Wang-Mu didn't realize that, or saw the sarcasm but chose to take it at face value, it was none of Sprout's business. *He* wanted to read the books, but he'd talk to Wang-Mu about it later.

"I assume," said Ela, "that everyone here agrees that we should accept Sprout's report as originally given, with augmentations from the vidrec. Anyone to the contrary?"

Nobody spoke, nobody moved.

"Then the report is accepted, and we will all study it to form the basis for further action," said Ela.

Peter chuckled.

Sprout saw that Wang-Mu made a subtle gesture to him. He assumed it meant, "Shut up," but in the nicest possible terms.

"You are amused?" asked Ela.

"Nobody ever 'accepted' Wang-Mu's and my reports," said Peter.

"Nobody ever doubted them," said Ela. "And you brought back Royal Son and Dog."

"Can I get dressed in regular clothes now?" asked Sprout.

"First get your hair cut," said Ela. "Not all the bird crap came out of your hair, and cutting it shorter will probably be easier than finding a useful chemical solvent."

18

Talker: I can witness your conversation from here. No need to come inside.

Peter: Thank you

Jane: What is it that's so important you wanted to say it in the presence of the Hive Queen?

Wang-Mu: We were discussing Quara, and her efforts to make sure we don't inadvertently do what happened when the Formics first came to Earth.

Talker: What happened on Earth was my fault. I had never conceived of sentient beings who could not speak mind to mind, as my Sisters and I do.

Wang-Mu: As soon as you realized your mistake, you stopped trying to colonize Earth. But you knew of no way to communicate this to us. And we ended up killing all the Sisters except you, in your cocoon, left behind for Ender Wiggin to find.

Talker: You were discussing that tragedy of errors, and?

Wang-Mu: And Peter thought of something I thought was very important.

Jane: And yet Peter lets you talk for him. Are you Peter's Talker?

Wang-Mu: He did not think it was as important as I did.

Peter: I think it's important. I just think it's also obvious, and telling you in this formalized way will make my embarrassment all the more.

Jane: He's shy.

Wang-Mu: In a pig's eye.

Peter: A Hive Queen came to Earth with one goal, to prepare the planet for settlement by her and her brood. She set to work, and all the human resistance was just a pesky primate that had some weirdly sophisticated tools. She kept interpreting events according to the framework she already had in mind.

Talker: Until some of those primates snuck into the scout ship and blew it up from the inside. Using our own tools against us. Too clever and dangerous to ignore.

Peter: But to the humans, *our* purpose was to repel a destructive invader, who was destroying our croplands, killing our people, making Earth uninhabitable for human beings. We had to repel the invaders, so that was *our* single-minded purpose.

Talker: It's sometimes good to remind ourselves of ancient history.

Peter: It isn't ancient history. We're acting out the same tragedy of errors right now.

Talker: Nobody's trying to colonize Nest.

Peter: *We* know that. And I believe that the ravens and keas and Engineers trust us, at least to a degree. Us, and also Sprout, probably to a greater degree.

Wang-Mu: Just as that Hive Queen came intent on terraforming and colonizing, we came with the sole intent of finding the source of the descolada and trying to determine its function. We've made some progress, but we have much, much more to learn.

Peter: That's what Nest is to us. A source of data. But what are *we* to the Folk of Nest, the underground people who left birds and their tree-swinging cousins on the surface as their first line of defense against intruders? What are *we*, as the birds and Engineers come to trust us?

Talker: You are strangers who can appear anywhere, whenever you want, whose box of a spaceship can instantaneously jump to any part of the sky. Strangers with technologies they never dreamed of.

Jane: And we are humans who answered their offering of the descolada genome with cryptic genetic codes and not a word of language. And now our emissaries are making friends with their watchdogs, so they are no longer a line of defense at all.

Peter: Everything we do and say is filtered through that perception of us as terrifying invaders who cannot be kept out.

Jane: And that perception is accurate.

Peter: Just as humans perceived the Formics' terraforming as a brutal assault, how do the Folk of Nest perceive our actions? Spies, seducers, turning their allies into our allies. They have been hidden for millennia, and now they have been found by humans with terrifying, irresistible technology.

Jane: If they think we're irresistible, then they shouldn't resist.

Wang-Mu: We aren't killing anybody. Not one feather of one bird fell because of us.

Peter: But the Folk were underground. They didn't witness any of it. They only know what the birds and the Engineers tell them. And now, because they like us or respect us or whatever it is they feel toward us, the Folk can't trust them to make an honest report.

Talker: You think we may have war whether we like it or not.

Jane: War would be impossible. We will simply disappear when we perceive a threat.

Wang-Mu: Sprout didn't, he stayed and endured his punishment, and I'm not sure what they'll conclude from that.

Jane: They should conclude that we mean no harm.

Wang-Mu: Or that we sent a completely unqualified terrified child who froze up when he was attacked.

Peter: They can't attack us in any way that they believe we will recognize as an attack.

Wang-Mu: But they *will* attack us. They must. They believe we are their worst nightmare come true.

Talker: What do you suggest? Abandoning your mission?

Wang-Mu: We must find out all we can about the descolada.

Jane: But "all we can" must certainly mean "all we can learn without getting killed."

Peter: We need to think what form their attack might take. A trap, an ambush? Certainly. But we can escape from any trap, and they know it.

Wang-Mu: They have to find a way to attack us without our knowing we have been attacked.

> —Conversation: Jane Ribeira, Hive Queen (via Talker), Peter Wiggin, Si Wang-Mu quoted in Plikt, "Peter Wiggin as Ender's Heir"

Jane had gone off with Peter and Wang-Mu, presumably to visit either the pequeninos or the Hive Queen. Still, Thulium realized she must have been able to devote some attention to the leguminids, because it was while Jane was gone that Father came back.

Along with Aunt Carlotta and her husband, Yuuto, and Uncle Andrew and his wife Mayumi. But Father's wife, Thulium's mother, Airi, was not with them.

"She did not choose to come," said Father.

"That's not enough," said Carlotta. "Thulium will take it all personally."

You don't know how Thulium will take anything, Aunt Carlotta. But instead of saying this, Thulium held her tongue.

"Fine," said Father. "*If* you care, Thulium, her decision had little to do with you. Because she met your brothers, she declared herself to be incompetent to contribute to any child-rearing in my family. Unfortunately, she hadn't met you. She might have come, if she had, but it wasn't my choice."

Uncle Andrew chuckled. "I believe that Jane sent the people she wanted to keep out of her way, you and the twins foremost, Sergeant."

"Quite likely," said Father. "But she didn't leave me much time to make my case."

"We're here," said Yuuto. "And since we *do* want to meet our long-missing children, why are we still out here chatting with Cincinnatus's daughter?"

"I'm pleased to meet you, too, Uncle Yuuto," said Thulium. Then she bowed in greeting. "Aunt Mayumi, I'm happy to have a chance to know you."

Mayumi bowed slightly in return. "I see that to some degree, you are different from your brothers."

"I am proud to hear it," said Thulium. "If you find that I resemble them in any way, I hope you'll tell me, gently but clearly, so I can change."

Mayumi smiled at that. "I hear that you and all the children have turned out to be very bright."

"We're all scientists," said Thulium. "We are entrusted with adult tasks and fulfil them well."

"What adult tasks?" asked Father.

At this point, Sprout and Blue came out of the building and shyly approached their father, Yuuto. So Thulium thought they weren't listening when she answered Father, "I work in the Quarantine Bay, analyzing data collected from the surface of Nest."

"What is Nest?" asked Uncle Andrew.

"It's the name the natives use for their own world," said Thulium. "We used to call the planet Descoladora."

"You've spoken to the natives?" asked Father.

"Some of us have," said Thulium.

"Sprout has," said Blue, proudly. "They pooped and peed all over him."

That created a dead silence.

"We'll show you all the vids," said Sprout. "Not as bad as it sounds."

"I think the missing information here," said Thulium, "is that the natives who performed said acts upon Sprout's person were birds. Kea parrots to be exact. And Peter and Wang-Mu spoke with a raven named Dog."

"Ravens? Keas?" asked Father.

"They're fully sentient," said Thulium.

"I'll decide *that* for myself," said Father.

"And trigger an interplanetary incident?" said Sprout.

"You went down to the surface of the planet that sent us the descolada?" asked Father.

"They didn't do it," said Sprout, "but we have plenty of time to lay that out."

Father looked intently at Thulium. "Have *you* been down to the surface?"

"I left as soon as the keas started harassing us. They took all our gear and I realized I couldn't properly do my job, so I . . . left."

"And I stayed," added Sprout thinly.

Aunt Carlotta uttered something that might have been "Hmmm?" or "Hmmmph!"

"Thulium, I don't know what kind of failure of adult supervision this represents, but you are *not* going back to the surface of that planet."

Thulium said nothing, because she knew that he couldn't control her location in space ever again.

"You have your defiant look," said Father. "But I think the adults around here will understand that I am to be reckoned with when I say that anyone who transports you to the surface of Descoladora or anywhere else without my consent will pay severely."

"Will you kill them, Father?" asked Thulium.

"Thule," said Sprout.

"Stay out of this, Sprout," said Aunt Carlotta.

"He can't control where she goes, not anymore," said Sprout. "That's just a fact, it's not defiance or brag or anything else. Just a fact."

Thulium knew that because Sprout's own parents were there, and perhaps because Father had some respect for Yuuto's physical prowess, Father could not face down Sprout the way he would have on the *Herodotus*. So he turned back to Thulium.

Whereupon, with the characteristic wrenching in her gut, Thulium went Outside and In, placing herself next to Sprout with her hand on his shoulder.

Father took a moment to find where she had gone.

Not being a fool, and, more importantly, not wishing to *seem* a fool, he said nothing to show his consternation and, quite likely, fear. "Quite a trick you've learned," said Father, eventually. "Or did Jane do that for you?"

Thulium knew Father well enough to know that her ability to dodge away from him would not be enough. She didn't want to be at war with him, so that meant she had to *win* that war immediately and completely.

So Thulium took herself *and* Father Outside and In, and this time brought him to the place on the riverbank across from the entrance to the hive house, and within sight of the fields being worked by Formic laborers.

Father looked a bit dizzy—but he had been transported before. He understood what had happened.

But the fact that she could carry him with her wasn't her entire point. She looked out toward the laboring Formics. So did Father.

"Everybody thinks they were all destroyed," he said.

"Everybody is supposed to think that. But Ender Wiggin brought her here in her cocoon and reestablished her. They're growing the food that feeds many worlds. Small populations, but still—the Hive Queen is our ally now."

"Who is this 'our' whose ally she is?" asked Father.

"Those of us working on the descolada problem. And visiting the world of Nest to help with our study."

"I have just forbidden anyone to—"

"I have just shown you how useless it is for you to forbid anyone. You're my father, and I love you, but I am a full member of this research team, and I have the power to go wherever in the universe I choose. Forbidding me to do this will only make you look foolish. And if you try to interfere with my work, I'll send you back to Nokonoshima for you to work things out with my mother."

"Don't make threats you can't—"

Finding the location of Nokonoshima in Father himself—not his memory, not his mind, but, Thulium could only suppose, his aiúa—Thulium took him there, and then immediately returned herself to Lusitania, where the others were still gathered. "Father is stubborn," said Thulium.

"It takes multiple demonstrations?" asked Sprout.

"Is that really *you* causing this jumping around?" asked Uncle Andrew.

"It's her all right," said Sprout.

Thulium noticed that he did not even hint that he, too, could do the same stunts. Well, keep it hidden, Sprout, she thought. I won't tell.

"But it's time to bring him back," said Thulium.

This time she didn't go herself. Since she knew where he was, she merely caught hold of him, brought him through the Outside, and set him just a few steps away from the others.

Father looked calm, because that's how he always wanted to look, especially when he was frightened or awed. Instead of speaking to Thulium at all, he looked to Sprout and Blue. "Jane brought us back here. Was there any purpose in it? Is there work for us to do? Or should we try to conceive more children, since the ones we already have are now severed from our parental care?"

Thulium knew that now was the time to speak. "Father, you are not severed from anything, beyond what you did yourself during our lives on the *Herodotus*. All of us lived in terror of you—and of the twins, to whom you were absurdly indulgent. So stop looking for someone else, some adult, to blame and punish for alienating my affection. There is no such person. Except yourself. *You* alienated my trust and affection and you've spent my whole life doing it. You kidnapped me away from my mother and taught me to do anything to avoid provoking your rage. So if you want to return to a fatherly role toward me, you need to spend a little time figuring out just how a loving father talks to his very independent daughter, and shows his affection for and trust in her. Then act out that part as best you can until you actually mean it."

"You think I don't love you? Or respect you?" asked Father.

"I think the menacing tone you were trying to conceal, and failing, is your own answer. I think if you do love me, you've hidden it from yourself so it won't interfere with this hyper-manly show you are always putting on in order to bully and dominate your siblings and the cousins."

"You talk to me this way, while asking me to love you?"

"I'm not asking you to love me," said Thulium. "I personally believe that you can't. I only said that until you show me love and respect, you will have no further influence or authority over me. I said it in front of witnesses so there can be no mistake. Now go to bed."

And with that she transported Father to his assigned room in the compound.

Carlotta turned to Sprout. "Is it your turn now to make that speech to me?"

"Have you ever treated me as Uncle Sergeant treats Thulium?" asked Sprout.

"I hope not," said Aunt Carlotta.

Sprout hugged her. And Yuuto placed a hand on Sprout's head. Sprout raised a hand to lay on top of his father's hand. "Welcome, sir. I would say 'welcome home,' but this isn't your home, and it isn't our home. But it's where we're working for now, so . . . I'm glad you're here."

"And I'm glad to meet you, Brussels," said Yuuto.

"When you have time," said Sprout, "I have a very funny vid to show you."

"I hope it will include the time that birds pooped and peed on you," said Yuuto.

"Remind me not to be there," said Aunt Carlotta. "I don't think I want to see."

"Oh, you do," said Thulium. "Because Sprout was extraordinary. He was *great*."

And Sprout's smile told her that if their friendship had been damaged when he stayed behind on Nest, it was healing well.

19

Thulium: After three thousand years or so, their population must be in the tens of millions. Hundreds of millions.

Sprout: Or they control their own reproductive rate.

Thulium: Or they don't all live underground.

Sprout: We know that. The Yachachiyruna are partly underground and partly in the forest.

Thulium: So let's say the Folk really do live underground except at harvest time and planting time. They didn't *always*. They must have begun their colony on the surface where the sun shines.

Sprout: Probably.

Thulium: Why did they make the move underground?

Sprout: I bet you think you know.

Thulium: They found out that the ravens and keas couldn't share the surface world with humans. The Yachachiyruna were fine—I think they're the ones that have educated ravens and keas so well in human languages and history and all. But the only way to keep the peace was for the humans to live as far as they could from the mischief of the keas.

Sprout: They're just playing.

Thulium: Savagely and selfishly. So the Folk gave up the surface, except for crops, and underground they set up a water and sewer and ventilation system and then carved out whatever they needed. The birds couldn't thrive down there—nothing for them to eat, and they need room to fly. So the birds live on the surface, and the Engineers swing around in the trees, and you can't tell me that there isn't a substantial group down below who deeply resent the bargain their ancestors made and are agitating to return to the surface, which would mean war. And now you and Peter and Wang-Mu make friends with the ravens and keas and the Engineers, and you've set us up as allies of one side and foes of the other.

Sprout: For reasoning based on guesses based on hypotheses based on doubtful premises, you've built a pretty elaborate structure.

Thulium: We need to meet with the Folk. And we shouldn't be led to them by the surface dwellers. We should go straight down. Appear among them without intermediaries.

Sprout: Because people always trust visitors who magically appear in their house.

—Conversation: Thulium and Sprout
quoted in Plikt, *Leguminidae*

Peter and Wang-Mu arrived in the meadow near the Council trees, and in a few moments a raven dropped down into the grass.

"Are you Phoenix? Or Dog? Or some raven we haven't talked with before?"

The bird flew up to Wang-Mu's shoulder. "Greetings, Royal Mother of the West."

"Well, we know you're not Royal Son," said Wang-Mu.

"So at least you can tell keas from ravens."

Peter decided it was time for him to speak up. "We can tell corvids from parrots, and we can tell hawks from vultures."

"We have no vultures in our world," said Dog, for Peter now recognized her voice and style of speech.

"Do the Folk underground still have the frozen embryos of falcons and other predatory birds?" asked Peter.

"Why would you want to know?" asked Dog.

"They have obviously been selective about what Earth species they introduced into this world. I think part of your understanding with them is that they will never introduce more predatory birds into the Nest," said Peter.

"We fear brood parasites far more than flying predators. We can deal with hawks and falcons, but brood parasites attack us in the nest, killing our own babies so we'll raise theirs."

"I can't imagine that ravens or keas would be fooled," said Peter.

"We are the birds who speak with humans," said Dog. "We have to speak for all the birds, and try to keep them safe."

"Do they appreciate your intervention on their behalf?" asked Peter. He could feel Wang-Mu growing more anxious. He was treading in perilous territory now, he knew.

"Those that understand, yes," said Dog. "But what difference would it make if they were all ungrateful to us? They still need us, and we will still stand for them."

"Because there is a history of conflict between humans and birds," said Peter.

Silence.

Dog flew off Wang-Mu's shoulder and disappeared in the trees.

Peter immediately lay down in the grass. "It's a little damp," he said. "Either a heavy dew this morning or it rained last night."

"Not afraid of damp," said Wang-Mu, lying down close by. They knew Dog might be three minutes or three hours in her conversation with the Council, and they didn't want to wear themselves out with standing around uselessly.

"I'm betting," said Wang-Mu, "that you have now proven Thulium's theory."

Peter said, "One of her guesses. It doesn't rise to the level of a—"

"The separation of sentient species did not arise out of mutual convenience. It arose as a way of settling either a war or a chronic conflict that everyone feared might turn into war."

"That's what I think we're confirming here," said Peter.

"And what difference will it make, knowing that?" asked Wang-Mu.

"It's easier to make good decisions when you have more information," said Peter.

"And you think Thulium may be paranoid and overly suspicious, but she also might be right," said Wang-Mu.

"She may be little, but she's smart," said Peter.

"When we know almost nothing except by rumor," said Wang-Mu, "our guesses are neither smart nor dumb. What's dumb is to trust those guesses and take irrevocable actions based on them."

"But taking no action at all is also dumb."

"The great human dilemma," said Wang-Mu. "We always act, or fail to act, based on insufficient information. And yet we muddle through, recovering from our mistakes as best we can."

"Quote from Han Fei-Tzu?"

"No," said Wang-Mu. "I think I was quoting *you*."

"Ah," said Peter. "No wonder it sounded so wise to me."

"If it sounds wise, I must be quoting someone?" asked Wang-Mu.

"If you want to take offense," said Peter, "then it doesn't matter what I actually say."

At which point, a raven fluttered over them and landed on Peter's knee, which happened to be upraised at the moment. "Yes," said Dog. "In the second century of the colony, some humans were so furious with the kea that they started making traps for them and caging them where they could do no harm to humans' projects. When the ravens saw it, and heard the grieving of the free keas, the ravens declared a relentless guerrilla war against the village of humans who had done this thing."

"Guerrilla war?" asked Peter.

"We carry no weapons but our talons and beaks," said Dog. "But we are as good at mobbing our enemies as the keas and crows. The humans could go nowhere, do nothing out in the open without constant bombardment, pecking, tearing. Everything they built we broke or weakened. And when that proved not to be enough, we began pecking at their faces, tearing their ears, causing them to bleed down over their eyes. We never blinded any of them, though we could have. We wanted this to be a war whose scars might heal."

"How did they fight you?" asked Wang-Mu.

"They tried to swat us out of the air. They reinvented the bow and arrow, but they were horrible marksmen. To avoid us, many of them in that village took refuge underground. We were content to let them escape us that way, as long as they weren't out where they could be annoyed by the keas."

"Then what?" asked Wang-Mu.

"We opened the cages and set the keas free," said Dog. "That was the foundation of our alliance."

"Peace ever since?" asked Wang-Mu.

"Every few centuries, some group of humans gets on about taking back the surface, with slogans like, 'We made them smart, now make them obedient.'"

"Ah," said Peter. "They acted and talked like humans."

"But they didn't make us smart," said Dog. "We made ourselves smart, during the voyage and after, when we controlled our mating and child-rearing."

"Slogans don't have to be accurate to be effective," said Peter.

"Why does this matter to you?" asked Dog. "It's all history."

"One member of our team suggested that the longer we wait to meet the Folk underground, the more suspicious of us they might become," said Wang-Mu. "If any of them feel resentment against ravens and keas, won't they mistrust us as allies of the birds?"

"Do you really think," asked Dog, "that after the way your craft appeared in our sky and hopped around instantaneously, and after you appeared on the surface without any kind of craft at all, they would mistrust you because you were friends with *us*?"

"Fair point," said Peter.

"I have seen your home planet, Lusitania," said Dog. "I already reported to the Yachachiyruna that your level of technology on the planet's surface is not superior to our own. Only your means of travel."

"That's true enough, on Lusitania," said Peter. "But you met the Hive Queen. She has all the memories of her species. She knows how to build extraordinary starships and death-dealing surface weapons. She knows how to burn your planet to cinders. She will not do it, but don't judge our technological capabilities solely on the basis of what we have on hand. If it came to war, nobody wages more terrible war than the Formics."

"Except the humans," said Dog.

"Well," said Peter, "that goes without saying."

"Your war would not be against birds, but against humans," said Dog.

"There is no war," said Wang-Mu. "There will be no war. Because we will not raise any weapons against you, and if you raise a weapon against us, we'll simply go away."

Dog walked on Peter's knee, circling while thinking of what to say, it seemed. Her claws bit through the fabric into the skin of Peter's knee, causing tiny stabs of pain. Yet her movements also tickled him so he wanted to laugh and complain at the same time.

"I have an idea," said Dog. "Take whatever samples you can gather in the next couple of hours, and then leave. Go back to your planet. Take your box out of our sky. And then forget that you know of the existence of Nest."

Peter thought: That may be the wisest advice we'll ever get.

And he also thought: We haven't yet learned enough about the descolada.

Or do we have enough data now that if we left Nest completely, we could work out the descolada's mysteries on our own?

"It is not our decision to make," said Wang-Mu.

"When you say that," said Dog, "you mean that you, Royal Mother of the West, and your husband, Peter Wiggin the Second of That Name, cannot make the decision about your future course of action without winning the consent of the other members of your team."

"Yes," said Peter. "As you also need to consult the Council of Ravens."

"But Peter Wiggin," said Dog, "will you advocate for your leaving Nest and never coming back?"

"I will tell them your proposal, and I will rehearse for them all of the arguments in its favor."

"But also the arguments against it?" asked Dog.

"He won't have to do that," said Wang-Mu. "The others will unite to present those counter-arguments, and they will overwhelmingly decide to come to Nest and meet with the underground Folk."

"Don't come with them," said Dog.

Peter felt Wang-Mu preparing to speak, and he knew she wanted to say what *he* wanted to say: Why not? But he touched his hand to her hand, and they both said nothing. Peter felt that Dog was giving them a warning, but that she could not be more explicit than she already had been. She was advising them to stay away for their own good. She was warning them that if they went down to meet with the Folk in their underground lairs, it would come to no good.

And yet the descolada researchers *would* come again, and go underground, and whatever dire consequence Dog foresaw would happen.

All I need to do, said Peter, is to stay on Lusitania with my wife and my gestating child. Let the others go without me. I'm not their leader—I'm not a leader of any kind, not even to Wang-Mu. They don't need me. If we stay behind, we will be safe.

That's what I'm going to do, he decided. I'm going

to stay on Lusitania when everybody else overrules us and comes back down here.

Now the question is, will Wang-Mu stay with me? Or will she decide to put our child at risk by joining the expedition?

And then what choice would I have, except to change my mind and go?

———

Thulium had learned to speak and understand Japanese at an early age, though she tried not to show the others what she was doing. They would mock her for yearning for her mother so much that she would try to learn the language of Nokonoshima. Aunt Carlotta was the only one who guessed, and that was probably due to Sprout, who noticed Thulium's actions more than anybody else. Carlotta said to her one day, "You do know that on Nokonoshima, everyone speaks Stark, just like every other planet in the Hundred Worlds."

"I assume," said Thulium. "But that doesn't mean that I shouldn't learn Japanese, so I can read ancient books and watch ancient vids."

And that's as far as the conversation went.

Thulium realized that her mother's refusal to join Father on Lusitania was a rational choice, but it didn't mean Mother did not wish to meet her only daughter. The twins she *had* met—Thulium knew them too well to think they might have made a good impression.

She also knew herself, and how bad an impression she, too, was likely to make.

But if I go to Nokonoshima, to Airi's house in Tochoji, and I do my best to be patient and kind and loving and obedient, then if she still doesn't like me, that only means that she would not have loved me no matter how events had gone. And I will let go of that childish fantasy.

What she absolutely would *not* do was transport Mother Airi to Lusitania against her will. Not just because Jane would never tolerate such a thing, and would surely send Mother back at once, but also because love does not compel. That was the lesson that growing up with Sergeant as her father had taught her: Love does not compel. Love like Aunt Carlotta's for her children. And for Thulium herself.

Walking along the streets of Nokonoshima, Thulium could feel the furtive glances of the people she passed. They were too polite to stare openly, except a few very small children. But she could see that her Lusitanian garb was sadly out of fashion here—and probably had never been in fashion anywhere. Thulium thought of going into a shop and buying local clothing, but before she tried it she remembered that she had nothing that would pass for money here, and that her Stark would have a pronounced accent.

She didn't want to create a stir, just find her mother.

She appreciated the fact that ancient characters were rarely used on signs—the roman alphabet of Stark and English was used on every world. So she was able to find the street she had heard mentioned. It had many apartment buildings, though none was more than two stories high. This colony was too new and uncrowded to need high-rise buildings. Still, it would be a challenge to enter every one of the buildings and try to find her mother's name on a mailbox or address list.

But what was she thinking? She walked behind a delivery truck parked on the street and then made her twisting jump into the lobby of the first apartment building. She searched the listed names and then asked the man who seemed to be the guardian of the place, "Does Airi live here?"

"No one by that name," he said. "I'm so sorry to disappoint you."

She believed that he actually meant it.

In some buildings, she had to leap floor to floor because the names were beside the doors instead of in a central place. But the process was still far faster than it would have been had she been required to climb up and down stairs.

And then she came to a block of standalone houses, narrow and close together, but with no shared walls. The third house she checked had the name Delphiki on the mailbox. Since that was obviously not a common Japanese name, Thulium walked to the door and clapped.

Soon the door opened, and an elderly lady bowed to her. Thulium's heart sank. Her mother could not possibly be that old.

"No, no, don't be disappointed," said the old woman. "I am not Mrs. Delphiki. That will be my daughter, who owns this house."

"Is your daughter's name Airi?" asked Thulium.

Apparently her emotions showed on her face.

"If I am not guessing wrong, I believe you are my long-lost granddaughter, Thulium."

The woman extended her hands, and Thulium bounded forward and they embraced long and hard. "My father never told me that my mother lived with *her* mother," said Thulium.

"I took great pains to make sure I was off visiting friends when he lived here. He and I did not get along."

"He doesn't get along with anyone," said Thulium.

Grandmother changed the subject, as any polite person would. "Please come in and sit with me. Airi will be home from the market very soon now, and then you can prepare dinner with us."

"I have no experience with cooking," said Thulium.

"But after tonight, you *will* have had some experience."

They sat in the front room, on comfortable chairs, and Thulium listened as Grandmother told stories of when Airi was young and had friends and was pursued by fine young men.

"And then a strange man came from another world," said Thulium, anticipating where it all ended. "And he ruined her life."

"He fulfilled her life," said Grandmother. "Airi was madly in love with him, and she bore him three babies—twin boys, and a daughter. Her husband insisted on giving them nonsensical names—rare earth elements?—but Airi thought, I will get used to any name, just to have these children in my life. You lived here, in this very house, for three weeks, Thulium. You crawled in your first week, your body developed so quickly. It was going to be thrilling to watch you grow, because unlike your brothers you had a sweet and loving disposition. Then one day Airi came home from market and her babies were gone."

"Were *you* here?"

"I was," said Grandmother. "I asked him where he was taking you. He said, 'To the park,' and since he had often done that, why would I doubt him? By then the twins were sturdy walkers, so your father carried you and led them out, and so I told your mother when she got home. We waited up all night for him to bring you home."

"He didn't even tell you we were gone?" asked Thulium.

"After the spaceship was out of Nokonoshima's atmosphere, he sent a message by ansible. A text message, not even a vid. And that was when your mother's life ended."

"But she's alive!" said Thulium.

"Of course," said Grandmother. "But she takes little interest in anything. Your father did provide for her—he bought this house, as well as several apartment buildings to provide her with a good income. At first she wanted to refuse all his aid—he had her babies, why would she care about his money? But I am her mother, and I prevented her from doing something flamboyantly stupid in her grief and rage."

"So Father did provide for her."

"Oh, the widow Delphiki is well known for her charitable works and her kind treatment of her tenants. You see that we live simply, not lavishly, so there is always money for her to help those who need it."

Then they talked of other things, half in Japanese and half in Stark, until the door opened and a strikingly lovely woman entered the room, carrying two mesh bags of vegetables and fruits.

Airi stopped when she saw her mother's face. Then she looked where her mother was looking.

"Are you . . ," asked Airi.

Thulium rose to her feet, then bowed deeply before her mother. "I apologize for my father's decisions and actions, and I grieve that I did not have a chance to grow up in your care."

Airi embaced her and wept, and then they sat together, her mother's arms about her, and talked and talked. Thulium didn't notice when Grandmother got up. Only when Grandmother returned and told them that supper was ready did Thulium realize she had left the room.

They ate together, a traditional Japanese meal, or at least the version that was traditional in Tochoji. They talked gently with each other. Only when the food was gone and the bowls were taken into the kitchen did someone ask the question that they were afraid to ask.

"Thulium," said Airi. "Did your father bring you?"

"No," said Thulium. "I brought myself. No one knows that I'm here."

Grandmother nodded and said, "This next generation was bound to be miraculous."

"Do you have to go back?" asked Airi.

"I have responsibilities," said Thulium. "We are on the verge of crucial decisions and decisive actions."

"Will you stay this night?" asked Airi. "A night with my own daughter under the same roof?"

"I would not stop talking to you until you fell asleep," said Thulium, "and then I would stay awake memorizing your face. Yet it's almost morning now on the planet where we live and work, and I will need to have some sleep before I get back to work. So I need to leave in a few minutes."

"I'm sure that was a weakness in your Japanese," said Airi. "The word you meant to use was 'hours.'"

"Minutes, dear Mother Airi," said Thulium. "But a thousand hours of remembering this beautiful evening, the happiest in my life."

"Change the worlds, my daughter," said Airi. "I always knew you would."

"Anyone can change the world," said Thulium. "But to change it for the better—that's always the challenge."

More things were said, and eventually it was well over an hour before Thulium stood in the middle of the sitting room and said her good-byes.

She would not hide her power from Mother Airi and Grandmother. Thulium stood there in their plain sight, and then she was on Lusitania as the first blush of dawn appeared in the eastern sky. She arrived outdoors, on the meadow beyond the fence. She meant to run to the gate and then catch a few hours of sleep, but instead she lay down—collapsed, rather—and wept for joy and sorrow.

I will never regret meeting my mother, thought Thulium, though it makes me miss her even more. And Grandmother is a blessing I had never thought possible—how can an orphan like me have a grandmother?

It was there, weeping, that she fell asleep. Hours later she awoke feeling stiff and damp, but she quickly recovered her limberness and walked to the gate. "Did you sleep well?" asked the pequenino on watch.

Of course they had known she was there. Nothing passed on Lusitania without the pequeninos knowing it.

"I did," said Thulium. "Thank you for letting me use your beautiful bed for a few hours."

"You are always welcome here, Thulium," said the pequenino. Thulium wondered if she knew him, if he was one of the pequeninos from Q-Bay. But the thought soon passed out of her mind. She could hardly tell pequeninos apart, even though she could plainly see that there were many different facial structures among them. It was a sign of carelessness and inattention on her part, she knew that. And yet she was still too full of her visit with her wonderful mother and grandmother to trouble herself about anything as trivial as telling pequeninos apart.

20

Quara: What Ruqyaq told Sprout might well be true. Our initial analyses told us that the descolada code they sent us at first had only trivial differences to the virus we've known for so long.

Ela: Well, that was foolish of us, to think that *any* differences were trivial.

Quara: I think so. But we all agreed to that error, until Sprout told us that here the descolada did *not* behave as a destructive disease.

Ela: I assume you've found the points of difference.

Quara: Two, in fact. And each of those genes is off by one broken molecule. In *our* version.

Ela: You're saying that their copy is the original, and ours is defective?

Quara: I've run functional simulations based on your earlier studies of how the descolada progressed in our cells. The Nest version enters the nucleus and splits the entire genome, connecting it to a neutral protein strand that prevents the genes from being active in any way. It's a complete record of that creature's genome.

Ela: The Recorder virus.

Quara: Then the simulation shows the Nest version of the descolada, with the captured genome, leaving the nucleus and the cell and then eventually leaving the body. It does not propagate inside the original host, because this switch here *keeps* it from activating the replication sequence inside the host body.

Ela: But in our descolada, the anti-replication switch is broken.

Quara: And so the descolada *does* replicate, eventually taking every cell in the body, tearing apart its DNA, and then using the nucleus to create new copies of itself.

Ela: And the other broken gene?

Quara: The simulation doesn't know what to do with it. So I thought, what does the Recorder virus do that our descolada never did?

Ela: Record?

Quara: That's why you're head of this project, dear sister. When I studied the Nest Recorder virus, that other gene seems to be the switch to create the neutral strands that the host DNA attaches to.

Ela: Everything that the Recorder virus does that is useful, our version doesn't do. And everything ours does that is most dangerous, theirs doesn't do.

Quara: Without clinical trials—which would be unethical to attempt—we can't be sure, but it makes sense. My question is, was the breaking of those genes deliberate, in order to weaponize the descolada? Or could these two occur by collisions with cosmic radiation during the passage from planet to planet?

Ela: For only two variations to occur, in the two places that would make the descolada most destructive—can that just be the random chance of mutations?

Quara: Leaving the genes broken but present is sloppy work, if it was deliberate.

Ela: But consistent with the mutations we've seen from worlds without a significant ozone layer or other shield. Sloppy.

Quara: In just the right places. Or wrong ones, depending.

Ela: So as far as we know, some ancient species might have created the Recorder virus to make records of every living creature on every planet that uses the DNA system of reproduction, so that when the viruses were collected and read out, a database of life could be assembled.

Quara: An obviously mad project, considering that they might eventually collect so much information that there'd be no place to store it or interpret it or index it so you could find and retrieve any of it in the first place.

Ela: Well, when it comes to mad projects, we're the team for it.

Quara: One thing is certain—our descolada virus certainly did not originate on Nest. Ruqyaq's story seems to be supported by the evidence of the virus genomes.

Ela: In that case, we already have all the data we need, don't we?

Quara: Oh, biological curiosity invites us to explore how genomes of various earth biota have changed in the intervening years, but you're right—we've troubled these innocent people enough.

Ela: And birds.

Quara: When I said people, I was including the birds and the Engineers.

Ela: Of course. That's the best attitude.

> —Transcript: Ela and Quara Ribeira
> as quoted in "Conversations in the Box"

Just because Peter and Wang-Mu had already decided to heed Dog's advice and remain on Lusitania instead of going back did not mean that they should not attend the meeting of all the members of the descolada project.

Ela allowed Quara to explain that it seemed more than likely that the destructive descolada virus was a broken copy, coincidentally broken in the most dangerous possible places. It was most likely that most versions that arrived on planets would still be Recorder viruses, harmless and scientifically full of potential.

"Maybe someday we'll meet one of the ships sent

out by the Recorders to collect and catalogue the viruses that worked properly, creating libraries of genomes," said Quara.

"And maybe their star went supernova a hundred million years ago, on the far side of the Milky Way," said Sergeant.

"So glad you're here, Cincinnatus," said Jane. "That seems to me the most likely outcome. Not necessarily the nova, but the high probability that if they survived, they lost interest in the Recorder virus project and forgot all about it. After all, the virus they sent out was a harmless data collection device."

"Unless it wasn't," said Sergeant.

"Sprout talked with Ruqyaq again this morning," said Jane, "and he passed along an invitation from the Folk, to come tonight to a banquet given in our honor."

"A trap," said Sergeant.

"Quite possibly," said Jane. "History and mythology are full of such traps, where guests are slaughtered because they trusted in the good will and honor of treacherous hosts."

"We don't even know these people," said Carlotta.

"We have to meet them sometime, for that situation to be rectified," said Quara.

"But why all of us?" asked Miro. "That seems a strange request."

"And it's one that they can't verify. If we arrive with a certain number and say that it's all of us, how can they argue?" asked Quara.

"As long as the group we send contains every person they've met on the surface of the planet," said Ender Delphiki.

"And it won't," said Peter, who could no longer keep silent. "Wang-Mu and I will not go back."

"Do you think what Dog said to you was a threat?" asked Jane.

Peter said nothing.

Wang-Mu said nothing.

"We can explain," said Ela, "that because Wang-Mu is pregnant, you will not transport her through our method anymore."

"We need a name for 'our method,'" murmured Boss, Ender's son.

"I have one already," said his older sister, called Little Mum by the cousins. "I call it detouring. We never go anywhere directly, right? Jane carries us Outside and then back Inside to another location. So no matter where we go, we take a detour."

"A short cut, you mean," said Boss.

"It seems to me that the two of you have already had this argument," said Carlotta.

"We have, but I won," said Little Mum.

Boss merely rolled his eyes.

"Detouring is fine," said Jane. "New names will evolve as long as this mode of travel is being used. But Ela, will you forgive me if, time being so short, I simply cut to the chase? Which of you want to accept this invitation?"

Hands went up.

As far as Peter could tell, everybody was eager to go except him and Wang-Mu. A part of him wanted to be part of the company by raising his hand. But he did not. And Wang-Mu did not. They stuck to their resolve.

"What armaments will we bring?" asked Sergeant.

"None," said Ela. "We will be outnumbered."

"Thermopylae," said Sergeant.

"Please recall that the Spartans only held the pass for a few hours, and then they all were killed," said Ender, who was used to countering any idea of Sergeant's with logic and precedent.

"There won't be any fighting," said Jane. "The instant conflict seems imminent, we will all leave. Those who can do so will transport themselves; I will bring the rest."

"You're assuming that you'll detect an imminent attack," said Sergeant.

"Yes," said Jane. "They're still human. If violent desires don't show, fear will, as will deceptive intent. Human beings have been my study all my life."

"We have no choice but to trust you," said Ela. "You've never let us down."

There was a momentary silence, till Sprout raised his hand. "Ela, Jane. Why aren't there any Formics or pequeninos here at this meeting?"

"The Queen and the fathertrees barred their children from coming with us to Nest," said Jane.

"But they've been part of everything else we've done," said Sprout. "Fingers in particular has done as much as any of us. Well, almost anyone."

"Which one is Fingers?" asked Little Mum.

"The one who looks exactly like a pequenino," said Ender.

"The one who takes care of our computer systems," said Miro. "You all know him, because he's the only one you ever call on to help you deal with a computer problem."

"I knew him even before he embraced that nickname," said Ela. "A very bright and industrious rapaz."

"We have plenty of time to get to know all the pequeninos who work with us by name," said Miro. "They all look completely distinct to me, but I know that for others there's a learning curve."

"My intention," said Ela, "is to address everyone at the banquet, and tell them that we plan to leave Nest for good, as of tomorrow. With the assurance that we will not add their world to any database or atlas."

"We're really going to leave behind a world with

four intelligent species, all of Earth origin?" asked Ender.

"They aren't specimens," said Ela. "We have been told that they want us to leave. If, when I make this announcement, they beg us to stay, then we can hold off for a few days and negotiate a time for us to leave."

"Can't we ask the ravens and keas for volunteers to come with us?" said Sprout. "Say, a dozen breeding pairs of each?"

"I thought you of all people," said Carlotta, "wouldn't want to bring any keas along."

"A dozen pairs isn't enough. Fifty pairs would be a small gene pool," said Quara. "But it's a good idea. If they can find a hundred of each species to consent to it."

"There's nothing for them here on Lusitania," said Miro.

"But our other colony worlds aren't as bare as Lusitania," said Jane. "I think there are eight that are worth trying. As long as the keas agree to behave."

"They'll behave like keas," said Sprout. "You can't forbid keas to play, any more than you can forbid humans to talk."

"Then we may restrict them to one continent—and warn humans to stay away," said Jane. "There are ways to make it work. Our little colonies are refuges for endangered sentient species. We can add a few more, I think."

"The Engineers?" asked Sprout.

"They are still part of the Folk," said Jane.

"They winter with them underground. But if they *ask* to come, as permanent colonists and not as tourists, we can find out how the Folk feel about it."

"Are we done here?" asked Sergeant.

"I suggest," said Peter, "that Sergeant be left behind here with us."

Dead silence.

Peter rose to his feet. "Sergeant's hostile and belligerent attitude, along with his skepticism about all decisions made by the project leaders, makes me fear that he will do something that will provoke an incident with the Folk."

"I will not," said Sergeant.

"And if you do, who will stop you?" asked Peter.

"If you plan to take my daughter with you," said Sergeant, "I will be there too."

"Your daughter will go where she likes," said Jane, "as you well know. However, I think that if Cincinnatus wishes to go, we shouldn't leave him behind."

"How magnanimous of you," said Sergeant.

"We already have his promise to commit no provocations," said Jane.

"He's not even part of the project," said Ela.

"Only because Jane sequestered all three of the Giant's children on Nokonoshima, on a fool's errand," said Sergeant. "But she chose to bring us back, and now we *are* part of the project, since we know as much about genetics as any of you, having repaired our own twisted genome years ago."

"Cincinnatus is right," said Jane. "I haven't heard a real reason, other than personal dislike, for me not to transport him. Anything else?"

Sprout raised his hand again. Peter realized for the first time that this hesitant, shy-seeming child was not one to hold back. He seemed timid, but Peter suspected he was as fearless as Thulium.

"Thulium isn't here," said Sprout.

"That is true," said Jane.

"Is she going with us or not?" asked Sprout. "She won't want to be left out."

"I know where she is," said Jane.

"Where?" asked Sprout.

"Where she chose to be," said Jane.

"Will we see her on Nest?" asked Sprout.

"I expect so," said Jane. "As you said, she's not likely to miss this."

———

The descolada team stood in a circle in a meadow. A moment before, they had been in the same formation on the lawn outside the compound. A few pequeninos and Formics were there to see them off, but there were no speeches. A few of them had put canteens on their belts, but nobody had packed food and nobody carried a weapon.

As soon as they arrived on Nest, they heard the crashing of waves against the shore not very far away. There was a shelf of sand that blocked the view of the breakers, but beyond that they could see ocean stretching on into the distance.

"Why here?" asked Sergeant. "An underground civilization can't be built this close to the ocean."

Jane said nothing.

"They must be constantly patching leaks," said Sergeant.

A few keas rose up from the grass, and everyone with canteens put their hands on them, but these keas seemed not to be in a playful mood. One kea flew up to Sprout's shoulder. "Where is my Royal Mother?" asked the kea.

"Royal Son?" asked Sprout. "She's pregnant, and didn't want to endanger the baby."

"There's no danger," said Royal Son. "And she was pregnant when she came before."

"Maybe she didn't yet know," said Ela. "Are you our guide?"

"We are all your guides. We have promised the Raven Council, no pranks, no misleading you, no false paths. We will take you to the passage down to the human Folk in this part of Nest."

"We're ready," said Sprout.

"Is it far?" asked Sergeant.

"Far can mean so many different distances," said Royal Son, "I can't answer, except to say that no human has ever found this distance taxing. But if you need to rest, stop. We'll notice and wait for you."

So they set out, and even the cousins, with shorter legs, had no trouble keeping up.

Sprout walked beside Jane, so he could ask questions. "Why is Uncle Sergeant with us, and Valentine is not?"

"She was afraid that as the oldest among us, she would be regarded as the chief of our party," said Jane.

"What's wrong with that?" said Sprout.

"It was her preference, as it was Peter's and Wang-Mu's."

"So now who will they think is our chief?" asked Sprout.

"Don't worry, Sprout," said Jane. "It probably won't be you."

"Don't be sure," said Miro. "Sprout was our best diplomat. He earned enough credibility to hear Ruq-yaq's history."

"Oh my," said Jane. But Sprout knew she and Miro were teasing him.

Though what if they weren't? What if he was greeted with great honor? Sometimes young people could be honored for their deeds. Not as often as they deserved, perhaps, or maybe far more than was good for them; but those who knew what he had done might give him respect.

Thulium should be here, thought Sprout. Yes, she fled the keas' onslaught, but she was right—they were going to be relentless and why shouldn't she get away? He had been a fool for staying. Until he was no longer a fool. Thulium had earned her place here.

How would she know where they were, so she could join them? Jane seemed awfully cavalier about it.

The distance was only a little more than a mile. Away from the river's mouth, the ground rose upward to a height at least thirty meters above the sea. Down below the hill, there was still a beach, bright yellow in the daylight. Sprout wondered what it was made of, because it didn't seem like the normal color for silicon dioxide sand.

What mattered, though, was not to stray away from the group. He realized that a couple of keas were trying to herd him away from the brow of the hill and back to the little flock of Ribeiras and Delphikis.

An awful thought occurred to him. The Folk might be perfectly sincere in their invitation to share a meal in their underground habitat. But they might also be planning to kill everyone capable of—what was the new term? Detouring.

But they were the least killable people in the world. The Folk couldn't be stupid—Ruqyaq proved that. Different as his body was, he was still part of their society. They all must know how impossible it would be to use any kind of weapon against them.

I am limiting myself with words like "impossible," thought Sprout. Instead of rejecting the idea that they had any useful weapon, Sprout should try to imagine what kind of weapon they would use. A silent projectile weapon that was undetectable until it struck? For that matter, bullets could travel faster than sound so they would easily be silent until after they hit the target. Would it be bullets?

Where would the Folk learn to practice shooting? They did no hunting on the surface, surely. No stray bullets could be allowed to strike a bird or one of the Yachachiyruna by accident.

Nothing's impossible. And even if an attempt would fail, that didn't mean the Folk wouldn't try it.

They had nothing to gain by killing anybody, Sprout told himself.

The Folk's main goal probably wouldn't be murder. They wanted to get the Box out of the sky and make sure it never came back. They would erase all knowledge of Nest from the human universe.

Except two of the most prominent visitors to the surface were missing—Peter and Wang-Mu. And also Thulium, who came only once—but arrived with Sprout.

What are their weapons? What is their science? From Ruqyaq, Sprout had learned that the Yachachiyruna were the engineers, the technicians, the builders. If they had any weapons, then as machines they would surely be created by the engineers. Yet Ruqyaq did not seem to be a treacherous sort of person, a calculating person. He enjoyed telling stories; he seemed to like talking to Sprout. Would he have built weapons designed to kill intrusive visitors like the humans of the descolada project?

They came to a doorway built into a recessed place in a rocky cliff. They were on high enough ground that they could go down fifty meters without reaching sea level, so Sergeant's concern about a leaky roof was probably not a problem. The caverns here would be dry. Except maybe leaking groundwater from above them. And if they lived underground, they'd make sure that it wouldn't be leaky and promote the growth of mold.

The door opened automatically—or had a kea pecked on some hidden control? Maybe some observer had opened it remotely.

Inside, there was plenty of room for them all to enter. The walls were smooth but didn't seem to be made of metal. Or wood. Plastic, then? Not a texture or feel that Sprout was familiar with. He wanted to see if he could scratch the surface, but he had nothing to scratch it with, and anyway, what kind of impression would it make if his first impulse was vandalism?

The floor shuddered a little and Sprout thought, Did they think they could make us fall through a huge trap door and die on the stalagmites below?

Nonsense. Why was he so afraid? It was just a large elevator, one that could probably raise and lower a hundred people at a time. At harvest time, they might bring enough people up to the surface to need to make several trips, but with a ten-person elevator they couldn't possibly bring a few hundred harvesters up and down in a reasonable time.

The elevator went down a long time, but there was no way to gauge how fast they were moving. Had they reached sea level? Deeper? Or only a dozen meters at a very slow pace?

The floor shuddered again, and then the back wall rose up and a vast room opened before them. It did not seem to be a cave at all—the walls were straight and smooth, the ceiling complete and solid, and the floor wasn't stone. The room was cooler than the air on the surface, because that's how it was in caves—but it wasn't bone-chilling. It didn't feel like what Sprout imagined a deep cave would feel like. The air was clean and fresh. Their ventilation system must be superb.

Sprout had a sudden thought, and he tugged on Jane's hand. She stopped, and so did Miro. Sprout looked up at her, not sure if he dared to speak aloud.

Jane mouthed words and whispered very softly. "Look at me. I can read your words even if you make no sound at all."

Sprout spoke accordingly. He didn't even whisper, just mouthed these words:

"Their weapons will be biological," he said. "That is their most advanced science."

Jane squeezed his hand and nodded. "If you're

right," she whispered very softly, "we are probably infected already."

"It's a crazy idea," said Sprout, this time with a bit of a whispery sound.

"Your fear is rational," said Miro. "Fearless people are fools—and quite often dead fools."

"I'm monitoring everybody's vital signs," said Jane.

Reassured, Sprout let go of her hand and moved with the others into the room.

There were tables arranged in untidy bunches, as if nobody cared whether it was convenient to walk among them. The keas were no longer with them—they must have stayed on the surface. But they saw humans scattered among the tables. Tall, well-nourished people, so however they handled agriculture here, it must be working well.

The introductions were all among adults; the children were not really ignored—Ela said their names—but the Folk directed all their attention toward the adults in their party. That saved Sprout the trouble of trying to figure out polite things to say.

Their speech was a fair-sounding Stark, but with an accent that made it hard for Sprout to understand them. It was as if some consonants were said so far back in their throats that the sounds could barely escape. And the vowels—a lot of words seemed to use "ee" and "ah" and "oo" as their only vowels, even when other vowels were required. So it was all odd.

But at least they hadn't evolved some weird system of tones or something. No doubt the limited vowel set was inherited from Quechua or Aymara, or both. And Stark, being based on English, had an extravagant set of vowels and diphthongs. Without any corrections from contact with the Hundred Worlds, why *wouldn't* their Stark pronunciations glide in directions more comfortable to them?

Ela, at the front of their party, stopped cold. The

others quickly stopped, too. Ela's gaze seemed to be fixed on the dais at the far end of the room. They were almost in the center of the vast cavern, so now was the first time they could have made out the features of the people on the dais.

There were several highly elaborate chairs in the middle. Only one of them was occupied, apparently by a child. A princess of some royal family?

Miro lifted Sprout up so he could see better.

It was Thulium.

She had come down here ahead of them. She might even have appeared right here in this room, skipping any journey from the surface. Sprout knew well that you could never put anything past Thulium. If she thought of it, she'd figure out how to do it, and then she'd *do* it, without asking permission or informing anybody of what she had done.

Thulium had appointed herself the first ambassador to the Folk, as Peter and Wang-Mu had first met the keas and ravens, and Sprout himself had first met a Yachachi.

But knowing Thulium, Sprout feared that she had said too much or too little, or had chosen words that would make all the wrong impressions. And she hadn't been at the meeting, where the plan of announcing the complete departure of all offworlders was explained. Thulium had no idea of the plan, and yet she had preempted it with whatever she decided was the right thing to say.

Sprout felt a flash of anger at her. How dare she!

And then his normal calm returned to him. They had treated her well enough. She was dressed in some fine clothing of a style and fabric that Sprout didn't recognize. It certainly wasn't the clothing Thulium would have arrived in.

Unless it was a Japanese costume. Yes, that's what it was. She went to visit her mother on Nokonoshima,

Sprout realized. Of course she did. Uncle Sergeant couldn't persuade his wife to come with him, but Thulium would never allow that to keep her from meeting her mother. And Airi would have given her some fine clothing to wear on her return trip.

Did Thulium go directly from Nokonoshima to here? Was she that skilled now that she could go to a place where she had never been, and pass through solid rock to reach a subterranean cavern?

Eventually he'd find out what she did. She would tell him. He would be proud of her for her accuracy and audacity. He would be resentful of her for having such contempt for the rest of the group. But he would only show the pride in her. The admiration he felt for her. Because he was quite sure that others would express their anger at this stunt. He would not need to be part of *that* chorus.

A man of the Folk, wearing an elaborate headdress, stood beside Thulium's chair and spoke. His voice was amplified and every word was clear—there wasn't any reverberation. "Our dear friend Thulium has brought her friends to us as she promised she would. Thulium, please tell us all their names."

Thulium stayed in the chair, and her voice, too, was amplified clearly. She named each of them in turn, and to Sprout's surprise, a spotlight shone on each of them, as if the light operators already knew who was who. Maybe they did.

"Come join me at the high table," said Thulium. "All things delicious and healthful await you here."

They must have given her that script. She would have scorned such flowery and overformal verbiage, unless she was trying to be diplomatic.

Wouldn't that be nice, if Thulium had learned to be tactful?

The whole party walked toward the front and stood where various men and women directed them.

Everyone had a chair, though nobody but Thulium had one of the finely decorated thrones.

Except that as soon as Sprout got on the dais, he slipped behind the thrones and stood directly behind Thulium's seat. He gave her no sign that he was there—he figured he was small enough that nobody out on the main floor of the place would notice him. Any attempt to communicate with Thulium would make him visible and obvious to the audience.

But then curiosity got the better of him. He stepped between two thrones and looked right at Thulium. She didn't turn her face to look at him at all—maybe her peripheral vision didn't see him.

They had her face thickly caked with makeup that looked chalky, far too white. Her features had been painted over the white, so that it seemed a miracle that Sprout had recognized her.

Then he looked more closely. There was an unevenness to the white substance, or maybe it had been applied over seriously bumpy skin. But Thulium didn't have any bumps on her skin. She had a very clear complexion.

Instead of dismissing his worried thought, Sprout immediately took action to see what was really happening with her skin. He flashed out his hand and with his fingernails scraped away the layer of white on her cheek.

The white stuff flaked and fell off. And underneath it, Sprout could see what looked like dozens of small blisters. His fingernails had opened some of them, and a clear fluid had burst out of them. Was this just an allergic reaction to the white face paint?

Or was the white face paint there to conceal the pustules?

Sprout called out, "Jane!" as he turned Thulium's face so the bare place on her cheek faced Jane.

A few people were moving to try to intercept Jane,

but that was useless. And Sprout noticed that others, including the ones who seemed to be the highest officials, were cheerful enough about Sprout's discovery.

As if they had already won a war that wasn't supposed to start.

"Take her," said Jane to Sprout. Then, more loudly, she reached out her arms to all of the party. "To Q-Bay," she called. "Now."

In a moment everyone who had gone up onto the dais was packed into Q-Bay—not just the isolation chamber, but the offices just outside it as well.

"Silence," Jane commanded. "Ela, roll call."

In a moment, Ela answered, "All here."

Quara spoke up. "I'll send a message to all the staff—don't come inside. This whole building is now quarantined."

"Good," said Ela.

Sprout saw that Jane was standing directly in front of Thulium. Fearing that the onslaught would be terrible, Sprout immediately went to Thulium and held her hand.

But Jane was not rebuking her. "How many hours were you there, my love?" asked Jane.

"Yesterday afternoon," murmured Thulium. Sprout was relieved that she could answer at all. She looked weak and frightened.

"When did the pustules appear?" asked Jane.

"This morning when I woke up. They sting badly when they break."

"Other symptoms," said Jane.

Thulium told her of a blinding headache, sparks dancing like comets across her vision, congestion that made her short of breath, and violent diarrhea since she got up.

"Everyone was very kind," said Thulium.

"They give you a fatal disease," said Jane, "against

which all of *them* have been inoculated, and then treat you kindly as you die."

"Will she die?" asked Sprout.

"It's what I deserve," said Thulium. Then she gasped for air.

"Oxygen," said Jane, and at once Ela had an oxygen mask over Thulium's face.

"Should we intubate you?" asked Jane. "So you can breathe?"

Thulium pulled her face away from the mask. "Not yet," she said. Then she pushed her face back into the mask.

"I don't know how long we might have stayed," said Jane, "if we hadn't had Thulium there early to show us the symptoms of the Folk's biological weapon."

"Do you recognize the disease?" Miro asked Ela.

"No," said Ela. "But we'll be looking at her blood and tissues and find ways to treat the symptoms, at least, and the underlying disease as soon as possible. Whatever is happening to Thulium will happen to the rest of us in twelve hours."

Blood and tissue samples were taken and placed in the various microscopes. Team members knew how to read the samples, and quickly identified the two microorganisms that were savaging Thulium's body. One of them attacked the red blood cells; the other was encasing the nerve cells in her limbs and face "Progressing inward," said Quara, who was administering the internal examination. "But so far, nothing shows up in her internal organs."

"So maybe we still have time," said Jane.

"Thulium," said Ela, "we're going to have to experiment on you. We'll try every treatment that seems to have a reasonable chance, and we'll be attacking these little beasts outside your body to see what kills them. But you're our test case."

Thulium nodded. "Don't let it escape from this building," she whispered.

"We've already got negative pressure everywhere," said Miro.

Everything moved so quickly that Sprout couldn't keep track of who was doing what. But while everyone else was busy at various tasks, Sprout found that Uncle Sergeant sat beside Thulium's bed, holding her hand.

Everyone spoke their findings aloud, and Sprout had no problem understanding everything that they learned. Which mostly consisted of treatments that would not work.

Every now and then Thulium herself made a suggestion. Sometimes Ela replied by saying, "Do it," to one of the others. Sometimes Ela replied to Thulium, "Already tried it. Dead end."

Through it all, Sprout did nothing useful. With Thulium's father holding her hand, even that job was unavailable to him. But he had never worked on pathology, and now was not a good time for him to get someone to train him.

So he leaned against a far wall and tried to tell if his own symptoms were appearing yet. Whatever is happening to Thulium will happen to all of us. Find a cure, please.

Did the ravens and keas know the plan? The Engineers? Were they complicit, or were they deceived as the Lusitanian party had been?

This could not have been known to Dog the Raven or Royal Son or Phoenix or Ruqyaq. But Ruqyaq might know the principles underlying this disease—it was surely part of Engineer science. If they could only talk to him, they might make faster progress toward a cure.

But this was war. Just because you liked someone before the war started didn't mean he was still your friend now that hostilities had begun. If Sprout went to Nest now, no one would lead him to Ruqyaq. The people of Nest might well assume that, having been betrayed himself, Sprout would readily betray anyone who helped him.

Sprout was as helpless as he felt. He wondered if the heat he felt in his face was rage or fear or the first onset of the fever.

Thulium, please live. You're the best of us. If all the rest of us are saved, but you die, then the people of Nest would have scored a terrible blow.

If Thulium dies, thought Sprout, I'm going to make sure that every starmap and atlas in the Hundred Worlds shows the exact location of Nest, and what the underground people of Nest did under pretense of hospitality.

21

Peter: If the disease is manufactured, or if our people were deliberately infected, it's an act of war.

Queen: As it was when your people killed the Formic worldshapers who were merely carrying out their duties.

Peter: Our visitors to Nest never killed anybody. We were doing our best to make it clear that we were *not* colonizers.

Queen: We never killed anybody, either. We just brushed aside interfering animals that never answered our efforts to communicate.

Peter: I am not blaming you or your sisters. I'm saying that we have been bending over backward not to give offense.

Queen: But do they believe you?

Peter: Why shouldn't they?

Queen: Because you can travel instantly between worlds. Because your sophisticated starship is an airtight box with a life-support attachment. And because they are also human, so they will judge your honor and integrity and compassion by their own.

Peter: Oh. Yes, that makes sense.

Queen: I traveled with . . . Ender Wiggin long enough to learn of all the trickery that humans use on each other, all the backstabbing, all the lying. We Hive Queens cannot lie to each other, because our only communication is total communication.

Peter: So are we at war with the humans of Nest or not?

Queen: That's *your* decision. But I think it's quite likely that they're at war with *you*.

Peter: That's what we're most afraid of.

Queen: Why? Do they have ships that can reach Lusitania? Do they even know where Lusitania is? As long as you don't go back there, then there cannot possibly be war.

Peter: So we'll try to cure this disease, and never return to Nest.

Queen: You will return once. You know why.

Peter: Because we weren't attacked—well, not in a serious way—by the birds or the Engineers.

Queen: You have given us multiple worlds, and the pequeninos, too, so that we can't be wiped out in a single disaster.

Peter: Yes. We have a duty to offer that to them, too. They can't live here, though.

Queen: Nothing for them to eat. And nobody willing to put up with the keas.

Peter: Not even you?

Queen: Come back to me if you can't find a cure for the disease. Especially if you think Thulium might die. I want to speak to her one more time. It *is* important to me.

—Memorandum of conversation:
Peter Wiggin and Hive Queen
as cited in Demosthenes, "Boundaries of War"

Thulium was wide awake the whole time. She kept wishing she could sleep, but her mind kept racing. How could they fool me? How could they see me, a child, and choose to infect me with a deadly disease? How did I give them offense? Why didn't I sense their hostility? Why did I believe all their flattery and phony honors? What did I care about sitting on a throne at a great banquet?

They thought I was a child and I was, an ignorant, trusting child.

These thoughts repeated again and again. She tried to empty her mind and sleep, but she never slept, even as she felt sicker and weaker, as if something was eating every cell in her body from the inside out.

Time passed. Sometimes the room was bright with outdoor light, and sometimes with the ceiling lights. Sometimes there were people in the room with her, talking about her but making little sense. Sometimes she was poked with needles, and now she had a tube down her throat so she could breathe, but speech was impossible. That was fine, she had nothing to say. The only thing that came to mind was, I'm sorry I'm sorry I'm sorry. And, now and then, Let me die, study my cadaver, and learn to beat this disease before anybody else dies.

One time, and only once, she decided to transport her father to Nest. The twins, too. If anyone could figure out a way to wreak vengeance upon them for Thulium's death, they would do it.

I don't want vengeance. She drove away the thought of transporting Father anywhere. She was too weak anyway. She'd probably leave him stranded Outside, and then *she* would be as much a murderer as the Folk of Nest.

"Isn't there something productive you could be doing?" asked Miro. His words were challenging, but Sprout detected no malice in his voice—not even irritation. "I think you'll feel better, Sprout, if you do something to help us with this thing."

"Since we're all going to die soon anyway," said Sprout, "what will my poor skills do to advance our case?"

"We won't know until you do it," said Miro.

"And your contribution is to look for idle team members and goad them to keep working," said Sprout.

"I couldn't find anything better to do," said Miro.

"I'm not doing nothing, Miro," said Sprout. "My best friend in the universe has the most advanced case of this plague, and so I'm sitting here trying to think of how these supreme breeders and geneticists would go about giving us a disease that we couldn't cure."

"How would they know what we could cure?"

"We sent back genetic codes from the Box, in

answer to the codes they sent us. They know a lot about the kind of genetics we know."

"Do you think they created something that has no DNA or RNA or anything familiar?"

"I don't know," said Sprout. "But since they probably didn't start developing this until after the Box first appeared—or maybe not till after Peter and Wang-Mu first went to the surface—it is most likely based on something they're familiar with. Here's what I think. It's not based on any Earth-born species. Not a virus, not a bacterium, not a fungus, not a protozoan—nothing from Earth. They've had thousands of years to study the microorganisms of Nest. Maybe there was one that caused them a plague a thousand years ago, and now every baby on Nest is born with the altered gene that gives complete resistance to the disease. So they could freely infect us because everybody else in that room was born immune to it."

"I think you've been using your time better than I have," said Miro. "I'm going to play back our conversation with the others. It's possible we're looking in the wrong places for the wrong things."

"Or it's also possible that I'm delusional in the throes of this disease."

"But as a leguminid, even your delusions are probably informative."

———

Peter and Wang-Mu accompanied the dinner team when they brought food to the quarantine building. They set it outside in the open air, then walked back many yards. They watched two or three of their friends come out in hazmat suits and bring the food inside. Disposable containers were used. The concrete pad where they laid the bags and baskets was disinfected after they went inside.

Meanwhile, Peter tried to understand how the study of the disease was progressing. He couldn't enter the quarantine building, and Jane, talking to him through the jewel, would say useless things like, "They've eliminated thousands of possibilities." To which Peter would reply, "If they eliminated them, then they weren't possibilities after all." And she would say, "They know which avenues are not worth exploring. That's progress."

Then the most important question: "How is Thulium?"

"She doesn't know she's delirious," said Jane. "When she's conscious, she constantly apologizes, but doesn't seem to hear us telling her that she's completely forgiven."

"Because she knows she isn't," said Peter. "She knows people are only saying that because she's going to die."

"We don't know what the course of this disease is supposed to be," said Jane. "The incubation period is only about twelve hours. But her exposure must have been more intense, because the rest of us are all progressing much more slowly than she did. Yet she also continues to live. Her heart is beating a little faster, her blood pressure fluctuates weirdly, but no organ has failed."

"Is it possible they didn't intend it to be fatal?" asked Peter.

"How can they guess how this much stress on the body will affect different people? Thulium might have been swept off immediately. Instead, it may be that the leguminids have far greater strength than the Folk of Nest could have guessed at. Sprout also seems to have great resistance—or perhaps just a weaker infection."

"What can I do?" asked Peter.

"Keep bringing us food," said Jane.

"The Hive Queen wants to see Thulium before she dies. She says it's important to her."

"So we take Thulium, sick as she is, on a parade across the open meadows of Lusitania?" asked Jane.

"Come on. You only need to ask the Hive Queen where she and Thulium should meet, where there's no risk of infecting the Formic workers," said Peter.

"Thulium is not clear of mind," said Jane. "Communicating may be hard."

"Is there any chance of her mind getting *clearer* before she dies?" asked Peter.

"It seems unlikely," said Jane.

"I've given you the message," said Peter. "I'm surprised she told me and not you. But now you know, and the next move is yours."

———

When Miro told others about Sprout's suggestion, some of them rolled their eyes; Quara said, "That's the only possibility I've been exploring"; and others responded by sitting there thinking for a while.

It was one of that third group that came up with the first real progress. They all gathered around Carlotta's station. "It's been visible all along," said Carlotta. "Look, here, here, here." She laid down printouts of images of the infected cells that were taken within the first hour. "This spot here, and then here, hugging the surface, only an atom or two in thickness would be my guess. And nothing like genetic material in it."

"So it just clings and then what, takes vids of how the cell works?" asked Quara.

"Sarcasm isn't helpful," said Ela, "especially since you don't know any more than the rest of us."

Quara was temporarily stilled.

"Can we take a series of time-lapse images and see if they're changing?" asked Ender.

"I think that anything under the slide, being dead, won't show any movement," said Carlotta.

"And a living sample won't hold still," said Ela.

"How about a brand-new sample that doesn't know it's dead yet?" asked Sprout

"Here goes," said Carlotta. She swabbed the inside of her wrist with disinfectant, then used a scalpel to scrape an infinitesimally thin patch about a half-centimeter wide from the inside of her wrist. She showed no pain, though it must have hurt. When Sprout suggested a fresh sample, he didn't expect Carlotta to act so quickly.

Ela had the patch of skin between two slide plates and into the imager within five seconds.

"Mother," said Sprout, reaching out with a gauze pad for Carlotta's wrist.

She pressed it in place while Miro bound it down with tape. "Thulium doesn't have much time," said Carlotta. "If I have anything she needs, it's hers, without hesitation. We all feel that way."

Sprout wondered: Would Thulium's own father have taken a patch of his own flesh, without flinching and without hesitating? It was a good thing to know Mother's courage and stamina when she was needed by someone she loved.

They took repeated images, at first ten per second, then one per second, then one a minute until an hour had passed. The computer, instead of printing them, made them into a sequence. Ela displayed it on all the screens in the room at once, so everybody could get a close look.

The slightly thicker patch moved. It was sliding along very slowly in the ten-per-second sequence. In the one-per-second, it moved quickly and left several parts of itself behind. Each of those parts grew, not thicker, but wider on the inside of the cell wall.

"Is it doing anything other than reproducing? Does the cell wall still function?" asked Miro.

"Without blood circulating, we can't really test that," said Carlotta.

"We can't test absorption, but is the cell still secreting waste?" asked Ela.

"Yes," said Sprout. "Just like normal. As if there were nothing there."

"Well, if it does nothing," said Ela, "if it interferes with nothing, what's causing the pustules on the skin, the fever?"

"Auto-immune? Hyper-immunity?" suggested Little Mum.

"All possible," said Quara. "But I've been scanning through older samples, blood samples, and they all have those patches."

"So what is it?" asked Sprout. "It's too small to be a one-celled creature—there's no room for a nucleus. But without one, how does it reproduce? If it's dividing, what gets passed to each new iteration?"

"Such fine questions," said Ela. "Let's divide that sample, and look at the old samples, and see if we can isolate them and get greater magnification."

Everyone set to work, assigning themselves to a task unless somebody said, "Mine already," and after everybody had called out what they were working on, Ela mentioned a couple of other things to be explored. "Just look for these along the way. Be alert to them."

After six hours of intense close work with slides and images, hypotheses and discussions and arguments, they had learned a few things.

First, viewed from above, the objects emerged as wormlike, wriggling slightly as they moved across the inside of the cell wall. Yet they were nowhere thicker than two atoms deep, and they weren't particularly complex molecules, though they were all carboniferous.

"It's like worms with amino acid blocks as segments," said Quara.

"A parasite, then," said Miro, "not a virus or bacterium or fungus."

"It's making its new copies out of the available materials in the cell," said Ender. "What do they do, kill the cell by using up everything inside it?"

"If so, where are the dead cells?" asked Little Mum.

"Do they shrivel away to nothing?" asked Sprout. "Do they burst? Do the worms propagate themselves to other cells without breaking the original host cell?"

It was midnight when Jane finally said, "We know far more than we did this morning. But do we know yet how it kills? How it makes us sick?"

Nobody had the answer. "Just speculation without evidence," said Sprout.

"Good speculation, though, Sprout," said Miro. "You gave us the kick we needed, got us unstuck."

A few murmurs of agreement.

But Jane held out her hands for their attention. "The Hive Queen wants to see Thulium before she dies."

"You can't take Thulium or any of us, not even yourself, into the hive house," said Miro. "We don't know if this bug will infect Formics or not."

"The Queen has asked me to meet her in the open air out in the meadow beyond the fence," said Jane.

"Why can't she just communicate with Thulium's mind, the way she does with you?" asked Sprout.

"Thulium's mind isn't very coherent just now," said Jane, "and anyway, I don't know why the Queen wants her. Maybe it's not a conversation."

"Surely you don't think the Hive Queen has a *cure*," said Quara scornfully.

"I don't think anything," said Jane. "But remember

that she can alter her own genes during egg-laying to bring forth hundreds of different kinds of creatures, suited to one particular purpose or another. She does things at a genetic level inside her eggs that we need machinery to do."

"Going outside might kill Thulium," said Sprout.

"Leaving her inside while we continue to fail to find a treatment probably *will* kill her," said Jane.

And without further discussion, Jane, Thulium, and the examining table Thulium was lying on were gone from Q-Bay.

A couple of seconds later, though nobody noticed at the time, Sprout was also gone.

———

"I didn't invite you here," said Jane, when Sprout appeared a few meters away and trotted toward them.

"Are you bringing the Queen," asked Sprout, "or is she coming on her own?"

Jane didn't answer, because no answer was necessary when the Queen appeared on the lawn under the starlight. Talker was with her, as were two of the slug-like helpers that tended to the eggs in the hive house.

"This is so dangerous to you," said Jane.

Talker replied, "Don't distract me."

The Queen lifted both slugs up onto Thulium's body. One writhed down her leg, the other up across her chest. Here and there they left holes in Thulium's clothing, small ones, with the skin bleeding a little under them. Biopsies, thought Sprout. We're seeing Formic surgery.

Then, long before the slugs had traversed Thulium's whole body, the Queen pulled them off and attached them to her abdomen. She stood upright for a few moments, then bent and curled herself into a ball on the ground.

"Patience," said Talker. "I now speak my own words.

The Mother is scanning the new creature, the tiny one inside the cells of the body."

"What is she looking for?" asked Sprout.

"What I felt of her intentions was first, to see what the intruder was doing, second, how it was doing it, and third, how to render it harmless or kill it without harming the host cell."

"That's the whole project we were working on back in the quarantine building," said Sprout.

"The Mother uses different tools and different senses."

The Hive Queen uncurled herself, but remained lying on her side on the ground. Then she rolled over on her back. The two slugs were changing somehow—with slight undulations, like a snake swallowing a mouse, they were growing, and patches of their surfaces seemed to be changing color.

"What are they doing?" Sprout asked.

"Hush, Sprout," said Jane.

"I don't know," said Talker. "The Mother is filling them with the substance of her own body, shaped for whatever purpose she has conceived of."

The two slugs suddenly were free of their connection to the Hive Queen. They slid off her abdomen into the grass.

Talker reached out to Jane and Sprout. "She is exhausted. Will you pick up the carriers and put them back on Thulium's body?"

Jane instantly picked up the near one, while Sprout ran around the Hive Queen to pick up, in trembling hands, the slug on the far side.

"On bare skin," said Talker.

Jane pulled up Thulium's shirt far enough to expose her stomach. Jane held out her carrier over the skin, but Sprout hesitated. The carrier was heavier than he had expected. And he was afraid of doing it wrong.

"At the same time," said Talker. "Each is useless alone."

Using all the strength and stamina of his arms, Sprout held out his carrier and then, looking at Jane's eyes, he mirrored her action. As near as he could tell, the two carriers attached themselves to Thulium at exactly the same time.

The carriers didn't move across Thulium's body. They just sat there, undulating very slightly.

Sprout wanted to ask, to demand, How long is this going to take? But he already knew that even the Hive Queen didn't know. Whatever was happening to Thulium, if it was going to be curative, if it was going to remove all the microworms from her cells, it would take time. There were so many cells to reach.

Sprout reasoned that the carriers couldn't possibly be cleaning up one cell at a time—the sun would probably turn into a brown dwarf or something before they could finish *that* job. So most likely the carriers were either releasing some kind of toxin or anti-parasite that would chemically destroy the worms, or they were releasing hunter-killer organisms born of the Hive Queen's eggs, which would move through Thulium's body killing or removing or disabling worms as they went.

He remembered a story about how on the planet where Ender Wiggin was governor, they had discovered that one group of the Hive Queen's children had survived. Not warrior Formics or even workers. But rather sluglike creatures, about like the carriers, Sprout realized now, that would eat into the rock and inside their bodies separate gold from everything else. They gave out pellets of gold, and then much larger deposits of earth. They moved like earthworms through the stone, ingesting and egesting. This was how the Hive Queen created machinery for mining. She created workers—or larvae—that could selectively separate rock into its constituent parts. Sprout had read that there was some controversy about whether this meant that Formics were not actually tool-using creatures, until somebody pointed out that they came to Earth in starships much more sophisticated than the ones humans were using. Definitely toolmakers and tool users. But among the Formics, miners were born, not made.

So had these carriers been born for a new purpose? Or was this their job with all the hatching eggs in the hive house? Did they come to an egg, deposit something in it, and then the egg would hatch a larva all set to become what the Hive Queen had determined that it should be?

The Hive Queen didn't change the eggs inside her ovaries, thought Sprout. She changed them after she laid them. Their destiny was injected, not inborn.

Or I'm completely wrong, Sprout reminded himself.

The first hint of dawn was appearing in the east. Talker said, "Thulium's situation was very bad."

"Yes," agree Jane.

"I don't know why she wasn't already dead," said Talker.

"We wondered the same thing," said Jane.

"Every cell of her body is strong, and many were adapting to the invasive tissue, building new cell wall material around it, isolating it," said Talker. "This would not have saved her, but the adaptation slowed the progress of the disease."

"Without your intervention, what would have happened?" asked Sprout.

"Death," said Talker. "But I see that you are asking how death would come. I believe that at a single time, all the worms at once would have torn open every cell wall. There would not be enough of Thulium left to call her remains a dead body. She would be a pile of cellular garbage, a molecular wastebin, and all the worms would dissolve into spores that would float away, ready to be inhaled by another host."

"Vicious," said Jane.

"A deliberate creation," said the Hive Queen. "This did not arise by natural selection or random mutation. It was adapted from a life-form unrelated to Earth life, so it must have been found on Nest and changed into this lethal form."

"So they were trying to kill her. To kill us," said Sprout.

"I think they might also have been gathering information," said Talker. "I think perhaps the people of Nest might have been trying to discover how she was able to transport herself instantaneously."

"They wouldn't have found it," said Jane.

"No," said Talker. "The worms could never have found the aiúa."

"Still," said Jane. "I don't marvel that she lacked the strength to transport herself back to Q-Bay. By the time she knew she was sick, she was already weak."

Talker said nothing for a long moment. "She didn't transport herself?" Talker finally said.

"Well, I didn't take her," said Jane.

Then Talker looked at Sprout.

"I did it," said Sprout. "Jane, you told me to. You said, Take her."

"I said nothing of the kind," said Jane. "I reached out to *all* of our party, but she was already gone. With you."

"Then I—Jane, I heard you, even though you said it softly."

"You heard your own mind telling you what must be done to save Thulium," said Jane. "You've done well today."

Sprout knew that he should be bursting with pride. But all that was on his mind was this: "Talker, is the treatment working? Does the Mother know?"

"You should call her the Queen," said Talker. "She is *my* mother, not yours."

"From this day on she is my mother *and* my queen," said Sprout, "if she saves Thulium's life."

"She doesn't need more children," said Talker, "especially not children as uncontrollable as you leguminids. But she can always use friends."

"Then she is my friend," said Sprout.

"She knows now what that word means, when spoken by you," said Talker, "and she welcomes your friendship and gives hers to you in return."

Jane raised an eyebrow at Sprout. "I hope you realize that a serious pact was just made."

Talker made a sound like a hoarse laugh, or gravel spilling on tin. "Sprout understands it every bit as well as you, Jane."

———

The sun had not yet risen when the carriers slid off Thulium's stomach and onto the grass beside the examining table.

"Take the carriers into the quarantine building," said Talker. "They will do their work much more quickly on people who are not as infected as Thulium was. When everyone is free of the parasite, leave the building for an entire day, and the carriers will cleanse every surface."

"Then we return them to you?" asked Jane.

"There will be nothing left of them," said Talker. "Now the Mother asks you to carry us home."

"You won't be bringing the infection into the hive house?" asked Jane.

"The Mother knows how to take care of her own."

The next moment, the Hive Queen and Talker were gone.

Sprout picked up his carrier from the grass. Jane picked up hers.

Then they were back inside Q-Bay.

Thulium opened her eyes. "I'm sorry," she said. "I should have come down to Nest with the rest of you."

"Yes, you should have," said Jane. "But we all understood and forgave you at once, even those who thought they were angry at you. And we're all happy that you're alive."

"Can we take her vital signs?" asked Ela, from out in the laboratory.

"No," said Jane. "Instead, one at a time you will lie down and receive the treatment the Hive Queen created." She held her carrier up where they could see it. Sprout also raised his.

"Ick," said Little Mum. "Do we have to *swallow* that?"

"Or does *it* swallow *us*?" asked Blue.

"It rests on your skin and injects you with the treatment the Hive Queen prepared."

"A magic potion," said Miro.

"As far as *our* science is concerned, yes," said Jane.

"Shouldn't we keep samples of the parasite to study?" asked Quara.

"Do you plan to create a version of your own? Are we beginning a cycle of biological warfare?" asked Miro sharply.

"Of course not," said Quara. "But this is a different principle of life here and we—"

"Abstract science must make way for survival," said Jane. "If you work with these parasites, someone will be infected someday and it will spread throughout the world. We *had* to study the descolada—but we also had it contained. This can never be contained. Do you understand?"

"She didn't actually say that," said Sprout.

"She didn't say it to *you*," said Jane.

Jane insisted that Sprout receive the treatment first, to show others how it worked. She probably figured that Sprout would have fewer trepidations about receiving the creatures, since he had already seen it work and had handled one of them himself.

So he lay on a table in Q-Bay and Jane and Miro put the carriers on his bare stomach. He could feel that something was passing through his skin, but there was no pain, as if the darts piercing him avoided all the pain-generating nerves. Instead of taking half the night, his procedure was done within a half-hour. "I really wasn't as sick as Thulium, was I," he said, when the carriers slid off him.

"Or the carriers are working faster," said Jane, "now that they have experience."

Everyone got a turn. Jane sent people out of the building as soon as their cure was complete. But she allowed Sprout to stay, because she wanted him to apply his carrier to each person, simultaneously with hers. Apparently Miro was only a substitute, when applying the carriers to Sprout.

When Jane, Miro, and Sprout were the last three in the building, and everyone had been cured, Sprout asked Jane, "Did you know that the Hive Queen could find a cure?"

"I didn't know. I barely hoped. As did she. But what else was there to try, with Thulium nearer and nearer to death?"

"I know you didn't invite me out there," said Sprout. "But I'm glad I went."

"I'm glad you came," said Jane. "Your wisdom in this case—or the foolishness of your devotion to Thulium—led you to make a choice that helped us all."

Sprout didn't allow himself to grin, though the pride he felt demanded it. "I need to go talk to Thulium, now that the work is done."

Miro put a hand on Sprout's shoulder. "First go tell your father that you performed bravely and brilliantly."

"I can't tell him that," said Sprout. "I only just met him."

"Then we will," said Jane. "Go to Thulium. You'll know what to say to her."

Sprout ran outside and went in search of her. It didn't take long to find her. She was waiting for him outside the barracks.

"I told them to save you some supper," said Thulium.

"You mean the twins didn't eat it all?" asked Sprout. Sergeant had demanded that the twins be returned to Lusitania, when it looked like Thulium might die.

"The cooks always hide most of the food when they're around."

She turned to lead him inside to the mess hall. Without even glancing, she reached out her hand and took his. Hand in hand, they went to finally eat the kind of banquet they had thought they would get in the caverns of Nest. Apparently the cooks were glad they had survived the disease, too.

22

Dog the Raven: All five of the worlds you propose seem acceptable, though there may be unforeseen complications.

Hive Queen: There always are.

Dog the Raven: If there are human colonies on all these worlds, however, I don't see how the keas will be able to live there in peace.

Hive Queen: Three of the worlds are either in a Pangaea continental formation, or the continents are so close together that keas could easily fly from all of them to any other.

Dog the Raven: Which means that ravens and other corvids could do the same.

Hive Queen: The other two worlds, however, have at least one continental landmass that is too far from any other for keas to make the flight.

Dog the Raven: Or ravens.

Hive Queen: The question is, my sister, do you want to share a continent with the keas, and with no humans, or do you want to share a continent with humans, and no keas.

Dog the Raven: Why can't we establish two breeding populations of ravens, one on each?

Hive Queen: But you agree that sequestering the keas will be better for everyone.

Dog the Raven: It will be better for the keas. Humans tend to want them all dead.

Hive Queen: When humans arrived in the keas' original habitat, New Zealand, the keas mercilessly attacked the sheep the settlers brought with them. The humans responded as if it had been a declaration of war.

Dog the Raven: I assume the keas merely enjoyed playing with the sheep.

Hive Queen: Eventually the humans will forget or ignore the treaty restrictions, and they will come to settle and exploit the continent of birds.

Dog the Raven: It's our business to make sure we're ready.

Hive Queen: For war?

Dog the Raven: Has anyone ever won a war against the humans?

Hive Queen: I'm the only one who ever fought one. That is, my sisters did.

Dog the Raven: We drove them underground.

Hive Queen: Stalemate, not victory.

Dog the Raven: Will there be a place for the Yachachi-yruna?

Hive Queen: They are part of the Folk.

Dog the Raven: They are *not* part of the Folk, even though they live with them in winter.

Hive Queen: Invite them. If they choose to come, the Travelers will transport them.

> —Dog the Raven's account of her conversation with the Hive Queen quoted in Demosthenes, "Deliberate Dispersals"

There was little discussion about who would go back to the surface of Nest. Peter said, "Wang-Mu and I are going." Wang-Mu said, "Our only friend among the keas is Royal Son. I am the Royal Mother of the West." And it was settled.

They came back in the earliest dawn, before sunrise, to the spot where they had first met the keas, where Royal Son had begun to talk to Wang Mu. Where, later, Sprout had been mobbed.

This was the hour of the day when many birds did their foraging. Humans were usually in bed. It was a fairly undisturbed time.

But no birds were about.

Peter and Wang-Mu each turned around several times, searching.

Wang-Mu whispered, "It seems impossible that none of them have seen us."

"It *is* impossible," said Peter softly. "Should we call for Royal Son?"

"Sounds can be heard by anyone," whispered Wang-Mu. "They cannot be called back."

"Are we afraid of the Folk? Aren't they under-ground?" asked Peter.

"All bets are off," said Wang-Mu. "For one thing, the Folk must certainly fear our retaliation for their attempted massacre. Maybe they have laid an ambush for us here on the surface."

"Why would they imagine we would ever come back?"

"Because they know," said Wang-Mu, "that you and I were not with the party they infected."

"And they want to kill all the Detourists. The Trav-elers."

"Let's wait a little longer before leaving. Give the keas a chance to decide whether to recognize us."

"By now they should have stolen everything we're carrying," said Peter.

"Or wearing," said Wang-Mu.

Every minute the light increased and the ground be-came more visible. And then Wang-Mu saw a little splash of bright, shiny green in the grass. And another.

She reached down and picked it up. A dead kea.

Peter picked up a kea, too. There were dozens all around them. Hundreds, maybe—they couldn't yet see how far the slaughter had carried into the distance.

Wang-Mu put the bodies of two keas into her satchel. Peter did the same with his.

"If Royal Son were coming, he'd be here," said Peter.

Wang-Mu took his hand.

Everyone was waiting out in the lab when they re-turned to Q-Bay. Procedures now were so disregarded that Miro approached the door to open it. Peter and Wang-Mu both signaled him to stop.

They opened their satchels and laid the birds on an examining table.

Miro turned and asked everyone in the lab, "Who does birds?"

"We've never had any birds but xingadoras to examine," said Fingers. "And their anatomy is different from any birds from Earth."

"We need autopsies of the dead keas," said Peter. "Not healing. How did they die?"

Soon the anatomists and geneticists were taking samples and opening up corpses. Peter and Wang-Mu underwent their checkups, especially their hands, since they had held the birds and any biological agent might be stuck to their skin. When they were sanitized and pronounced clean, they went out into the lab, looking at slides and vids as they came onto the various monitors.

Miro, Jane, Sprout, and Thulium gathered around the station where Wang-Mu sat down. Peter knelt on the floor beside her, till Miro pulled up a chair for him.

"How many keas died?" asked Sprout.

"We saw no living keas," said Wang-Mu.

"There were dozens of dead ones scattered randomly across the grass," said Peter. "It never got light enough for us to see farther, but it could have been hundreds."

"Did you call out for Royal Son?" asked Sprout.

"We did not call out at all," said Wang-Mu. "We didn't know who else might hear."

"Very wise," said Miro.

"And no ravens showed up?" asked Thulium.

"The Queen says that Dog is still alive," said Jane.

"Then we have to go back," said Peter.

"We have to find out as much as we can about how they died," said Jane. "Nobody goes back till then." Jane looked pointedly at Thulium, who nodded her consent. Everyone knew why.

"We have a mission," said Peter. "If the Folk have come to the surface to kill birds, then we have no time to waste."

"If their weapons kill humans, we have all the reason in the world to wait," said Miro.

But the answers didn't take long, because nothing showed up. "They didn't die *of* anything," said Quara. "They just died."

"Maybe Ruqyaq knows," said Sprout.

"Maybe the Yachachiyruna invented the weapons," said Little Mum. "Maybe they carried out the massacre."

"I'm going back," said Peter. "I owe it to Dog."

"I owe it to Royal Son," said Wang-Mu. "We don't know that all the keas are dead."

Fingers spoke up, without raising his gaze from his holo. "Take a hundred Formic soldiers with you," he said.

The words hung in the air.

"That depends on the circumstances," said Jane. "And on the Queen's willingness."

"We won't go back to the same place," said Peter. "We'll go to the meadow near the Raven Council."

"Good plan," said Jane.

"They might all be dead, too," said Thulium.

"If that's the case," said Peter, "if they've committed xenocide against the keas and the ravens, then I think we should turn Sergeant loose underground."

"We will not do that," said Wang-Mu. "If the Folk killed the keas we found, it can't have been a unanimous choice by all the Folk. We don't punish all for the crimes of a few."

"In war you do," said Thulium.

"We are not at war," said Wang-Mu. "And we are not the judges of Nest. All we are is the hope of moving as many sentient creatures away from Nest as we can."

"If there are any keas left," said Sprout, "we won't lack for volunteers to join us."

"The two of you won't go alone and unsupported," said Miro. "And this time, you go with a box."

"And we bring back all the birds that will fly inside," said Sprout.

"Are there drying racks?" asked Ela. "Shelves? Hat racks? Something they can roost on? They can't all fit on the floor."

It took about twenty minutes to fill the Box with possible roosts. Nobody rode inside it—Jane would bring it along. Miro, Ela, and Quara insisted on coming. So did several of the cousins, pleading that it wasn't fair for Thulium and Sprout to go to Nest again and again. Jane silenced them with a glare.

"Go first," said Jane to Peter and Wang-Mu. "I'll land the box about thirty meters away."

Peter and Wang-Mu hardly had a chance to look around before everyone else in the expedition arrived. Sprout and Thulium arrived at the same time, but separately; Wang-Mu was pretty sure Sprout had brought himself, without any need for Thulium's help. Quara, Miro, and Ela looked around at the plants, seeing whatever it was that ecologists and xenologers looked for in a new world.

Peter and Wang-Mu, without discussion, walked toward the Council trees, and when Wang-Mu knelt in the grass, so did Peter. Wang-Mu spoke aloud, but did not shout. If the ravens were there, they would hear her. "Can Dog or Phoenix speak to us? Or is there someone else who can talk to us?"

There was a rustling in the leaves, and then a naked man with long arms and hands for feet swung down and sat in the grass before them.

"Ruqyaq," Sprout greeted him.

"This isn't a safe place for birds," said Ruqyaq. "They have all moved away west and north."

"How did the keas die?" asked Peter.

"Were there survivors?" asked Wang-Mu.

"Were the ravens also slaughtered?" asked Sprout.

"Did you know they were going to do this?" asked Thulium.

Ruqyaq held out his hands. "There isn't time for a story," he said. "Did you come to carry away the keas and ravens? Because almost all of them beg you to take them."

Jane turned to the others. "The only destination is Lusitania, the meadow beyond the fence. Plenty of time to transport them to the right colony worlds later."

"Should I lead you to where they are gathering?" asked Ruqyaq.

"Can we trust you?" demanded Thulium.

"What an annoying child," said Ruqyaq. "Sprout, I want to go with you too. I can't live with these crimes committed by the Folk."

"First," said Miro, "what is the nature of the weapon that killed so many keas. Will it harm us, too?"

"I assume it's a combination of ultrasound and infrasound," said Ruqyaq. "It's a weapon I designed for riot control twenty years ago. It keeps the peace underground."

"So, not utopia after all," said Thulium.

"No one ever said it was," said Sprout.

"Can you point me in the right direction?" Jane asked Ruqyaq.

He rose to his feet and turned to point west-northwest.

Instantly, they were all standing in a different meadow, with different trees around them. The box was still thirty meters away. And Ruqyaq was still standing and pointing.

"Oh," said Ruqyaq. And then, "Oh," again.

To Wang-Mu's great relief, she saw the fluttering of bright-colored wings. There were living keas here.

And ravens, though as usual they kept their distance, watching, waiting.

Sprout stepped forward, away from the group of humans. "If you want to go to another world, go into the box."

Immediately, keas swarmed into the open door of the box. While keas were still queued up outside, Jane called out, "When you see you're on another world, all of you leave the Box. You will harass no humans, you will steal nothing, you will break nothing."

Then the box disappeared. "I need ravens now!" called Jane. "Ravens come and gather here in the grass."

At once the keas flew away from the area she indicated, and ravens flew in, not vocalizing at all, but with the beating of their wings making a rushing sound, like the crashing of waves.

The ravens hadn't all settled themselves when they disappeared.

Then the box reappeared, its door open, with no birds inside. Keas again swarmed into the box.

To Wang-Mu it seemed as if the supply of birds was endless. Ten, twenty, thirty times Jane sent the box as well as loose birds on the grass.

"Can we help you?" asked Peter.

"Don't interfere with my bandwidth," said Jane.

Peter turned to Wang-Mu. "So I guess I can't ask if she's sent Dog or Phoenix or Royal Son on to Lusitania."

"I have," said Jane. "All three. Now shut up."

At last there were no birds left—except for a few that hovered off in the distance, apparently ravens and keas that had no wish to go, even under threat of death from the weapons of the Folk. That was when there emerged from the trees a band of humans, all naked and long-armed and short-legged, male and female, carrying no possessions.

"Can we trust you to come to our world in peace?" Miro cried out to them.

They knelt in the grass.

And they were gone.

They waited a few more minutes. Jane called out once, "Now is the time. We will not come back."

Three more of the Yachachiyruna came out of the trees and ran toward them. They disappeared in mid-run.

Jane turned to the others. "Peter and Wang-Mu, Thulium and Sprout, take everybody back. Miro, bring the box. And me. Bring me. I'm exhausted."

"The meadow?" asked Miro.

"Too many birds there," said Peter. "Q-Bay. Except for the box."

They arrived in Q-Bay and immediately rushed outside. Now they could see clouds of birds, flying, dipping, sometimes chaotic, sometimes with astonishing order, like watching vids of schools of fish in the sea. Jane said, "Let's all go to that clear area just beyond the fence."

When they were standing in the appointed place, the swarming of the birds ended. They all alit in the grass, making a patchwork carpet of bright keas in this patch, black ravens in that, all facing the humans.

"I can't divide you into your tribes and leks," said Jane loudly. "You need to divide yourselves into your breeding populations. Don't make any mistakes, because once I take you to your new colony world, you can't change your minds."

The birds swarmed again, seeking out their companions. Wang-Mu noticed that the ravens seemed to fly in pairs as they gathered into groups.

A raven fluttered out of the group and landed

on Jane's shoulder. Wang-Mu recognized Dog. Jane apparently heard her say something, and called out, "Ravens who want to be on the same continent with the keas, I need two breeding populations of you. To my left. Keas, divide into two groups. And yes, that means I don't trust you to behave around humans."

The sorting continued.

"If you think you chose the wrong group, change now!" called Jane.

A few hundred birds flew from one group to another.

And then they were all settled. Jane had her arm around Miro's waist. Sprout and Thulium walked to her and touched her arm.

"Should we?" asked Wang-Mu.

Peter said, "I think they'll be enough to sustain her. She'll ask for us if she needs us."

One by one the color-sorted patches of birds disappeared.

"I wonder if anyone has warned the colonies what's coming," said Peter.

"She won't send them to human-populated places," said Wang-Mu. "We'll go around and tell them all what happened, and inform them that they're sharing their world, not with two other alien species, but with four or five or six."

The Yachachiyruna were all still gathered near the edge of the woods. "We don't have to send them off yet," said Peter.

"They'll take some getting used to," said Wang-Mu.

"And they eat what humans eat. They'll *have* to be taken to the human colonists on each world. Or maybe they'll all go to the same world. There may be only one breeding population of the Engineers."

"Wherever they go," said Wang-Mu, "that colony will have the best designed and built and maintained machinery."

"Remember that the Formics do fine with metal-work," said Peter. "But yes, there will be advantages to having Quechua-speaking Engineers living in the trees. Has to be a world with branchy trees."

Jane and her companions leapt to a place near the Yachachiyruna, but Peter put his arm around Wang-Mu and said, "I know you're not tired at all, and I know you wish we knew where our raven and kea friends were sent. But for right now, our baby is very tired, and she won't nap till you get to sleep."

"Nonsense," said Wang-Mu. "The baby sleeps on its own schedule. Not she, not he. It, till we know. We don't want anybody to think we're hoping for one sex more than the other."

They detoured to the barracks, inside their own room. "Did we have breakfast?" asked Wang-Mu.

"Yes," said Peter, "but a nice combination of lunch and supper would be nice about now. Let me call the mess hall and ask if they can send something over."

By the time the food arrived, they were both asleep. Anticipating this, the cooks had prepared meals that could wait outside the door of their room until morning.

———

At the forest's edge, Ruqyaq asked Jane, "Can we stay here?"

"No," said Jane.

"You think the Lusitanians won't accept us?"

"They probably will," said Jane. "But there are no trees you can swing on or nest in. They are all the surviving remnants of dead pequeninos. Every tree is sacred here."

"Ah," said Ruqyaq. "Those are stories I would like to hear."

"We may bring you back for a visit from time to time."

"I assume that we're too naked to be tolerated by most of the humans."

"This is a good Catholic colony," said Jane. "So are all the others."

"How dressed do we need to be? Loincloths are easy, and they don't interfere with our mobility very much, but it's hard for us to put on shirts and take them off."

"Covering your private parts would be a very good start," said Jane. "And if the women among you could cover their breasts, that would also help."

"Then may we stay a few days, while we get cloth and needles and thread to make our coverings?"

Jane grinned. "I'm not your ruler, you know. I'm just your bus driver."

"Oh, you're our ruler, like it or not," said Ruqyaq. "We knew it was only a matter of time before the Folk decided they didn't need us so much anymore. They'd either kill us or they'd keep us underground, where they could control us."

"They do understand, don't they, that if we wanted to harm them, they couldn't keep us out of their caverns," said Jane.

"Maybe they think, because the underground world is so vast, that they could hide from you," said Ruqyaq.

"They probably could," said Jane. "But not forever. Fortunately, we're not interested in Nest anymore, now that those willing to emigrate have left the place."

"I'm afraid for our brothers and sisters," said Ruqyaq. "I did my best to explain what you are and what you can do, but either they don't fear the Folk as much as I do, or they fear you more than they should."

"Everyone chooses and then lives with the choice," said Jane. "Most people regret most of their choices—at least a little."

Sprout walked up to Ruqyaq. "When you leave Lusitania, I won't have any more of your stories."

"Foolish boy," said Ruqyaq. "Jane will show you where I am, and then you can come to me whenever you want. What does distance mean to *you*?"

23

Cincinnatus: I don't want to be here anymore.

Jane: We have a nice array of brand-new colony worlds you can reside on.

Cincinnatus: I have little to contribute when the primary object is mere survival.

Jane: It's hard to think of a world where most people aren't constantly engaged in exactly that project.

Cincinnatus: You dragged me here, me and my children. Then you sent me off to retrieve my wife, who never really loved me and hadn't changed her mind. You've sent me hither and yon and you know what? I liked my life better on the *Herodotus*.

Jane: The ship is still in perfect condition, and it would be fairly simple to restock the supplies. Say the word and I'll send you up.

Cincinnatus: With my children.

Jane: If they choose.

Cincinnatus: Nobody wants the twins. They're very clever but also quite malicious and they egg each other on. My task will be to keep flying at relativistic speeds until we come to a world that we want to live on, at a time when they've matured enough to be tolerable.

Jane: That sounds like an excellent plan.

Cincinnatus: And Thulium will make the voyage—

Jane: If she chooses to go with you.

Cincinnatus: She's eight years old and I'm her father.

Jane: If she chooses.

Cincinnatus: I have already chosen for her. She's a minor child.

Jane: No sir. She's an extremely important child, a major child, and she has in her the power to go wherever she wants, at any time she chooses. How will you get her on that spaceship and *keep* her there if she doesn't want to go?

—Transcript of conversation: Jane Ribeira and Cincinnatus Delphiki as quoted in Plikt, *Leguminidae*

Brussels Delphiki thought of himself as Sprout, most of the time, and thought of his little brother Delft by the nickname Blue. It was a convention born aboard the *Herodotus*, when their whole world consisted of the three children of the Giant and their seven children, the cousins. Sprout had always felt overwhelmed by the sheer energy of the others. Both he and Blue were of a quieter disposition. Not necessarily introverted, but lacking the need that the other cousins seemed to share—the need to insert themselves into every conversation, every argument, as if they had proof that no conversation was real or important until they had contributed to it—or mocked it.

Sprout just listened. He formed his opinions, but rarely voiced them when the whole circus was going on, everybody outshouting everybody else, the interior of the ship echoing with every spat or frolic. Later, in the quiet of Carlotta's family compartment, Sprout would tell his comments on the arguments of the day to his mother, while Blue listened, tucked under her arm.

If Blue spoke, it was only to echo what Sprout had already said. Every now and then Sprout would take him to task for it. "You have ideas of your own, Blue. You have no need to echo mine."

"I do if you're right."

"I'm not always right, Blue."

"If you don't think you're right, then why do you say it?" asked Blue.

It was such a reasonable question that Sprout gave up and let Blue be his little echo as much as he wanted.

But now and then Blue noticed something and said something that reminded Sprout: The boy had a brain in his head, and he saw things through his own eyes.

So on a particularly sunny but not-too-hot day, as they walked across Bird Meadow, as they now called the place beyond the fence where all the birds had gathered before dispersing to five different worlds and seven different continents, Sprout decided to tell Blue something he had been thinking for several days now.

"I don't think I want to be called Sprout anymore," said Sprout.

"It's your name."

"My name is Brussels Delphiki," said Sprout.

"You were named for a city on Earth," said Blue. "As was I. The nicknames are better."

"Brussels is easy to say, and it was the capital of a country," said Sprout. "Delft is hard for a lot of people to say—I bet the Portuguese speakers here on Lusitania will turn it into, I don't know, Del-ee-fee-chee Delphiki."

"Yes, that's exactly what they do with my name," said Blue. "So I'll stick with Blue, thanks very much."

Not an echo today. That was good. "But if I really want to be called Brussels, will you call me that?"

Blue was very quiet for a while.

Then he stopped walking and pointed over toward the trees they were approaching. "Is that a raven?" Blue asked.

Sprout looked where he was pointing. "I don't see it."

"Big and black and shiny. In the sunlight it was as if lots of other colors were trying to escape from it. A black hole of a bird."

"Sounds like a raven," said Sprout.

"Then it's a raven."

"They all left Lusitania," said Sprout.

"Then this is a robot raven that stayed behind to keep us company," said Blue, the little smartass.

Finally, Sprout saw it. And it was definitely not a robot. "Dog!" he said, loudly enough that the bird could hear.

The raven flew toward them, like an arrow. And close behind came another raven, a little smaller.

"Dog is a stupid name for a bird," said Blue.

"As Blue and Delft are stupid names for a boy," said Sprout.

The first raven came to rest on the grass about two

meters in front of them. The second raven alighted on Sprout's shoulder.

"Are you Phoenix?" Sprout asked, and the bird on his shoulder said, "Yes."

"Dog, Phoenix," said Sprout, "I thought you went when the others left, a week ago."

"Nine days," said Blue.

"Arbitrary constructs," said Phoenix. "You humans and your calendars."

"*You* pay attention to the years," said Sprout.

"We pay attention to spring, summer, autumn, winter," said Phoenix. "Those have something to do with survival. The Stark names for days are weird, tied to Norse gods, and the Portuguese speakers on Lusitania call the days, 'Second market, Third market,' and so on. We don't have markets, or gods."

"Those names all had historical reasons," said Sprout. "What do *you* call the days?"

"Yesterday, today, tomorrow," said Phoenix. "And sometimes, 'Remember that day when we . . . ?'"

Sprout turned to Dog the Raven. "Madam Dog, leader of the Raven Council, why are you here instead of being on a new world with your people?"

"There's enough food here to feed two ravens."

"What, seeds?" said Sprout. "The amaranth is ripe, yes, but what about when winter comes?"

"We'll move indoors with you," said Dog, "and take sandwiches from your lunch trays in the mess hall."

"That would work," murmured Blue.

"One mating pair is not enough to start a viable breeding population," said Sprout.

Phoenix answered first. "I'm a male and Dog is a female but we have never mated. We're partners because we both speak human languages well."

"Well, if you never mate," said Sprout, "the whole problem of a viable breeding population goes away."

"Laying eggs," said Dog, "is tedious. It takes a lot out of me. But if I want to raise a brood or two, Phoenix will do."

"I'm honored," said Phoenix.

"Really," said Sprout. "Why didn't you go with your people?"

Phoenix fluttered off Sprout's shoulder and came to ground ten centimeters away from Dog. The size difference was very plain. Dog must be older than Phoenix, and Phoenix must be fairly young. Not a full adult.

Then Sprout realized what the birds were signaling. "Let's sit down, Blue, and hear what Dog and Phoenix have to say."

Even after they were all seated, Dog preened a while before she finally began to speak. "Sprout, you are one of the wisest of the humans, and one most open to learning new things."

Sprout accepted the salutation without false modesty.

"Blue," said Dog, "you are like your brother, though not yet as accomplished. You are both patient and willing to listen. Will you hear my tale?"

Sprout wondered, briefly, whether Ruqyaq learned his storytelling patterns from the ravens, or the ravens learned them from him.

"Please tell us," said Blue.

Sprout simply kept his gaze focused on Dog the Raven.

"There is a reason why I was able to hear the voice of the Hive Queen in my mind, when I first came to this world," said Dog.

Then she waited.

Sprout thought over what she had said, and replied, "Is it because ravens already talk to each other mind to mind, without words?"

Dog nodded her head, as did Phoenix.

"So when the Hive Queen looked for sentient life, using the method the Queens have always used," said Sprout, "she found you to be a viable partner in conversation."

"From her," said Dog, "I learned that this connection of the minds, of the heart—"

"The aiúa," said Blue.

Sprout look at him in surprise.

"I know about it," said Blue, testily.

"I learned that the connection could reach infinitely far," said Dog, "and yet take no time at all. Like the way you Travelers fly."

"So you're still in contact with all the ravens, on all seven continents?" asked Blue.

"I didn't know if it would work for us—none of us is as mighty as the Queen," said Dog. "So I let them all go, and waited here to discover if I could stay in contact with them."

"Can you?" asked Blue.

"Yes," said Dog.

"So you're still head of the Raven Council?" asked Sprout.

"I'm the representative of the ravens to the Travelers and the Geneticists. Other Council members serve as ambassadors to the keas on their world, and to the humans and Formics and pequeninos. We have had to expand the Council, so that every liaison is represented, and all our knowledge can be pooled."

"But it condemns you to isolation," said Blue.

"It keeps anybody from challenging you for leadership," said Sprout.

Dog the Raven made a gruff, raucous sound—not the cawing of a crow, but it would certainly pass for laughter. "I am at the center for now," said Dog, "but I won't live forever. Still, the liaison with the Travelers is the most important position of all, because you Travelers are the only ones who can save us if one or another of our colonies should be in danger of failing."

"I'm not a Traveler," said Blue.

"I don't think Jane intends to have a lot of traffic between the worlds," said Sprout. "Not that way."

"She's still transporting food and other supplies from Lusitania to all the human colonies," said Dog. "It will cost her nothing if a raven or two wants to hitch a ride."

"Jane doesn't want anybody to be a prisoner," said Blue.

"A wise boy," said Phoenix. "He should be allowed to breed."

Dog turned to Phoenix and said, "Humans let anybody breed."

"Oh," said Phoenix.

"And these two are so young they can't inseminate the eggs of the human female."

"Oh," said Phoenix. "I just thought they were small, like me."

So Phoenix wasn't necessarily younger. Just small for a raven.

"Dog the Raven," said Sprout, "I honor you for your sacrifice in remaining here. But when we're sure we've resolved the matter of the descolada, it's unlikely that all the Detourists—the Travelers, as you call us—will remain on one world."

"It will be interesting to see what the Council asks me to do, if I'm still alive at that time."

"How old are you now?" asked Blue.

"Wild ravens on Earth rarely lived to be twenty years old," said Dog. "But during the voyage, as we bred for intelligence and speech, we also achieved ever greater ages. I am already twenty years old—Earth years—and expect to live at least ten more years, and possibly twenty."

To Sprout it seemed unthinkable, to look forward to so brief a life. But then, anyone could die at any time, so anyone who counted on a full lifespan was delusional. You die when you die. Till then you live.

"I'm content with whatever life I get," said Dog. "Laying eggs shortens the lifespan of females, yet the species must go on, and I am expected to breed."

"As long as you remain on a world with almost no other birds," said Blue, "you must be lonely."

"We ravens are usually content to journey two by two. We change partnerships, but there's a human saying, 'Two is good company, three is crowded.'"

"So you don't usually flock," said Sprout.

"We do, when there's a need," said Dog. "Two ravens can't mob a hawk and make it go away."

"And there's something worse than being alone, or just the two of us," said Phoenix.

"What's that?" asked Dog.

"We might be forced to be the only ravens among a population of keas," said Phoenix.

The two ravens made their gronk-gronk sound.

"They'd have our feathers off us in ten minutes," said Phoenix.

"But I miss them," said Dog.

"Me too, the stupid clowns," said Phoenix.

"Do they talk mind-to-mind, the way you ravens and the Hive Queen can?"

"Not that I know of," said Dog. "And not all ravens are equally adept at it."

"How are the colonies doing?" asked Sprout.

"They're all eating well," said Dog. "The Travelers chose well, sending us to worlds bountiful with insects, grubs, worms, nuts, and seeds."

"Any predators?" asked Blue.

"Three of our seven colonies are on worlds with hawks and falcons, but we're smarter than they are, and we're bigger than other corvids. Hawks quickly learn to leave ravens alone. We're not their prey—not when there are small mammals and fish to be had."

"Then I won't worry about you," said Sprout.

"But if I ask you to take me to another world," asked Dog, "will you do it?"

"Jane would have to show me where it is, first," said Sprout. "Then I can find it again."

"Visit all the colonies," said Dog. "Tell me about them when you do."

"Me too?" asked Blue.

"You can't detour yet," said Sprout.

"But you can take me with you," said Blue.

"Why not?" said Sprout.

"Why not indeed," said Dog. "Blue may learn how to Travel just from doing it frequently with you."

Blue grinned. Sprout worried.

"You'll always be needed, Sprout," said Dog. "Don't begrudge your brother the chance to have a power you like having."

"Right," said Sprout. "That would be wrong, for me to even *want* to keep it from him."

"None of the other humans know that we're here," said Phoenix. "Will you tell them now, or keep it secret?"

"What do you *want* us to do?" said Blue.

"I don't know," said Dog. "I would like to see Peter and Wang-Mu again, so you could tell *them*. And Jane and Miro—of course they should know."

"The only Traveler you haven't mentioned," said Sprout, "is Thulium."

"She's a remarkable human," said Dog. "Even cleverer than you."

"I know," said Sprout.

"But still somewhere between crazy and stupid," said Phoenix.

"You're wrong," said Sprout. "Neither one. But frightened sometimes and wildly overconfident at other times."

"Therefore crazy," said Phoenix.

"And she sometimes overestimates her own knowledge and skills," said Sprout.

"Therefore stupid," said Phoenix. "You only reject 'stupid' and 'crazy' because they're on your list of not-nice words."

"Are you telling me not to tell her?" asked Sprout. "Because I think she would benefit from talking to you often. I think it would help her learn how to be less . . . crazy and stupid."

"Tell her, then," said Dog. "Or better yet, bring her here without telling her."

"How will I know when you're here?" asked Sprout.

"Where else would we be?" asked Phoenix.

"One of us will always be nearby," said Dog, "and will call the other if you come."

"The Council of Ravens, back on Nest," said Sprout. "Now I wonder—were there a bunch of other ravens there, meeting in those trees? Or were you talking to them all in your mind, from a great distance?"

"It was rarely more ravens than me and Phoenix," said Dog. "We're not crows. They're such annoying extroverts."

"Were there crows on Nest?"

"Almost every kind of bird except the ratites and the raptors," said Dog. "The Huapaya couldn't deal with giant birds inside a spaceship. And no condors or other birds with vast wingspans were awake for the trip."

"You have a long and amazing history," said Sprout.

Dog paused before answering. "Our history is completely dependent on humans for our transportation through space. But we honor humans for letting us ravens breed ourselves. Humans were not good at recognizing the traits we value most."

They regarded each other in silence for a long time.

"Come speak to me from time to time," said Dog. "Either of you, together or separately. I want to learn from you about the special humans called leguminids. We have a lot of knowledge that you'll never hear from Ruqyaq, because he doesn't know it."

"We have some stories, too," said Blue. "We had our own voyage in the *Herodotus*, for more centuries than the Folk of the *Ark*."

"Then we will also listen to your tales," said Dog. "Good-bye."

With that, she took wing and flew away. But instead of going into the trees, she spiraled upward, then began a show of acrobatic moves in the air, she and Phoenix dancing together, or so it seemed. It was beautiful to watch these large birds flying on their broad wings, black crosses in the sky.

And then they swooped down and went into the shadows of the trees. They disappeared the moment they entered the shadows.

"Thanks for taking me with you today," said Blue.

"Thanks for noticing the ravens, so we could go to them," said Sprout.

"I think they would have sought us out whether I saw them or not," said Blue. "They know you."

"Maybe," said Sprout.

They headed back toward the gate in the fence, because it was getting on toward mealtime.

"Do I have to call you Brussels?" said Blue.

"No," said Sprout. "Not yet."

"Not ever. Please?"

"We'll see."

"You sound like an idiotic grownup when you say that."

"What's idiotic about it?" asked Sprout.

"It's a grownup way to say no, without a child realizing their request has been rejected."

"Yes," said Sprout. "But apparently it doesn't work on you anymore."

"Never did," said Blue.

"Always did till now," said Sprout.

24

Quara: I understand that as a matter of interplanetary peace, we can never return to Nest. Especially now that we've taken so many refugees with us.

Ela: Then what is this conversation about?

Quara: We're not diplomats. We're not a government. We're not even a military force. We're scientists. And we haven't finished our work. We have no definitive answers about the descolada virus.

Ela: Do you still believe such answers are to be found on Nest?

Quara: When they thought of us as enemies, they attacked us. A biological attack. Why should we be sure that they didn't alter the Recorder virus to function as the descolada?

Ela: And then they launched it into space with no concern about where this terrible weapon would land? Their attack on us was directed against a particular threat that landed on their world, uninvited.

Jane: They did invite us to dinner.

Quara: Finding the descolada, its source, the likelihood of running into it again on other worlds —how can we abandon that work and leave the whole human species—all the sentient species—exposed to this terrible bioweapon?

Ela: Don't beg the question, Quara. The whole issue is *whether* it was made as a bioweapon, so don't talk as if that had already been decided.

Quara: We have a responsibility.

Thulium: Stop. All these points have been made now. It's time to think.

Quara: Your specialty, yes?

Ela: Don't be mean to a child, Quara.

Thulium: What if we already have all the data we need? What if we simply haven't analyzed it right? What if we need to conduct experiments to test hypotheses?

Quara: What experiments can we possibly conduct? Spread a very fine net across a hundred light-years of space and see how many descolada viruses we catch?

Thulium: I can think of a few useful things to try. So can you, if you open your mind to possibilities you haven't already thought of—or to some you already rejected.

—Excerpt from transcript: Ela, Quara, Jane, Thulium, Sprout as quoted in Plikt, *Leguminidae*

Some of the experiments could only be performed in computer simulations. The descolada virus was too virulent and too intelligent, if that was the right term, for experiments with the actual virus to be safe.

But the simulations were solid—they'd proved accurate many times before—so Sprout took over running the many iterations of the sim to determine what the result would be if only one of the two key genes on the Recorder virus was broken. They were able to confirm that each break would always result in some descolada-like behaviors; only when both were broken did Recorder become descolada.

Then they ran simulated cosmic radiation damage, to see what the probability was of striking those particular genes during passage through space. Then the resulting deformed molecules had to be simmed to see how the descolada would perform with those breaks.

The result was that no other mutation they found, no other broken genes, resulted in a viable infectious agent like the descolada. Any other changes either did nothing or killed the virus.

"I think that proves it was made to be a weapon, deliberately," said Quara, when Sprout presented his results.

"It proves nothing," said Thulium. "We're scientists, remember? We're not trying to *prove* anything. We're trying to *dis*prove our own hypotheses, and then if we fail we regard it as temporary possible confirmation of our guesses."

"What's your alternate hypothesis, then, Thulium?" said Quara. "Why were these two genes broken, and no others?"

"I have an idea," said Blue.

Thulium looked impatient.

Sprout intervened. "Blue knows way more about the descolada than we knew six months ago."

"Tell us your idea, Blue," said Ela.

"It's not a simulation," said Blue. "We don't understand either the descolada or the Recorder virus well enough to build a decent sim. But we have vacuum chambers, don't we?"

Everyone knew the answer was yes.

"The descolada responds to its environment," said Blue. "It knows when it's inside a host's body, when it's in sunlight, when it's in water or atmosphere."

"It seemed to, on Lusitania," said Fingers, who had been helping Sprout run the simulations. And since he carried a version of the descolada in his body, because pequenino reproduction and transformation still depended on it, he had a special claim on their attention.

"What we've only guessed at," said Blue, "is whether the descolada or the Recorder can survive in cold hard space."

"Put the viruses in the vacuum chamber?" said Quara. "That won't show anything."

"Said the omniscient Quara," said Miro.

"Shut up," said Quara. But she made no more protest.

"Don't use the descolada or any version of it," said Blue. "Use the Recorder and see what happens to it."

"We can't possibly see the molecule inside the chamber, and the moment we take it out to examine it, it won't be in vacuum anymore," said Thulium.

"Such a Schrodinger moment," said Miro.

"Not the big vacuum chamber," said Blue. "The little one, with the clear window into it."

"Shrink it down more inside," said Sprout. "Make it so the Recorder virus has to be right up near the window."

"Might work," said Ela. "Worth trying."

Because it was Blue's idea, he supervised the crew working on building the tiny vacuum chamber and inserting a version of Recorder. The back wall was a color-killing black, while a series of variable-colored lights could play through the field from different angles. The microscopes were snapping high-speed pictures and taking vids at every useful depth of field. Finally Blue said, "That should be enough as a test of concept."

Sprout was proud of his little brother, but also afraid what it might do to him if his experiment turned out to show nothing.

It took a while to find which stills showed the clearest pictures. The equipment couldn't show individual atoms, but it gave a fuzzy picture of the shape of the whole molecule. At first they looked at the most recognizable stills—Recorder exactly as it existed on Nest.

But Thulium quickly scanned through the stills with that sort of image and snorted. "*All* of the stills we've chosen are from the first second after insertion. We're seeing only what we put into the vacuum, not how it responded."

Now they looked at the later pictures. The images seemed to resist clear resolution. "It looks like the viruses have shrunk down to a tiny fraction of their regular size," said Quara.

"But thicker," said Blue.

"And all of the images from later in the process show the same thing. Shrunken or cut-down viruses," said Miro.

"Or reconfigured ones," said Thulium. "Time for the vids, even though the resolution won't be as good."

It took many viewings of the first five seconds after insertion before they began to understand what they were seeing. It was Ela who finally put it into words. "In a vacuum, the Recorder folds itself repeatedly, like a fan, like pleats."

"More like a string being folded back and forth upon itself," said Blue.

"What we need to do now is determine what that means to exposure to cosmic radiation," said Thulium. "Here's my guess, based entirely on Blue's insight. The way the Recorder virus folds, only the outside of each bend is exposed to radiation, and therefore mutations would be most likely to occur at those fold points."

They had to run the experiment several times, and at one point Peter and Wang-Mu went to another world to buy a higher-resolution microscope. Finally, though, they had clear enough images to see that Thulium was exactly right. Instead of the break points in the descolada being two among billions of genes, they were two among 88 genes exposed and weakened at the fold points.

"Any genes broken by radiation during transit through hard space," said Quara, "would kill the virus, except those two. But the chance of those two occurring randomly, given the configuration of the folded virus, is not unlikely. Those are the only mutations that would result in a living but changed virus. Now I can believe the descolada was not deliberately weaponized."

"I think there's some kind of encapsulation going on, after it's folded," said Blue. "Can we run some different colors?"

By the end of the next day, they understood that once the Recorder virus hit near-vacuum, it folded up and then built a microthin film around itself, to protect it and, perhaps, contain it so it wouldn't spontaneously unfold.

"It's an amazing design," said Sprout. "No spaceship needed. Just go out into space, eject a few million Recorder viruses in the general direction you want, and they'll build their own tiny life-support and isolation chambers."

"Why didn't we see it before?" asked Carlotta. "We're supposed to have decoded most of the genome."

"It's probably controlled by the sequences we couldn't decode," said Ender. "It happens."

"We should have seen it," insisted Carlotta.

"It's not a failure of leguminids or of Ribeiras," said Jane. "It's just the simple fact that until you think of a thing, you haven't thought of it yet."

They all sat or stood around, maybe thinking of how profound yet obvious Jane's aphorism was. But Sprout was thinking, Good work, Delft Delphiki. You've earned your place among the scientists for sure.

"Good work," said Ela. "Everybody get something to eat and a good night's sleep. No celebration, just sleep, because we've got some decisions to make tomorrow."

———

The decision was the obvious one. Had they solved the whole descolada question? Thulium was the one who said, "Science isn't done until it's published," and everyone agreed that they needed to send several short reports and a long, detailed paper demonstrating the differences between Recorder and descolada, how the descolada on Lusitania was neutralized, and describing the behavior of Recorder in a vacuum.

They put the names of the entire research team, including those of the pequeninos who had worked with them. The Formics who had been part of the project had no names, and since they could not reveal the existence of Formics anyway, no harm done. Ela's name came first, as head of the team. But everyone was aware of which bits of research each person had done. "Dead ends are part of the achievement," said

Ela, "because until we exhaust many possibilities, we can't have any confidence in our results."

When it was all written up and ready to transmit by ansible to the Hundred Worlds, Jane made them wait. "This will have little impact unless it comes with a story." So they waited for Plikt and Valentine to draw up some fairly brief monographs that included accounts of the work of the Ribeira family and the leguminids. Jane was never mentioned; nor was detouring; and no account mentioned Nest in any way. The Hundred Worlds had heard plenty about the terrible danger of the descolada, so they would have a context for the stories that were sent along with the scientific papers.

On the day when Jane said, "All done. All sent. Getting acknowledgment of receipt from some. Many," Ela made a simple proposal. "There are a whole lot of superb geneticists on Lusitania right now, and there's still plenty of follow-up work to do. Nevertheless, I declare the descolada project to be at an end. We never found the point of origin, but it doesn't matter. We now understand the benign intent of the makers, and we have disseminated a course of action for any world that runs across a mutated Recorder virus. So the project is complete, and you're all fired."

They laughed and applauded and a few of them wept.

Then, over the next few days, they started forming up in small teams to research this and that. About half the former team members asked to be transported to one or another of the new colony worlds, to study the native flora and, if there was any, fauna. The rest were happy to stay on Lusitania, which now had most of the best equipment available in the Hundred Worlds. Only four considered and then decided to leave Lusitania and go to one of the older worlds with great and famous universities.

They worried that they had no credentials, but Jane only laughed. "I'll send you copies of the reviews of older papers that have had your names inserted as co-author. You have all the credentials you'll need, as long as you want to study xenology or genetics."

The leguminid cousins had their own meeting, and grudgingly permitted their parents and Miro to attend, insofar as parents were available. Thulium was fine being an orphan, and she accepted Carlotta and Yuuto as foster parents.

"We're children," said Little Mum. "That's how we look, and despite our manifest brilliance, that's what we *are*."

"Speak for yourself," said Thulium.

"I can't imagine a stupider waste of time than going to some civilized world," said Boss, "picking an elementary school, and trying to tolerate the company of children who don't know anything about calculus or the Peloponnesian War."

"That's not even on the table," said Carlotta. "There's no place for us in the regular academic system of any nation on any world. But I also don't want us to be confined in a tube hurtling through space with no outside human contact at all."

"Father already has the *Herodotus*," said Thulium, "and it would be a waste of money to buy another near-lightspeed ship."

"Not that there's any chance of any of you running out of money in our lifetime," said Yuuto.

"You've seen our financials?" asked Little Mum.

"I've seen that the list of the leguminid holdings would take me a year just to read," said Yuuto.

"Where shall we go?" asked Boss. "I want to go everywhere and see everything."

"A lovely thought, impossible to achieve," said Ender's wife, Mayumi. "I can assure you, once you've seen your first dozen flocks of sheep on grassy slopes and meadows, you've seen them all."

"I intend to do some traveling," said Thulium, "sometimes with company, if you want, and sometimes alone. I'm going to visit my mother and grandmother at least once a year, and probably more often. I'm going to visit the ravens and keas—on the colony worlds, I'm not violating the rules and returning to Nest. But in between trips, this is where I want to be. As long as Miro and Jane are here—"

"We plan to be," said Miro.

"And Wang-Mu and Peter, too," said Thulium.

"At least till the baby is born, they've assured me," said Miro.

"And I want to come back home to the place where I know I'll see the cousins. You've been my whole life, till the last six months. I don't want to lose you, not now, not ever."

Boss laughed. "Come on now, Thulium, what if we're trying to get away from you."

"Then tell me what I'm doing to annoy you, and I'll stop," said Thulium.

"Just a joke," said Boss. "You're fine, and I want a place to come home to, as well. Can we still use this building? Will there still be support staff?"

Miro shrugged. "The project won't be picking up the bill anymore. But if you'll authorize Yuuto to pay out the expenses, this can become the property of the leguminids. It's not as if real estate on Lusitania is going at a premium."

"And will we someday meet the actual people of Lusitania?" asked Sprout. "The regular citizens?"

"We'll start getting them used to you right away," said Miro. "These are good people. Just remember that what seems normal to you will be very strange to them. And watch what you say about religion. It means a lot to these people, so be respectful or, failing that, silent on the matter."

They all understood, or said they did. Lusitania was officially declared to be their home.

"And keep Q-Bay fully equipped and at least a skeleton staff," said Thulium. "You never know when we might come home with some bug or other creature."

"Another heavy expense that won't even be a blip on the family finances," said Yuuto.

They sat around in silence, until Sprout finally spoke up. "I guess we're about to start having actual lives now."

"Saving the world isn't a lifetime career," said Ender. "Just a hobby for a while."

25

Plikt: What I ask is simple enough. You have access to your own memories from the past three thousand years.

Jane: As well as all the written records that have been digitized.

Plikt: It's your own memories I need. You were in Ender's ear for most of his life, seeing all he saw, hearing all he heard.

Jane: And hearing whichever of his thoughts he chose to share with me.

Plikt: To write the final document of my Speaking of his death —

Jane: You want to write *The Life of Ender* to stand parallel with *The Hive Queen* and *The Hegemon* and *The Life of Human*.

Plikt: Doesn't he deserve such treatment? More than his brother ever did.

Jane: But he deserves as good a Speaker as the writer of those works, and you are not qualified.

Plikt: I know. But with your help, with your memories and perceptions, I can come closer than I can without.

Jane: So I should help you make a project that is a botch from its conception into somewhat less of a botch?

Plikt: Yes. It's all that's within my reach, and nobody else is reaching.

> —Memorandum of conversation: Jane and Plikt
> from Plikt, "Notes on The Life of Ender"

"Please let me come with you," said Thulium.

Wang-Mu looked at her carefully. Was she sincere, or had she merely improved her ability to pretend to be a caring, sensitive person? So much evidence pointed both ways.

"We can't stop you from coming," said Peter, "so why ask?"

"I want to be part of the conversation," said Thulium.

"So, talk whenever you want," said Peter. "We'll listen."

"I want to be a respected part of the conversation."

"That will depend on what you say," said Peter.

Wang-Mu knew it was time to intervene. "Thulium, I know you think we cheated when we went to the surface of Nest without you."

"I was offended and hurt and angry, yes," said Thulium. "But by the time you got back, and definitely after that, I realized that it would have been crazy for me and Sprout to go at the same time. You would have had to think about protecting us the whole time."

"What has changed?" asked Wang-Mu.

"I've grown up a little. Not just smarter, but wiser, too. I almost died from the bioweapon of the Folk, which hit me hardest because of my own stupidity in going first, and going alone."

"This is all good news," said Wang-Mu. "But it doesn't explain why you want to go *with* us."

"The keas are insane," said Thulium. "If I go to them alone, I'll be lucky if I get treated as mildly as Sprout did."

"Kea poop is a good thing to avoid," said Peter.

"But you have a friend among the kea. A friend who seems to be a leader. Are you going to the world where Royal Son is living?"

"Yes," said Wang-Mu.

"Please let me meet him and his tribe under your protection."

Wang-Mu knew what was really happening. Though Thulium treated her Aunt Carlotta as a kind of foster mother, Carlotta couldn't be her mother in all the ways that Thulium needed. In other cultures and other eras, mothers would introduce their daughters in society, giving them standing and asserting protection. Thulium was asking Wang-Mu to be her sponsor with another species. And for Peter to be her protection, though Wang-Mu knew Royal Son's relationship was primarily with her.

But it was more than that. Peter had been assigned to love her, back when they thought Peter would be the one helping her detour. But what happened, inadvertently, was the development of a far greater philotic bond between Wang-Mu and Thulium. With me, she not only feels safe, she feels known.

"Peter," said Wang-Mu, "what if Thulium stays with me, and only contributes to a conversation when I tell her it's all right?"

"She won't abide by any such rules," said Peter.

"I know why you believe that," said Thulium, "but—"

"This is a conversation," said Peter, "between Wang-Mu and me. Between husband and wife, deciding whether to take a child into a conversation which she has not earned a place in. This is not a time for you to plead your own case."

Wang-Mu smiled at Thulium, to soften Peter's words.

"Wang-Mu is speaking *for* you," said Peter, "far better than you could possibly speak for yourself."

Wang-Mu could see that Thulium already had a retort in her mind, in her mouth, ready to be spoken. But she did not speak.

"If she makes a mistake, my love," said Wang-Mu to Peter, "let me smooth over any misunderstanding. I believe I will be able to do it, though I think it will never be necessary."

"Royal Son and all the other keas will wonder why we brought her, what her purpose is," said Peter.

Wang-Mu took a few steps to the bassinet where baby Fei-Tzu was sleeping. She picked up the baby carefully, not waking him, and handed him to Thulium. At first Thulium shrank back—when would she have ever handled a baby in her life?—but then she understood, if not everything, then something, and she reached out and took the baby from Wang-Mu.

This time, finding himself in unfamiliar hands that did not hold him in familiar ways, he woke up, and began to whimper softly.

"What am I doing wrong?" asked Thulium.

"Absolutely nothing, except for the horrible mistake of not being me or Peter," said Wang-Mu.

"Well, I plead guilty to that."

"Rock slightly back and forth. It's a pattern all parents learn, and while it doesn't always work, it improves your chances," said Wang-Mu.

"It worked for me," said Peter, getting into the spirit of this. Wang-Mu knew that Peter recognized that she was determined to bring Thulium—and he would join her in trusting Thulium with the care of their little boy in order to bring it off.

Within a half-hour, Thulium had been taught and had practiced feeding the baby, changing his diaper, singing softly to him, and getting him back to sleep.

"I'm obviously not an expert," said Thulium.

"Stay with me and help me with the baby for a few days before we go."

Peter did not remind her that they had planned to leave today after lunch.

Thulium agreed.

So it was that when Jane led them for the first time to the continent where keas lived, Thulium was with Peter, Wang-Mu, and little Fei-Tzu, holding on to the backpack that held the supplies for the baby.

"Where are the keas?" Peter asked Jane.

"This is the continent where they live," said Jane. "I didn't stay to see where they built their nests."

"But they could be anywhere," said Peter. "How big is this continent?"

"The size of Africa, back on Earth," said Jane.

"How are we supposed to find them?" asked Peter.

"By looking in the right places," said Jane. "All three of you are very smart. Figure it out." And with that, Jane was gone.

They were on fairly level ground. There were mountains visible in the distance, though with clouds gathered along the peaks it was hard for Wang-Mu to decide whether the mountains were snow-capped or not. "What do we know about keas?" she asked.

"They were the only alpine parrots on Earth," said Peter. "They lived in the mountains and high forests of the South Island of New Zealand. They must have flown there as ordinary parrots, and then became keas on that island."

"So should we look in the mountains?" asked Wang-Mu.

"Well-watered mountains, I imagine," said Peter. "Forests need water."

"There hasn't been time for any Earth flora to take over anywhere, so are we even sure what a forest will look like here?" asked Wang-Mu.

"The vegetation will be thick and lush," said Thulium. "If there are no predators, the keas will nest on the ground; if there are trees with strong wooden branches, they'll nest in the trees."

Wang-Mu saw Peter looking at Thulium for a moment before he said, "So how do we go about finding such a location? I don't want to try doing aerial reconnaissance, because I'm not Jane and we don't have a box."

"We could try reasoning," said Wang-Mu.

"We know nothing about this planet," said Peter.

"We know that Jane didn't take us to the arctic or antarctic zones," said Thulium. "The sun is fairly low in that direction, and I'll assume, because it isn't very hot, that it's still early in the morning."

"Well, that's something," said Peter.

"Judging from the trajectory of the sun," Thulium continued, "we're near the equator. I think we'll find that at noon, our shadows pool around our feet."

"So, this continent straddles the equator," said Peter, "and that's about where we are."

"This is a grassy plain, but it isn't yet in seed. And the keas evolved in a more deciduous environment, at a high elevation," said Thulium. "So perhaps we should simply move either north or south, until we find mountains and forests. At this latitude, we're likely to find only jungles, grasslands, or deserts."

Wang-Mu looked at Peter and smiled. "Good advice is good advice," she said.

"Would you like me or Wang-Mu to lead the way?" asked Peter.

"What if I take you with *me*?" asked Thulium.

"No," said Peter. "*You* will take the backpack with you, Wang-Mu or I will hold the baby in its wrap, and whichever of us doesn't have the baby, that's the one that leads. That's plenty for any of us to keep in our minds while detouring."

Wang-Mu could see that an argument had already leapt to Thulium's mind, but the girl held her tongue, and Wang-Mu was pleased.

"The baby is the most important," said Thulium mildly. "But the diapers, wipes, and food and drink for him will make this trip much easier. Thank you for trusting me with that."

"Wang-Mu," said Peter, "you have the baby, so I'll explore ahead first."

"Me first," said Wang-Mu, and, still holding the baby in the wrap, she leapt.

As soon as Wang-Mu arrived, she walked up a rise of ground and saw that there was no apparent danger nearby. She turned back and could barely see the others in the distance. Prairie land like this was convenient, but as soon as they reached trees, beckoning wouldn't work. But it could work now, so she waved. And then beckoned.

A moment later, Thulium was there, with all the supplies.

"He said he'd wait to make sure nothing got left behind," said Thulium.

"Don't be offended," said Wang-Mu. "He's just careful."

"I get it," said Thulium.

When they got into rolling ground, and then trees,

and finally the slopes of a snow-covered mountain range, Wang-Mu calculated that they had detoured so far that they were out of the tropics. The air was markedly cooler, especially near water or among trees.

"They might have gone north," said Thulium.

"We had to choose a direction," said Peter. "And if we need to go back to where we started, we don't have to do it in baby steps."

They began to climb, and whichever of the Wiggins moved ahead, they couldn't wave—now they had to detour back and tell the others it was safe to follow. They could all sense each other well enough that they didn't have to go by line of sight. They just knew where they needed to go.

They had journeyed a significant amount of the circumference of this planet when the sun began approaching the western horizon. "At this elevation, the baby will get cold," said Thulium.

"Oh, we'll go back to Lusitania and sleep in our beds tonight," said Peter. "We're not insane."

Wang-Mu laughed lightly at Thulium's consternation. "We won't spend a night here, Thulium, until we know it's safe."

"Snakes," said Peter. "Scorpions."

"Surely when the colonists got here they didn't release such dangerous Earth creatures," said Thulium.

"We don't know the native life here. Lions hunting by night are a danger in Africa. We don't know if there are native creatures here to which we look like prey," said Peter.

"I don't believe Jane would have established colonies on worlds with dangerous predators," said Thulium.

"She had no time to explore any of them," said Peter, "beyond ascertaining they had a breathable atmosphere, plenty of water, lots of photosynthesizing plant life on land, and were inside the goldilocks climate zone."

"That was already kind of a lot," said Wang-Mu.

"And the colonists were armed," said Peter. "Plus they had Formics with them."

"And we don't," said Thulium.

"Baby Fei-Tzu likes sleeping on his mattress in his bassinet in an air-conditioned house," said Wang-Mu.

"And so do I," said Thulium, laughing. "I wasn't criticizing your plan, I was just surprised by it."

The sound of fluttering wings interrupted them. There was still plenty of sunlight, and they could pick up the bright colors of the keas flying toward them. Only a dozen or so.

They whirled chaotically around the human party, and skimmed just over the baby, as if deciding what it was.

A kea perched on Wang-Mu's shoulder. "Good evening, Royal Mother of the West."

"Are we near your home forest?" asked Peter.

"You've been in it for your last three jumps," said Royal Son. "But I was far off to the east, where it's already nearly night, and it took time for them to find me and tell me you were here."

"By far off, do you mean—" Peter began.

"Not far for people who can travel between worlds," said Royal Son. "But a half-hour's journey for us."

Wang-Mu interrupted the technical questions with the matters that seemed more important to her. "Royal Son, we want you to meet *our* son, Fei-Tzu."

Royal Son said, "I must change my name now, for there really is a royal son in your family."

"Treat this baby as your brother," said Wang-Mu, "and keep your name. Fei-Tzu is blood of my blood, but you were my son before he was."

Royal Son nuzzled her neck with his head and beak.

"And we brought a girl to help us care for Fei-Tzu. Her name is Thulium."

"We saw her," said Royal Son. "She came with Sprout and stayed long enough for us to play with her a while. But then she left and didn't come back."

"I was afraid," said Thulium. "And I was angry. The keas had taken all my equipment."

"We didn't take your eyes and ears and fingers and feet," said Royal Son. "But I understand. I'm glad to know your name. And you'll notice that you are not being played with today. This visit is far too important for us to want to be annoying."

"Can we come back tomorrow, when we have the whole day to visit your people?" asked Wang-Mu.

"That is a fine idea," said Royal Son. "Many will gather from our farthest reaches."

"Is this world a good place for you?" asked Peter.

"All our adult females have had at least one brood, and some have had as many as three."

"So there's plenty to eat," said Peter.

"Not for *you*," said Royal Son. "You'd have to visit the human colony on the other continent, where we don't go."

"Are the seeds and fruits here nourishing to you?" asked Peter.

"Jane told us that she chose only worlds with compatible proteins in the biosphere when considering where to send us."

"Jane thinks of everything," said Thulium.

"No," said Royal Son, "because she doesn't know everything. But she knows many things, and thinks of many things, and her actions are always intended to benefit us."

Wang-Mu chose to speak again. "Royal Son, would the other keas care about meeting little Fei-Tzu, or would he be boring, since he can't play?"

"You freed us from the domination of the Folk Below," said Royal Son. "We didn't know how much we longed for freedom until you came and spoke to us, Royal Mother of the West."

"What about the ravens?" asked Thulium. "There are ravens on this continent too, aren't there?"

"Yes, Child Who Can Vanish," said Royal Son. "There are several who are kind enough to condescend to talk to mere keas."

Thulium laughed. "Come now, you surely don't think of yourselves as inferior to ravens."

Royal Son laughed, too. "Sarcasm," said Royal Son. "That's a game we're very good at."

Another bird, this one standing amid the grass, said, in a voice only a little less clear than Royal Son's, "We are no longer subject to the laws of the Raven Council," said the bird. "We are thus twice liberated."

Wang-Mu thought this was unfortunate, because she wasn't at all sure the keas were capable of rational self-government. But since humans weren't either, she supposed the keas would have to learn how to work things out with each other and with the ravens. It was not her responsibility.

"Should we come back to this spot?" asked Peter. "In the morning?"

"This is the best place," said Royal Son, "because you know and we know where it is."

"And the ground is level," said Thulium, "so if you put the baby in the grass he won't roll downhill."

"We take our leave of you," said Peter.

"We rejoice to see you, now and tomorrow," said Wang-Mu.

"It was nice to meet you," said Thulium. "Thanks for not pooping on me."

Royal Son laughed as he flew down from Wang-Mu's shoulder.

"Now?" Peter asked.

"Ready, Thulium?" asked Wang-Mu.

Thulium's answer was to disappear, along with the backpack. A moment later, back in the Wiggin home, Wang-Mu was pleased to see that Thulium had already begun preparing for the pre-bedtime diaper change.

"Poor Fei-Tzu got more sun than he's ever had before in his life," said Wang-Mu, stripping off his clothes.

"He was never in full sun," said Thulium. "I was watching, and I don't think he got a sunburn at all."

"Humans need sunlight to be healthy," said Wang-Mu. "You were very good with Fei-Tzu today, Thulium. Thank you."

Thulium said nothing, but Wang-Mu could see that she was pleased.

Over the next week, Wang-Mu and Peter, with Thulium, visited the keas every day. They brought Fei-Tzu with them only once, then left him with Ender and Mayumi and their children after that. By the end of the week, Thulium had her own friends and favorites among the keas, and had learned ways that humans could take part in some of their games. She even thought of a couple of simple-minded games that only the young keas would play with her—but that was fine with her. She was a child too, wasn't she?

When Peter announced that this was their last day of all-day visiting, Royal Son laughed. "Yes, your visits make it hard for us to forage, and young mouths need to be fed and we need to have food laid aside for winter. In these mountains, winter will likely be terrible, though we have plans for coping."

"You were generous to give us so much time among you," said Wang-Mu.

"Thank you all for taking me in," said Thulium.

"You are now our friend in your own right," said Royal Son, "and you don't need older humans to come with you, if you want to come alone."

"Thank you," said Thulium. "But I am still a little afraid. I saw the vids of what happened to Sprout that time—"

"It will never happen to you. Remember that we felt like prisoners before, and our frolicking had madness in it. Fury. We knew Sprout had never harmed us, but we also recognized that he was of the same species as the Folk Underground. We tested him. But you have already passed our tests, and played with us and with our children. You are welcome, you are honored, you will be treated as a guest, not a spy."

Thulium smiled and then put her arms behind her, in imitation of a posture the keas frequently took. Then she bowed deeply, as the keas bowed to each other.

And then they were gone.

Once they were home, and Thulium said goodnight to Fei-Tzu and then went home to Carlotta's house, Wang-Mu and Peter talked for a while in bed.

"I can see she's adopted you as a kind of mother," said Peter. "If you want her to live with us, I won't mind."

"No," said Wang-Mu. "She would think she always has to care for Fei-Tzu. Let's make her welcome when she wants to come, and speak to her sociably and also, when appropriate, intimately, like good friends who have shared journeys together."

"I can do that," said Peter.

"And so can I," said Wang-Mu. "I already have enough children in that bassinet in the other room to occupy my life for the next few years."

"Not too many years," said Peter. "I want to have children while I'm still young enough to get down on the ground and play with them."

"Since you never had parents," said Wang-Mu, "how do you know that that's an important part of being a father?"

"Because Ender Wiggin had a childhood, and a father and mother, and so I know what a father is and what he's supposed to be and do."

Wang-Mu was happy that he was so openly speaking of the deep Andrew Wiggin memories that were attached to his aiúa. It was making him kinder and less fearful of the opinions of others. It was making him more loving to her and the baby. And to Thulium, which pleased Wang-Mu for reasons she herself didn't understand, because there was no reason Thulium should have been so important to her.

It's because she needs me, and I know how to give her what she needs, thought Wang-Mu. She's a hungry bird in my nest, and even though she didn't hatch from my egg, she's no brood parasite. I can nurture her and still have plenty of time and love and attention to give to little Fei-Tzu.

And I will visit my other adopted son, a kea named Royal Son, not so often that he tires of my visits, but not so rarely that he feels forgotten. He needs to feel the love of a human being, so that he'll know that not all humans are evil. With any luck, the humans of his world will leave the keas' continent alone forever. Or at least until both species have converged in their evolution enough to share the same habitat in peace.

That *can* happen, Wang-Mu told herself. Though she could think of no examples in history where species had treated each other as fellow citizens, as siblings, as equal friends.

As long as there's never a profitable market in kea feathers, thought Wang-Mu, they'll probably be safe.

———

Cincinnatus put up with the twins' delaying tactics for about half an hour. Then he picked them both up and carried them to their separate bedrooms.

"We want to sleep in the same room," said Lanth.

"I don't," said Dys.

"Liar," said Lanth.

Cincinnatus tossed Dys into his room and closed the door, and then tossed Lanth into the other room.

"This isn't my room," said Lanth.

"It is tonight," said Cincinnatus.

He palmed the doors closed, so the boys couldn't open them from the inside unless the ship went into emergency mode.

Peace at last. It didn't bother him that both boys were pounding on their doors or walls with their feet. The *Herodotus* was tough enough to stand it.

"Spare the rod and you'll spoil those boys," said a man.

Since there was no other human on the ship, Cincinnatus knew at once whose voice it was. "Graff," he said. "Didn't anybody purge you from the ship's computer?"

"You can't actually do that," said Graff. "I *am* the ship's computer."

"You have nothing to say that I want to hear."

"Fine," said Graff. "I'll just go and talk to the boys."

"Leave them alone," said Cincinnatus. "You spent your career destroying children. I'm not going to let you do your work on mine."

"Did I destroy Ender Wiggin? Did I destroy your father?" asked Graff.

"You turned them into weapons of war," said Cincinnatus.

"And you've spent their childhood turning your twins into far less effective weapons—but weapons all the same."

"They're naturally competitive," said Cincinnatus.

"They're naturally bullies," said Graff. "I would never have admitted them to Battle School."

"There were bullies in Battle School," said Cincinnatus.

"There are bullies in every army and police force and bureaucracy in the human universe," said Graff. "But in Battle School, nobody was *just* a bully."

"You certainly have a low opinion of my children," said Cincinnatus.

"I have a very high opinion of Thulium," said Graff. "Somehow she grew up to be teachable, despite her upbringing."

"Meaning that she's disloyal to her family and easily persuaded by strangers."

"Sergeant," said Graff, "did you have some *theory* behind the way you raised your kids?"

"'Sergeant' is the nickname my brother and sister gave to me when we were little, and I was the bossiest. They aren't here. To you my name is Cincinnatus Delphiki."

"I'm glad to hear it. The great Roman general who went home and farmed after the war was over."

"The Giant gave us names that reflected his thoughts and feelings," said Cincinnatus. "I'm not required to live up to that name."

"Cincinnatus," said Graff, "you are every bit as gifted as Carlotta and Andrew. Maybe even a little brighter. Please don't be at war with me."

"Awkward, obvious flattery won't make us friends," said Cincinnatus.

"There are only you and your sons on this ship," said Graff. "I spent my life studying children and how to train them. I learned many things that don't work, but also a few things that do. Now that you're having to deal with your obnoxious twins all day every day, wouldn't you like some advice on how to tame them?"

"Tame?" asked Cincinnatus.

"Domesticate. Civilize. Choose your word," said Graff.

"They're tamed right now."

There was still loud pounding on the walls and doors of their rooms.

"They sound tamed," said Graff.

"They give up after a while, if I ignore them," said Cincinnatus.

"Do you intend to keep them with you forever?" asked Graff. "Or do you count on the government of whatever planet you release them on to incarcerate them for the crimes they are bound to commit within hours of arrival?"

"Their choice."

"They aren't fit to make choices," said Graff, "because you haven't prepared them to make any. Did you raise them, *do* you raise them, so they can live a life of crime?"

"That wasn't my plan," said Cincinnatus. "And, unlike you, I'm not at all sure that's what I've done."

"You know that's exactly what you've done and are still doing," said Graff.

"And you could do it better?" asked Cincinnatus.

"I can't do it at all, since I can't pick them up and throw them into a room and lock the door behind them."

"You can lock the door," said Cincinnatus.

"Should I unlock it and let them out?" asked Graff. Cincinnatus sighed wearily. "Please, please don't."

"You don't like your children," said Graff.

"I don't like children," said Cincinnatus. "But I love Thulium."

"You were hurt to learn that she resented you and wanted to be free of you."

"I couldn't disagree with her decision," said Cincinnatus. "I still don't know if she was trying to get away from me or from her brothers."

"I think both," said Graff. "Cincinnatus, you don't

want to listen to my voice and you'll automatically want to reject any suggestions I make. But I can give you an article to read every morning that will give you some ideas about how to civilize the boys and turn them into something that a woman might one day want to marry and a business manager might someday want to hire."

Cincinnatus laughed. "Where is the Planet of Fools where such women and such managers live?"

"Will you read the articles I give you?" asked Graff.

"I'll read the first page of the first article," said Cincinnatus. "Then I'll decide whether to read on."

"Good," said Graff.

"You're a sim. Why do you care?"

"The grandchildren of Julian Delphiki are a precious commodity, not to be wasted because their father is still so angry and resentful toward *his* father that he has never functioned as a father himself."

Cincinnatus laughed dryly. "You've got me all sussed out."

"Yes," said Graff. "That's what your brother and sister both believe about you."

"They never said so," said Cincinnatus.

"They didn't dare, because of your mean streak."

"Mean streak?"

Graff waved a hand. "All right, your vicious streak."

Cincinnatus thought of the twins, how awful they had been to Thulium and, really, everyone, including their mother, when they met her. Cincinnatus also thought of how Andrew and Carlotta avoided him and said as little as possible, behavior that had begun back when he tried to convince them to kill the Giant because he used up too much of the ship's resources. Just because he faced hard realities and they . . .

"I need some counsel," said Cincinnatus. "The Giant wasn't much of a father. All talk, mostly talk about science."

"He didn't have the freedom of movement to dandle you on his knee," said Graff. "He filled the hold of the ship. But he lived only for you and your sibs. He loved you. He gave up his life with his wife and normal children, in order to keep you alive long enough for a cure to be found for the side effects of Anton's Key. That was his sacrifice. Now what will you sacrifice to save *your* broken children?"

Cincinnatus wanted to shut down the ship's computer to eliminate this ghost. But that would kill them all, so he wouldn't do it, because . . .

Because the boys were precious to him, and they were broken, and maybe Graff's shadow would be able to help fix them.

"Thank you for your help," said Cincinnatus.

"Thank you for giving me a chance to be of service," said Graff.

"How did you get to be Minister of Colonization back in the day?" asked Cincinnatus. "You don't sound like much of a politician."

"First, I tell the truth to power, whether they like it or not," said Graff. "Second, I make alliances and networks everywhere so I can get around the clowns who try to thwart me. And third, I won the Third Formic War."

"Oh. Yes. That," said Cincinnatus.

"By using your father and Ender Wiggin as my puppets," said Graff.

"And will you make *me* your puppet now?" asked Cincinnatus.

"No," said Graff. "I don't want puppets on the *Herodotus*."

"What *do* you want?" asked Cincinnatus.

"A family," said Graff.

"*My* family," said Cincinnatus.

"If you use your head and your heart, yes, it will become a family, and the family will be yours."

"Not yours," said Cincinnatus.

"I know what I am," said Graff.

"The ghost in the machine," said Cincinnatus.

"No," said Graff. "I'm just the machine."

"You don't believe that," said Cincinnatus. "You think you're still a person."

"I'm not insane," said Graff. "Here's what I think. I believe that *you* are still a person. Prove me right."

"I don't care what you think I am," said Cincinnatus. "Help me to be a father, and that'll be enough."

———

Sprout led Blue into the clearing, and then started beating on a hollow log with two sticks.

"Should I do it too?" asked Blue.

"He's coming," said Sprout.

"You're calling him?"

"I'm calling everybody who wants a tale," said Sprout.

In a few moments, the rustling of the leaves announced the arrival of people from every direction. Most of them were young Yachachiyruna, though there were also several ravens. The Yachachiyruna wore breechclouts now, which Sprout was grateful for. He was naturally modest himself, and appreciated their concession to his feelings.

Ruqyaq arrived last, because, as he had once told Sprout, it wasn't worth coming if there wasn't going to be an audience. But he had also said that Sprout and whoever he wanted to bring would always be audience enough for him.

Ruqyaq had met Blue before, but now he sized up the boy with a keen eye. "Aye, you hairy beast," he said to Blue. "If only you had four hands instead of flat feet, you'd be courted by a good number of Yachachiyruna."

"Females, I hope," said Blue.

"Don't hope," said Ruqyaq. "They're never going to mate with you. Because if we're still human enough to mate with people like you, we're far too human."

Blue blushed and laughed, and Sprout laughed too. The Yachachiyruna of this world lived on two different continents, and used boats to pass between them. One of the continents was dominated by the fast-growing human colony and the Formics and pequeninos who dwelt alongside them. Another continent was given to ravens, whom the Yachachiyruna sometimes visited. And this third continent was where the Yachachiyruna mined for metals and coal, and made their factories on the leeward coast, where the prevailing winds would usually carry away the smoke of manufacture.

"This is our Earth," Ruqyaq had once told Sprout. "Nest was merely a training ground, where we learned our science and engineering and languages. But here, we can become one nation and then several nations and perhaps many nations, with languages developing freely. Here we can have a history of our own."

Sprout wished that he could believe that humans and Yachachiyruna would always get along and respect each other's borders, but he knew too much of history to have much real hope of it.

"I have a tale, a brief tale, to begin with today," said Ruqyaq.

Everyone fell silent.

"It's a story of two brothers, who were kidnapped away from their father when they were little, and raised in a metal cave for many years. But their mother was with them, and taught them to be kind to each other, and kind to other children trapped in the cave.

"The brothers were curious about the worlds where people lived under the open sky and felt sunlight and warmth on their skin in the day, and grew cold in the winter. And one day they were magically taken from the cave and placed in a world where they had never been before. There were strange magical creatures there, and also there were diseases that had once threatened to kill everybody. And there was a strange kingdom full of perils but also wonders, like talking birds and creatures who swung in trees and had hands for feet."

Sprout didn't understand why Ruqyaq was telling a story that was obviously about Sprout and Blue. But he could see that Blue was enthralled, so he said nothing; and besides, why would Sprout want to interfere with a master storyteller?

"I wish I could tell you," Ruqyaq continued, "that the brothers were able to slay the enemies of their people and save their family from danger, but that would be a lie. They fought alongside their comrades and they were brave and clever, so when the victory came, they had earned their place in the triumph. But it is not the story of that war that I wish to tell.

"Instead, the first time the older brother visited the strange kingdom, he was set upon by some of the magical birds, who tormented him and came close to slaying him. But with remarkable courage, he refused to fight with them. None of the birds came to harm at his hands, and finally they gave up trying to kill him, and gave him great honor, as a powerful foe who refused to flee but also refused to fight. Not one of the birds had suffered any harm from him, even though he had suffered much harm from them.

"So the birds led him to a feeble old wizard, who had almost no magic, but who had some tales to tell. And the wizard told the older brother the story of his people and many other things about the strange magical kingdom.

"In time, the brothers and their friends decided to leave the magical kingdom forever, because there could never be trust and peace between them. But the older brother remembered the feeble old wizard, and the birds whose respect he had earned, so when he went back to the world he had come from, he took with him all the people of the old wizard who wanted to come, and all the magical birds who wanted to come, and he gave them lands where they could be safe.

"And in all of this, his younger brother was in complete agreement, for when the feeble old wizard met the younger brother, he learned that the older brother had told him everything, so it was as if the younger brother was not a stranger at all. He already knew and loved the magical birds, and he already knew the feeble old wizard's stories so well he could tell them all himself.

"That is why, whenever the brothers visited the lands they had given to the birds and the wizard, they were received as kinsmen, as providers, as fathers to the people of these lands, for they had been saved and brought out of captivity into a land rich in fruits and nuts, in seeds and insects, in soil that could grow crops and rocks where metals could be mined. Everything was owed to these brothers, and songs were sung about them in all the languages of the birds. The end."

The other Yachachiyruna gave the grunting sounds that were their version of applause, and the ravens also made approving sounds.

"What did you think of my story?" asked Ruqyaq.

"I think you gave the brothers credit for far more than was in their power to do," said Sprout.

"You are mistaken," said Ruqyaq, "for if you had not listened to my story and told a believable version of it to the other Travelers, we would not have been transported to the freedom and plenty we now enjoy."

Sprout gave it a little thought and realized that Ruqyaq was right, at least to a degree. The vids of Sprout's experience with the kea and with Ruqyaq had been a vital part of the descolada project's understanding of the peoples of Nest, and even though it was Jane who had done all the transporting, she was responding to the desire of Sprout's heart, to save his wonderful new friends from the dire enemy that had already slain so many keas.

"It was a good story," said Blue. "I hope to live such a life as to make it true."

Ruqyaq laughed at him. "How I wish you could swing through the trees with me! It's so exhilarating, like flying and yet always close to the earth, with the smells of life all around."

"I wish I could, too," said Blue. "But I'm not foolish enough to climb a tree and try to keep up with *you*."

"I know," said Ruqyaq. "You would certainly fall and die or be crippled, and that would take all the pleasure out of it for me."

"And for us," added Sprout.

"Unless being dead is very pleasant," said Ruqyaq. "That's a tale I can't tell, because nobody has come back to report on it."

"You said this was the first story," said Sprout. "Do you have another?"

"It's not really a tale," said Ruqyaq, "because it's both true and not very interesting."

"True stories are best," said Blue. "Even if they're not designed to be entertaining."

Sprout was proud of his brother, now that they were both becoming men. As in the story, he was glad that the two brothers were close, so that what happened to one might as well have happened to the other.

Ruqyaq changed branches, so that now his feet were touching the ground as he sat on the branch. "I need my feet connected to the soil for this story. It's about the makers of the Yachachiyruna."

"About how they made you?" asked Blue.

"Only at the end," said Ruqyaq. "I must tell you *why* they became the people who could make us out of themselves."

A silence fell upon the clearing.

"They lived among the high mountains, our ancestors, who spoke the holy languages of Quechua and Aymara."

"And Guaraní," murmured one of the Yachachiyruna.

"Keep silence," said another.

"There was nobody among the Huapaya who spoke Guaraní," said yet another.

"Should have been," said the first.

"Are we done with old and pointless disputes?" asked Ruqyaq.

His fellow Yachachiyruna muttered apologies and fell silent.

"I will call them the mountain people," said Ruqyaq. "Nobody in the wide world knew they existed, except tribes that lived in the jungles to the north and east, or along the seashore where they fished for their food. But in this isolated place, with no one to teach them, they taught themselves.

"There was a plant that had no real use, except that it formed little knobs of hard flesh underground. And now and then, in times of famine, some of the mountain people would dig up one of these knobs and try to eat it. It was hard to eat and had an unpleasant flavor when they ate it raw. And if they washed it before boiling it or roasting it, the people who ate it became very sick.

"They learned that they could roast it and eat it as long as they left the dirt on the skin of the knobs, for the dirt apparently contained the antidote for the poisons.

"They became so skilled with the preparation of these little knobby roots that the knobs became an important source of food for the mountain people even when there was no famine. They began to plant them, and nurture them, and by choosing which of the knobs to replant and nurture, they made the roots more delicious and less poisonous.

"This shows that already the mountain people understood how to genetically alter a living thing by selective breeding. And they didn't confine this skill to the potatoes which became their gift to the whole world. There was another plant, related to the potato vine, that produced tiny red berries that were tart and sweet and delicious. The berries could be collected together and crushed and boiled to make a sauce, and the mountain people began to breed them to give more and more berries, and bigger and bigger ones.

"The cultivation of these berries became widespread, and when they reached another people far to the north, they carried the breeding even farther, because these people did understand breeding, but they did not realize that there is a time to stop making changes. This is why they took a perfectly fine little cereal grain and bred it larger and larger until the grain grew into huge cobs covered with massive grains. The yield per hectare of ground was great, and by drying and grinding these huge grains they could feed large populations in every season, so they were very pleased with themselves.

"But when they got their hands on the berries that the mountain people had bred, they did the same ridiculous thing—they grew the berries to be big fat fruits, and all the delicacy and beauty was gone.

"The mountain people, though, remembered to keep all things in proportion. The desert people from the north gave the world maize, and it was a good gift, ugly as the giant cobs had become. The mountain people gave the world potatoes, the most complete and nutritious crop ever grown on Earth. And both peoples created tomatoes. The mountain people made them sweet and juicy. The desert people made them huge.

"Did the world thank the mountain people? Of course not. They were enslaved and oppressed. But they kept alive the heart of the mountains, and when the day came that they could go out into space, they became once again great miners and hewers and builders, and they also became great breeders, though now they chose to be breeders of birds.

"Some of them had befriended and studied ravens and keas, because they were the smartest of all birds, smarter than any of the other animals that humans had worked with. The Huapaya kept breeding them carefully, to be smarter and smarter, until the ravens understood human speech and grasped the way the humans were breeding them.

"At that point, when the Huapaya fled the realms of Earth to escape an invading enemy, the ravens took over their own breeding, until all the ravens could understand human speech and many could speak it. They learned to operate machines that the humans made for them, until at last the ravens, and to a degree the keas, became sentient beings, equal partners with the humans, equally entitled to freedom and prosperity, equally capable of acting cooperatively to improve everyone's lives.

"But in the spaceship, the mountain people did as the ravens did—they bred themselves. They had enough science to alter their own genes directly, so they could create a race of humans who no longer had flat feet, but could grasp with four hands, and swing through null-gravity environments, and grip both tools and the pipes and beams that they clung to. These new people were trained as engineers, repairing the spaceship, making new parts, inventing new machines, improving everyone's life.

"They were not human anymore, by then. They had the minds of humans, the desires, the memories, the lore of humans, but they could not interbreed without losing the improvements they had been given. When they reached the planet Nest, they could swing through trees and travel much faster than the regular Folk, and the Yachachiyruna befriended the clever birds and proved that they could all live together in harmony."

Sprout had already heard a version of this story, but the surrounding Yachachiyruna seemed to hear it as their own epic.

"We are the heirs of the mountain people," said Ruqyaq. "We control our own evolution as the ravens do. We satisfy our own desires as the keas do. We build machines better than any other humans, and invent whatever we need. Someday, just as all humans now cultivate and eat potatoes, all humans will come to us for machines. And in the meantime, we will breed ourselves into ever greater perfection. We are the mountain people."

And among the listeners there came a chant: "Yachachiyruna. Yachachiyruna." Even the ravens joined in.

When silence returned, Ruqyaq spoke in a normal voice to Sprout and Blue. "I know, Sprout, that I told you a version of this story before, but without the story of our heritage in genetic science. Your people are great geneticists, but so are we."

Sprout waited, but Ruqyaq said no more.

Then he understood what he was being asked.

"Ruqyaq," said Sprout. "Friend of my heart. You are genetic scientists at heart, whether you do it by modifying genes or by selective breeding. My family also altered our own genes, to rid ourselves of a defect and to enhance our intelligence. We also separated ourselves from the rest of our species, though

Blue's and my existence shows that we can still inter-breed with regular humans."

"Our stories then are very different, but also very similar," said Ruqyaq.

"Would the Yachachiyruna wish to learn what my people know of genetic science?" asked Sprout. "Perhaps we can all grow wiser by pooling our knowl-edge."

Ruqyaq bowed his head gravely. "Sharing knowl-edge is a sacred thing, and if you teach us you will lose the advantages you have over us because you know so many things that we don't know."

"Will you use the knowledge we share to make war against us?" asked Sprout.

"I say that we will not," said Ruqyaq, "but I am only one. Likewise, you say that you would share, but you are only two."

"We are only two brothers," said Sprout, "but we are both superb students of genetic science. We two know enough in our own minds to teach you every-thing that is now known in the Hundred Worlds and among the leguminids and the Ribeiras."

"You truly know all of that?"

"We know how to access all of it, and we under-stand all the principles," said Blue. "This is not empty boasting. We are young, but we're pretty amazing."

Ruqyaq laughed. "That is the most modest bragging I have ever heard, and the most boastful modesty."

"Confer with your people," said Sprout. "If they agree to vow never to make war against flat-footed humans using the genetic knowledge we will pass on to you, then we will spend as long as it takes, coming to you frequently to teach and to answer questions, while you also teach us from your lore and wisdom."

Soon the gathering dispersed. Bidding a fond fare-well to Ruqyaq, and acknowledging and saluting

Yachachiyruna and ravens alike, Sprout and Blue returned home to their mother's house.

Blue took both of Sprout's hands in his. "What have we done, Brussels?"

"We will continue the work of Prometheus," said Sprout.

"And if the gods send an eagle to devour our livers," said Blue, "the ravens and keas will swarm them and mob them and drive them away."

"Why shouldn't the sentient species all share what they have?" asked Sprout.

"You notice they didn't ask us to share the secret of detouring," said Blue.

"Jane wants that ability to die with the people who now know how to do it. The power of going anywhere instantly is more than any person should have," said Sprout.

"Except us?"

"So far we're using it fairly and wisely, to the benefit of all," said Sprout.

"We think, then, that we're superior to all the peoples we aren't giving this power to?" asked Blue.

"We have the power," said Sprout, "and we try to do no harm, but it would be better if no such power existed. When we're gone, it won't exist anymore."

"Until it's discovered again," said Blue.

"But that won't be our problem, and it won't be our fault," said Sprout.

"Because we'll be dead," said Blue.

"The dead commit no sins," said Sprout.

Then they went into the kitchen and annoyed their mother by snitching food that she was still in the midst of preparing.

"You boys!" she said, driving them out of the kitchen with a spoon.

"Don't you know that we're the heroes of the people?" asked Blue.

"Yes I do know that," Mother replied. "But that doesn't mean you aren't still brats."

Then, on impulse, Sprout grabbed his brother and half-dragged him back into the kitchen. There the two of them hugged their mother tightly, and refused to let go.

"How can I cook if you crush me like this?" she demanded. At the same time, though, she hugged them back fiercely.

"Thank you, Mother," said Sprout.

"For what?"

"For choosing to bring us into this amazing universe," said Sprout. "And for giving us minds capable of understanding the blessing we've been given."

Blue laughed. "What *he* said," he murmured.

"On balance," said Mother, "it's worked out pretty well so far. Now get out of the kitchen and let me finish. Your father and Thulium will be here soon, and I want to be able to serve as soon as they arrive."

"We *are* heroes of a story," said Blue. "Ruqyaq said so."

"And he's no fool," said Mother.

They each snitched one more bit of a couple of different things, but they knew their mother was only pretending to be angry, because she was proud that they liked her cooking well enough to want an early taste.

As Sprout lay in bed that night, wishing he could sleep but knowing it would be a while before he managed it, he wondered if the right thing for him to do would be to stop using the power to detour, and merely live within the limitations of normal life.

And he also wondered if he should take Ruqyaq aside and try to teach him how to detour, so that the power would be given to him to take his people somewhere else, if the need arose.

I will take neither course, he decided. I will use this

power in benign ways that meet my needs and don't harm anybody else. But I'll obey Jane and teach it to no one, not even my own children if I ever marry and have babies. I won't teach it to Blue, even though I know he would use the power wisely and well. Because power is worthless without boundaries and the self-control to respect them.

Then he thought of all the amazing things that were bound to happen in the future, and he felt a stab of regret that even if he lived to be old, he would only see a tiny portion of the future, and would die before anything ended.

Because it would never end.

Acknowledgments

Readers of the Ender novels, the Shadow books, and any others in that same future universe have long been aware that none of the main story threads have been resolved in more than twenty years.

Not that each book lacked an ending; on the contrary, knowing that I was not going to resolve the crucial question of who designed the descolada virus, I made sure that each book had its own ending.

Why did I wait for so long? Oh, I can come up with all kinds of reasons, but from the very start—from the time that I thought up the descolada virus as the reason for the hypersimple ecology of Lusitania—I had no idea who created it or why, what world or star system or galaxy they lived in, and how the virus was propagated across space.

I thought of all kinds of possibilities and played out many stories in my mind. They all ran aground on the reef of motive: What possible motive could any civilization capable of creating such a tailor-made virus possibly have for afflicting other worlds randomly with such savage destruction?

Along the way I received suggestions from many readers who, in the absence of any decisions by the author, had made up their own speculative stories. The most common one was that the creators of the descolada were the descendants of Bean. Until I wrote *Shadows in Flight*, that remained a possibility, though an unlikely one—I would have needed more time than I could afford in order to have Bean's descendants make the virus, propagate it, and have it work its damage upon the world of Lusitania.

But *Shadows in Flight* laid that issue to rest. Once I came to know Bean's children, strange as they are, I knew that nothing as arrogant, destructive, and selfish as the descolada could possibly have come from them.

That left me with one choice that I kept coming back to: The descolada planet had once evolved higher life forms, but in waging biological warfare on each other, they reached a point where all that was left was the artificial viruses. I had toyed with that idea in an early short story, but the fundamental problem was, I didn't want to write a novel that depended upon creating an alien species with no physical existence higher than the microbial.

Creating the alien culture in *The Abyss* was hard enough; why set myself a project that, if I did it extremely well, would still be incomprehensible and uninteresting to the vast majority of readers?

The goal of writing fiction is to put a story into your readers' memory. How can you accomplish that if you are unclear and uninteresting? Maybe it would have been an entertaining experiment, but my readers have not waited twenty years for me to give them an arty, meaningless ending. I don't want to leave my readers in uncomprehending awe, I want them to receive stories they can believe in and care about.

My breakthrough came with Jennifer Ackerman's lovely books *The Genius of Birds* and *The Bird Way: A New Look at How Birds Talk, Work, Play, Parent, and Think*. I was so delighted by the things I learned—and by Ackerman's obvious empathy with and admiration of the smartest birds on our planet—that I thought: What if some space-faring community on a generation ship made it their project to breed these birds for intelligence, rather the way dogs and horses have been bred for attributes that humans considered useful? What if, when they arrived at their new colony planet, the birds were ready to compete with humans for dominance?

While the ravens were my primary species to play with—despite Poe's gloomy view of them and Diane Setterfield's depiction of ravens in *Bellman & Black* as vengeful, just, and with long memories—what I really fell in love with were the kea parrots of New Zealand, which are too smart and playful for *our* own good. I didn't have to make them all that much smarter than they already are in order to have them function as I needed them to.

Meanwhile, I played games with the construction of the virus that entered Lusitania so destructively hundreds of years before. Finding its origin was beyond the scope of the characters of *The Last Shadow*, but what they could do was speculate about its transmission between star systems, and how it might have been mutated by cosmic radiation along the way.

In a way, it turned out to follow the creative recipe that I discovered quite by accident at the very beginning of my career. Take one idea that you've been struggling with, combine it with a completely unrelated idea that you've also been working on, and see what comes out of the effort to reconcile both ideas into one coherent story.

You don't necessarily end up with a strong story about *both* ideas; but the interplay of the unrelated ideas in your brain brings out the best of your storytelling. Book after book has arisen that way—only rarely by design—just as it took the imposition of two sentient bird species into my story about the struggle to understand and control the descolada virus to bring *The Last Shadow* to life.

Since the book ends without ever actually finding a world of origin for the descolada, perhaps some readers will be disappointed. But novels must resemble reality as well as fulfil our dreams and wishes, and in reality some historical and scientific questions remain mysteries because discovering the answers would require acquisition of data that we do not have, that we cannot reach.

When the characters in *The Last Shadow* have analyzed all the data and speculations that are available to them, and reach a conclusion which, to them, is sufficient, then I think I have done all a novelist can do, without breaking the contract between reader and novelist. When you can't pull magic out of a hat to solve a problem, readers and writers are bound by something like the limitations of the real universe.

At the time of *The Last Shadow,* there is a means of traveling instantaneously to anywhere. But with so many star systems and planets, even a thousand ships would not be enough to make a serious dent in the number of Goldilocks planets that might have given rise to life, and which therefore cry out to be discovered and studied.

So the characters, being wise, close the book on the question, having found all the answers available. If their decision turns out to be even partly wrong, it is a later generation that will need to resolve it. But I am not the novelist who will recount that adventure.

There are many people who have been of great help in the years leading up to and including the writing of this book. First, Aaron Johnston's powerful storytelling in the Formic Wars novels, which laid the groundwork for the entire Ender series, helped clarify my thinking about many things; his fiction also helped keep the Ender universe alive in the minds of many readers. Aaron and I developed the worlds and cultures and characters and outlines together—but all the flesh and blood, all the words and paragraphs of the finished novels came from Aaron. I'm proud to have partnered with him.

Then there are the two men I dedicated this book to. Ben Bova picked up the novelette *Ender's Game* from the slushpile at *Analog* magazine back in 1974, asked for revisions, and then bought and published the story that resulted.

Years later, I realized that *Speaker for the Dead* would only work if a grown-up Ender Wiggin were the main character, and that this version of the story could only be told if I published a novel version of *Ender's Game* with serious revisions in the denouement to set up *Speaker*. I met with Tom Doherty, who already had *Speaker* under contract, and told him I needed to write a novel version of *Ender's Game* first. "Same terms as *Speaker*?" he asked. "Yes," I said, hardly believing that he was giving me my answer on the spot. A handshake, and I went home, set aside *Speaker* for a while, and madly wrote the first (and basically last) draft of *Ender's Game*.

So the book you're holding in your hands—the book that I assume you've already read before coming to this acknowledgments section—really had its roots with Ben and Tom.

I made demands on my editor for decades, Beth Meacham, that I have never made of any editor before or since. She saw every chapter almost as soon as I wrote it, and either made suggestions that invariably helped in the writing process, or gave me the go-ahead that lent me confidence to proceed. She has been a stalwart and valuable friend and counselor throughout almost my entire career.

For decades now, I've regarded the audiobook production as the best first edition of my fiction. I write in an oral style; my books are meant to be read aloud. And for almost my entire career, my books have received superb audiobook productions under the direction and guidance of Stefan Rudnicki and his family of narrators. If you have listened to this book instead of reading with your eyes, you know why I am grateful to him for the high quality of his work.

My wife, Kristine Allen Card, as always read every chapter as it spewed out of my printer or arrived as a PDF when I was traveling. She never writes a word of my books, yet her imprimatur is on every aspect of my storytelling that actually works. Our friend, Erin Absher, also read, responded, and advised.

Cyndie Swindlehurst brought a lawyer's attention to detail when she gave *The Last Shadow* its first copy edit, so we could turn in to Tor a clear and coherent story that did not contradict itself or the books that came before. After the superb job she did, she undertook to give the manuscript a final pass in order to make sure it was the best it could be. I'm glad I can trust a good lawyer to never miss any of the fine print.

Meanwhile, my children and, now, my grandchildren show me over and over again that when I write about the intelligence of children, I have not far exceeded what is possible for real highly verbal children. I have seen them struggle; I have seen them overcome their struggles. My adult children have found work that they love and have been quite successful at it; my grandchildren are all completely different from each other, demonstrating the amazing variety and vitality of human life.

To any of them who physically resemble me, I

apologize. To those who are incessant talkers, I attest that you can, in fact, make a career of that. And because they are all kind and generous human beings, I can affirm that I am prouder of them than of any book or play or poem I've ever written.

THE ENDER SAGA

ON AUDIO